WHITE

ROSE

AND

THE RED

UNIVERSITY PRESS OF FLORIDA

Florida A&M University, Tallahassee
Florida Atlantic University, Boca Raton
Florida Gulf Coast University, Ft. Myers
Florida International University, Miami
Florida State University, Tallahassee
New College of Florida, Sarasota
University of Central Florida, Orlando
University of Florida, Gainesville
University of North Florida, Jacksonville
University of South Florida, Tampa
University of West Florida, Pensacola

WHITE

ROSE

AND

THE RED

H.D. (writing as Delia Alton),

edited by Alison Halsall

UNIVERSITY PRESS OF FLORIDA
Gainesville · Tallahassee · Tampa · Boca Raton
Pensacola · Orlando · Miami · Jacksonville · Ft. Myers · Sarasota

First cloth printing, 2009
First paperback printing, 2010

Library of Congress Cataloging-in-Publication Data
H. D. (Hilda Doolittle), 1886–1961
White rose and the red/H.D. (writing as Delia Alton); edited by Alison Halsall.
p. cm.
Includes bibliographical references and index.
ISBN 978-0-8130-3370-9 (cloth)
ISBN 978-0-8130-3551-2 (pbk.)
1. Siddall, Elizabeth—Fiction. 2. Authors' spouses—Fiction. 3. Artists' models—Fiction. 4. Rossetti, Dante Gabriel, 1828–1882—Fiction. 5. Pre-Raphaelites—Fiction. 6. Pre-Raphaelite Brotherhood—Fiction. I. Halsall, Alison. II. Title.
PS3507.O726W55 2009
813.'529–dc22   2009011117

The University Press of Florida is the scholarly publishing agency for the State University System of Florida, comprising Florida A&M University, Florida Atlantic University, Florida Gulf Coast University, Florida International University, Florida State University, New College of Florida, University of Central Florida, University of Florida, University of North Florida, University of South Florida, and University of West Florida.

University Press of Florida
15 Northwest 15th Street
Gainesville, FL 32611-2079
http://www.upf.com

Contents

Illustrations

A Note on the Edition

In her 1931 lyric "Red Roses for Bronze," modernist poet and prose writer Hilda Doolittle (1886–1961) meditates on the transformative potential of art, the quasi-mystical process by which organic red roses are recast in bronze. By "hammering" and "fashioning," the speaker attempts to preserve the vibrant red roses with a solid "weight of bronze" (*CP*, 211). Weighing the substantiality of the artifact in comparison with the fragility of the natural object, the artist strives to make concrete the essence of her/his lover, hoping to catch the flicker of a "slightly mocking, / slightly cynical smile" in the bronze's tangible presence.

Sculpting a statue or designing a monument is analogous to H.D.'s process of fashioning a novel about the Pre-Raphaelites, *White Rose and the Red* (1948), which in turn makes and remakes the legendary icon, Elizabeth Siddall.[1] *White Rose* presents key members of the Pre-Raphaelite movement (Dante Gabriel Rossetti, William Morris, John Ruskin) from the perspective of Elizabeth Siddall, Rossetti's controversial model, muse, and wife. By focusing on pivotal moments in Siddall's life with Rossetti, this novel mythologizes the struggles endured by nineteenth-century women in the artistic sphere, and employs a woman known primarily for her role as artistic inspiration to comment on the complex relations of artistry, identity, and corporeality. *White Rose* also insists on the continuities that exist among members of the Pre-Raphaelite Brotherhood and H.D.'s own modernist contemporaries, thus emphasizing the dynamic interchange between literary past(s) and present. My editorial project recovers H.D.'s provocative attempt to situate Elizabeth Siddall (her face, her body, her artistic efforts) at the center of an avant-garde group of artists, and to reimagine the many factors (gender, class, spiritualism, aesthetic desire, addiction) that shaped her life and posthumous reputation.

H.D.'s reinterpretation of historical events and myths from a feminist perspective is typical of her work in general, especially her poetry. In *Trilogy* (1944–46), she revises the stories of Mary, the mother of Christ, Mary Magdalene, and the goddess Aphrodite; in *Helen in Egypt* (1961), H.D. returns to the myth of Helen as the putative "cause" for the Trojan War. *White Rose and the Red* is entirely consistent with this lifelong project. In the novel H.D. unveils a figure who had, until the 1980s, been overlooked in literary and artistic criticism.

White Rose in no way positions itself as the "authentic" version of Siddall's life, however. In its dialogue with Violet Hunt's biography, *Wife of Rossetti* (1932), H.D.'s elusive novel adds another layer to the mysterious palimpsest that is Elizabeth Siddall. Since her death on February 11, 1862, Siddall has functioned more as a cultural icon than as an actual woman, and readers have puzzled over the many versions of her that circulate in memoirs, art history, and literary criticism. H.D.'s *White Rose and the Red* is not so much a tomb to commemorate Siddall as an artist as it is the figuration of a dead woman *as* a work of art, by which Siddall's dynamic spectre continues to circulate.

White Rose and the Red is published here for the first time in its entirety, as H.D. would have wished it. H.D.'s novel about the Pre-Raphaelites is a challenging text to edit, let alone read, which may explain why it has remained buried in the archives for close to seventy years. Though the prose may at times seem contrived, and the pacing uneven, the text's extensive treatment of the Pre-Raphaelite Brotherhood, its intricate intertextuality, and the teasing out of complicated narrative strands are entirely consistent with H.D.'s poetics—all the while adding a new, and relatively unexplored, aspect to our perceptions of H.D., *Imagiste*. As the accompanying introduction demonstrates, *White Rose* is historically invested in Victorian arcana and invokes the Pre-Raphaelite Brotherhood and their personal and artistic histories to continue H.D.'s textual investigations into the nature of the visual.

Another testament to H.D.'s impressive creative productivity during and immediately after World War II, this lengthy text furthers her interests in biography and memoir, and proves once again how wide-ranging were her fields of research. Expanding H.D.'s fascination with the image and with visual art, *White Rose* demonstrates a profound investment in the literary and artistic circles against which modernists defined themselves. Not only does this novel about the Pre-Raphaelites enter into a clever dialogue with the novel that immediately precedes it, *The Sword Went Out to Sea* (1946–47), but also it engages with pointed questions about female artistry and authenticity in vogue among nineteenth-century literary critics and Pre-Raphaelite historians. In this way, H.D. cleverly precedes contemporary modes of questioning by almost half a century.[2]

Four typescript drafts of *White Rose and the Red* are housed among the H.D. papers in the Yale Collection of American Literature at the Beinecke Rare Book and Manuscript Library. The unblemished appearance of the fourth typescript (YCAL MSS 24, Box 27, Folders 758–63), and the fewer substantive errors it contains, convinced me that this draft would constitute the most effective copy-text. From the first to the fourth drafts of the novel, H.D. made no substantial emendations. Evidently, she had a clear conception from the beginning of the direction *White Rose* would take. Consistently structured in seven parts, each typescript includes the epigraph from *Richard III* and the explanatory note. The early typescripts of *White Rose* are clearly works in progress: there are numerous interlinear, typed emendations, and corrections of brief sections made in H.D.'s hand. Changes made between drafts one and four, however, are concerned not with the ideas themselves but more with formatting, spelling, phrasing, and the length of the paragraphs.

Throughout the four typescript drafts of *White Rose*, H.D. underlines and thereby highlights allusions, specifically titles of plays, books, individual Pre-Raphaelite paintings, popular magazines, and particular lines of poetry. Often the sources of these intertexts are not clarified, which enhances the elusiveness of H.D.'s text. She also underscores formal and important names (like the *Order of Sir Galahad*), as well as connections she makes to Elizabeth Siddall's ancestral images (*Per Bend Vert and Gules: an Eagle displayed*). Phrases that are repeated earlier in the novel are underlined, as are significant expressions to which she wishes to draw attention. In the first part of the novel, for example, Siddall muses, "'I am the *Bridge* between them'" (*WR*, 42): the underline highlights the metaphorical connections among William Morris, Dante Gabriel Rossetti, and Siddall herself, as well as refers to an early version of the painting *Found* that Rossetti worked on at various stages throughout his career. Such underscored passages are reproduced in italics in this edition.

H.D. carefully emended each typescript of *White Rose* in pencil, employing carets and arrows to indicate where to insert marginalia and interlineations. Generally, her emendations are legible; the corrections appear to have been added at the proofreading stage. Caroline Zilboorg and Robert Spoo respectively describe H.D. as a "notoriously bad speller" with "unorthodox" punctuation.[3] *White Rose* is no exception. In her novel H.D. commonly misspells (regardless of language) locations and proper names. Clear typographical errors, proper names and foreign words that are misspelled or lack appropriate accent marks have been silently corrected. Following the precedent set by Cynthia Hogue and Julie Vandivere's edition of *The Sword Went Out to Sea*, I have not standardized H.D.'s American and English spellings. In this respect, I agree with Caroline Zilboorg, who interprets H.D.'s use of both spellings as "important evidence of her expatriate identity."[4] I have also shifted the punctuation from outside to inside the quotation marks, according to American usage.

Although it was very tempting to gloss all of the intertextual allusions in extensive endnotes to the edition, I refrain from doing so in an effort to allow readers to consume the novel *as* a novel. As much as possible I attempt to provide in the introduction enough information that will allow present and future readers to recognize the significance of *White Rose and the Red* to H.D.'s poetics, the remarkable investment H.D. made in nineteenth-century historiography, as well as to highlight the particular complexities the novel adds to our understanding of this important modernist writer. Writing to her ex-husband Richard Aldington in 1953, H.D. reveals her desire to make *White Rose* and *The Sword Went Out to Sea* available to readers: "In time, the things will be placed," she writes hopefully. "It must be just the right moment and the right publisher—but that will come, when indicated."[5] Easy as it might be to dismiss *White Rose and the Red* as being inaccessible to a wide reading public because of its difficult intertextuality and destabilization of a teleological narrative movement, its complex stylistics and profound fascination with Pre-Raphaelite history provide an exciting new lens through which to view H.D.'s interest in the nineteenth century and her theorizations of the visual. In her return to the Pre-Raphaelites, H.D. fashions her own "weight of bronze" and effectively, hauntingly monumentalizes "red roses and white."

Acknowledgments

I have been very fortunate in being surrounded by a professional and personal community who has offered me unwavering support. Without funding provided by the Social Sciences and Humanities Research Council of Canada, and the Office of Research Administration and CUPE 3903, York University, this project would not have been possible. Sincere thanks go to the generous staff at Yale's Beinecke Rare Book and Manuscript Library and the Frost and Scott Libraries, York University. I would also like to thank the Shaffners, executors of H.D.'s estate, and the New Directions Publishing Corporation, agents for the estate, for permission to publish *White Rose and the Red*.

It is a very special pleasure for me to extend my gratitude to the colleagues, friends, and family who helped see this project through to completion. Most profound thanks go to Lesley Higgins for her erudition and her invaluable advice as my mentor. David Latham was a kind and conscientious reader—his patience in answering questions about Pre-Raphaelite lore and editorial particularities was invaluable. Inspirational and rigorous, Jonathan Warren challenged me to "dig deeper" and to diversify my methods. I wish also to thank the H.D. critics Susan Stanford Friedman, Donna Krolik Hollenberg, Adalaide Morris, Cynthia Hogue, Julie Vandivere, and Caroline Zilboorg, whose work has invariably helped me to understand (or begin to) the intricacies of H.D.'s prose. I especially appreciate Jane Augustine's very helpful insights about H.D.'s spiritualist experiments and for her reading of an early draft of the book's introduction.

Amy Gorelick has supported this project since she learned of it. Enormous thanks are owed to her and her remarkable editorial staff at the University Press of Florida (project editor Jacqueline Kinghorn Brown and copy editor Beth McDonald), and especially to Cassandra Laity and Helen Sword for their very helpful reviews of a manuscript draft of the book. Their important research has shaped my own view of Victorian modernisms, and it was with great pleasure and respect that I read their comments.

Thanks also to my esteemed friends and colleagues, Joel Baetz, Elicia Clements, Tom Cull, Jaspreet Gill, Kerry Manders and Natalie Neill for their generous proofreading and intellectual engagement.

I could never have completed this project without the encouragement from my family—Albert, Mary Lou, and Colin. My final thanks are reserved for Anne Benedetti for her confidence in me and my work: her unflagging support helped me see this project through to completion.

Abbreviations

CF   H.D., Typescript. "Compassionate Friendship." H.D. Papers, Yale Collection of American Literature at the Beinecke Rare Book and Manuscript Library.

CP   H.D., *Collected Poems.* New York: New Directions, 1986.

DA   "H.D. by *Delia Alton.* Ed. Adalaide Morris. *Iowa Review* 16, no. 3 (1986): 179–221.

HE   H.D., *Helen in Egypt.* New York: New Directions, 1961.

PR   H.D., Typescript. "Pre-Raphaelites." H.D. Papers, Yale Collection of American Literature at the Beinecke Rare Book and Manuscript Library.

S   H.D., *The Sword Went Out to Sea (Synthesis of a Dream), by Delia Alton.* 1946–47. Gainesville: University Press of Florida, 2007.

T   H.D., *Trilogy.* 1944–46. New York: New Directions, 1973.

TF   H.D., *Tribute to Freud.* 1956. Rpt. Boston: David R. Godine, 1974.

WR   H.D., Typescript. *White Rose and the Red.* H.D. Papers, Yale Collection of American Literature at the Beinecke Rare Book and Manuscript Library.

These texts are cited parenthetically and are followed by page number(s).

Introduction

"But I'll go on talking. We are legitimate children. We are children of the Rossettis, of Burne Jones, of Swinburne."

H.D., from *Asphodel*

"Elizabeth Siddal was to become a figure of history and romance."

Francis Bickley, from *The Pre-Raphaelite Comedy*

White Rose and the Red (1948) was underway as early as Christmas Day 1947, when H.D. wrote to Richard Aldington and alluded to a novel about the Pre-Raphaelites that she intended to produce.[1] "I get deeper and deeper into the Pre-Raff scene and have been making notes for another possible volume," she comments. "A book first—maybe a play after—I see it in scenes and the costumes fascinate me."[2] Violet Hunt's 1932 biography of Elizabeth Siddall, Richard Aldington's preparation of an anthology of aesthetic poetry, and the 1948 exhibit of Pre-Raphaelite work at the Whitechapel Gallery inspired H.D. to return to the poets and aesthetic movement she first learned about in her early twenties.[3] On display at this 1948 exhibit were works by William Morris, John Everett Millais, William Holman Hunt, at least five Dante Gabriel Rossetti drawings featuring Elizabeth Siddall, and, most important, watercolors and drawings by Siddall herself.

It is no coincidence that the Pre-Raphaelite centenary exhibition in 1948 should correspond with the date of H.D.'s *White Rose and the Red*, especially in a society still suffering from the aftermath of World War II.[4] Devastated by the strain brought on by the war and Lord Hugh Dowding's rejection of her séance messages, H.D. experienced a severe mental breakdown in February 1946, though this did not in any way affect her creative output. While recovering in the Klinik Brunner, Küsnacht, near Zurich, she delivered *White Rose*, her "labour of love" (*DA*, 193) as she called it, her fictional investigation of the Pre-Raphaelites. As H.D. no doubt realized, curiosity about an artistic movement that predated her by almost a century paralleled the Pre-Raphaelites' curiosity about artists from the medieval and pre-Renaissance pasts. Both H.D. and the Pre-Raphaelites looked to the past in an effort to understand their respective presents, which were characterized by cultural and political change, and even outright revolt.[5]

In February 1944, H.D. describes her energetic writing period during the war to a former classmate: "I have never worked so hard as in the past few years—a terrific creative urge that, I suppose, is a sort of 'escapism' but a cerebral drug, too that has kept me sane and alive—the writing is crazy, if you will—but has acted as a sort of safety valve."[6] In *White Rose* H.D. finds the peace and sustenance necessary to cope with the recent trauma. At once escapist and nostalgic, comforting and invigorating, H.D.'s interrogations of the past propel her creativity; she works tirelessly through her wartime experiences by connecting with another place, another time. "I am very happy with the book. I hope I do not finish it for some time, as I love it and live it so much," she wrote to Aldington in July 1948, summing up the professional and personal influence the Pre-Raphaelite movement had over her.[7] H.D. describes the hope and relief that her examination of this British nineteenth-century past and its own experiences of war (the French invasion scare of 1852; the Crimean War of 1854–56; the Sepoy Mutiny in India, 1857; and the fright over another French invasion in 1859–60) provides as an alternative to war-decimated Europe. Interested in destabilizing rigid notions of linear history to emphasize the inheritance and transformation of the Victorian past by modernist writers, H.D. returns to the nineteenth century to highlight its parallels with the political excesses of the twentieth. In *White Rose* H.D. draws attention to the refreshing continuity that exists between her chaotic present and the nineteenth-century past.

H.D.'s fictional interpretation of Elizabeth Siddall's experiences with the Pre-Raphaelites coincides with her interest, evident in *Trilogy* (1944–46) and *Helen in Egypt* (1961), in reclaiming previously marginalized figures from Greek, Roman, and Judeo-Christian myths, and repositioning them at the center of new cultural narratives.[8] In *Trilogy*, Our Lady of the Snow carries a book whose pages "are the blank pages / of the unwritten volume of the new" (*T*, 103); the volume also resituates Aphrodite and Mary Magdalene as inspirational goddesses. Similarly, in *White Rose* H.D. produces a new volume about the Pre-Raphaelites, this time told largely from the perspective of Siddall, a continuation of H.D's musings about the instinctual forces of love and war that have shaped history since the Middle Ages. Of particular interest to H.D. is the dismantling of a masculinist Pre-Raphaelite cult of beauty, which she achieves by deploying Siddall as the epistemological center of the narrative.[9]

Draft typescripts of *White Rose and the Red* were dated by H.D. herself as having been composed in 1947 and 1948.[10] This fascinating novel has remained unpublished until now, submitted to publishers but rejected because of its elusive narration; its destabilization of teleological narrative movement through an emphasis given to vision, trance, and thought transferences; and the difficulties experienced by readers in categorizing it.[11] Susan Stanford Friedman is not alone in her inability to classify H.D's novel about the Pre-Raphaelites. Cassandra Laity describes it as H.D's "autobiographical novel"; Donna Krolik Hollenberg identifies it as a "fictional biography"; and H.D. herself considers it to be a "romance" (*DA*, 195).[12] In keeping with H.D's clever play with generic categories, it is interesting to note that she initially conceived of *White Rose* as a play: "The future, I think, should have a 'stunner' in the way of a 'grind' [a poem]—a play, I think would take like anything in a year or so in London. I am so afraid that someone else might push in, that I am not speaking of any of this outside. I can SEE those people, and hear them talking."[13] H.D. goes on to suggest that Greta Garbo could perform Siddall (*CF*, 81), Ralph Richardson could play Morris, and Laurence Olivier, Rossetti![14] This initial conception of the Pre-Raphaelite story as a "play" and as a "grind" parallels H.D's interest in dramatic representation and in the performative, as well as her tendency to disrupt rigid generic and historical parameters in her prose.

Although it appears that H.D. did not discuss *White Rose and the Red* with many friends or colleagues during the writing process, she certainly solicited responses from Richard Aldington and Norman Holmes Pearson. Chiding H.D. for her cryptic style and allusions in her war novels, *The Sword Went Out to Sea* (1946–47) and *White Rose*, Aldington claimed that the hybrid nature of both, and their lack of "clear-cut genres," would make them unappealing to a commercial publisher and to a "common reader."[15] Aldington, however, was a generally astute critic of the text: he and H.D. exchanged at least sixteen letters in which they discussed the novel's structural and thematic details at length. Due to his familiarity with nineteenth-century artists (honed in his preparation of an anthology of aesthetic poetry), Aldington was a useful resource for critical and biographical works about the Pre-Raphaelites. After sending H.D. the two-volume *Life of William Morris* by John Mackail (1899), he recommended that she read Walter Pater's essay on "Aesthetic Poetry" because of its analysis of William Morris as a poet, and discussed Morris's socialist activism at length. Overall, he was relatively encouraging about her novel, as a letter from August 1948 attests: "I am very glad indeed to know you are continuing with the book [*White Rose*] and that you are enjoying it, and hope it will last."[16] H.D.'s letters to Aldington emphasize the significant dialogue about the Pre-Raphaelites that they shared for at least two years. Over the course of their correspondence H.D. shared with Aldington her impressions of Violet Hunt's *Wife of Rossetti* and described the creative process that evolved from outlining a play to producing an entire volume.

H.D.'s letters to Norman Holmes Pearson, devoted friend and first curator of her papers at Yale University's Beinecke Rare Book and Manuscript Library, also explain the process of shaping *White Rose*. In a letter dated August 14, 1948, H.D. thanks Pearson for sending her research materials, particularly the bibliography of Morris's literary and socialist works, a "most useful and valuable list of Morris treasures," which formed her principal reading list.[17] Pearson and H.D. exchanged at least fourteen letters in which they address different aspects of the novel. In November 1948 Pearson expresses his delight "both with the beauty of the imagination and with the beauty of the prose." He goes on to exclaim that he was "particularly taken" by the characters and "the formalizing concept of the book-within-a-book, which gave it depth and luminosity."[18] Not all of Pearson's responses to *White Rose* are complimentary, however.[19] In fact, Pearson suggests that part 1, chapter 3 (the encounter between Rossetti and the medium, Norton Ely) is "unduly lengthy," and that the final book with its "leisurely ending" is "not so well integrated with the whole as the first ones had been." He goes on to criticize H.D.'s shift in focus away from Elizabeth Siddall's artistic potential and expresses a dissatisfaction with the ending: "Perhaps simply because you have her [Siddall] less concerned with her own aspiration for creativity, and remove her from the scene," he maintains, "the last book seems more like the beginning of a new volume than the end of another."[20]

As the few thematic differences between the four draft typescripts demonstrate, H.D. resisted Pearson's advice. Corrections on the drafts are more concerned with typographical elements and inconsistencies in punctuation and spelling than with the substantial revision and re-sculpting of her ideas. Pearson's opinion of the novel, however, was favorable overall. In the same letter he generously expounds upon the crystalline beauty of her prose. "The total result of the impression on me of this first section," he begins, "is that the first two books of it are written with a delicacy of prose, imaginative power, and formalization which ranks it among the finest things you have done, and in some ways perhaps the best of the prose so far. It seems to me to be highly successful, and a sheer delight to read. I cannot praise it enough."[21] Emphasizing the importance of this unpublished novel to H.D.'s oeuvre, Pearson praises the intricacies of the prose as well as the imaginative power involved in H.D.'s fictionalized re-telling of Pre-Raphaelite history.

As her extensive correspondence with Aldington and Pearson makes evident, H.D. did not, as Lawrence Rainey claims, intend for this novel to be available only to a small coterie of writers.[22] In a letter dated September 16, 1948, H.D. expresses her determination to publish *White Rose* and *The Sword Went Out to Sea* as part of a prose trilogy, and announces to Aldington that she has sent the novels to her New York editors at Macmillan for comment.[23] In December of the same year, H.D. informs Pearson that she is waiting to hear back from Macmillan "before re-sorting or re-writing."[24] Although there is no record of Macmillan's response to her submission, these letters to her friends and critics emphasize H.D.'s determination to present *White Rose* before the public. This edition represents the actualization of this desire.

Although at times obtuse and difficult to follow, *White Rose and the Red* pays tribute to a nineteenth-century legacy that shapes modernists like H.D., T. S. Eliot, and Ezra Pound. This edition allows readers to view firsthand H.D.'s exploration of Pre-Raphaelite visual culture, as well as to witness how her evocation of key Victorian figures participates in her interest in Victorian and Decadent artists.[25] Especially when coupled with *The Sword Went Out to Sea*, *White Rose and the Red* gives readers a refreshing insight into H.D.'s "visionary politics" of the 1940s, her new way of seeing provoked by World War II.

"Pre-raphaelitish slush": H.D. as a Writer of Prose

In *White Rose* H.D. produces a novel that blends elements of literary biography, historical fiction, romance, and the roman à clef.[26] Her notes (YCAL MSS 24, Box 27, Folder 764) clarify the liberal approach she takes to the Pre-Raphaelite movement's history: "It will be obvious to any student . . . that I have taken certain liberties, in order to fit the picture into the frame. . . . I have quoted freely from Violet Hunt, whose *Wife of Rossetti* has been severely criticized [. . .] that it contains much that is unreliable & mythopoeic. The myth, however, sometimes contains or suggests that reality that is the source and inspiration of all poetry" (*PR*, 7–8ʳ). This characterization of Violet Hunt's biography as being "mythopoeic" helps one to understand H.D.'s own tendency to mythologize the Pre-Raphaelites, especially Elizabeth Siddall, in order to explore heterosexual power relations that span the two centuries, and to draw attention to issues of ownership and possession of the female figure that mimetic art affords the artist— issues that H.D. was also addressing at this time in her poetry, in *Trilogy* and *Helen in Egypt* specifically. From this mythology and even methodology there emerges a central narrating consciousness (that of Siddall herself); a narrative that eschews linearity in favour of repetition, incompletion, and a complex intertextuality; and an original, novelistic hybrid that foregrounds the social realities and spiritual preoccupations with which Siddall as artist had to contend.

In *White Rose* H.D. inventively engages with the biographical genre, more particularly with Hunt's 1932 biography, countering the genre's focus on fact by presenting her own fictional interweaving of biography, romance, and history from the perspectives of Siddall, Morris, and at times Rossetti. In her personal writings H.D. goes so far as to draw a direct parallel between her own struggles as an artist and those experienced by Siddall (*DA*, 194). The affinity H.D. feels for the Pre-Raphaelites emerges in her description of them as "familiar, *familiars* almost. I have known them somewhere, perhaps because of my early devotion to their legend. I know more about them or sometimes seem to know more about the Rossetti-Morris circle than I do of my own contemporaries. . . . It is the sense of continuity that inspires me, the feeling of intimate communion or communication that renewed my faith at the end of the war-years" (*DA*, 194–95). The term "familiar" is richly overdetermined, given the focus in *White Rose* on spectres from the past that haunt the principal characters, as well as the memories and visions that the three central characters share. Highlighting the intimate connection

H.D. feels for Siddall and the Pre-Raphaelites, the term "familiar" also calls attention to the spiritualist association she makes between previous writers and her contemporaries.[27] In this way, H.D. emphasizes the refreshing link with the Victorian past that she turned to for support in the chaos during and after two world wars.

Critics also choose to read *White Rose* as a roman à clef, encouraged in part by H.D.'s own descriptions of her prose. H.D. admits that she develops a dialogue among her short stories and unpublished writings because many of the characters (albeit from different historical periods) recur, but are referred to by different names (*DA*, 219). In her analysis of the Victorian poets on H.D., Cassandra Laity interprets H.D.'s novel about the Pre-Raphaelites in this vein, with Richard Aldington becoming Rossetti, D. H. Lawrence standing in for Morris, and H.D. playing Siddall herself.[28] By recasting her modernist contemporaries as Victorian artists, Laity argues, H.D. attempts to return these male modernists to their Victorian "other" selves.

For Laity, H.D.'s fictional histories that rewrite her involvement with the Imagist circle—*HERmione* and *White Rose*, specifically—describe the modernist break with the nineteenth century and H.D.'s painful initiation into a patriarchal sexual politics associated with her confining role as muse to Lawrence, Aldington, and Pound. To this end, by situating Elizabeth Siddall as the nucleus of *White Rose*, H.D. rethinks the history of the Pre-Raphaelite movement from a strong female perspective, and in this way attempts to create a "cultural myth of womanhood from which to fashion a female modernity."[29] For Laity, H.D.'s new figuration of the muse as femme fatale is a direct response to the modernist masculinism with which H.D. and modernist women writers in general had to contend. Siddall's beauty, enigmatic silence, and intensity radiate beyond the frame of the male gaze and provide, for H.D. at least, a sense of erotic, linguistic, and political empowerment.[30]

However compelling, Laity's claim that Siddall's paradoxical role as failed woman browbeaten into submission and sexualized femme fatale seems inexact given the increasingly marginalized role Siddall plays in H.D.'s novel. Siddall certainly holds a position of paramount importance for William Allingham and Walter Deverell, the man who introduces her to Rossetti in part 1 of *White Rose*. Her role as model, muse, and love of Rossetti, not to mention as a visual artist and poet endorsed by the great John Ruskin, is certainly a focus in the novel's first half. *White Rose*, however, depicts the gradual separation, first geographical and then emotional, of Siddall from Rossetti, as she travels to Paris, Nice, Hampstead, and eventually to Sheffield for art instruction, and as Fanny Cornforth and Jane Burden (later Morris) supersede her as Rossetti's love interests. Moreover, frequent mention is made of Siddall's ill health and her addiction to laudanum. Part 7 concludes with "L'envoi," the sending on of Siddall into death; the climactic moment in the novel reminds readers of the devastating impact Rossetti had on an often fragile woman.[31] That said, Siddall undoubtedly functions as a locus for H.D.'s examination of the issues of artistry and authenticity that preoccupy Victorian and modernist artists alike. By indicting Rossetti's exploitation of Siddall as a model and muse, H.D. develops an identity for Siddall separate from that of Pre-Raphaelite icon through an engagement with her art, spiritualism, and ancestral images.

One of the most important aspects of *White Rose and the Red* is the dialogue it carries on with *The Sword Went Out to Sea*, the first novel in the trilogy H.D. wrote under the pseudonym, Delia Alton. Thanks to Cynthia Hogue and Julie Vandivere's important introduction, the intricacies of *Sword*, and the stylistic and thematic preoccupations common to both novels are more readily apparent. Most obvious is the overlaying and doubling of characters and narrative patterns.[32] Although nowhere near as allusive as *Sword*, which requires a key to the characters to decipher the densely woven patterns that connect them, *White Rose* demonstrates the recurrence of character types throughout history and literature, signalled immediately by the novel's title and epigraph. Alluding to the heroic character of Richmond in Shakespeare's *Richard III*, who proposes that "We will unite the white rose and the red" (5.7.19), the book's epigraph establishes the text's various projects: H.D. proposes to reconcile the binary suggested by the juxtaposition of two different families (York and Lancaster) through the intervention of a Richmond figure, first William Morris and then Godfrey Lushington. The title also emphasizes the equal attention the novel devotes to Siddall, the white rose, and Rossetti, the red, two figures united in desire and matrimony, but mutually irreconcilable.

After all, H.D.'s novel about the Pre-Raphaelites is as much about Siddall's identity vis à vis Rossetti as it is about the subjectivity she develops away from him. One of the principal ironies of this epigraph and title, then, lies in the realization that however much the characters struggle to unite these roses, the roses remain divided at the end by Siddall's death. In the conflict that invariably separates the principal lovers H.D. also incorporates the archetypal *héros fatal* that recurs throughout her oeuvre, specifically in *Sword* in the figures of Ezra Pound, Richard Aldington, Hugh Dowding, and J. J. Van der Leeuw. Dante Gabriel Rossetti and William Morris are versions of this *héros fatal*, figures with whom Siddall falls in love and by whom she is betrayed or abandoned. Both Rossetti and Morris fail to become Siddall's ideal lover, an archetype she associates initially with Walter Deverell, later with the mysterious Gregor, whom she perceives in her medievalized dream visions, and finally with Algernon Swinburne.

Through her interactions with such figures, Siddall develops an association of love with death in *White Rose*. "If she married him, she would die" (*WR*, 40), Siddall muses to herself about Rossetti. In coding this relationship according to the conflicting instincts of eros and thanatos, H.D. demonstrates the continued influence of Freud on her thinking from their sessions in the early 1930s.[33] From Rossetti, Siddall gains an identity as an artist and as a woman; however, her relationship with him brings with it inevitable betrayal, as Rossetti becomes involved with Annie Miller (William Holman Hunt's model), Fanny Cornforth, and Jane Burden. The contrast between "white rose" and "red" thus signals the conflicting forces of ice and passion, personified in Siddall and Rossetti respectively. Likened early on to lilies through the allusion to Rossetti's painting *The Blessed Damozel*, Siddall is depicted as being woefully unsuited to the self-absorbed passion of Rossetti.

The intimacy Siddall develops with William Morris in *White Rose* is one of the more fascinating inventions H.D. contributes to Pre-Raphaelite literary history. Morris's poetry and prose resonate throughout *The Sword Went Out to Sea* and *White Rose and the Red*. In fact, *Sword*'s final chapter, "Goldwings," functions at once as an open-ended conclusion for *Sword* and an entry into *White Rose*, as this reference to Morris's poem "Golden Wings" allows H.D. to draw links among nineteenth-century London, Paris, America, and an undefined period in the Middle Ages, and to evoke tropes of courtly love to characterize the power politics that govern the interactions among Rossetti, Morris, and Siddall. The prosaic setting of nineteenth-century London disappears into the vague, ethereal settings of the medieval dream to which Siddall constantly returns, prompted in part by the poems from *The Defence of Guenevere* collection Morris reads and sends to her. "Two Red Roses Across the Moon," "The Tune of Seven Towers," and "The Eve of Crecy" offer up a host of evocative images, the decoding of which gives Siddall's life meaning.

In *White Rose*, the friendship that develops between Siddall and Morris is first provoked by Rossetti's story, "Hand and Soul" (1849); it initializes their shared thought transferences.[34] Eventually, during the course of this relationship, Siddall becomes associated (through conversation and trances) with Margaret de Liliis from William Morris's story "The Hollow Land." Morris's belief in this associative link is reinforced when he happens upon Rossetti's painting *The Blessed Damozel*, whose visual interpretation of the line from the poem, "*She had three lilies in her hand*" (*WR*, 109), he in turn associates with Siddall herself. "Granted that the picture had been painted by Rossetti, granted that the girl in the picture was Rossetti's rose—that did not alter the fact that she was Florian's lily, de Liliis, Lis" (*WR*, 118). Morris's likening of himself to Florian de Liliis from his own story provides the quasi-romantic link to Siddall that is one of the more significant additions H.D. makes to Pre-Raphaelite lore.

Further, Siddall associates herself with Flor (a variation of Florian), Iseult (interestingly, the one literary figure about whom Morris completed a painting), and the medieval woman Blanchefleur, all characters who appear in various incarnations in *The Sword Went Out to Sea* and re-appear in the medieval dream associations Siddall makes with William Morris. These figures, who remain enigmatic in *White Rose*, and are animated in *Sword*, allude to the idea of "living a story" that *Sword* and *White Rose* share. Fiction and "reality" merge in these trances that allow Siddall to become different women throughout history and literature. "Watching a play, reading a book or hearing an old mystery-story is living it, if one has the artist's passion," Morris tells Siddall. "I'm living your story with you" (*WR*, 219). In H.D.'s deft narrative turn, Morris's references to the interrelationship between art and life culminate in the use of his poem "The Defence of Guenevere" to alert Siddall to Rossetti's infidelities with Fanny Cornforth (through its depiction of the triangularization of desire between Guenevere, Launcelot, and King Arthur). H.D.'s gift for inter- and intratextuality is vividly displayed in *Trilogy*, as well as in *The Sword Went Out to Sea* and *White Rose and the Red*.

In *Sword*, images of the spiral shell, the pleats of time, and the bee-lines point to radial patterns that permit the movement backward and forward that is so central to H.D.'s conception of time. "Past, present and future became one," Delia Alton muses in her trances with the medium Ben Manisi in *Sword*. "The distant past and the near past merged" (*S*, 64). It is through this juxtaposition and superimposition of present and past—London during World War II, Athens in fifth century BCE, Rome at the time of Julius Caesar, and Normandy on the eve of the 1066 Norman invasion of Britain—that H.D. demonstrates the ubiquitousness of love and war throughout history. Mirrors and crystals in *White Rose* in turn suggest the refracting of history and the linking of fiction and reality. Moving away from a classical—

and by implication aristocratic and patrilineal—model of history, H.D. fore-grounds a distinctly nonlinear relationship to the past.[35]

Similarly, by juxtaposing past states in her narrating present, the fictional Siddall experiences the literal living through of the past, both recent and remote, through her séances and thought transferences. In *White Rose*'s ability to highlight the "present-ness" of the past, it captures the dynamic "now" of the Pre-Raphaelite movement, focalized through Siddall and cen-tered around the years 1848, 1856, 1860, and 1862.[36] This "now" is almost wholly made up of memories, however. Shared thoughts and dreams point to a mysterious, unspecified past that Morris, Siddall, and Rossetti share. In her visitation and re-visitation by memories, Siddall's narrating present is also one in which she recalls and anticipates the future: "It was remember-ing and at the same time *remembering in the future*," she muses to herself. "Had she thought that, or had someone thought it for her?" (*WR*, 312). The dynamic "present" that H.D.'s Pre-Raphaelites inhabit thus depends on a juxtaposition of past and future, facilitated in large part by the thoughts and dreams shared by the three characters.

In turn, H.D. calls attention to the linking of different temporal states with the Pre-Raphaelite present (and, by extension, the "present" of the Pre-Raphaelites with that of her modernist contemporaries) by the trope of reincarnation. In *White Rose*, reincarnation is a reminder of the constant evocation of the past, a deliberate conjuring up of the past that is propelled into the future. "'But why bother about reincarnation?' Rossetti asks. 'We go on reincarnating backward in time, ordinary time, one's own childhood. I found my own delirium in Dante, in the *Vita*, though he presumably was grown-up when he had his'" (*WR*, 274). H.D.'s use of reincarnation denotes at once the impossibility of escaping the past and the reworking of such memories to suit the needs of the characters in the present. H.D.'s evocation of the links among past, present, and future through the trope of reincarna-tion approaches T. S. Eliot's notion of time in *Four Quartets* (1943) where he states: "Time present and time past / Are both perhaps present in time future, / And time future contained in time past."[37] H.D.'s preoccupation in *White Rose* with the perennial presence of the past eventually culminates in 1961 with *Helen in Egypt*, in which Helen characterizes the re-telling of the same story over time as a form of collective inheritance, as a narrative that she has inherited, lived through, forgotten, and eventually rediscovered in an endless cycle of remembering and forgetting (*HE*, 57).[38]

Novels fired in the kiln of war, both *Sword* and *White Rose* foreground images of personal and collective trauma as emblematic of humanity's terrible inheritance. In *Sword*, the "whiz-bang" that resounds throughout suggests the omnipresence of war that is at once personal (as we see through Delia's mental illness that worsens as the buildings crumble around her) and communal. Warfare and slaughter are global and historical occurrences, Delia realizes in an increasingly bombed-out London, through her juxtapositioning of contemporary London, and ancient Knossos, Athens, and Delphi. In *White Rose* the Battle of Waterloo (1814) preoccupies Elizabeth Siddall's father; the American Civil War (1861–65) and the vexed issue of the South's secession form the backdrop to the conversations between Rossetti and the medium, Norton Ely, and his talk about the runaways that Miss Cathy and Miss Mary, the Fox sisters, were working with;[39] the Crimean War (1853–56) and Indian Mutiny (1857) plague Siddall in part 6. "There had always been war" (*WR*, 68), Norton Ely states wearily, alluding to warfare as the instinctual drive that links present with past. The very title of H.D.'s novel, alluding to the war of the Roses, serves to remind readers that history is made in and through deadly conflict.

Despite the creative opportunities afforded by this blending of literary biography, historical fiction, romance, and the roman à clef, the novels are very challenging. Literary techniques such as time-shifting and narrative disruption, repetition, and dense allusiveness in *White Rose*, *The Sword Went Out to Sea*, and *The Mystery* initially made these novels too challenging for readers and thus unappealing to prospective publishers. (Ironically, the difficulty H.D. encountered in marketing her novels commercially was one that the Pre-Raphaelites experienced almost a century before.) In a letter to H.D., Richard Aldington refers to the cryptic style and form of *The Sword*, which would make it too complex for the popular publisher: "This book is going to be difficult in its present form—I mean from the commercial publisher's angle. Always the problem is: How to present new non-popular material in a form which the publisher will and the public must accept. You have not done it. Publishers all believe in Napoleon's dictum—they like 'clear-cut genres.' 'How are we to classify this?' they ask anxiously. If the answer is 'Fiction' or 'Biography' they are enchanted—if 'Essay' gloom! Now, from the publisher's point of view this is part fiction, part essay and can only be classified as 'Occult.' Difficult—the field is instantly limited."[40] Aldington had not exaggerated the challenges—he confirmed in June 1947 that a publisher had refused *Sword* because of its generic indeterminacy.

This productive and provocative inability to classify *White Rose and the Red* (as well as *The Sword Went Out to Sea*, for that matter) is precisely what makes it such an exciting text. *White Rose* is a remarkable and unusual modernist text: a significant addition to H.D.'s canon that helps readers and critics alike understand the significance of nineteenth-century literature and the visual arts for an important modernist poet and prose writer and for modernism more generally. The novel demonstrates H.D.'s lifelong commitment to women throughout mythology and history who struggled to assert their importance as artists and persons. In doing so, *White Rose* parallels the recovery movement within recent criticism of the modernist period—work undertaken by Bonnie Kime Scott, Georgina Taylor, Shari Benstock, and Cassandra Laity—which counters the perception of modernism as an elitist movement of male writers, opens up the field to a description of plural modernisms, and resurrects narratives of late Victorian and modernist women writers as they struggle to define themselves within and against canonical conceptions of the Victorian and modernist periods.[41]

H.D.'s prose shares its dense intertextuality and generic fluidity with Dante Gabriel Rossetti's art and literature.[42] Like H.D., Rossetti employs a mythopoeic method through the study and juxtaposition of sources from different historical periods. Just as H.D. combines Greek, Roman, and Egyptian myths in her revision of the Helen of Troy narrative in *Helen in Egypt*, she mythologizes Siddall, Rossetti, and Morris in *White Rose* for her explorations of spiritualism, art theory, and heterosexual power relations. The literary appropriations practised by the Pre-Raphaelites (their use, for example, of the Middle Ages), which situate aesthetic and erotic ideals in past literary and artistic traditions, anticipate H.D.'s use of myth and her eventual appropriation of the Pre-Raphaelites and their sphere to create a (small) world empowering to women.

Pre-Raphaelite Spectres

In *Tribute to Freud* (1956), the figure of a haunted house highlights the ghostly connections that link present and past, a metaphor that resonates throughout *The Sword Went Out to Sea* and *White Rose and the Red*. "We are all haunted houses" (*TF*, 146), the narrator of *Tribute* announces cryptically. By way of this analogy, the narrator calls attention to the haunting of the human mind by forces of the unconscious and traces of yesteryear. The ghosts that inhabit this haunted house are also emblematic of the traces of the nineteenth century that are bound up in modernist practices of self-definition. Modernists like H.D., Pound, and Eliot produced manifestos of the "new" that tried to exorcise or conjure up (or both) spectres of the nineteenth-century literary past in their modernist present. Some of these ghosts materialize and hover in the narrating present of H.D.'s novel about the Pre-Raphaelites.

As we know, modernists defined themselves in relation to and against the traces of that which came before—and some of those spectres were distinctly Victorian. T. S. Eliot's belief in the need for "a continual extinction of personality" from all aesthetic works and Ezra Pound's focus on formal innovation and poetic "hardness" sought to reject "pre-raphaelitish slush," the Victorian tendency to include overtly personal sentiment in poetry.[43] Nevertheless, the trace of the Victorian past is part and parcel with modernist state(s) of being. Instrumental in many of the modernist manifestos is an obsession with the incarnation of the past—textual, historical, cultural—in the "new" modernist present. Even though the first issue of *Blast* (1914), edited by chief "outlaw" Wyndham Lewis, called for the need to BLAST "years 1837 to 1900," modernist self-definition in part depends on a paradoxical rejection *and* appropriation of poetic conventions from the literary past.

For example, Pound develops his lyrical voice by experimenting with Italian, Greek, Roman, and Anglo-Saxon lyric traditions, with Japanese and Chinese aesthetics and ideogram, and, more specifically, with Robert Browning's dramatic monologue. Eliot juxtaposes Eastern and Western philosophies, contemporary and popular forms of art, and canonized European texts in the cataclysmic masterpiece that is *The Waste Land* (1922). James Joyce and H.D. re-deploy the epic genre and figures from Greek and Roman mythology in their masterful, mythopoeic depictions of contemporary Dublin and London.

H.D.'s *White Rose and the Red* willingly acknowledges the Victorian spectre as a part of modernism rather than insisting, as T. E. Hulme maintains in his essay "Romanticism and Classicism" (written c. 1912), that the Victorians simply do not figure in the modern literary canon. In her re-telling of Pre-Raphaelite history from the perspective of Elizabeth Siddall, H.D. breathes life back into her Victorian predecessors in an effort to analyze the inheritance that many of her contemporaries ignored or silenced. Her insistence on the "continuity" (*DA*, 195) that exists between members of the Pre-Raphaelite movement and her own contemporaries emphasizes the productive interchange between literary past and present.

Interestingly, H.D. is one of the few modernist writers who openly acknowledges that Victorian poets and prose writers (particularly the Pre-Raphaelites) played a pivotal role in the development of her aesthetic beliefs.[44] When she first encountered Pound in Philadelphia in 1901, he was praising medieval troubadours and Provençal poetry, and more important, the work of Dante Gabriel Rossetti, William Morris, and Algernon Charles Swinburne for their unusual subject matter and technical innovations. *End to Torment* (1979), H.D.'s memoir of her friendship with and brief engagement to Pound, recounts the early days when the young and amorous Pound recited Rossetti and Swinburne to her, as well as such Morris poems as "The Gilliflower of Gold" and "The Defence of Guenevere," two poems that are omnipresent in *White Rose*.[45] Morris's commitment to artisanship, and the links between text as literature and as aesthetic object were eventually taken up by Pound, who championed the precise crafting of modernist poetry and prose.

Pre-Raphaelites and modernists shared a rigorous intertextuality that demanded much of their readers and viewers, as well as an attention to detail and an objectivity that strove to return poetry and prose to a state of crystalline purity. Both as poets and visual artists, the Pre-Raphaelites were initially inspirational to modernists like H.D., Pound, and Eliot because of their systematic rebellion against artistic conventions of the time, as well as their curiosity about artists from the medieval and pre-Renaissance pasts.[46] Eventually, however, male modernist poets denounced Victorian work as being flawed by aestheticism and, worse, by a distinctly feminine sentimentalism. At work in the rejection of a Victorian aesthetic by the principal male modernists is a rhetoric that situates "dry, hard, classical verse" as being more "masculine" than the ornamental and "feminine" Romantic and Victorian poetry.[47]

Such masculinist norms about art surfaced in an age that was witnessing the emergence of women into more socially and politically engaged positions of power. This particular turn away from the Victorians was also a homophobic response to Walter Pater's aestheticism, the sensationalism promoted by the Oscar Wilde trials, and the consequent identification of the late-Victorian aesthete as a sexual deviant.[48] In fact, as Pound's *Hugh Selwyn Mauberley* (1920) suggests, the death of the effeminate Aesthete is necessary for the birth of an improved modernist (and masculinist) poetic.

As H.D.'s *The Sword Went Out to Sea* and *White Rose and the Red* demonstrate, the process of living is one whereby humanity learns to coexist with memory, and, more important, with ghosts from the past. So much of H.D.'s *White Rose* involves the spectral presence of past temporal periods, and even *revenants*, the ghosts of dead friends or lovers who materialize and hover in the narrating present. In effect, *White Rose* rarely narrates the "here and now" of mid-nineteenth-century London; instead, it focuses on

Siddall's retrospections about and reinvocations of the past. Coming in at close to 600 pages in draft typescript form, H.D.'s novel reads like a Victorian triple-decker, intimately steeped in cultural history and Victorian apocrypha, emphasizing memory and vividly recalling imagined scenes from the Middle Ages, and the seventeenth and eighteenth centuries that have been inherited collectively by Siddall, Rossetti, and Morris. In this reanimation of the past, then, H.D. demonstrates that the dynamism of Siddall's present is inflected by timeless and time-bound narratives of love and warfare. For Siddall, spectres of the past provide a spectrum of creative possibility, offering insight into a global inheritance of personal and martial conflict, all viewed from within the matrices of artistry, identity, and corporeality.

In this way, the symbol of the palimpsest is extremely productive to describe H.D.'s engagement with the Pre-Raphaelites. As an emblem for overwriting, it highlights H.D.'s invocation and transformation of a partially erased story, namely that of Elizabeth Siddall—woman and artist—in relation to and defined by the P.R.B. In its interaction with previous stories, the palimpsest also draws attention to H.D.'s dialogical relationship with Victorian precursors, one that interacts with and reformulates the literary past informing the author's modernist present. By reconceptualizing the history of the Pre-Raphaelite movement from Siddall's perspective, H.D. re-envisions the Pre-Raphaelite narrative and conjures a renewed incarnation of Siddall's ghost. Modernists, such as H.D., Pound, and Eliot, are renowned for their almost manic search for a sense of cultural inheritance. As *The Sword Went Out to Sea* and *White Rose and the Red* show, H.D. found hers in the historical and literary past. Indeed, it is her cryptic relation with the nineteenth century that constitutes her particular Victorian modernism.[49]

"Yeux Glauques": Elizabeth Siddall as Pre-Raphaelite Icon

H.D.'s interest in Elizabeth Siddall as artist rather than as wife of D. G. Rossetti was partly a response to Pound's portrayal of her in *Hugh Selwyn Mauberley*. To address the colossal waste of war and the economics of power, *Mauberley* employs Siddall's image to highlight the rift that developed in the early twentieth century between viewing writing as commercial product or the product of careful craftsmanship. According to this multipart and multifaceted poem, the senseless destruction of the war-machine has not promoted clear perception but rather the grey-green gaze of postwar "Yeux Glauques." The synecdochical, "vacant" eyes by which readers come to recognize Siddall allude at once to the Pre-Raphaelite fascination with the female body and the exploitation of the female model/muse by Rossetti, her "last maquero."[50]

The "Yeux Glauques" of Pound's Siddall refer also to the tension between the conservative morality of Robert Buchanan, demonstrated in his essay about the "fleshly" content of Rossetti's poetry,[51] and Pre-Raphaelite sensuality, a tension H.D. develops in *White Rose and the Red* in Morris's condemnation of Rossetti's overtly sensual painting, *Bocca Baciata* (1859) (see figure 7). For Pound, and Morris in *White Rose*, this conflict between aestheticism and morality is staged around the spectacle of Elizabeth Siddall's beauty. Rossetti's reputation as an artist was solidified in large part by the exploitation of Siddall's enigmatic beauty through the production and circulation of pictures of her.[52] The destructive influence that this relationship with Rossetti and the art market had on Siddall is highlighted by the emphasis Pound gives to her "half-ruin'd face," the personification of which Violet Hunt and then H.D. explore in their respective works. Siddall's spectral "Yeux Glauques" that lurk at the heart of Pound's *Mauberley* provocatively allude to masculine spectatorship and consumerism, issues that implicate both artist and model. In turn, H.D. builds on the power of this visual image in her novel, which situates Siddall at the center of a Pre-Raphaelite narrative and foregrounds her interactions with ghosts through the medium of the spiritualist séance.

Yet, disappointingly, Siddall loses agency in *White Rose*, and her death/suicide is mourned in the final pages of the novel. Functioning as a refrain throughout the novel, William Allingham's ballad "The Cold Wedding" is a powerful intertext as it uses the image of a wedding to announce the death that awaits the pale bride and bridegroom. This ballad surfaces repeatedly to call our attention to the sensational death that all know awaits Elizabeth Siddall herself.

In 1932 Violet Hunt published the first biography of Elizabeth Siddall, *Wife of Rossetti*, and it was this biography that served as H.D.'s main source for *White Rose and the Red*.[53] An epigraph to H.D.'s novel clarifies H.D.'s intention to modify Hunt's interpretation: "We are immeasurably indebted to the late Violet Hunt, for her reconstruction of the period, and we have profited by her recording the names of many of the minor characters in this narrative, though we differ in our attitude and approach to *The Wife of Rossetti*" (*WR*, 7). Hunt's biography focuses in particular on the damaging effects that Rossetti's neglect had on Siddall. Sensationalistic and melodramatic in its attempt to capture the marital tensions of the couple, Violet Hunt's desire to produce the truth about a woman who has been relegated to the margins of the Pre-Raphaelite movement fails. Hunt deprives Siddall of any personality altogether: she describes her as being "virtuous, static, almost characterless except for a natal obstinacy."[54]

The "static" quality of Hunt's portrayal of Siddall comes from an account based on personal memories of figures associated with the Pre-Raphaelite Brotherhood, and from gossip gleaned from diaries and letters. Despite her attempts to reveal Siddall's personality, Hunt characterizes her as a perennial consumptive (there are repeated descriptions of her ailing body) and reduces her poetry to an allegory of the sad events in her life. Unlike Hunt's biography, which compiles a host of different interpretations of Siddall's character from various men and women associated with the Pre-Raphaelites, H.D. registers most of the events between the years 1849 and 1862 through the consciousness of this artist and model. In this way H.D. begins the transformation of Hunt's "static" version of Siddall into the dynamic one developed by later feminist critics and art historians.

In *White Rose* H.D. enters into dialogue with many of the versions of Siddall circulating in autobiographical and biographical portraits of the Pre-Raphaelite movement over the years. Part of the mystery surrounding Siddall resides in the many contrasting versions of her that circulate in art and criticism. In 1989 Jan Marsh published her fascinating exposé *The Legend of Elizabeth Siddal*, a biographical history of the stories about this woman from the nineteenth century to the present. Marsh shows the various characterizations of Siddall as languishing maiden, manipulative partner, suicidal hysteric, poet, artist, and exploited model. During her lifetime, Siddall was perceived more as the dependent and lover of Rossetti than as an artist whose talent was officially recognized by the great Victorian arbiter of art, John Ruskin, and by Harvard Professor of Fine Arts, Charles Eliot Norton.[55]

After her death, biographers invoked her in terms of absence and loss because of her macabre identity as Rossetti's dead beloved, and the model for Millais's painting of the drowned *Ophelia* (1851–52) and Rossetti's *Beata Beatrix* (1864–70). All served conclusively to link Siddall's beauty with death (see figures 5 and 6). The lasting impression of Siddall, as H.D.'s novel makes clear, is of a woman known for her frailty and recurring illnesses, her great beauty, her poetic feeling, and her identity as Rossetti's model, muse, and wife. Yet, H.D.'s emphasis on mirrors, trances, and dream visions also foregrounds Siddall's ontological instability and suggests that therein lies her heroine's subversive potential, a subjectivity not confined by Rossetti's subjugating measures or his critics.' Rather than present Siddall as a woman on whom viewers look, H.D. directs the viewer's gaze through Siddall's eyes, eyes that witness firsthand the legacy of neglect that characterizes Siddall's relationship with Rossetti.

The different versions of Siddall rendered and disseminated since her death in 1862 are sites of cultural anxiety, as the increasing numbers of articles and books testify.[56] At stake in these versions are worries about femininity, identity, authorship, and women's artistic labour, issues that H.D. investigated in poetic and prose forms throughout her career. The complexity of Siddall's image, however, stems from her elusiveness. Although omnipresent in biographies of the Pre-Raphaelite movement, Siddall enjoys a legacy that strangely hinges on an absent history, one that has invited fictional reconstructions, much like H.D.'s speculations in *White Rose and the Red*. A lacuna that exists in the midst of dualisms, Siddall lurks between health and illness, art and politics, beauty and horror, life and death.

By fictionalizing Siddall in a novel about the Pre-Raphaelites, H.D. adds her own version to the genealogy of "Siddall," and in this way contributes to the tradition in twentieth-century art and literary criticism that seeks to recover marginalized art sisters. H.D.'s sympathetic portrayal of Siddall in the 1930s and 1940s anticipates work done in the 1980s and 1990s by such feminist art historians as Griselda Pollock and Deborah Cherry, and literary scholars like Jan Marsh and Pamela Gerrish Nunn, who highlight the female artists (both visual and literary) affiliated with members of the Brotherhood in an effort to rethink male-centered views of Pre-Raphaelitism.

Of limited importance in H.D.'s *White Rose* is the emphasis given to the communities, circles even, that Elizabeth Siddall develops with women. These Sisterhoods attempt to re-envision the exclusive male, homosocial bond of the Pre-Raphaelite Brotherhood. Rossetti, Holman Hunt, and Millais (in the first Brotherhood of 1848) and Rossetti, Morris, and Burne-Jones (in 1856, the second phase of the Pre-Raphaelite movement) developed a mutually supportive (and almost exclusively male) society. Letters passed between members of the movement and their patrons, encouraging each other to pursue their artistic goals, defending work (Pre-Raphaelite or otherwise) bought by Brothers, and suggesting new subjects for paintings. This Brotherhood in *White Rose* is a distinctively male sphere, as is indicated by its name, the Order of Sir Galahad.

As H.D.'s novel demonstrates, although this "magic-circle" (*WR*, 48) of Brothers is a useful configuration for male self-promotion, it is marred by the power politics implicit in the relationships among the members, the artists and models, and the artists and their patrons. H.D.'s Siddall does not attempt to join this Brotherhood; instead, she remains "a-part," blocked from participating in this male sphere but involved in its powerful tensions as the lover and wife of its leader (Rossetti) and the beloved of one of the Brothers (Morris). Writing, painting, and table-tipping become the activities that help her to cope with feelings of exclusion and loneliness.[57] The Sisterhood H.D. develops in the trances experienced by the Siddall figure, the "Greensleeves circle," harkens back to the triumvirate Siddall first forms with her biological sisters to enrich her sense of familial identity, and to the unofficial Sisterhood of artists and women's activists Siddall organizes with Anna Mary Howitt (referred to as Mary in *White Rose*), Barbara Leigh Smith, and Bessie Parkes. The groups H.D. creates as counterparts to this male Brotherhood attempt to supply the personal and spiritual support that Siddall's relationships with men lack. The relevance of the circle of these "Ladies of Greensleeves" is compromised, however, by the fact that they only appear to Siddall in trances and dreams, and the comfort they offer is all too transient.

Through her sustained evocation of Elizabeth Siddall and the Pre-Raphaelites in *White Rose and the Red*, H.D. acknowledges the importance of the nineteenth-century past in her chaotic modernist present. Evidently, Siddall as a spectacle of youthful beauty and decay haunts H.D. in the 1940s. Yet the decision to conclude her novel with Siddall's sensational death/suicide unfortunately solidifies popular representations of Siddall as a languishing maiden and dead beloved. Siddall's tomb is juxtaposed with Rossetti's *House of Life*, that "fiery sonnet-sequence" (*WR*, 322) folded in her cold, dead hands. Using Siddall to comment on the problems of representation, literary and visual, H.D. breathes life into a figure who appears to haunt the imaginations of at least two modernists (Pound and H.D., respectively). "We all thought we knew her," claims Debra Mancoff in her fascinating study of this enigmatic artist, model, and muse. "Elizabeth Siddal [. . .] came to us wrapped in the shadows of myth."[58] The conclusion of H.D.'s *White Rose* proves that the genealogy of "Siddall" is indelibly marked by the now-mythical tales that have circulated about her since her death in 1862.

Elizabeth Siddall's own drawing "A Woman and a Spectre" (n.d.) (see figure 9) poses many of the questions H.D. asks about the privilege of artistic representation. Title and drawing render a causal connection between a woman and a ghost—Siddall formally highlights this connection with the pencil lines that depict the spirit emerging from the body of the dead woman. These lines imply that, to some extent, woman *is* a spectre, the phantom figuring a thematic and ideological excess that hovers over this spectacle of dead femininity. The emergence of the spirit from the dead woman's pubic region reinforces the sexual spectacularization of femininity, of *dead* femininity at that. Intersecting over the dead woman's genitalia, the lines of spectre and woman call attention to Siddall's particularly gendered figuration of spectrality. From the dead woman's corpse arises the apparition of the madwoman: the eyes of the spirit are haunted and haunting.

In this drawing, Siddall participates in the Pre-Raphaelite fascination with women—and with her own image—that H.D. eventually analyzes in the late 1940s. "A Woman and a Spectre" in this way captures the transformation of woman into *revenant* in a more violent fashion than Rossetti would in *Beata Beatrix* (1864–70), a painting that foregrounds Dante's beloved Beatrice poised on the threshold of death. A memorial to his wife, Rossetti's painting figures this woman as the beatitude of his (and Dante's) idealized vision. But Rossetti's Beatrice is a far cry from Siddall's (and H.D.'s) tormented phantom. Rising from an inert corpse, the ghost in Siddall's drawing connotes decomposition rather than idealization, trauma instead of ease.

In addition, the inscription scrawled on the verso of Siddall's drawing articulates the difficulty in apprehending the "real" Siddall. The note reads: "By Lizzie I think"; Jan Marsh observes that this note is "probably by WMR [William Michael Rossetti]."[59] A casual note, probably written by her brother-in-law, suggests that the drawing is probably by Elizabeth Siddall. Neither the picture nor the note is signed; W. M. Rossetti and Marsh speculate about the drawing's original author. Rossetti's and Marsh's glosses thus point to the double conjecture involved in the drawing's lack of signature. The phrase "By Lizzie I think" juxtaposes familiarity and uncertainty, a lack of ceremony (implied in the use of a personal name), and a careless ambiguity about the author's identity. This explanatory note sums up the predominant Pre-Raphaelite and modernist tendency to take Siddall for granted, and the rare struggles to apprehend Siddall in and through literature and visual art. W. M. Rossetti's supposed attribution of this drawing is not surprising given its engagement with illness and death, themes that are linked typologically with Siddall herself (and are in turn solidified at the end of H.D.'s elusive novel).

In its entirety, *White Rose and the Red* presents a fascinating portrait of the Pre-Raphaelite Brotherhood and its interpersonal politics from a feminist perspective. Siddall is the ideal subject for H.D.'s investigation of the Pre-Raphaelites because of the creative potential that arises from the development and deployment of this enigmatic figure as the text's narrative centre, its vital "Yeux Glauques." Drawn no doubt to the shadows of myth that characterize Siddall's legacy, H.D.'s revision of her history complicates this idea of the nineteenth-century woman as a pale, withdrawn, sensitive being by suggesting that the creative power of the female artist emerges in her dreams and trances. By centering on Siddall's spiritualist experiences, H.D. attempts to develop the depths of a woman whose fame, up until then, was associated primarily with her luxurious red hair and her grey-green eyes.

Notes

NOTES TO "A NOTE ON THE EDITION"

1. In the spelling of Elizabeth Siddall's surname H.D. participates in a controversy that would continue into the twenty-first century. Over the course of her association with the Pre-Raphaelites, Siddall's identity as a woman and an artist was complicated by the many nicknames (Lizzie, Liz, Guggums, Guggum, Gug, The Sid, Miss Sid, Miss Siddal, Ida) she was given by members of the Brotherhood, names that crop up in *White Rose*. Critics, biographers, and historians have argued for years over the correct spelling of her surname, spelling it "Siddal," "Sudel," or "Siddall." Deborah Cherry and Griselda Pollock suggest that in art historical criticism, Siddall has been predominantly recognized as a beautiful model, as the beloved of Rossetti, and, most of all, as an enigma whose mystery and elusiveness are enhanced by the various names and identities that she was given ("Woman as Sign in Pre-Raphaelite Literature," 207). The existence of Siddall as a stable, knowable person is also undermined by the loss of her date of birth from genealogical history. H.D. addresses this element of the Siddall myth in her novel as well. In the creation of *White Rose* H.D. replicates the uncertainty of Siddall's identity by changing the spelling of Siddall's surname in the draft stage of the writing process. In the four typescript drafts of *White Rose and the Red*, H.D. substitutes the spelling of "Siddal" (in the second draft) with "Siddall" (in the fourth). In this edition I employ the latter spelling (Siddall), which is the one that H.D. used in the production of the final typescript.

2. The importance of H.D.'s feminist critique of the Pre-Raphaelite Brotherhood becomes especially clear when reading criticism from the 1990s that recuperated work by previously unrecognized Pre-Raphaelite female artists. See, for example, Clarissa Campbell Orr, *Women in the Victorian Art World*, for a general revision of male-centered approaches to Victorian aesthetic circles. See Jan Marsh, *Pre-Raphaelite Sisterhood*, for a much more specific re-reading of the Pre-Raphaelite movement from a distinctly feminist perspective.

3. Caroline Zilboorg, introduction to *Richard Aldington and H.D.: The Later*

Years in Letters, vii. Robert Spoo, "Editing H.D.'s *Asphodel*: Selected Emendations and Notes," 13. The editions of H.D.'s works that were published prior to this edition of *White Rose and the Red*, specifically Spoo's edition of *Asphodel*, Jane Augustine's edition of *The Gift*, and Cynthia Hogue and Julie Vandivere's recent edition of *The Sword Went Out to Sea* were very helpful in the preparation of this edition.

4. Zilboorg, *Later Years*, vii.

5. Ibid., 194. The time is propitious for the publication of *White Rose*, as Cynthia Hogue and Julie Vandivere's edition of *Sword* was published in 2007. *White Rose and the Red* is the middle text in a trilogy of war novels written by H.D.'s author persona, Delia Alton, which includes *The Sword Went Out to Sea* and *The Mystery*. The *Sword* (whose title was taken from William Morris's lyric, "Sailing of the Sword") is based on séance communications that Lord Hugh Dowding and Delia had with dead or "lost" R.A.F. pilots in London 1945. In *The Mystery* H.D. explores her Moravian ancestry, inspired by the history of Count Zinzendorf. Jane Augustine's edition of *The Mystery* is currently in process. These exciting publications will clarify and complicate our reception of H.D. as a writer of prose.

NOTES TO INTRODUCTION

1. Writer Richard Aldington (1892–1962) helped found the Imagist movement in 1912 with Ezra Pound (1885–1972), and Aldington and H.D. became lovers in 1912 and married in 1913. Aldington saw active service in France and Flanders; however, he and H.D. did not live together after his demobilization in 1919. They separated finally in autumn 1919, but continued to write to each other until H.D.'s death in 1961. H.D. felt deeply about Aldington, and he appeared in several of her prose works, *Asphodel* and *Bid Me to Live* specifically. Aldington was also one of H.D.'s principal readers of *White Rose*.

2. Zilboorg, *Later Years*, 110. Richard Aldington and H.D. discuss the process of writing *White Rose and the Red* at length in a series of letters that span the better part of two years (1947 to 1949). See Zilboorg, *Later Years*, 93–110, 126–30, 137–39 passim. In this exchange they speculate about the possible influence that a younger William Morris could have had on Siddall, an invention to Pre-Raphaelite history that H.D. develops in detail in the second half of *White Rose*. Zilboorg's edition of these letters as well as her glosses are very helpful in understanding the genesis of H.D.'s novel about the Pre-Raphaelites.

3. A folder labelled "Pre-Raphaelites" (YCAL MSS 24, Box 51, Folder 1289) housed among the H.D. papers at Yale's Beinecke Rare Book and Manuscript Library contains the catalogue for the 1948 exhibit on the Pre-Raphaelites, held at the Whitechapel Gallery from April 8 to May 12. On the cover of the catalogue is a reproduction of D. G. Rossetti's *Portrait of Elizabeth Siddall* (see figure 1). This catalogue demonstrates Rossetti's obsessive attempts to capture the essence of his lover and eventual wife. Such pictures as *Beatrice Denying her Salutation to Dante* and *The Salutation of Beatrice* were on display, as was the *Portrait of Miss Siddall*, and at least four other pictures in which Siddall is the primary subject.

4. H.D., *The Sword Went Out to Sea (Synthesis of a Dream), by Delia Alton*, 25. In *Sword* the author persona, Delia Alton, suggests that her method of coping with the war was to celebrate the riches (especially the literature) of England.

5. The year 1848 marked the Chartists' revolt in England and the antimonarchist rebellion in France. And 1948, the year H.D. completed her novel about the Pre-Raphaelites, reminds one of the value of artistry in the wake of war, a theme H.D. explores in detail in *Trilogy*. H.D.'s major investment in the Pre-Raphaelites in the 1930s and 1940s anticipated the national and international attention given to the centenary.

6. Letter dated February 8, 1944, H.D. to Mary Herr, a former classmate from Bryn Mawr, quoted in Donna Krolik Hollenberg, *Between History and Poetry: The Letters of H.D. and Norman Holmes Pearson*, 19.

7. Zilboorg, *Later Years*, 126.

8. In its fictional investigation of women in relation to the Pre-Raphaelite Brotherhood, *White Rose and the Red* shares similarities with Margaret Hunt's *Magdalen Wynyard, or, The Provocations of a Pre-Raphaelite* (1872), Violet Paget's *Miss Brown* (1884), and Olivia Shakespear's *Rupert Armstrong* (1898). Interestingly, these late-Victorian authors also had connections with or were influenced by the Pre-Raphaelites. Margaret Hunt (1831–1912) was the wife of the landscape painter and water-colorist Alfred William Hunt, and mother of Violet Hunt (1862–1942), author of *Wife of Rossetti*, one of the source texts for H.D.'s novel. Both Violet Paget (1856–1935) and Olivia Shakespear (1863–1938) were women of letters with connections to the Victorian aesthetes and early modernists: Paget was an acquaintance of Henry James, Walter Pater, and Oscar Wilde; Shakespear was Yeats's first lover, lifelong correspondent, and confidante, and the mother of Ezra Pound's wife, Dorothy Shakespear.

9. The Pre-Raphaelites popularized particular types of beauty in the nineteenth century, most specifically the modest maiden with quasi-spiritual attributes, the golden beauty, the enigmatic femme fatale, the languishing maiden, and the dying woman. See Elizabeth Prettejohn, *Rossetti and His Circle*, 9, 10, 16, 24. For a more detailed analysis of these types of the Pre-Raphaelite "stunner," see Jan Marsh, *Pre-Raphaelite Women: Images of Femininity in Pre-Raphaelite Art*. In *White Rose* H.D. humanizes many of these "types" of beauty. However much H.D.'s novel engages with ideals of beauty projected onto the female models associated with the Pre-Raphaelites, *White Rose* disappointingly does not dismantle many of the myths surrounding Siddall's continual illnesses and her death/suicide.

10. In "Compassionate Friendship" (YCAL MSS 24, Box 38, Folders 1011–1014), a document in which she describes the genesis of much of her literary work, H.D. refers to the winter of 1948 when she finished *Red Rose and the White* (*CF*, 54). This version of the novel's name is typical of H.D.'s play with names and naming in general. This work is unpublished, held among the H.D. Papers, YCAL/Beinecke.

11. In 1948, H.D. wrote to Aldington, expressing an interest in publishing *White Rose* and *The Sword Went Out to Sea* as part of a prose trilogy, and announced that

she had sent the novels to her editors at Macmillan for review. Zilboorg, *Later Years*, 127. Susan Friedman, in *Penelope's Web: Gender, Modernity, H.D.'s Fiction*, describes *White Rose* as having been "probably rejected" by publishers (365).

12. For Susan Stanford Friedman's evaluation of *White Rose and the Red* and *The Mystery* as unsuccessful autobiographical or historical novels, see Friedman, *Penelope's Web*, 357. See Cassandra Laity, *H.D. and the Victorian Fin de Siècle: Gender, Modernism, Decadence*, xiv, for her characterization of *White Rose* as fictional autobiography. See also Hollenberg, *Between History and Poetry*, 69.

13. Zilboorg, *Later Years*, 103.

14. Ibid., 103.

15. Ibid., 94.

16. Ibid., 124.

17. Hollenberg, *Between History and Poetry*, 75–96 passim. The letters between H.D. and Norman Holmes Pearson collected and analyzed in Donna Krolik Hollenberg's edition are an invaluable resource when learning about the shaping of *White Rose* for publication.

18. Ibid., 82.

19. Barbara Guest, *Herself Defined: The Poet H.D. and Her World*, 287. Guest is no fan of *White Rose and the Red* either, characterizing it as a work that interfered with H.D.'s other, more "sensible" writing.

20. Hollenberg, *Between History and Poetry*, 83.

21. Ibid., 83.

22. See Lawrence Rainey, "Canon, Gender, and Text: The Case of H.D.," 102–7 passim. In his contentious essay Rainey distinguishes between a perception of H.D. constructed by literary and feminist critics in the 1980s, and the "actual" H.D. suggested by the poetry and prose she published during her lifetime. By insisting on this distinction, Rainey depicts H.D. as an economically privileged writer whose work was too precious and too idiosyncratic for widespread publication. Not only does he maintain that her work was intended only for a small coterie of friends, Rainey also insists that it was published primarily because of Bryher's connections with the Contact Publishing Company. ("Bryher" was the name taken by Winifred Ellerman [1894–1983]. Writer and philanthropist, Bryher was H.D.'s life-partner until H.D.'s death in 1961.) In the same essay, Rainey contends that H.D.'s novels and romans à clef, like *White Rose*, held no interest for most readers as they took as their subject obscure people, and were directed towards, and were only of interest to, what he labels a literary "aristocracy" and "elite." Rainey concludes that H.D.'s contributions to various avant-garde magazines (forty-three reviews and articles, but he does not specify) indicated an unwillingness to participate in the modernist critical institution. Rainey also fails to account for H.D.'s active involvement in communities of modernists that thrived on literary dialogue and critical exchange. Georgina Taylor's study, *H.D. and the Public Sphere of Modernist Women Writers*, outlines the networks of writers in which H.D. actively participated, working as a literary editor for the *Egoist*, planning three Imagist anthologies with Amy Lowell and Richard

Aldington, and preparing the two Poets' Translation Series with Aldington for the
Egoist Press. As well as her critical contributions to the *Little Review*, the *Egoist*, and
the *Adelphi*, H.D. contributed reviews and commentaries to the avant-garde film
magazine *Close Up*, another collaborative project that involved Bryher, Kenneth
Macpherson, and H.D. during the late 1920s and 1930s. These avant-garde journals
were not the casual outgrowth of a select coterie of artists; H.D. was undeniably
taking part in a wider communicating public, one whose dynamic discussions were
enriched by the arrival of new participants and new ideas.

23. Zilboorg, *Later Years*, 127.

24. Hollenberg, *Between History and Poetry*, 84.

25. Cassandra Laity theorizes about this interest in Victorian and Decadent artists in *H.D. and the Victorian Fin de Siècle*.

26. Friedman, *Penelope's Web*, 72. Friedman's study of H.D.'s prose initiated the
critical investigation into the hybrid nature of H.D.'s narratives. In *White Rose*, William Morris describes the Grail stories, so resonant in H.D.'s novel about the Pre-
Raphaelites, as being at once "legendary," "symbolic," and "historical." Through this
superimposition of historical modes and literary types, H.D.'s novel questions strict
notions of linearity and generic composition. Morris goes on to tell Siddall about
Swinburne's appropriation of Malory's tales, a project that also juxtaposes literary
modes: "You must see Algernon. He was the first to bring the poetry of Provence
actually, to my notice. It is the Grail story, but history. I knew it was real, but real in
another sense—that is, legendary, symbolic. But apparently, it is both history and
legend" (*WR*, 213). The weaving metaphor implied by Friedman's title, a dominant
trope in much of H.D.'s poetry and prose, signals the continuous process of reworking and transforming temporal and generic modes that is at the core of H.D.'s poetics.

27. *White Rose* develops D. G. Rossetti's connections to the nineteenth-century
spiritualist movement, and in so doing builds on the importance of spiritualism
and the séance table that *The Sword Went Out to Sea* explores in such detail. H.D.'s
preoccupations with spiritualism, psychoanalysis, cosmology, and the Kabbala have
been extensively documented by critics before me, most specifically by Susan Stanford Friedman in *Psyche Reborn: The Emergence of H.D.* and Helen Sword in *Ghostwriting Modernism*. See also Timothy Materer in *Modernist Alchemy: Poetry and
the Occult*.

Describing the Pre-Raphaelites as her *"familiars"* (*DA*, 195), H.D. emphasizes the
direct connection she developed during World War II with the Pre-Raphaelites over
the Morris and Co. table that sat in her London living room. H.D. began holding séances with the Eurasian psychic, Arthur Bhaduri, in 1941, among a "circle" of eight
inquirers at Walton House (which she called "Stanford House"), where the International Institute for Psychic Investigation was located. By January 1942 H.D. wanted
more personal attention than the group of eight provided, so Bryher arranged for
a "home circle" with the required minimum four members. H.D., Bryher, Bhaduri,
and his mother May met at Lowndes Square every Friday evening until mid-1944.

My thanks to Jane Augustine for several e-mails June 13, 2007 and July 5, 2007, drawing from her own work in progress, *The Poet and the Airman*, in which she clarifies H.D.'s spiritualist involvements in the 1940s.

In October 1943 H.D. attended a particular lecture on spiritualism that affected her profoundly. Lord Hugh Dowding, Air Chief Marshal of the Royal Air Force (R.A.F.) and author of the spiritualist treatise *Many Mansions*, was the speaker. In the ensuing months, H.D. corresponded with Dowding, describing to him particular images she had seen in séances and had begun to associate with him. Late in the summer of 1945, inspired by Dowding's alleged communications with lost R.A.F. pilots, H.D. received messages from a group of airmen killed during the Battle of Britain; they warned her about the dangers of atomic warfare. H.D. turned to Dowding for help in analyzing these messages, but he replied in February 1946, dismissing her visions as trivial. Susan Friedman attributes Dowding's rejection to be the cause of H.D.'s severe illness in 1946 (*Psyche Reborn*, 175). H.D. describes the breakdown that ensued in the opening chapters of *The Sword Went Out to Sea*.

Spiritualism is an extremely fruitful discourse in *White Rose*: it allows Siddall (and H.D.) to engage actively in literary creation, to make veiled allusions to Arthur's Round Table and the Templar Knights, to juxtapose noncontemporaneous events, and to question a strictly linear view of history. It also provides compensation for Siddall's lack of emotional fulfilment with Rossetti.

28. Laity, *H.D. and the Victorian Fin de Siècle*, 119. Laity identifies H.D.'s return to the Pre-Raphaelites as a kind of revisionism that provided her with an "alternative sexual/textual program for a 'female' modernism" (117). My analysis of *White Rose* has been immeasurably shaped by Laity's analysis of H.D.'s difficult novel.

29. Ibid., 118.

30. Ibid., 144.

31. Siddall's health issues have long been of interest to critics, further reinforcing the view of her as a fragile figure. For responses to Siddall's illnesses that are contemporaneous to Siddall and the Pre-Raphaelites, see Oswald Doughty, *A Victorian Romantic: Dante Gabriel Rossetti*, 262–304 passim, and Evelyn Waugh, *Rossetti: His Life and Works*, 56, 107, 110. For more contemporary analyses of Siddall's health problems, see Jan Marsh, *Pre-Raphaelite Sisterhood*, 48–49, and Isabelle Williams, "Elizabeth Siddal: The Health Issue," 53–70. Siddall's weakened condition is a central aspect of the myths associated with her; so too is her death. After experiencing a devastating stillbirth in May 1861, Siddall's mental state was clearly affected; she became dependent on laudanum, which eventually led to her death/suicide in February 1862. Siddall was buried in the Rossetti family grave in Highgate in 1862. Rossetti had the coffin exhumed in 1869 in order to retrieve the manuscript book of poems he had buried with her. This bizarre exhumation has become central to the legend of Elizabeth Siddall.

32. *The Sword Went Out to Sea* features a "painted-lady," a woman who is in turn linked to the author persona, Delia Alton, and to an unspecified other time in England. Given the complex intertextuality of both *Sword* and *White Rose* I suggest

that the "painted-lady" of *Sword* is none other than Elizabeth Siddall herself; this reference confirms the sustained dialogue between these two texts in the trilogy of war novels.

33. For a thorough examination of the impact of Freud on H.D.—and Bryher especially—see Susan Stanford Friedman's edition, *Analyzing Freud: Letters of H.D., Bryher, and Their Circle*. See also H.D's memoir, *Tribute to Freud*, for details about this period in her life. In *White Rose* the allusions to Mr. Greenacre are another interesting off-shoot of this conflict between the life and death drives. Mr. Greenacre, a grocer who lived near the Siddalls in London, murdered the laundress, Hannah Brown, a week before their wedding day, allegedly to inherit the money his fiancée brought with her. Siddall muses towards the end of *White Rose* that the Ladies of Greensleeves that she sees in her visions offer compensation for her nightmares about this violent man. Mr. Greenacre is another element that H.D. takes from Violet Hunt's biography of Siddall. See Violet Hunt, *Wife of Rossetti*, 120–21.

34. Rossetti's short story "Hand and Soul" outlines the history of the artist figure, Chiaro dell'Erma, who is granted a vision of his soul, personified as a beautiful woman, who advises him to appropriate her as his inspiration.

35. Eileen Gregory, *H.D. and Hellenism: Classic Lines*, 2.

36. This concern with the dynamism of the "now" parallels the Pre-Raphaelite concern with the mutable moment, especially evident in the sonnets that make up Rossetti's *House of Life* (1881), each of which presents "a moment's monument." Dante Gabriel Rossetti, *Collected Poetry and Prose*, 127.

37. T. S. Eliot, *Four Quartets*, 13.

38. Complementing this idea of time as being repetitive, circles in *Sword* and *White Rose* call attention to the links between and among people and particular time periods. It is significantly through her séance circles, her "home circles" as Delia Alton calls them in *Sword*, that she establishes "networks of secret workers" from different episodes in history (*S*, 131). Around the "Round Table," the Morris and Co. table that sat in her London living room, Delia talks of the Knights of the Round Table, whom she eventually associates with the lost R.A.F. pilots with whom she was communicating.

39. In this passage H.D. refers to the beginnings of the spiritualist movement, first developed in North America in 1848 with the phenomenon of the "Rochester Rappings," the mysterious noises that the sisters Margaret and Kate Fox claimed to hear at Hydesville, near Rochester, in upstate New York. Margaret Fox eventually revealed that she and her sister produced the rappings by throwing their big toes out of joint. See Ernest Isaacs, "The Fox Sisters and American Spiritualism," 104. The section in *White Rose* about the Fox sisters renames them (Mary and Kathy, as opposed to Margaret and Kate) and relocates the site of their séances to a Connecticut farm.

40. Zilboorg, *Later Years*, 94.

41. See Bonnie Kime Scott's anthology, *The Gender of Modernism* (1990) for the important expansions it makes to the modernist canon. See also Georgina Tay-

lor's fascinating analysis of H.D. and the spheres of influence through which she navigated in *H.D. and the Public Sphere of Modernist Women Writers, 1913–1946: Talking Women* (2001).

42. For a more sustained analysis of Rossetti's importance for the modernists, see Jerome McGann, *Dante Gabriel Rossetti and the Game That Must Be Lost* (2000).

43. T. S. Eliot, "Tradition and the Individual Talent," in *Selected Prose*, 40. Ezra Pound, *Literary Essays of Ezra Pound*, 387.

44. Modernist links to the Victorians are undeniable. In his *Autobiographies*, W. B. Yeats acknowledges: "I was in all things Pre-Raphaelite. . . . We were all Pre-Raphaelites then" (141). Not only was Evelyn Waugh the nephew of William Holman Hunt, but his first two books focused on the Pre-Raphaelites: *P.R.B.: An essay on the Pre-Raphaelite Brotherhood* (1926) and *Rossetti: His Life and Works* (1928). Ford Madox Ford's first book was a biography of his grandfather (*Ford Madox Brown: a record of his life and work* [1896]), and he produced several essays about the movement: *Rossetti: a critical essay on his art* (1902) and *The Pre-Raphaelite Brotherhood: A Critical Monograph* (1907). In spite of these clear connections, modernists emphasized their distance from their literary and artistic precursors.

45. Hogue and Vandivere's edition of *The Sword Went Out to Sea* provides an important gloss to this friendship with Ezra Pound. In this roman à clef Pound emerges as Allen Flint, and Delia Alton (H.D.'s author persona) reads poems by the Pre-Raphaelites with him (*S*, 56).

46. For an expansive treatment of the Pre-Raphaelites, see Elizabeth Prettejohn, *The Art of the Pre-Raphaelites* and Tim Barringer, *Reading the Pre-Raphaelites*. The two principal movements of Pre-Raphaelitism originated in the years 1848 and 1856, respectively. Reacting against the aesthetic conventions of their day, William Holman Hunt, John Everett Millais, and Dante Gabriel Rossetti inaugurated the Pre-Raphaelite Brotherhood in 1848, a movement featuring art that rebelled against such academic traditions as pyramid structure, scale of coloration, and complacency of style encouraged by Sir Joshua Reynolds (first president of the Royal Academy). Inspired by John Ruskin's *Modern Painters* (1843–60) to "go to nature," the Pre-Raphaelites imitated and adapted the bright colors and verisimilitude of depiction of fifteenth-century Italian art. Ruskin's encouragement to give "truth to nature" aimed to produce an objective depiction of the external world rather than an idealization of the human figure, and suggested that this intense scrutiny of nature would reveal higher truths. Critic William Michael Rossetti, sculptor Thomas Woolner, painter James Collinson, and painter and art critic Frederic Stephens soon joined the three founding members of the group, which prided itself on innovation and collaboration.

In contrast, the second wave of Pre-Raphaelitism, represented principally by Rossetti, William Morris, and Edward Burne-Jones, stressed an interest in medieval subjects and themes inspired by Sir Thomas Malory's narratives in *Le Morte d'Arthur*, a visual sensuality, and a move away from realism in favor of the careful staging of subjects. Arthur Hughes, John Roddam Spencer Stanhope, and Valentine

Cameron Prinsep joined Rossetti, Burne-Jones, and Morris in producing the medievalesque mural paintings in the Oxford Union Debating Chamber in 1857. Ruskin's *Stones of Venice* (1851–53) encouraged Morris and Burne-Jones to study medieval art and architecture, as well as to use art for social critique. Turning to medieval England as a model for Victorian reform, they adopted a set of artistic axioms that stressed the values of work and community, not to mention the dynamic qualities of Gothic architecture.

Although this second wave of Pre-Raphaelitism was interested in all things medieval, there was no longer a sense of unity in terms of the overarching style shared by members of the movement. Holman Hunt's religious scenes, inspired by trips to the Holy Land, stand in sharp contrast to Morris's growing interest in household decoration and the Arts and Crafts movement. Moreover, Morris's interest in the socialist implications of Gothic architecture was not shared by Rossetti or Burne-Jones, who eschewed overt sociopolitical involvement. Rossetti's later portrait *Bocca Baciata* (1859) exemplifies his gradual deviance from early Pre-Raphaelite principles in favor of an open sensuality (see figure 7). In *White Rose*, Morris uses this painting, which vividly demonstrates Rossetti's aesthetic changes, to describe Rossetti's infidelities to Siddall.

47. T. E. Hulme, *Speculations: Essays on Humanism and the Philosophy of Art*, 133.

48. See Lesley Higgins, *The Modernist Cult of Ugliness: Aesthetic and Gender Politics* for a cogent examination of the gender norms enforced through modernist aesthetic ideologies. Chapter 1 employs Ruskin and Whistler to explore problems involved in modernist legitimizations of idealized beauty and highlights the misogyny that shapes their different views. Chapter 2 reveals the homophobic energies with which male modernists made an "enemy" of Walter Pater. I am especially grateful for Higgins's analysis of the interface of modernism and social constructions of gender differences.

49. The fascinating cross-pollination of Victorianism and modernism is a topic about which much important criticism is still being produced. Carol Christ's *Victorian and Modern Poetics* spearheaded this examination of tropes and themes that link Victorian and modernist literary traditions. See also Peter Faulkner, "Pound and the Pre-Raphaelites," 229–44. Laity's analysis of the Decadent writers on H.D. is also important in the configuration of a Victorian modernism, as is Jerome McGann's exploration of Rossetti's influence on modernists.

50. Pound, *The Selected Poems of Ezra Pound*, 65.

51. In October 1871 Robert Buchanan (under the pseudonym Thomas Maitland) published the inflammatory essay "The Fleshly School of Poetry: Mr. D. G. Rossetti" in *The Contemporary Review*. In it he accuses Rossetti of extolling "fleshliness" as the supreme end of poetic and pictorial art. Buchanan's rhetoric achieves the height of hyperbole when he suggests that members of the fleshly school of verse-writers (specifically Rossetti and Swinburne) are "spreading the seeds of disease broadcast

wherever they are read and understood." This passage is quoted in Carolyn Hares-Stryker, *An Anthology of Pre-Raphaelite Writings*, 238.

52. Elizabeth Siddall as a spectacle of youthful beauty and decay is reinforced by the versions Rossetti completed of *The Blessed Damozel*, John Everett Millais's *Ophelia* (1851–52), and Rossetti's posthumous painting, *Beata Beatrix* (1864–70) (see figures 4, 5, and 6). The process of painting *Ophelia* remains one of the myths associated with Siddall. The story goes that, while posing for the painting, she played dead and became ill in the process. The creation of Millais's gorgeously evocative painting, representing the beginning of Siddall's interactions with the Pre-Raphaelites, eventually culminates in Rossetti's painting, *Beata Beatrix*, an oil painting he completed after Siddall's death.

53. Violet Hunt (1862–1942), daughter of Alfred William Hunt and novelist Margaret Hunt, was a feminist, novelist, self-proclaimed wife of Ford Madox Ford, and a friend of H. G. Wells and Henry James. Hunt's literary reputation stems from her Kensington salons where she entertained Rebecca West, Ezra Pound, Joseph Conrad, Wyndham Lewis, D. H. Lawrence, and Henry James. H.D. and Bryher were longtime friends of Violet Hunt, and in a letter dated August 24, 1947, H.D. claims that she originally suggested the title for Hunt's *Wife of Rossetti*: "I gave her the title of the book, oddly enough; she wanted to call it Elizabeth S[iddall]—but I said the majority of the people wouldn't be taken by the name" (Zilboorg, *Later Years*, 103).

54. Violet Hunt, *Wife of Rossetti*, viii.

55. Siddall participated in the 1857 Russell Place exhibition. Her work was so well-received that Ruskin asked to become her patron, paying her 150 pounds a year for her visual art. Charles Eliot Norton purchased *Clerk Saunders* for forty guineas, and the picture was included in a show of British art in the United States (see figure 8). Although H.D. does not refer to any of Siddall's visual art in *White Rose*, she was certainly aware of her work as an artist. The catalogue for the 1948 exhibit on "The Pre-Raphaelites" lists Siddall's *The Haunted Wood*, *Clerk Saunders*, *Sir Patrick Spens*, *Madonna and Child*, and *The Eve of St. Agnes*, works that H.D. would presumably have seen.

56. For criticism that specifically addresses the influence of Siddall on Rossetti, or vice versa, see Violet Hunt's biography, Ford Madox Brown's *The Diary of Ford Madox Brown*, and Georgiana Burne-Jones's *Memorials of Edward Burne-Jones*. For a more contemporary analysis of Elizabeth Siddall, see Maggie Berg, "A Neglected Voice: Elizabeth Siddal," 151–56, Debra Mancoff, "Is There Substance Behind the Shadows? New Works on Elizabeth Siddal," 21–29, and Beverly Taylor, "Beatrix/Creatrix: Elizabeth Siddal as Muse and Creator," 29–42. For dissertations about Siddall, see Lila Hanft, "Woman in an Artist's Studio: Pre-Raphaelitism, Female Authorship, and the Construction of Gender" and Amy St. Jean, "Unearthing Elizabeth Siddal: The Voice and Vision of a Pre-Raphaelite Artist and Poet." Kim Morrissey has also written a play about Siddall, *Clever as Paint: The Rossettis in Love*. One of

the more bizarre examinations of Elizabeth Siddall's influence focuses on handwriting analysis. See Jack Joseph Challem and Barbara Reed-Stitt, "One Pre-Raphaelite Legacy: An Analysis of the Personalities of Dante Gabriel Rossetti and Elizabeth Siddal as Seen Through Their Handwritings," 12–24.

57. H.D.'s depiction of spiritualism as an active rather than a passive activity for redistributing grief, developed in *Sword* and *White Rose*, also anticipates a contemporary view of spiritualism among critics and historians. Recent criticism about the spiritualist movement in the nineteenth century has insisted that for women, it presented an opportunity for employment, communication, and public speaking (even if it was with the netherworld). See Mary Farrell Bednarowki, "Women in Occult America," 181. A concern for women's rights was a significant part of the spiritualist movement: in America, spiritualism advocated a woman's right to self-ownership in legal and social relations, control over her own property, and custody of her children. See Ann Braude, *Radical Spirits: Spiritualism and Women's Rights in Nineteenth-Century America*, 77. As Alex Owen demonstrates, the development of spiritualist societies in London, the Midlands, and the North coincided with controversies about sexual inequality and the increased agitation for women's rights (*The Darkened Room: Women, Power and Spiritualism in Late Victorian England*, 1). Since spiritualist culture provided professional opportunities for women, mediumship was a useful occupation for women seeking an alternative to a passive life in the Victorian domestic sphere.

58. Debra Mancoff, "Is there Substance Behind the Shadows? New Works on Elizabeth Siddal," 21.

59. Jan Marsh, *Elizabeth Siddal: Pre-Raphaelite Artist*, 69.

Figure 1. Dante Gabriel Rossetti (1828–82), *Portrait of Elizabeth Siddal (1829–62)*, 1854. Watercolor on paper, 18.1 × 16.1 cm. Delaware Art Museum, Wilmington. By permission of the F. V. DuPont Acquisition Fund/The Bridgeman Art Library, London.

Figure 2. Walter Howell Deverell (1827–54), *Twelfth Night*, c. 1850. Pen drawing. By permission o
private collection/The Bridgeman Art Library, London.

ure 3. William Holman Hunt (1827–1910), *Valentine Rescuing Sylvia from Proteus*, 1851. Oil on
vas, 98.5 × 133.3 cm. Birmingham Museums and Art Gallery. By permission of the Birmingham
seums and Art Gallery/The Bridgeman Art Library, London.

Figure 4. Dante Gabriel Rossetti (1828–82), *The Blessed Damozel*, 1875–79. Oil on canvas, 109.3 × 81.3 cm. Lady Lever Art Gallery, National Museums Liverpool. By permission of the Lady Lever Art Gallery, National Museums Liverpool/The Bridgeman Art Library, London.

Figure 5. John Everett Millais (1829–96), *Ophelia*, 1851–52. Oil on canvas, 762 × 1118 mm. Tate, London. By permission of the Tate, London.

Figure 6. Dante Gabriel Rossetti (1828–82), *Beata Beatrix*, c. 1864–70. Oil on canvas, 864 × 660 mm. Tate, London. By permission of the Tate, London.

Figure 7. Dante Gabriel Rossetti (1828–82), *Bocca Baciata (Lips That Have Been Kissed)*, 1859. Oil on panel, 32.1 × 27.0 cm. Museum of Fine Arts, Boston. By permission of the Museum of Fine Arts, Boston.

Figure 8. Elizabeth Eleanor Siddal (1829–62), *Clerk Saunders*, 1857. Watercolor gouache and chalk, 28.4 × 18.1 cm. Fitzwilliam Museum, University of Cambridge, U.K. By permission of the Fitzwilliam Museum, University of Cambridge, U.K./The Bridgeman Art Library.

Figure 9. Elizabeth Siddal (1829–62), "A Woman and a Spectre," n.d. Pen and brown ink on pale gray paper. Ashmolean Museum, University of Oxford, U.K. By permission of the Ashmolean.

WHITE

ROSE

AND

THE RED

By:

DELIA ALTON

We will unite the white rose and the red.

Richmond in *Richard III*

To

NORMAN HOLMES PEARSON

in gratitude for his suggestion

of continuing the story of the

Order of Sir Galahad

We are immeasurably indebted to the late Violet Hunt, for her reconstruction of the period, and we have profited by her recording the names of many of the minor characters in this narrative, though we differ in our attitude and approach to *The Wife of Rossetti*.

It will be remembered that manuscripts were freely circulated among the writers of the fifties of the last century, therefore we have in several instances, referred to books, prior to the date of publication.

The character of Godfrey Lushington, as outlined in this romance, is presented in a purely symbolic manner, for the sake of completing the old pattern and inspiring a new cycle of the original *Order of Sir Galahad*, founded at Oxford by William Morris.

Lausanne
Lugano

1948

PART   I

I

If only he would stop talking.

She had heard it all before but mostly from Mum and Annie. He read to them evenings and with his black scarf, his thin face and long hands, sitting with his book under the lamp, he might have been that other (the only picture in the small room), blackened, almost defaced, whose very name they had forgotten—Christopher, Mum said they said in Sheffield, but it was at best an indifferent likeness, perhaps only a copy and a bad copy at that, so it hadn't been sold up, along with the effects at Hope Hall. It was Dad's auctioneer cousin who said it would bring nothing. Let Charles Siddall have Christopher Siddal—leaving out that one "l;" his grandfather had added it, after the failure of the flax and bankruptcy.

It was Anna Grant de Hope who married Jacobus Sidall—and again in her thoughts, she spelt it differently, though Gabriel said she was Sidal really—de Grant de Hope.

Sudel or Suddel was carved on some of the oldest tombstones. Gabriel said he would take her to Hope Dale to see the carvings on the church front and "inside, there is sure to be," he said, "*Per Bend Vert and Gules: an Eagle displayed*, somewhere."

That was the Greaves quartering.

Who would expect Dad to talk about his family? He had cut her short once when she was a little girl. She had never forgotten. She had not asked him again.

It was about the later coat that he was talking, *Three Birds and the word Honour.*

It was after Harry began to call her the ginger-cat, that she had chosen the Eagle. They were the *Three Birds*, it was Annie's idea really. Annie, Lizzie and Lyddie (Clara didn't count then) were *Three Birds*, Anna, Elizabeth and Lydia. There were seven of them altogether, that is counting Charlie. Annie and Charlie were both born in Sheffield; Charlie died there. She, Lyddie, Clara and the two boys were born in the old house, number five, which Dad had taken over for his business. "This is number eight, Kent Place," she said to herself. It was necessary to remind herself of the *Three Birds*, having remembered Gabriel's joy in his discovery of *Gules* and *Eagle displayed*. That is what she had wanted to ask Dad—what are *Gules*?

She had not asked Dad, neither had she asked Gabriel.

Nor had she told Gabriel that she had chosen the Eagle. She had told no-one. Moreover, to be on the safe side, she had kept the *Three Birds*, that is her share in them. "I am Elizabeth Siddall," she said to herself and that in the beginning was the bird in the middle.

She had left her room and come across the river, dressed up (for to dress as she used to, was "dressing up" now) in the very dress she had worn at Mrs. Tozer's. She kept it carefully for these occasions. It was as if Dad were an actor or a clergyman, talking out of a book and talking about honour. She did not say, "I am engaged to marry Mr. Rossetti," for that wouldn't have made any difference. She had come to say something else, at last secure. But she might have been a prospective governess being interviewed, whose credentials are not satisfactory. This would not be the drawing-room itself, but a small ante-room. There would be a garden outside. The new sheds and houses had encroached on their old play-ground and you could hardly see the masts now, at Wapping. She was playing her old game again, she must not let them know (not even Gabriel) that she was *an Eagle displayed*.

She could almost bless Harry now. It was like that. It was even like that afterwards, with "the very knife he did it with." Mum said it couldn't have been, but that didn't make any difference. It was the way Harry lunged out at her, pretending to be Mr. Greenacre. She was to have married him.

Then, when she thought of the bride (as she always did before going to sleep), that night for the first time, she could count the pieces. She went on counting them, severed arms, legs, the head caught in the weir. She counted them carefully and then something happened. She was no longer afraid.

She could go on with her work in the parlour under the lamp, and not say anything, and wait for Annie or even Lyddie to shout, "Now, stop it, Harry, that's long past." Later, they all agreed that Harry wasn't quite right and James, a grown lad now, in the shop with Dad, made it his own concern that Harry stopped plaguing his three sisters, for it was three still; though Annie had got married, Clara had joined the ranks of the *Three Birds*.

That is why she blessed Harry and if only Dad would stop talking, she would ask him if that new school had agreed to keep on Harry. It was Harry hissing and spitting "gin-gin-ginger-cat" that had driven her to take refuge in the fancy that her hair was like the feathers of a golden eagle. But she had to remember that she was also one of the *Three Birds* and the first now and "an example to the others;" she heard her father saying, "you are an example to the others and—my favourite daughter."

. . . . . .

If only Lyddy would come in. Could she interrupt him to ask him about Lyddy? Lyddy had had the room to herself, and that was another reason for moving across the river. It wasn't only Gabriel, though it was all Gabriel. Lyddy could never sleep lying down.

"I wanted Mum and Lyddy and you, all together—to tell you the news." But he thought it was something else.

"Your mother went with James to fetch Lydia from your Aunt Day's."

Lyddy was in Aunt Lucy Day's shop now; she slept there, working-days.

No-one had ever crossed the river to Cranbourne Street, not that she remembered, to fetch her home from Mrs. Tozer's.

"Do they always call for Lyddy on Saturday?"

"When I can spare James."

"Why?" asked Elizabeth Siddall.

At least he had stopped talking about honour or perhaps that is what he was still saying, but saying it differently and saying it about Lyddy. It wasn't the crowds and anyway, she liked walking alone. What had happened that they had gone to Aunt Day's shop to fetch Lyddy? She could not really believe that they went often. She had been so happy when Mum's friend, out of her Euston Road days, had said she could work in the shop. She had been in there with Mum when she was a child, and admired Mum's old friend who wasn't married then. But she married Mr. Tozer. He was a little old gentleman and it seemed funny, a man in a bonnet-shop. But his father was, he said, French, and he spelt his name differently. It was something about war that brought them to England, and he called her *mademoiselle* and said, would she like to help them.

He gave her some scraps and she made a pin-cushion for Mum's Christmas. She never forgot Mr. Tozer.

He had even helped her with Dad's present. Annie was hemming the handkerchiefs and Mum always gave Dad the black scarf. Mr. Tozer said, what did Dad do? Gentlemen had their preferences. He would like something for polishing the cutlery perhaps? But he had the soft pieces sent from Sheffield, she told him, from the same place where her grandfather got the chamois. And Mr. Tozer said, that would, anyway, be in the way of business and the shop, he understood, was now separate. Christmas was for personal-like reminders. His own Dad was easy enough to plan for. It was always the same from that nice place in Haymarket—it was old too, and they remembered their clients from year to year and preferences. Times are different, they always remarked friendly, and the old gentleman (he was dead now) was the last, as he remembered, to say, "Mr. Toussier—your father's usual mixture?" But Dad, she had to tell him, didn't take snuff.

She didn't know why but she couldn't tell even Mr. Tozer that Dad played the violin.

She thought of the times she had hemmed the black square of that special soft cotton and of how she had scolded Clara, more than once, for polishing the table with it.

"But I always know where to find Dad's duster," Clara told her.

The violin-case was standing in the corner.

The leather folder with the music was lying on the table.

She realised that she was sitting "tight in her chair," the way she had so often sat, lifting her head from her sewing, about to take a deep breath, as Annie flung down her scissors, and (firm as Mum and grown-up now and going to be married) rapped out, "Harry, no more fooling." It was for Mum's sake they stood it. Mum said he was growing too fast and all lads were a bit wild at that age.

It was Mr. Tozer's idea really.

He even cut the rounds of velvet for her, but he let her measure and cut the inside circles of ordinary cloth to wipe the pens on.

The black velvet pen-wiper was still on his table in the office.

On the black velvet, she had embroidered the eagle that was stamped on the music folder. It was not, Annie said, their Eagle. Annie said she thought it was a Church Eagle from the Cathedral where Dad's father had sung in Sheffield. There were other animals (Annie remembered the Cathedral) carved on the choir-stalls, a Lion, a Bull and there was an Angel that went with them.

She had asked a question, it seemed a long time ago, but it couldn't have been, for Dad had gone on talking and when he said, "it's these roughs about, at war-time," she remembered that the question had been about Lyddy and why did James and Mum call for her.

She asked again, "Do they always call for Lyddy?" and he answered,

"Not always—only lately; crowds get out of hand, excitable, almost like the last war."

She made an effort. "I am Elizabeth Siddall," she said to herself, "and I can't remember the last war," and then she remembered how Mr. Tozer had explained or tried to explain it to her, how they were looked after by the friend of Mr. Tozer's former master, who had been—who had been . . . it was the flash of the knife in the lamp-light that she hadn't even seen then, for then there was no Mr. Greenacre and the snow that fell and fell, but there was a word that Mr. Tozer said that flashed broader than the Greenacres that had been their play-ground and brighter than Dad's polished silver and sharper than any steel in Sheffield. It was a Doctor Guillotine who had invented it, but her head caught in the weir.

"War," she said, trying not to ask a question. She was only prompting. Now she wanted him to go on talking, even if it was about war. Mr. Tozer had talked about war, how kind they were; they had been friends, his father's master and the English gentleman, and then everything changed and it was Frenchie, Frenchie and throwing stones at him and barking and howling, "Come on, Tozer." He laughed, Mr. Toussier, when he told her.

Of course, it had all started with her going to work in the shop. She had wanted to help them, surely Dad knew that. And Mrs. Tozer was a friend of Mum's, and Mum and she both remembered Mr. Tozer. And Dad knew (or perhaps he didn't) how his teaching her to keep the books for him and checking up on the accounts, had really given her her place there; Dad said she was good at numbers. She was happy when Mrs. Tozer called her out of the shop, into the little office and said, "Lizzie, just see what's wrong here," and she could sit there, after she got the sum right, nursing Tabby and warming her toes at the tiny fender. She remembered when it happened.

Mrs. Tozer said, "Thanks, Lizzie, and now will you give a hand to Jenny and Ellen; that buyer had all the bonnets down." She was reaching up, she was taller than the others, putting the boxes back on the upper shelf, when she felt something. She turned with her arms still lifted. It wasn't a face reflected in the window. It was a face in the window.

It was two faces.

They were looking at her, that was the strange thing about it.

. . . . . .

But she mustn't think of the faces in the window, until she found out what Dad meant about war. Yet somehow the faces in the window and Mr. Allingham by the street-lamp on the corner, bowing to Ellen and Jeannet did not encroach nor confuse. It was going on there, and it was going on here, at the same time. It was that Mr. Allingham who was looking in the window.

"I am twenty-two," thought Elizabeth Siddall, "I was seventeen then."

They said they were alone, Ellen and Jeannet that evening; would she walk with them? They knew she didn't like meeting strangers.

"It's Miss Sid," said Jeannet. She would drop them as soon as she could. It was a gentleman from Ireland, Ellen had explained afterwards, substantial. They had met him looking round the shops and had asked him if they could help him. He said, "Yes, girls know best what girls like;" he was taking them presents back to Killarney. He had the pleasantest way of speaking. He was official. It was something to do with ships, but by way of customs or controlling. They hadn't really expected to see him again but in return for his confidence, they had told him where they worked. Oh, he knew Leicester Square and all that neighbourhood. He spent all his time in London, at the play. He did say he was going back, so Jeannet really was surprised to see him. He turned to "Miss Sid" but he didn't embarrass her by saying anything. She felt, he felt she wanted to get away.

But she didn't get away.

. . . . . .

" . . . the Crimea," Dad was saying.

"But that's far off."

"War is never far off—it doesn't depend on where you send your soldiers. It's the same."

"It can't be, Dad, that was different, that was only across the channel, that was—"

"One remote country, in no way racially related to England, or even you might say to Europe, may be the cause of final and complete disaster."

He was thinking, she felt, about how he missed going out that time, with the Midland Division, he had set his heart on. He was only fifteen, then the war was over. He used to talk to James about it. James was older now than Dad was for Waterloo. Nobody talked about war in Chatham Place. It only came to her notice, really, last summer when she stayed with Gabriel at Scalands. It was Barbara Leigh-Smith saying she wished she could go out there and Gabriel saying,

"They won't take you, Barbara, even in your riding-breeches."

And Barbara saying, "But they're taking Florence."

"And who is Florence?" Gabriel asked her.

"My cousin Florence, Florence Nightingale," said Barbara.

" . . . until things are readjusted." What did Dad mean by that? It wasn't like that war (his war) and it was far away and it would soon be over. They couldn't possibly want James. She said,

"It was twenty-four pounds a year that Mrs. Tozer gave me. It was out of Shakespeare. It was Viola he wanted. The Academy had already hung a picture and it was an honour for so young a man, though they said his father being head of Somerset House and the School of Design, helped give him his advantage. Mum told you all about it. Mum and me talked it over. She was not condescending, Mum said, Mrs. Deverell when she came to call and Mum said even the greatest ladies could spoil a visit by something you'd hardly notice, what Mum called condescension. Not that we need apologize." Elizabeth Siddall looked round the room.

"Mrs. Deverell didn't really want a bonnet. Mum said that was real proof of her son's intentions, his bringing his mother in to choose a bonnet, before even he spoke to me. It was, in fact, his mother asked me. 'But I must speak to your mother first,' she said. I remember how she said it. Mrs. Deverell asked me if I liked reading, she didn't ask me if I read Shakespeare, she just went on with it; did I not think Viola, someway, was reminiscent of Rosalind? I said, no, Viola was the sea and Rosalind was the forest. 'Oh, I mean,' she said, 'their doublet and hose. Would you mind wearing a page-costume, the jerkin comes almost to the knees, with pointy shoes and a Rosalind-sort of cap to hide away the aureole.' She meant my hair. It was my hair they wanted for their pictures.

"There was another Shakespeare, Mr. Millais' *Ophelia*. Mr. Hunt did Silvia and another Viola. Mr. Deverell didn't finish *The Marriage of Rosalind and Orlando* but Mr. Rossetti said he would finish it. Mr. Deverell had what he called *The Flight of an Egyptian Ibis* in mind but he didn't even begin. He wanted me to do *Ophelia* again. Mr. Deverell died a year ago last winter."

She waited for her father to say something.

"Mrs. Deverell came out through the garden and sat in the studio. She read aloud sometimes. Mr. Deverell had to work at odd hours because of his classes at the School of Design. Mr. Deverell was not strong and after his father's death, he overworked, looking after his mother and his sisters."

She was talking about Walter Deverell because she knew that Dad knew she was thinking about Gabriel.

She took the plunge suddenly. "Mr. Rossetti is concerned too, about his family, though Miss Maria and Miss Christina are very clever and teach at languages and Mr. William Rossetti is on the Board of Trade. They are still grieving for their father, who died a year ago last April. Miss Maria and Miss Christina took turns reading and translating. Mrs. Rossetti never left him. Mr. Rossetti was elderly and his work was Dante. Mr. Rossetti was going blind. It was for that reason that I did not wish to intrude. I found Miss Maria very pleasant but they are intellectually superior ladies. Miss Christina writes poetry."

The clock was ticking. If she started counting, beating out a rhythm, she would put words to it. Gabriel said her poetry was not good, she was trying to over-ride his admiration for Christina. But this was not true. She had scribbled in the stitched-together leaves of her wrapping-paper note-book, long before she heard of Dante Gabriel Rossetti.

> Soon must I leave thee
>   This sweet summer tide.
> That other is waiting
>   To claim his pale bride.

But that was after Walter Deverell walked across Blackfriars Bridge, that February morning. Stephens was leaning out of the window with her, so it wasn't just another of her fancies; "I thought Dev was too ill to be out," he said. It is true that it was snowing. He was too ill to be out but it was Deverell. He had died, they ascertained afterwards, at the exact moment that they saw him.

"Mr. Gabriele Rossetti was an authority on Dante; Mr. Gabriel Rossetti, his son, has now been entrusted with the rendering of the *Vita Nuova.*"

Still the clock was ticking.

"Mr. Gabriele Rossetti was for some time before his marriage, a close friend of—of—" She had forgotten the name of the gentleman in Malta.

"It was the Bourbons," she struck out wildly, she was beyond her depth now, "and the fight for freedom and him, Mr. Gabriele Rossetti being hidden in a cellar along with cholera victims and getting recalled at the last to life, because of some poems he had written. It was Lady Moore enquiring for the poet, Gabriele Rossetti, that led to their finding him.

"It was Lady Moore finding him and Sir Graham Moore bringing him to Malta and Gabriele Rossetti teaching Italian and learning English and writing the book about Dante and Divine Philosophy and circles and circles— you could not begin to understand it, even if you knew Italian—but Mr. Frere—I remember his name was Frere, the gentleman in Malta—and him, between them had mapped out what they called a system that spelt a different story, begun (Mr. Frere maintained) by the Knights themselves in Malta, and beyond them, the Crusaders."

. . . . . .

It was indeed difficult to explain. Was painting more important than poetry? Gabriel said yes, in her case. She had begun the sketches, partly because she wanted something to do—he didn't like to see her sewing. She never scribbled in a note-book when there were people around, as he did. He said he liked her drawings. They were not good.

That was the reason for her withdrawing or holding back the simple statement, the thing she had come to tell them. And now it seemed fabulous and impossible, after Dad giving her to understand that he would take her back in the shop and for more than Mrs. Tozer had given her, she having had that additional experience. It was no good, it was too difficult to explain, it spelt a different story.

"Mr. Stevens, one of the gentlemen," she said, "lived in the Tower."

Why did she say that?

"The Tower?" Dad had asked a question at last.

"His father was official," she said.

"Mr. Allingham—" what should she say about Mr. Allingham? "Mr. Allingham himself had a post at Customs—in Ireland. He came back and forth to London."

It did not explain Jeannet and Ellen and the elegant line of the dark blue broadcloth and the gentleman standing by the lamp-post. But how explain anything?

How could he believe that Mr. Ruskin had offered her one hundred and fifty pounds a year? That is, for the output of all the painting she might do in that year. She did not believe it herself.

"Miss Christina herself sat for her brother, in *The Girlhood of the Virgin*."

She had come to make a simple statement, to tell them about Mr. Ruskin and his offer. But she knew what her father thought about wastrels, spendthrifts, idlers with no set income, artists, painters and the harlots that sat for them. "Miss Christina was the Virgin," she had come back to Christina, the last person she would have thought to be appealed to, in this, her defence.

"They call *The Carpenter Shop* of Mr. Millais, the family party. That is, it was his own father stood for Joseph, and the little boy was—" She realized that her father did not know what she was talking about. "It is a study—Nazareth. You see outside, through the door left open. His mother kneels on the floor and He has been trying to help His father, and His mother holds open His hand, where the nail caught it. They are concerned with the little boy, cutting Himself like that and one of them brings a bowl with water for Mary to tie up His hand.

"They are not all religious. Mr. Hunt does historical pieces and things out of books and Mr. Brown, too." She remembered helping Emma Brown cut out the fleur-de-lis to sew on the king's coat. But she had not seen the finished picture and she did not remember the name of the king. She remembered how she had seen his likeness before she met Gabriel. That is, Mr. Deverell had used him for the Fool in *Twelfth Night*. Mr. Allingham had stipulated, before he brought Walter Deverell to look in the shop-window, that the lady, "Miss Sid," as he went on calling her, was (if she was what Walter wanted for his Viola) to sit only for him. That was in the beginning. Walter wanted to finish the picture; he expected the Academy would hang it, if he finished it in time. He wanted someone tall for the page, it wasn't her hair that time. Walter Deverell had painted himself for the Duke Orsino and it looked like him and the costume suited him. The other, he explained when he first showed the picture to her, was done from a friend who, also, was a painter. No, the Royal Academy hadn't yet hung any of his pictures. He did not mention his friend's name. "You remember the occasion," he said.

She did not fit in the grouping and the rough indication (already sketched in) of Viola, with any special scene in *Twelfth Night*.

But there was another occasion.

. . . . . .

It was late and they were alone, for Mrs. Deverell was ailing. There was a knock on the door but the door opened before Walter had time to lay down his brush.

"Oh," he said, "it's you, Gab," and he went on painting.

Gabriel flung down his cape. He brushed his hair from his forehead, combing the fingers of his left hand through it. His hair looked untidy, longer than Walter's, but it was the way he flung back his head. When he spoke, you knew that it was Feste, you knew it was the Fool, you knew that it was *Twelfth Night*. He was not as tall as Mr. Allingham. There was no elegant line of broadcloth, his coat did not match his trousers and his coat was a dark plum-colour.

"You'd better come back with me to my digs," he said, "it's cold here," but he did not turn and put on his cape again, as she expected. He made as if he were plucking a lute, but making a joke of it:

"*Come away, come away, death*, that is one of the best things I ever wrote," he said, "*And in dark cypress let me be laid.*"

But she knew the Fool's song in *Twelfth Night*. Why did he say he wrote it?

Come away, come away, death,
And in dark cypress let me be laid;
Fly away, fly away, breath;
I am slain by a fair cruel maid.
My shroud of white, stuck all with yew
    O prepare it!
My part of death, no one so true
    Did share it.

"Oh, Dev," he said, "did you know or do you think that cypress, in that instance, means not cypress, wreath, tree, funereal, you know—but just the colour or even the stuff—but he calls the shroud white, so it couldn't be the stuff, could it? Cypress means just black sometimes, not tree, wreath or anything. Why the devil must I go on like this? Probably those paraphrases of old Gab—Dante, you know—no, not Dante Gabriel Rossetti but Gabriele, the old gentleman. He's been working too hard. Old Antique knows more Italian than Maria and Christina put together, but dear mamma must have a rest sometimes. I can't say I helped much this evening, but the old blighter worries lest *come away, come away, death* should interfere with the final, pluperfect version, interpretation, illumination of his three-ringed circus. Those circles, you know, can't say I understand them, though I've explained them to you often enough, in my lucid Bacchic moments. Eh, what?"

He was looking at the picture.

"Your girl's a bit scrawny even for Viola," he said.

Deverell went on painting.

"I like myself, though, as Feste—but then, I always like myself, anyway.

"But then, there's this too. Does he mean by cypress, the cypress-wood box or coffin? I don't like the Elizabethans, do you, really? Of course, if you're like some people and have a pull with the committee and your Guv'nor runs a school for teaching imbeciles how not to paint and you do hack-work yourself, in your odd moments, and call it *Fête Champêtre* or *The Masked Ball* or whatever it was you called the last one—Dev, I positively blush to think I know you. That was a rotten picture the Academy hung last year; couldn't you have left it at that? But nothing succeeds like success and it's a pity—I will find myself on the line, after all the trouble I've taken to keep off it and to damn their stinking old Academy. And with that, too—Oh, so there's your model."

It was the first time Elizabeth Siddall had heard herself referred to as a model.

Deverell said, "I'm through painting. Get your things, Gab, we'll go immediately."

Automatically, as Walter Deverell stuck his paint-brush in the jar, she pulled off her cap.

"So that's who you are," said Gabriel Rossetti.

She was only wearing the jerkin over her dress, that evening.

She went on unlacing the strings.

She slipped her arms out of the sleeves.

She folded the jacket, as she always did, and laid it on the chair below the *estrade*. She laid the cloth cap on it. She did not look at Dante Gabriel Rossetti.

Her hair was not really coming down.

She found her outdoor coat, hanging on the peg behind the door, where she had left it.

Walter Deverell would understand her not saying good-night. He was putting away the easel.

He always left it standing. He was putting it away, so as to give her time to slip out.

"I don't think I caught your name, Miss, did I?" said Gabriel Rossetti. "Mine's Punchinello, yours to favour. I mean, Madame, yours to command. It was a night on the Rialto—no, not Shakespeare—this is another story; do you remember the moon? Come, don't say you have forgotten me?

"Madame, it was I, not Titian who invented your hair.

"I am poor brother Lippo, by your leave. Do you really like Browning? I don't. Taken all in all, he and the would-be laureate, I mean Tennyson, are provincial. And likewise, Mrs. Browning, O great god Pan by the river. It is, Madame, exactly what I mean. They never got out of Pimlico. Do you like poppies? You see the black coal in the centre. But Lor', Madame, we are not in Manchester—or is it Newcastle, they bring coals to?"

She was shivering, though it was not late and it was still mid-summer.

"I can't wait for Mum and James and Lyddy; will you tell them?" she said.

She was standing. She glanced down at the music-folder, with what Annie had told her was a Church Eagle, stamped or embossed upon it.

"It's by way of a commission," she said, "you'll tell the others. But for that—

"I mean, it's an undertaking and already paid for. It's for a year's work. I couldn't forfeit the promise I've made. I'll come back when I can stay and tell them properly. It's for—design and drawing. Mr. Ruskin wants a whole portfolio."

Her father said, "And who is Mr. Ruskin?"

II

How did cholera take people?

Perhaps that's why she was shivering.

Gabriel was staying at the Queen's Head, near Brown in Highgate.

It was about that calf.

Emma couldn't put Gabriel up in the house. Mr. Brown said he would be the Drover. It was a picture, unlike any of his others; Gabriel had begun it, even before she knew him. At least, he said he got the idea from a poem called *Rosabell*; it was writing to Mr. Scott about *Rosabell* that brought about their friendship. The idea of *Rosabell* was the same as Gabriel's own poem *Jenny*. Mr. Ruskin had wanted Gabriel to give up the idea; it was a modern subject. It was a girl crouching in a corner. Sometimes the picture was called *Found*, sometimes *The Drover*, sometimes *The Bridge*, and sometimes *Lost*.

Gabriel had even found the house here, fourteen Chatham Place, with the windows looking out on the river, when he was wandering about, trying to find a corner for the girl, who has gone on the town; a country girl like Emma Brown, but not like Emma Brown. Her lover out of the old days, finds her (Mr. Brown in a farmer's smock); he was faithful to her memory and he finds her crouching by the bridge, this very Blackfriars Bridge corner, but then Gabriel said he couldn't paint it there and stayed in Kew to be near a wall that he had found that would do better.

The cholera rumours had started again last summer, but she had stayed at her own room in Weymouth Street. It was not far off, so that she could be in and out, sitting for Gabriel. But she couldn't stay in Weymouth Street now that he was so far away as Highgate, and while he was away, it was something to stay in his rooms.

When they were married, he said, he would have a door cut through, back of the books in the hall. The hall joined the bedroom to the two front rooms. Gabriel said that would make the place twice as large as it was now. His study or his studio was the first room, but she was sitting in the long-room as he called it, where Maria and Christina had come in to take tea that day.

It was all right about Christina. She had told Dad, this afternoon, that Miss Christina was superior. So she was and she had a right to it. It was nice about the drawings. She just wasn't interested. She knew that what she wrote was what she wanted to write, when she said:

I can not give to thee the love
    I gave so long ago—
The love that turned and struck me down
    Amid the blinding snow.

And she had written that after their engagement. It took place formally, at Scalands Gate when she went down from Hastings, last summer. Gabriel was proud of her. Barbara's Aunt Julia was most gracious, the only real lady who had gone out of her way to be nice, since Mrs. Deverell. Not that Maria and Christina hadn't been nice, that is—well, you felt they had gone out of their way, as against their will and judgment. And she was at it again, judging Christina for judging her, and Christina was working at *Goblin Market* and Maria was helping with the *Vita Nuova*, and they were all being written up, now that Mr. Hunt had had his big success with *The Light*, and that modern picture that Gabriel said, Holman Hunt had stolen the idea for—from him. They were quite different ideas but they were both about a girl who had gone wrong.

Mr. Hunt's girl was Annie Miller in *The Awakened Conscience*. It was Mary Howitt who protested that Annie Miller was getting herself talked about with Gabriel. Mr. Hunt had stipulated, as Mr. Allingham had done with her, before he brought Walter Deverell to look in the Cranbourne Street shop-window, that Annie was to sit for no-one else, only he excepted Mr. Boyce. It was while Annie was sitting for Mr. Boyce that Gabriel got to know her, though they had all met her before. Mr. Hunt was having her educated with the intent to marry. It was Mary Howitt who thought with Barbara, it was a pity, Annie Miller throwing away her chances. And with Gabriel, it was only (he told Mr. Allingham) for a joke, "Hunt stole my picture," he said, "so I'm stealing his model."

Mr. Hunt's picture was a success, it and *The Light of the World*, last May at the Academy. Not that she liked Annie Miller. She didn't pretend to like her. She knew that Mary Howitt and Bessie Parkes, who Barbara always kept rooms for, at Scalands Gate, were working for her good. That is, Annie Miller's good, but it involved something that she had no care then to be discussed openly—about herself and Gabriel. As an engaged man, did Gabriel have the right to carry on openly that way and with the model, too, that one of his best friends was going to marry? At least, that is, Mary Howitt explained, what she had asked Mr. Allingham. Mr. Allingham was living in London now, writing; he was one of the contributors to Mr. Howitt's paper that had first printed Gabriel's *Sister Helen*. Mary Howitt would never take her eyes off her, wherever she was.

When she was thinking about ladies, she wasn't really remembering everybody. There was Mary's mother. The Howitts had the house at Highgate, the Hermitage, not so far from the Brown's. They would walk out there or go part way by 'bus. It was with Mary, almost idolatry, the way she looked at her. Mrs. Howitt said, "you understand the Spirits," naturally, like Mrs. Deverell talking about Shakespeare. It was there they had what Mrs. Howitt called their home-circle. Mr. Howitt was away on a long voyage and Mrs. Howitt asked if she and Gabriel would help them with their contact.

It was there at Highgate, that she got to know Barbara Leigh-Smith and Bessie Parkes and Mary. The Howitts had been Quakers but now they followed the new faith. You could say, yes, Bessie Parkes and Barbara were ladies, but they were fashionable young ladies, and Barbara always wore her breeches in the country and dragged back her hair. It was funny her taking the words out of Mum's mouth, about ladies and condescension. Mrs. Howitt wasn't so much of a lady as a sort of a little saint.

Quakers or Friends, as she called them, were like that, communing in the silence. It was different at the Howitts. All the same, there was comfort sometimes to be had at the séances at the Academy in Sloane Street. She might go there again.

. . . . . .

But there was no use going and asking, how does cholera take people? You picked up your own worry out of the air, and an answer came back to you that might mean almost anything. With that simplicity of Mrs. Howitt, just loving her husband and wanting word, for there had been no letters—he had sailed for the Gold Fields—the Spirits gave consolation and spoke simple words and spoke them very clearly. That is, it was what Mrs. Howitt called "Rapping Spirits," they could say yes and no, with one rap or with two raps, and letters like N for north and H for hope—Mrs. Howitt had a list of words they used—that was life-giving and inspirational. And Gabriel was gentle with Mrs. Howitt and with Mary, but he said at the end it was too slow and he went to the Academy for Spiritual Research, in Sloane Street.

She went there too, after the death of Walter Deverell.

They put ideas into your head and gave you comfort that way. It was a way that might keep you alive, if you lost hope. Not that she had lost hope, not that she didn't love Gabriel. But when she first began to realize that he was angry with her ("your chin, your chin, you've spoiled that line"), it was as if her heart were torn from her very insides, as if she must have someone, something, and there was no-one to go to, for she couldn't complain to the others about Gabriel.

She was happy at first—perhaps Mrs. Howitt could have told her it was spiritual pride, but Mrs. Howitt would never have said that. It wasn't just that Gabriel liked her. But did he like her?

He never said thank you, after a long hour's sitting.

It was how she came to think of Walter Deverell, he kept books by the *estrade* for her to read between times.

With Gabriel, there were no between times.

If she fell into a chair, just hanging on, exhausted, till she put on her coat, Gabriel would say, "Don't move" and she would wait there.

It was how she came to think of Walter Deverell.

And thinking of him, maybe got it into the air somehow. "It's a French name," the lady-medium said. There were four others in the circle. "It's for one of you five ladies." Nobody seemed to know any French "on the other side," as the lady-medium called it, and then she remembered Mr. Toussier. Maybe just thinking of Mr. Toussier, gave the lady-medium the idea that it was for her. She said, "It's a gentleman and it's something about Christmas."

She did not think of *Twelfth Night*.

"It's for this lady—no, it doesn't begin with T, the name of the helper who is calling. He says (indicating I'm right) it's for you. It's that way, Miss, many times, but you're sure to remember when you get home."

She did remember. She remembered before she got home. Gabriel had told her that Walter Deverell was descended from the D'Evrolles who had come in with the Conqueror.

. . . . . .

"Being what you are, how can anyone expect you to be other?" There were times when she remembered Gabriel's nonsense, like remembering something in a book, a play-book, something you've heard over and over, as if you were another actor, and yet heard it always for the first time.

"Strictly between ourselves,

     Lizzy, Lizzy,

     You make me dizzy,

and all my energy, my perfect and precise detachment, is required to get your chin right. If you painted, Lizzy, you would understand this, or even if you wrote poetry. No-one could expect you to be clever, endowed with the ambrosial locks and the dim, disenchanted eyes of Circe. But Circe in good time, and Medea.

"I do not care what you think of Tennyson. I say he never got out of Brixton. Or perhaps for reason of alliteration or assonance or mere crude rhyme or rhythm, which I can not expect you to follow, he remains and will remain to me always the perfect translator of Catullus; my favourite phrase of his correct and polished rendering is,

     Oh silver-shining Pimlico,

like a boot-black, polishing the boots of the perfect prince and his lady, looking like Mrs. Tibbs o' Sundays. But you didn't know Mrs. Tibbs, did you, O Queen Hermione? But it must be Guenevere, next time.

"You say I did not thank you for the *Damozel*. It was three months ago that I stopped working on the *Damozel*. What a memory you have. But the *Damozel* isn't finished, and why should I thank you, anyway; it is you who should thank me, for making you immortal.

"As to the *Bones of Venice*—"

But she stopped him.

She was, he said, dictating to him and he couldn't have that.

But he agreed with her afterwards about Mr. Ruskin—"The old sneak behaved like a gentleman."

She had never met Effie.

There was only one person who knew all about it, Emma said, and that was Mr. Ruskin's valet, Mr. John Hobbes.

But then Emma didn't like Effie, or the idea that Mr. Millais counted more with Mr. Ruskin than her own Madox Brown. Mr. Ruskin was not fair to Madox, Emma maintained. Emma said that Madox had run across Mr. Hobbes at the Working Men's College, where they took turns lecturing and giving lessons. Mr. Hobbes had gone in to explain that Mr. Ruskin must discontinue his teaching for a short space, for health reasons. He was going to the Continent.

"Mr. Hobbes' language was something terrible," said Emma. "Not that I don't suppose Madox told me everything." It was a delicate subject. "'Him,' said Mr. Hobbes, 'and her, after all he's done for both of them. And now people calling Mr. Ruskin a name you don't meet nowhere but in the Bible. Mr. Brown, if it's the last thing I do, I declare to you—but then with my all-but oath to Mr. Ruskin, you don't know anything, no more than I. What I *could* say—'"

But Emma said, "he grit his teeth in a manner that spoke everything and he was even at that minute catching his train," and that was all that anyone heard official, if you could say what Madox Brown said was hinted at, by Mr. Hobbes, the valet, was official.

"It was a scandal such as had not been heard in England, nor would probably not be heard again," so Emma said, and a man like him, so Madox said, with a mind like those crystal chandeliers he had all over the house (though Emma had never been there), reflecting like crystal-glass, so Emma said Brown said, and yet with a drawing-back as it might be, like those sea-medusas, like you get at Hastings (Emma had seen them, too, at Brighton), all feeling and nerves yet cold as crystal-glass; it was a contradiction, but that was genius, so Emma said that Madox Brown had told her.

The decree was granted to Euphemia Chalmers Gray (falsely known as Ruskin) on grounds of nullity.

But Elizabeth Siddall had always liked John Millais.

"The cold is due to the house-foundation being under water at high-tide," Elizabeth Siddall said to herself. At least, she could stay hunched in the basket-chair that Gabriel wanted to get rid of. Or she could get up if she wanted; it worried her that one window in the studio was closed, even though it was summer.

The window had been nailed secure because of the rattling and the draught last winter, but now it should be attended to, only Gabriel said he liked the light blocked out from that side and she hadn't the strength to drag a ladder all the way up the stairs, even if Mrs. Birrell had one. Gabriel had forbidden Mrs. Birrell to touch anything; Elizabeth was sure there was an accumulation of dust behind the long single curtain that was actually tacked into the wall below the ceiling. It was beautiful cloth, some old piece Gabriel had picked up but it should have been cleaned and hemmed before he hung it. The curtain was hung when Mrs. Birrell sent the man to nail the window. Anyway, Gabriel did not like to see her sewing, and she had so little time to herself, that she liked to rest and dream, then. He would stop her, even in pulling out a table or folding up a length of drapery, in order to do a drawing. If it was a matter of long bastings for a surcoat or pinning loose sleeves over tight ones, for Saint Cecelia or Francesca, he didn't call it sewing—nor did she for the matter of all that, it was designing.

He had told her she was proud and put on airs, that her reserve was a sort of self-chastisement. He did not realize the self-control she practised, not to straighten a chair set at an impossible angle or a rug crooked on the floor. It was only natural to pick up a piece of drawing-paper that the draught was fluttering in the corner. As to pins—perhaps she had been too long at Mrs. Tozer's, but it was the same, anyway, at home. What would Mum think of her now? Idle—and the room looking like this.

True, the late mid-summer twilight softened the contours of the outlandish objects. Perhaps some of them were valuable. But she preferred the slim silhouettes of their few best pieces. They were bits that Mum had cherished and almost worn away with polishing. They were Sheffield. They were not rightly heirlooms, but at Mum's place, the lady took a fancy to her and when she was going to be married, gave her some old pieces out of the attic. "I shouldn't wonder," Mum said, she said, "if these old spindle-legs aren't Chippendale. The cabinet I know," she said, "is Flemish." It was the sort of feeling you got at Mr. Ruskin's in his own study that his mother showed her. Gabriel didn't like the house at Denmark Hill or anything about it. Downstairs, it was more crowded with heavy pieces, but she liked the stones and the shells he showed her. Yes, there were glass-crystals over the dining-room table and in the drawing-room. It was the way Mr. Ruskin said, "I was born to mourn over what I cannot save," that frightened and embarrassed her, as if he was quoting Scripture. She did not think he meant Effie, though there was a space above the writing-desk where Gabriel said a portrait of Effie had hung. She did not ask Gabriel if Millais had done the picture. John Everett Millais was Mr. Ruskin's best friend.

. . . . . .

Walter Deverell had not wanted her to sit for other people. His mother had made the arrangement and explained things to her. It was a shilling an hour for special work, five shillings for a full morning, seven-and-six for the whole day, and there were other things to consider, 'bus fares and so on. Elizabeth Siddall said she did not need the money, her work at Mrs. Tozer's was well paid for and she liked coming to the studio. Mrs. Deverell insisted on her having the usual School of Design fee for what she called the work, although Elizabeth insisted on the pleasure that it gave her to come there to Kew. She hadn't thought of giving up Mrs. Tozer's, until Mr. Hunt came in, one Sunday afternoon. Mrs. Deverell came over to the studio to ask first if she would mind; a friend of Walter's, she said, was planning to do another scene from Shakespeare and he didn't want to begin until he had seen Walter's picture, in case it might appear that he was taking Walter's subject. In fact, they were much alike, Mr. Hunt was doing Silvia in *Two Gentlemen of Verona*.

Mrs. Deverell presented Mr. Hunt and excused herself as there were other guests in the drawing-room.

Mr. Hunt said, not knowing anything about her, would she sit for him?

Walter Deverell said that Miss Siddall was not a model.

Walter Deverell tried to dissuade her from sitting to other people. She did not read now but they talked together, in the "rest." He told her that he had wanted to be an actor but the family were against it and he was glad now that he had stayed on at the School. The stage offered, at best, only a precarious living. He was interested in her writing but he said that that, too, would never earn a living.

She said, "I've been thinking it out, since Mr. Hunt came in last Sunday." She explained to him that twenty-four divided by twelve is two; that is, counting twelve months to the year, she had two pounds a month. The weeks were uneven, but counting four weeks to a month, she had ten shillings a week—but a little less. Counting five shillings a morning for two mornings in the studio, she had ten shillings, as it were, for the whole day. She had left out Sundays, but then there were those extra days at the end of every one of the twelve months. She would have free time to read, to write, even to do some dress-patterns for Mrs. Tozer. Even as a little girl, Mr. Toussier—that is, it was originally a French name—had helped her in some simple stitch-work embroidery. Mrs. Tozer was really very good to her and did not insist on her staying on late, but for the sake of Mr. Toussier who was dead, she liked to see orders filled in time, in the rush season. Mrs. Tozer didn't officially take in orders from the makers, but sometimes the buyers who had known Mr. Toussier in the old days, would rush in, for a special favour, with a last-minute ball-gown. They had really, though not officially, done some lovely costumes; the lace and drapes, Mrs. Tozer left to her discretion. Mrs. Tozer was better on the bonnets. Perhaps if she spent her time working on design, one of the big costumiers would take her for outside patterns. Mrs. Tozer, she knew, would sympathize with her ambition, but she must see out the season.

She remembered Walter Deverell was standing by the window.

"But I promised Allingham," he said.

She said, "Mr. Allingham was very pleasant the few times I saw him, but he wasn't particularly my friend."

He said, "Allingham may have had other—ideas for you. He might have— he might have thought he could help you with your writing."

"How could Mr. Allingham know that I did any writing?"

"Well—you might have told him."

"I only saw him those few times, and never alone."

She remembered, Walter Deverell came back and began scraping his palette.

"It's this way," he said, "I understand how you feel about your job. I feel the same way about mine. I resented it at first, now I don't think I could be without it. It sets a shape to the day, and all the time I'm teaching, I'm thinking how happy I'll be to get back to my work. Well—why do I call this work? This is my life and the other—the classes, family (interruptions even) set a sort of fence about a pasture. I might get slack and lazy or indifferent, if I could get to my painting any time of the day. Do you see what I mean?"

She thought she saw what he meant.

"I'm independent now and my mother says that it might be better if I had a place of my own to work in. It's cold here and the light's none too good, so we saw no reason for rebuilding this old shed. I've been looking for something, ever since we moved here. I'd save time and energy if my studio was nearer the School. I don't think you should give up your job entirely. But if your Mrs. Tozer agrees to take you part-time, I would be grateful if you would continue sitting for me. I have the *Ibis* in mind, there's *Rosalind* and then *Ophelia*. I personally see no reason why you should not help Hunt with his Silvia. It's only that I gave my promise."

She said she would be glad to sit for him, when he found his studio, if Mrs. Tozer would agree to part-time work.

Walter Deverell said he actually had a place in mind, but he had to wait till next quarter to move in.

The studio he told her was set back in a garden. It was number seventeen Red Lion Square.

But he did not tell her what William Allingham had told him.

. . . . . .

Mary Howitt helped Mrs. Howitt edit *The People's Journal* and *Household Words*, while Mr. Howitt was away.

Mrs. Howitt was working separately as well, writing a book on the new faith.

Mary should not have shown her the letter, but Mary didn't know Mr. Allingham then, and Mary didn't know that she had met Mr. Allingham. Gabriel took him out to the Hermitage, after they had printed *Sister Helen*; Mr. Allingham wrote poetry. But Mrs. Howitt made no reference to the letter when Gabriel presented Mr. Allingham to her and Mary in the garden.

Elizabeth wondered if Mary remembered the letter and the poem that Mr. Allingham had enclosed with it.

She wondered if Mary connected the name of the writer of the poem with this Mr. Allingham.

She didn't think that Mary did somehow, but she felt that Mrs. Howitt went out of her way to bring up the subject of the new faith.

It was as if somehow, something was understood between them.

It was a long letter and while she was reading the first page, Mary said, "but I thought this was a poem for *Words* or for the *Journal*. But I see it's confidential; I'll put it back with mother's private papers."

The address was written at the top of the page but Mary didn't then know Mr. Allingham or that he lived in Ireland. Perhaps she hadn't even seen the signature.

It was about an experience.

Would Mrs. Howitt send him word; he knew of her communications. He would be grateful for some sort of guidance.

A friend of his was doing a portrait of a lady. He had seen the lady in London and walking home with his friend, he was overwhelmed with a strange foreboding. Why should this be? He had stayed awake all night; he was returning the next day to Ireland. The poem enclosed could better explain his feelings. The poem, of course, Mrs. Howitt understood, was not for publication. It was called *The Cold Wedding*. He felt he was looking at the lady through a snow-storm. Why should he feel that his friend's portrait should bring disaster? His friend was a person of distinction, of high spiritual attainment.

> Ere she was born
> That vow was sworn;
> And we must lose into the ground
> Her face we knew.

Elizabeth Siddall could not have read the four lines more than twice, but she remembered them.

. . . . . .

She had seen Mr. Allingham only three times and "never alone," as she had told Walter, but actually she had only spoken to him once; how could she have told him about her writing?

Mrs. Deverell had asked her to Kew to look at the studio before the sittings began.

"We've already arranged the lamps," she said, "but it's hardly a place to work in. I'm afraid you'll get cold here. We think we can have a small stove fitted in the corner later, and I'm having some old curtain-stuff fastened up over the door and windows. By day, of course, Walter will need the windows but he can only work by day-light on Sunday—has he explained it to you? Walter says the light won't be too difficult, not for your sittings, as he has already finished himself (I'm glad you like it, he makes a good Orsino) and the Jester. Maria and Margaretta have promised to help Miss Black put up the curtains this evening. Ah, forgive me, my dear—I thought we were to be alone. Tell him to come in, Ann."

When Mr. Allingham bowed to her, when Mrs. Deverell said, "Miss Siddall," she wondered if she could claim to have met him before.

"Miss Sid," they had said, laughing by the lamp-post. He had not actually addressed her and she slipped off.

The second time was only a face in the window, and another face.

This was the third time.

She stood and instinctively dropped a little curtsy, the way Mum had showed them they did, at her lady's house in Sheffield.

"Walter even as a child, was always absorbed in Shakespeare," Mrs. Deverell said, after Ann had left the tea-things. "But except for a Mr. Garrick or a Miss Siddons, there's hardly a career in acting, is there? He was always casting everyone he knew for a part—now Miss Siddall—"

Mr. Allingham put down his cup and looked at her, as if he had never seen her before.

Elizabeth Siddall held her cup steady.

"Miss Siddall has agreed—she also is fond of Shakespeare—as a special favour, to sit for Walter in his *Twelfth Night.*"

Mr. Allingham said, "I trust Walter does a faithful likeness of Miss Siddall."

"He has done his own portrait excellently. There is something about Walter. He was hardly fitted for a solicitor's office—he may have told you how concerned we were about it. We couldn't have him go on the stage, but we agreed to his leaving his uncle Travel's office, if he would give up acting. Mr. Dyce and Mr. Herbert at the Academy, recommended his painting highly, so his father had no compunction about giving him an under-mastership at the Schools. But tell me about yourself, Mr. Allingham."

Mr. Allingham said, "I am off again to Ireland."

Mrs. Deverell said, "You prefer Ireland?"

"Oh no," said Mr. Allingham, "it's my work there. I find London attracts me more every time I come here. Besides my official work, I am doing reviews for a Dublin journal, news of things and people here, books and art. Mr. William Rossetti has also placed a few things of mine. William Rossetti, as you no doubt know, is now on the staff of the *Spectator*. I hope in time to make a livelihood of writing. Then I will stay in London."

Elizabeth Siddall felt that he was speaking to her, though he addressed himself to Mrs. Deverell.

"You enjoy the life in London?"

"Exceptionally."

"We are so busy at the Schools that I don't get about now, as I used to. But I hear much talk of books and people from my son. It is odd that I do not miss Wykeham and Spenser more. You will think I am, what a mother should not be, partial. I have heard Walter referred to as the handsomest fellow in London. He is singularly immune to flattery. It is not only his appearance; for all his indifference to society, I have heard from Mrs. Dyce that at the Academy, he was known for his exquisite manners. His nature is affectionate."

"Yes," said Mr. Allingham. "William Rossetti calls him troubadourish."

"You have been to their gatherings? My son tells me there are (at what he calls *casa Rossetti*) much come and go of famous characters, Mr. Mazini, Paganini—but they invite the piano-tuner and the dancing-master, as well as Father Gavazzi and the Maestro."

Mr. Allingham said he had not attended their formal gatherings but had spent pleasant evenings reading and discussing poetry with the two brothers.

"The sisters are likewise gifted. And I hear that Mrs. Rossetti is not only a brilliant linguist but a good cook. She is partly English; though her maiden name, Polidori, sounds Italian, my son tells me that he has heard it may be Greek. I sometimes worry foolishly, but Walter is not really strong and after coming back from the Rossettis', he seems sometimes to be burning with a fever and enthusiasm which I fear his body is too frail to withstand."

Mr. Allingham said, "Their inferences are not always sound but their enthusiasms are contagious."

"Their father's book has been printed, Walter tells me, but not circulated. How can that be?"

"The volume is perhaps a little too erudite for general circulation. No doubt it will find its place in time, in the universities and on the Continent. But I can express no opinion. The book is written in Italian with, I believe, certain explanatory notes in Latin."

"The book is political?"

"I should not say so. Only in so far as Mr. Rossetti's system, as I believe he calls it, would unravel or untangle certain ancient evils. But I am all at sea, here. I have heard of Machiavelli but for the life of me I don't know why I think of him now. Except that he, too, came from Florence. Something to do with an ideal king or ruler. Virgil led Dante through circles in the Inferno and apparently with penetrating acumen and a brilliant sense of historical parallels, Mr. Rossetti would untangle the threads, solve the riddle or enigma and apply Dante's criticism, say of the Italian tyrants, to the popes of his own day. There is no doubt, a fanatical ring about Mr. Rossetti's code or re-arrangement of letters, names and places, so that they spell in some instances (Gabriel tells me) other names and other places. But Italian spelt upside down, backward or anagramatically, can convey little to the uninitiate and nothing to one who has no Italian and whose Latin is at best fragmentary and unreliable."

"But Mr. Allingham—it savours of—what shall I say? It makes me think of Mr. Bulwer Lytton's *Zanoni*."

"Magic? I see, Mrs. Deverell, but I think I can assure you that the Conte de St. Germain and Caliostro would get scant welcome from Mr. Gabriele Rossetti. He is a devout man. He began his researches with an older brother, a priest, I believe in the Abruzzi."

"But you say he applied what he calls his system, to denouncing the evils of Rome?"

"He applied his system to show how Dante, guided by the poet Virgil, denounced or rather formulated the circles or the easy steps to Avernus. I do not say that Gabriele Rossetti goes so far as to apply his system to the evils of to-day."

. . . . . .

It was not only Gabriel. She could remember what other people said, like listening to a play, watching from the basket-chair, herself acting.

She could hear the words best when she was shivering or when she was frozen, too cold to shiver.

Not that she was actually shivering.

The tide-water lapped round the house-foundation.

There was only Mrs. Birrell in the basement. She was the caretaker, and Katy ran errands. There was Mrs. Birrell and Katy in the basement, in the corner-house at the bridgehead. The rest of the rooms in the entire row, were given over to solicitors, insurance, colonial societies, immigration and various welfare offices; the whole street was empty but for Elizabeth Siddall in a basket-chair, on the second from the top floor of 14 Chatham Place (the room at the end) and Katy and Mrs. Birrell in the basement. It seemed the city was deserted. True, it was August. True, there had been recent arguments, questions, debates and appeals in the House, about the river and about cholera.

Mrs. Birrell said it was the rats, but Gabriel said the rats didn't matter, if you called them wombats.

Madox Brown said there should be more emigration. He had done that picture, *The Last of England*, with Emma in a bonnet and shawl. He had taken no end of trouble with the bonnet-strings and the folds of the shawl.

Mr. Howitt felt the same about it but the friend who went with him to the Gold Fields, dissuaded him from staying; it would be too hard for a lady like Mrs. Howitt and for Mary.

She wouldn't want to leave England herself.

It started in Red Lion Square. It was easy getting there and Walter could work in lunch-time.

"What ho—" said Gabriel. He had come in without knocking. "Bill's in a stew."

Walter Deverell laid down his brush. "Let's have some lunch, Gab."

"I'll tell you about it first, Dev. I dropped my satchel and my easel in the hall here." He came back immediately. "And while we're about it, why disturb the lady?" He unrolled his drawing-paper. "I can work and talk at the same time, if you can't. Don't move, Madame. Emma said she couldn't have me, she's always saying that just as I begin to settle down to the *Bridge*. I can sleep at home but I want a place to work in. The sneaks stole my books and furniture at Newman Street, while I was at Brown's. That is to say, it was Bill's books mostly that paid the back rent. You're at the Schools all day. I can make do with this place and I can use your model. What an excellent arrangement this is. I got your address from the porter's wife, you know, Fanny."

Fanny?

Elizabeth Siddall did not want to think of Fanny.

Fanny called her the civet-cat.

But Fanny did not really matter, not that first year at Red Lion Square.

She could not now recall the exact sequence, there were preliminary sketches, then Gabriel would toss aside a sheet of drawing-paper and say, "We'll finish Saint George later. I must find a proper brocade first, for the Princess Sabra. I've a half-offer for a Triptych but I must do Dante. There's the *Salutation* and I must finish the *Dream.*"

The first drawing was a sketch for the *Salutation.*

She did not move when Walter said, "My hour's up."

Gabriel said, "Mine isn't."

Walter said, "The lady is not a model. I promised a—a friend, when she consented to sit for Viola, that she was not to be approached by any other artist."

"But I am not an artist," said Gabriel Rossetti, "the Academy don't like me."

Gabriel leaned back, he tossed the stringy lock out of his eyes.

"And moreover," said Gabriel, "I made no promise to nobody, about this or about any other lady."

Walter Deverell motioned to Elizabeth Siddall to go.

"St-tt—" hissed Gabriel, "one moment."

Walter Deverell went over to the easel.

"Now—almost enough for this, anyway—preliminary—my *Salutation.*"

Gabriel Rossetti laughed, a mirthless, high-pitched cackle.

She felt he was clowning, like he did with the lute, that first time she saw him.

He was not really laughing.

"St-tt—" he hissed again, but he sank back, though he still held the pencil.

Walter Deverell stood behind the easel.

"I'm sorry," he said, "Gabriel, but I can't kick you out."

"Not that I don't like Raphael, it's them that followed after. And them that followed them that followed after. A fashionable set-piece painter. Block in your pyramid formation, regard your colour and proportion it discreetly. Let light shine from this direction or from that direction, but never from any other. Mechanical rules laid down by Reynolds; there is no God but Raphael and Reynolds is his prophet. But you know all this, Dev."

......

And another day (she and Gabriel were alone in the studio):

"The blessed Damozel leaned out
    From the gold bar of heaven,
Her eyes were deeper than the depth
    Of waters stilled at even;
She had three lilies in her hand
    And the stars in her hair were seven.

I wrote that when I was nineteen and now I've found you, would you mind telling me if your lilies were the usual, or could they be white iris? But why white, you ask me, though you don't say anything. I see old Dev told you, discretion is the better part of valour. Did he ever do any talking? And you must have said something, sometime. He told you to keep quiet?"

She said (that was in the beginning, at Red Lion Square), "He told me to rest sometimes."

"He amused you, talking?"

"He talked about Shakespeare."

"Ha—a horse, a horse—Did he do Petruchio for you? Miss Clementina Black was Bianca. Did you see Clementina out there? Margaretta was Katherine. Do you think her as pretty as Maria? Stiffish, Spenser and dear Wykeham, the few times I saw them. Why d'you suppose he wouldn't tell me your name, that first time I saw you? Or would mamma not meet you?"

"It was Mrs. Deverell who first arranged my sittings for Viola."

"Ha—'I promised a friend' says Dev, speaking for the first time in his life like Wykeham, 'the lady is not a model; I assure you, my dear Rossetti, on my honour, I promised a friend that the lady was not to be approached by any profligate, thief, beggar or brother-artist.' He should have confided simply that you were Clementina's cousin from the country and he had promised mamma to keep an eye on you. It may be that Walter's doting mamma had a look at you, before she allowed you to take up headquarters at Kew. But Dev wouldn't have gone all pompous, 'my word as a gentleman—a friend,' if it had only been a promise to his mother. Who was the friend?"

She did not ask his permission, she trailed down from the *estrade*. He had folded a length of worn blue stuff about her shoulders. The stuff, he told her, had been rifled from the Polidori attic, "Only curtain," he said, "but I promised Aunt Charlotte not to cut it." She lifted the trailing blue and stood behind the easel.

"White rose—for service meetly worn—yellow like ripe corn—st-tt, we must get a little more gold in, for a' that and a' that—red-gold, not yellow. I blocked them in anyway, the iris, and I think you are right; blue is better for fleur-de-lis."

. . . . . .

It was Aunt Charlotte who paid the rent last time.

How could they manage the double rent, when "we are," as he said, "married."

And what more would marriage bring her than she had now—or what less?

She didn't think she would die giving birth to his child, but marriage had something to do with death.

If she married him, she would die.

She didn't really want to marry him, though she knew that Mary Howitt, Barbara and Bessie Parkes blamed Gabriel.

He was angry with Allingham; she remembered how he had stormed at her when he came down to Hastings, last summer. Mary had actually written to Gabriel, but how did Mary know (he asked her) that he—well—he and Allingham had taken Annie Miller to Madame Tussaud. A harmless little outing. Can't these sneaks leave me alone? What else did Allingham tell Mary? What the dickens does Allingham think he's doing?

"So you went to Madame Tussaud's?" She remembered the words in her mouth, the taste and sting of them and the strength she got from saying them. "Mr. Allingham told Mary nothing—and in any case, whatever got about, no-one mentioned Madame Tussaud."

"Lizzie," he stopped storming, "I almost suspect sometimes, you have a sense of humour. Or aren't you trying to be funny?"

"I can be funny without trying," she said.

"Mary wrote me you were dying."

"Well—what of it?"

"I tell you, Lizzie—and I went out to the Hermitage to tell Mrs. Howitt—"

"How was Mrs. Howitt?"

"Damn—I went out with Allingham, your precious Allingham who started all the mischief, to clear away—misapprehension. These misunderstandings—"

"Mary Howitt's waiting downstairs. Don't shout."

But he went out to the corridor and screamed down Mrs. Elphick's narrow staircase, "Come up here, Mary."

Elizabeth Siddall did not know why, but the scene was somehow familiar.

It might almost have been one of the old houses across the bridge, beyond the tanyards, or it might even have been Kent Place or Aunt Day's rooms above the shop in Pentonville.

Elizabeth Siddall was at home here, Mrs. Elphick might have been Aunt Day. It was Gabriel who had come from outside.

But there was more to it than just that. Say there was a row—not Mum and Dad—but like there was sometimes on that built-in court, the short-cut to the river, people hanging out of windows and shouting across that it was 'im or that it was 'er, and arguments about whatever it was that had caused all the commotion. Yes, she had had one of her attacks. What of it?

Elizabeth Siddall followed Gabriel and stood with him on the wooden platform that was like an *estrade*, at the head of the stairs.

Dad said she was good at numbers. She did not actually count her friends or number her adversaries, but she thought, "It's like what Gabriel calls Mr. Rossetti's Dante's three-ringed circus. I have Mrs. Elphick and most of High Street, Hastings; he has his brother to stand up for him and editors and journals—perhaps even Mrs. Howitt. But I have Mary Howitt."

Mary Howitt was standing at the foot of the stairs.

"This isn't the Battle of Hastings," said Elizabeth Siddall, "it isn't all that important. But why tell the town about it, Gabriel? Come back in the bed-room. Mary—" she heard herself speaking; even William Rossetti had said (Mary told her), "I never heard her speak other than correctly." There was patronage about it. She knew when she was speaking like Dad, almost out of a book, old-fashioned. Mr. William Rossetti was hardly one to comment on her way of speaking. As to Mum's friendly way of talking, that was equal and more than equal to Miss Maria's and Miss Christina's English—"governessy," Barbara called them. Mum got a sing-song in her voice too, sometimes, that was pretty. Mum was Welsh really, a Miss Evans.

But she must not think how her voice sounded, as she did when she pretended she was acting.

"It's about Scalands, Mary," she said, "and my going out there." That would please Mrs. Elphick if she were listening.

When she closed the door, Gabriel said, "I want this gossip cleared up, Mary. I went out to see your mother. Can't they leave a fellow alone?"

Mary was looking out of the window.

"I want to show you a new cove, I found," she said, "Lizzie. It was the turn of the tide when I went out there, and I couldn't get those brittle-star and feather-star, I told you about. Properly, you can only see them under water and my colour-box holds no vermilion or dye-purple that contents me. You can help me decide what blue edges the ordinary star-fish. You wouldn't think they could ever be blue, when you see them dried out. I can sketch in the background of seaweeds with my pencil, and colour afterwards. You can paint the flat shells or a dog-whelk at home—"

Gabriel interrupted, "Let there be no more gossip. I am not engaged to marry Lizzie."

Mary turned from the window. Elizabeth Siddall remembered—so long ago—when she had said to Mrs. Deverell, "Viola is the sea." Perhaps it was Mary speaking of dye-purple.

Mary said, "I forgot to tell you, Lizzie. I heard from my mother yesterday. She especially sends her love."

"Did you hear what I said, Mary?"

"She remarked about other things that have nothing to do with you, Lizzie, saying letters other than business or editorial, shouldn't be shown. People showing strictly private letters to other people is a breach of confidence or worse. It isn't honourable. I couldn't tell you what was in the letter that she spoke of, nor did she tell me. In fact, she would not read the letter that was handed to her. She handed it back to Mr. Gabriel Rossetti. It was his letter and it was written to him by me. Besides that, taking a daughter's letter back to show her mother—I don't know. Perhaps it's because mamma gets so many private letters, considering them as sacred, that we feel as we do. A letter is more sacred even than the word spoken."

One or the other of them must go. Elizabeth Siddall laughed. "I am the *Bridge* between them," she thought.

Or the circle in the middle, at this moment of their three-ringed circus.

Yes, Mary belonged with gallant Barbara, though she had an added grace and dignity, and there was Mrs. Howitt. She had forgotten Mrs. Howitt's book on the new faith, when she had connected her with editors and journals. She was thinking only of *Sister Helen* and people calling Gabriel a genius.

There was Mr. Allingham in their circle, and separate yet in no way inferior and never condescended to, by those in Mary Howitt's circle, there was her own circle, Mum and Dad, Lyddy, Aunt Day and other people; if it came to a row, there was, she had just realized, Mrs. Elphick and most of High Street, Hastings.

"Why are you laughing, Lizzie?"

"Won't you sit down, Gabriel?"

"Not while Mary's standing."

He had, people remarked, easy, charming manners. He had always been exceptionally gentle with Mrs. Howitt and with Mary.

"I am sorry that I showed your letter, Mary."

But there was something else that had offended Mary.

She did not look at Gabriel.

"It is odd sometimes, Lizzy, about honourable people—I mean, oh, spiritually honourable, you know, something that shows or glows in the way they ask a question; it may be just 'Miss Mary, how are you this evening?' And something shines out like the colour of the brittle-star or the feather-star. They look like other people, though perhaps there is something special in the way their Inverness cape seems different, ordinary but princely at the same time. They look like other people, all dried star-fish above the tide-line, and then something's somehow different—quite, quite different. Perhaps it is as mamma says, the Spirit is like water, the Sea—and suddenly, such a one, in the way he sweeps up his gloves from the console-table in the hall, seems to reveal himself, or in any other gesture, like flinging his cape with his right hand over his left shoulder. I mean, you see him with blue edged round him, like the under-water living star-fish. Then he is alive and he makes you alive with wonder. I am speaking without reserve, for so mamma taught me as a child, as her mother taught her. That is, to speak or write without fear and with no embarrassment, when the Spirit moves you."

Gabriel said, "Mary, almost thou persuadest me—"

"That Gabriel Rossetti should have taken a letter, wrung from me by my love of you, Lizzie, when you were so ill, out to the Hermitage to show my mother, is no matter. We sometimes think the same thoughts at the same time, mamma might even have written the letter for me. It is that the discretion and courtesy of Mr. Allingham should have been challenged and by Gabriel Rossetti."

"You look so pretty when you hold forth, Mary," said Gabriel.

. . . . . .

It was in no way her fault, she told Mary afterwards. Lyddy naturally was curious and they were all uneasy when she gave up Mrs. Tozer altogether and sat for Mr. Hunt for Silvia. That was the first outside person—she did not count Gabriel. But she gave up Mrs. Tozer because Gabriel wanted to rush through a picture for the Academy, though he said he would put the matter into the hands of his solicitor, if anyone suggested hanging it. The Academicians that Stevens brought in (no doubt prompted by Gabriel) didn't like it. Gabriel pretended he had never contemplated the Academy. "That sneak, Freddy Stevens, got Redgrave or Hornsley into the studio, to give an opinion." There were other pictures; if she gave up Mrs. Tozer, she must make up, and Mr. Millais and Mr. Hunt both wanted her. She had to explain to Gabriel that she could not sit for him for ever. And Walter Deverell was not working so regularly. He was not well.

She had taken Gabriel's extravagant statements at their face value from the beginning; he had given her the clue the first time she saw him, with "*Come away, come away, death*—that is one of the best things I've ever written."

It was as if she were painting the pictures herself, burning with his fire.

She could be quieter within, with Mr. Hunt and Mr. Millais. That was just a job that she was being paid for.

But Mum and Dad had to be told something, when she first had her own room across the river.

"It's confidential, Lyddy," she told Mary she had told her sister, "I'm working at design too, to put in time before—"

"Liz," Lyddy hugged her, "then you're going to be married?"

A little later she told Lyd that the design now was taking up more time, and she was working in Mr. Rossetti's studio as his pupil. It meant being odd hours in the studio, as she was sitting as well for Mr. Millais, and Gabriel had work out and commissions. Would Lyd tell no-one?

Elizabeth Siddall knew that Lydia would tell her mother.

By this time, Deverell had moved out altogether and Gabriel had found another place to work in.

They were not insistent, but she went out of her way to show Lyddy the house she lived in.

It was a nice room and the people at Weymouth Street were very pleasant, and as Gabriel was out of town that Sunday, she suggested to Lyddy that she might just like to stroll across and see the studio.

She explained to Lyddy that the bridge was Blackfriars, Whitefriars was across the river. This was Bridewell.

The street seemed empty, she told Lyddy, because it was all offices. Mrs. Birrell who was housekeeper in number fourteen, where the studio was, said it had at one time been residential.

Lyddy thought it all great fun, climbing the stairs past the polished nameplates of Mr. Keates, Consulting Chemist and that of Mr. Benthall. Lyddy looked out on the river and said the ships reminded her of Wapping.

The things, Elizabeth explained to Lydia, were some of them borrowed.

His aunt lent him brocades and satins for his pictures, and, sometimes, furniture. She had tidied up the place in Gabriel's absence, but she was seeing it through the eyes of Lydia and her mother.

"It looks like a curiosity-shop, I do admit it. I confess I don't like that chiffonier there, but I clear a space on the table; it's difficult working in the Weymouth Street bedroom."

"Does he sleep here?" said Lyddy.

"There's a little bedroom; if he's late working, he stays sometimes. He has his home to go to."

Elizabeth was glad that Lydia (prompted perhaps by delicacy) did not ask to see the bedroom.

Her mother seemed happier when Mr. Wheeler discovered Lydia.

"Liz and Lyd—I always said you had an influence on Lyddy, didn't I, Liz?"

"What's Lyddy done now?"

"The same as you and in somewhat the same manner. Your Aunt Day told me sometime back she was suspicious how often a certain gentleman stopped in for matches. You know your Aunt Day. Nothing too good for her girls, as she always calls you and Lyddy. Well, this Mr. Wheeler, she found out, was working on a paper in the City, working steady, a journalist with what Aunt Day called a column. I haven't yet met Mr. Joseph Wheeler—but it's funny how things happen, like Mrs. Deverell chancing by to look at bonnets, and having her son with her."

Elizabeth had told them she had first seen Mr. Rossetti when Mr. Deverell was working on the picture at Kew.

But Dad wouldn't be talking about honour, when he was telling her, this afternoon, about Lyddy. It was Lizzie, he was talking about. She would have asked him, if there had been time, why Mr. Wheeler didn't see Lyddy home, if Lyddy had to be seen home. She had noticed no more crowds than usual, rather less if anything, but this was another part of London. And Mr. Wheeler might have work too, on that column, as Aunt Day called it, keeping him overtime or taking him out of London, now that Dad brought it to her notice about war.

She had intended to settle in and maybe stay to supper, not frightened about what they might find out about Gabriel any longer, for she was formally engaged now, though Dad had not given his consent.

Gabriel had taken her to see his mother. Elizabeth Siddall was well aware that Mrs. Rossetti didn't want her in the family, any more than Dad wanted him, but Gabriel was her idol; it was idolatry and Mrs. Rossetti didn't want to lose Gabriel. You could see her hope was that Gabriel would change his mind.

She didn't like the way Mrs. Rossetti tried to find out things from Madox Brown. "But she didn't get anything from your old watch-dog," said Emma. Emma told her that Madox said, "I agree, they shouldn't marry. The lady should be better cared for. Gabriel hasn't enough to keep a wife on." Elizabeth didn't want Emma to go on. She did not want to know what Mrs. Rossetti thought about Gabriel's "model," as she called her, or "that girl from the bonnet-shop." Mrs. Rossetti could hardly say with her second son, "I never heard her speak other than correctly," for as far as she could recollect, she had said nothing.

Gabriel did all the talking.

He was good on these occasions and he was shrewd and business-like when his mind was on it, when he was getting the better of someone, like luring Annie Miller from Mr. Hunt, because he was annoyed that Hunt stole, as he said, his picture.

Gabriel could be patient and his easy negligence could hide a predatory something—what she meant was a cat stalking a bird. Harry had called her gin-gin-ginger and now there was that Fanny, the wife of Hughes who used to be the porter at Somerset House, calling her a cat too, a civet-cat, whatever kind of a cat that was. Fanny came to sit here sometimes, in the studio, but now she was engaged to Gabriel she could stop that simply by setting up her easel. Fanny didn't like sitting while she was around; Elizabeth knew that. It was Fanny he had found at last suitable for the girl in the *Bridge* picture.

"There is money in the *Bridge*," Gabriel told her, "that's why I want to finish it, so as to cut that door through, and make some alterations and improvements in the place here." He had already sold *Found*, but he was selling it again. "I have only to dash off another copy, but I must finish this first; I've sold *Found*. I've as good as sold *Lost*. This is the *Bridge*." It was the same picture.

She did not want to have another scene, not just now. It was all so confusing. How could he sell a picture that wasn't finished, and then sell it again? He had only changed the title. She did ask him, "What became of *The Drover*?" But that time, perhaps it was just as well, he didn't sense the taste and sting in the words and the strength she got from saying them. Fortunately, he didn't realize that she was being funny.

She was the Dove now.

What had she not been?

She was Ruskin's Princess Ida.

They had called her the Cid; they got that from Mr. Allingham still calling her "Miss Sid."

Who was Gabriel stalking? She was not taken in by his new attitude, always seeing her home and leaving the door open so that people passing on the landing outside her room at Weymouth Street could see her, could see him, whatever they were doing.

He was engaged to be married, in other words, to all intents and purposes, he was married, and he was free now, as the way was on the Continent, to have a mistress.

But it wasn't as simple as all that—and what did she know of the Continent and mistresses? It was things that concerned them in the plays, Gabriel took her to, in which Miss Herbert acted. Elizabeth would like to have been an actress. And it was not likely that Miss Louise Herbert, Mrs. Crabbe as she was, would look at Gabriel.

It was something else, and Dove though she might be, in the grey shot-silk she had made up in her own fashion, without hoops, to please him, she could sense things no Dove could be aware of.

It took her back to this afternoon again and *Three Birds and the word Honour*. She was, she had remembered, one of the *Three Birds* at home. But she remembered also that she was the Eagle, and the way she came to find herself the Eagle, was Harry spitting and making cat-calls at her.

This wasn't like home, but Gabriel was making outwardly the same distinctions. It was Fanny calling her the civet-cat that made her wonder. She was not afraid of Fanny.

She remembered how she was not afraid of Harry.

She was not afraid of Gabriel.

She was afraid of something that was stalking her.

And she recalled the ease and assurance of Gabriel's manner, she remembered how he had flung his challenge even to Christina that day he took her formally to see his mother.

"Oh," he said, "Ruskin—I'll arrange, Christina, for Lizzie to take you out there." It was his knowing how Christina, for all his admiration of her poetry, must wilt and wither inside, at the suggestion that she, Lizzie, "Gabriel's model" was socially (as far at least as Denmark Hill was concerned) her superior. For all of *Goblin Market*, Christina had not yet managed to meet Mr. Ruskin.

It was the way, smiling, you felt him feel Christina wither.

And then, that sudden turn-about at Scalands last summer. "Of course, I won't marry you, Gabriel."

There was Mum, there was Lyddy. She was one of the *Three Birds*.

There was Aunt Julia and Barbara and Bessie Parkes and Mary.

There was Barbara, "You're too good for Gabriel."

There was Bessie, "Gabriel says you've consented, at last."

There was Mary.

Elizabeth did not want to remember what Mary had said.

She thought of the letter that Mary wrote to Gabriel when she was so ill there at Hastings, and that other letter:

> Ere she was born
> That vow was sworn;
> And we must lose into the ground
> Her face we knew.

"Yes," she said, "Mary, I am going to marry Gabriel."

She stepped into the magic-circle of Gabriel's fame and influence.

. . . . . .

There were three circles, she had clearly reasoned; that day at Hastings when Gabriel, enraged at Mary writing to him about Annie Miller, had pronounced sentence on her: "let there be no more gossip, I am not engaged to Lizzie."

It was a life-sentence, she then thought, but oddly, she was not broken by it.

She could trump up an excuse about her illness, a "secret engagement," now cancelled and Dad would be pleased.

There were things she could do, even if she left off sitting for the painters.

Suddenly she was almost happy that he had behaved so badly.

There would be two circles, even as she had visualised them, Mum and Dad, Lyddy and Lyddy's children, and people who loved her. She could help Mrs. Howitt in the new centre, she hoped to model for girls, after The Working Men's College pattern. Barbara and Bessie Parkes helped in the old Rescue Home, but Mrs. Howitt wanted something "happier" she said, bright rooms and talks. "This is not the Battle of Hastings," Elizabeth had said to Gabriel, but it was a battle. And she had laughed—he had said, "why are you laughing, Lizzie?"—at the way (better than anything she had ever seen with Miss Herbert) Mary had refused to speak to Gabriel. They would refuse to speak to Gabriel. There was something stronger, even than that charm, that was, someone said, like a spell that Gabriel cast on people.

But the very thing that was standing, as you might say, at her elbow, waiting to rescue her, had betrayed her.

It was like a conspiracy.

It was *Three Birds and the word Honour.*

It was three circles certainly, out of Mr. Rossetti's book on Dante.

And maybe it was *Three Birds*, but one of them was *an Eagle displayed.*

It was a hawk really, like they carried on their wrists, like the picture in *The Triumph of Death*, an old book that John Millais's father had given Gabriel. It was, Gabriel had explained, a collection of engravings from old frescoes from the *campo santo* at Pisa. It was this very book, he had explained, that had started them in their ideas; these painters looked at things differently, they were pre-Raphael, that is before the Renaissance in Italy. The little flowers in the grass were all painted separately. And she, he said, who Bessie Parkes said Mr. Allingham had remarked on as "strange and affecting but never beautiful," was like those people on the *campo santo* walls that had peeled off. Mr. Ruskin said the same, she was like the pictures in the Missals that he showed them.

That special picture, *The Triumph of Death*, was what had most impressed them in the Lasinio book, as Gabriel called it. The book was in the hall, with loose papers and prints in folders, all untidy, on the shelves. If she touched the prints with their curled-up edges or the dusty folders, Gabriel would be sure to say that she had displaced the very thing he was looking for, to copy a door-way or a flight of steps, for the background of a Dante picture. The Lasinio pictures were about the same time as Dante. She had found some sort of comfort in the book, she did not know why; it was all so horrible. There were ladies and gentlemen in costume of the period, all riding across that sort of flower-meadow with every daisy showing separate in the grass. They seemed to be laughing and joking, all except the first pair, who already see what the others will soon see.

The lady has a hood with veils. Her sleeves are wide, the embroidery is indicated carefully; though this was only a print, you could imagine what the original was like. The first lady carried a hawk or falcon on her wrist. There is a cord fastened on the bird's leg. To her, that cord was the most important detail of the picture; she called it the *Gold Cord*. The dress swept almost to the ground; Elizabeth imagined the embroidered hem; there might be strawberry-leaves right round it, and little strawberry-flowers and now and again, an embossed, thicker knot of embroidered berries.

He, out of the same picture, wears an ordinary feather-cap, like a scene from Shakespeare. His sleeves were caught in at the wrists, as if for better drawing his bow.

These two see what the others, who are still laughing, will soon see. There is a ditch or fosse; three kings in open coffins lie there. It isn't just that they are dead; there was careful drawing, but this part was not impressive. The eaten-away faces and hands were only grotesque.

The look of sudden horror on the faces of the first two is intended to make you feel some kind of like horror, seeing a decomposing body.

Perhaps on the walls of the arcaded chapel of the *campo santo* at Pisa, the picture, before it began to peel away, might make you feel things.

Elizabeth Siddall had never been on a horse, and she did not accept Barbara's offer to take her riding, when she was at Scalands. Barbara rode astride.

"Why won't you come?" asked Barbara.

"I haven't the clothes," Elizabeth answered, but Barbara said her Aunt Julia's old habit would do nicely, and Aunt Julia didn't hunt now. But that wasn't quite what Elizabeth meant. Perhaps it was the saddle-bow that worried her. She felt it now, the cramp in her right leg, and she twisted her left foot round it, leaning sideways and loosening her right knee where it clamped in, under the saddle-hold. She was annoyed and breathless. It was her bird, but the others had gone on, her own party, ladies for the most part. Her outrider with the feather-cap out of a scene from Shakespeare, had left her where the road forked. Most of the gentlemen followed him into the forest.

She shifted the bird from her right wrist, and drew her left hand, still holding the reins, forward to receive it. She had forgotten the cord. It was looped about and wound in a ball, which, carelessly, she had left on her lap, instead of tucking into the saddle-pocket. The ball rolled to the ground and she jerked at the reins.

There was sand mixed with the moss and dried leaves of the clearing. They were not far from the sea.

The others had taken the sea-road.

They would be pounding ahead now, while she with her clumsy gauntlet, was trying to disentangle the cord from the reins, and all the time she had to hold her left arm, fairly steady, for the bird perched there.

If she dropped the reins altogether, her palfrey would consider it a signal to race on.

He was curveting in a circle, not knowing what she wanted.

Unless she balanced properly, the saddle would slip.

Elizabeth Siddall straightened and tightened her hold—but it was the arm of the basket-chair she was clinging to; she had been dreaming, but awake. She couldn't have been sleeping. There were no kings in coffins. That was out of the engravings from the Lasinio book, as Gabriel called it because it was edited by an Italian called Lasinio. The prints were copied from frescoes, many of which had now crumbled away. The book was from Florence (Firenze, it was written); she had worked out the date, MDCCCXXXII. She remembered the Roman numerals because that was the year she was born.

She was thinking of another book, when her right foot slipped from the stirrup.

It was a book they were reading. Was it something Gabriel told her? It was illuminated writing.

If her palfrey turned too quickly, he would tread on her, break an arm or . . . there were drawings in the Lasinio book of devil tortures . . .

Where was she?

By some miracle of wit, she had righted herself. She was standing in the moss and siftings of sea-sand. The bird, her familiar, had fluttered to her shoulder.

It was cutting out the costume for Francesca that made her think in costume, as if she were one of the ladies in the picture. Gabriel had done a number of sketches for *Paolo and Francesca*.

And the new dress of hers that made him call her the Dove and her objecting in herself to being called the Dove.

There was the same bird that she carried on her wrist, stitched on the saddle-cloth; it was their coat, *Per Bend Vert and Gules: an Eagle displayed*.

The palfrey was nosing for grass round the edges of the clearing. He dragged the gold skein, it was still tangled in his bridle. It lay in loops and tangles on the sand and moss.

She started winding the skein, she pulled off her left gauntlet, then the other.

She did not care to catch up with them now.

Perhaps he would come round through the forest, knowing someway, where she was, and meet her in the clearing.

. . . . . .

She could not remember what Gabriel had told her and what she made up, sitting there in the mid-summer darkness in the basket-chair, with the tide-water lapping round the house-foundation.

Paolo and Francesca were in hell, in the *Inferno* in one of Dante's circles; but she could not follow it and Gabriel made it no easier by saying that some of it was irony.

Beatrice was or was not his own soul, or the soul of a suppressed Church, the Church of Love—but wasn't it all like that? Here, she should be in heaven, engaged to Gabriel and already she was finding a way out, that is out of her impression that going to Madox Brown like that was not only to paint the cart and Brown in a farmer's smock, but to make it an excuse to be with Fanny, perhaps somewhere else that she didn't know about. What did it all matter? But for Mum and Lyddy and Dad, she had a mind to get away from Gabriel . . . she knew now she never could do that. So, in her dream (or maybe it was a sort of trance) she got away from worry. It was something driving you wild with worry, like Harry first rushing at her with a knife, "the very knife he did it with," that had driven her beyond being frightened. So now, when the cholera fear took her by the throat, so that she could hardly draw breath and she had fretted herself into a fever about what Gabriel might be up to, she got beyond feeling. Then, there was that shelf of sand and moss and someone else, not Gabriel, and she was waiting, while all the time her hands were busy untangling the *Gold Cord*.

It was a tangle but it need not be the death of her, for all that (beginning with Harry) they seemed to set Death about her. There was Ophelia dead or dying with the floating draperies, there was Mr. Allingham, though she wasn't supposed to know it, with that poem.

She thought of Lyddy and her old room at Kent Place.

She remembered how she was stiff then, as she was now, scarcely breathing and in the dark, like she was now, not wanting to light the candle because of Lyddy. Once Lyddy got to sleep, propped, almost sitting upright, she must leave her sleeping. Lyddy did not have dreams but she had the same terror and the memory of Mr. Greenacre, a large man in a farmer's smock, living almost next door with another woman to keep house for him; but it was Hannah Brown that he was going to marry. He was reputed well off, landlord of the row of cottages in Jane Place, but Hannah Brown had put aside her earnings and was said to have jewels, perhaps stolen from the lady she had worked for. It was his cutting her up . . . trying to recall the pieces, made her suddenly feel nothing.

III

But her mid-summer madness was interrupted or intercepted by Mr. Ruskin.

Ida must get out of England.

His choice for her was Switzerland, but she must stop off in Paris and see the Brownings.

No, he did not care to discuss alternative suggestions. Gabriel, however, found a travelling companion for Lizzie, one of the Pierce connection. Well, Ida might go to Nice, Ruskin finally consented, if she refused his gentians.

But "Ida must go South immediately . . . Paris will kill her," he was soon writing Gabriel.

Elizabeth Siddall had crossed early in September.

Gabriel was trying to get Ruskin to "advance" more money on pictures already sold, so that he could join Lizzie.

For the first time since their meeting six months ago, John Ruskin was in no way amenable to Gabriel Rossetti's suggestions. The crystal did not even reflect the molten rose of Gabriel's fanned-up embers. The famous, negligent manner and flattering insinuation caught no prismatic flash from the impenetrable Scot.

What had happened?

It was only the fare over that Gabriel wanted. Ruskin himself had said that Lizzie should leave Paris. He was simply going over to see her off to the South. But since the suggestion about the fare had been snubbed, Gabriel nonchalantly redeemed his call with "I only looked in to get a letter from you, to the Brownings."

John Ruskin reminded Gabriel that he had already met the Brownings, "write them yourself."

As to the fare to Paris, Ruskin said, "it is impossible, I am hard up."

Lizzie in the meantime, had taken it into her head to write Ruskin that she could no longer conscientiously accept his offer for paintings which she had not even begun and was sure she would never finish.

Gabriel had heard of Ruskin writing to someone last summer, from the Vaudois, of an experience he had had, lying in the grass and hearing dead soldiers talking. The letter couldn't have been entirely confidential, in any case, Freddy Stevens had got hold of the story. Gabriel thought that he might safely broach the subject. He suggested Ruskin joining him that evening, with another fellow, at the Academy in Sloane Street. Ruskin said, "on no account, Ressetti;" Gabriel noted the deliberate mispronunciation of his surname, "I have heard of their so-called psychic investigation. On no account and at no time will I go there to a séance."

. . . . . .

The other fellow was waiting as pre-arranged, in what Gabriel called the foyer of the Academy. Gabriel had dined after a fashion and wined out of proportion.

"Ressetti," he said, "a fellow called me Ressetti, before dinner. It's true, the guv'nor's father was a blacksmith—my guv'nor's, that is. His deals in wines, a better business altogether. Ruskin something-or-other and Domecq. Adèle Domecq broke his heart the first time; he kept a glove of hers eighteen years, even after the fatal Euphemia (Mrs. Millais as is) came trailing clouds of glory. Ever heard of Domecq?"

His friend said he had.

"Ever heard of Effie?"

"Who hasn't?"

"The sneak called me Ressetti—deliberate. Now why? It's true my grandfather was a blacksmith—what was his? Euphemia—I mean eupheuism—rosso, a horse? His name was della Guardia really, the blacksmith's. Who was Ruskin but a red-skin? My brother in Carmel—carnal—Carmelite—confession—confusion. What about the séance?"

"Let's have a smoke first," his friend said.

"What I say is, no harm waiting in the foyer. We can go in later. What I say is, do you think Rossetti is horse or rosette? My kingdom for—I mean blacksmith. What was his red-skin?"

His friend laughed.

"Everyone knows the story but Sco-Scotus gave fresh details the other evening, at a party. No, it was—"

His friend stopped him, "Ely," he said.

Gabriel staggered to his feet as Dr. Ely brushed past them on his way to the séance.

"Funny, his fish-eyes," said Gabriel, "do you notice? Even in this half-light, they go phosphorescent."

Gabriel staggered forward like a moth to the flame.

His friend dragged him back. "We can wait here. We'll go in at the break. The second part is always more amusing."

"Of Vasto, the Abruzzi, the counts of Della Guardia—why Rossetti?"

"It's something on your 'scutcheon, I'll wager, a rose or rosette," his friend said.

A late arrival left the street door open. The night air seemed a palpable presence in the dim hall.

"Br-rr," said Gabriel, "I never did like fresh air. Let's find a warm pub."

But his friend said, "I've got to wait here."

"For why, Gus?" said Gabriel.

"Well—er—he isn't certain how he'll feel, after his talk. I sometimes help him."

Gabriel Rossetti seemed suddenly sobered. "You mean it's all fake—or do you actually—see things yourself?"

"No," said Gus, "I'm a sort of secretary, and it's by no means all fake. He keeps the afternoons for maiden-ladies, for simple-Simon faith-healing and the mediums from Bayswater. He can't do everything and he can't waste his—his power. Depending who turns up—no, Norton Ely is no fake."

"I didn't know that you were in the business, Gus. You just say that."

"By no means, Gabriel."

Gabriel straightened in his chair. He reached for a cigar, but his hand rested on his breast-pocket and Gabriel Rossetti forgot the cigar. Those voices—those voices from the Abruzzi—the guv'nor's older brother who started him on Dante—a priest.

"You know Italian?"

"No," said Gus.

"Ely know Italian?"

"No," said Gus.

"You say you're not in the business, you're lying to me."

"No," said Gus.

"What do you do, anyway—and why do you tell me all this?"

"We're friends, aren't we?"

"I thought you were a painter—Charles Augustus—"

"Call me Manuel."

"You're a weird card," said Gabriel Rossetti, "but I like you. I'm sick of these damn' English—you really are a Spaniard?"

"Portuguese," said Manuel.

"Your English is too good."

"My father was a copyist at the Prado," said Manuel, "half English."

("He is no fool, is Gus," thought Gabriel Rossetti, "he wants something.") Gabriel tried to re-capture his vague stare, he felt the line tauten across his forehead, what his father had been wont to call the bar of Angelo, of Michaelangelo, a sign they said, of genius.

He thought of *casa Rossetti* and the crowd there. His mother had lived in retirement, since the death of Gabriele. Gabriel had loved his father.

There was Mazzini and Father Gavazzi, always tender with him. It wasn't that Pierce connection of his mother's. It wasn't Bloomsbury, it was Malta and Lady Moore and a refugee—a poet. What had the voice said?

The bar of Angelo glowed fiery but cold, across his forehead.

What had the voice said—inheritors?

War.

Not that he cared a damn for Balaclava.

"What do you want, Gus?"

"You know people."

"What sort of people?"

"Oh, interested in—in copies of old masters."

"I see. You mean Louis the Seventeenth?"

"Who's Louis the Seventeenth?"

"Louis Naundorf. But I've lost track of Louis. What about Caterina Cornaro?"

"Who's Caterina?"

"Another old friend; that sneak Browning's done a poem on her. I'm doing a picture for it—Queen of Cyprus."

"Caterina?"

"Well, one of her family once was."

Gabriel sank back in his chair. "Come out to a pub." He tried to re-capture his sodden insouciance. He thought of Ida de St. Elme whose lover had been a marshal of Napoleon.

He remembered Paganini, Michael Costa and again Mazzini.

"But the rest were dancing-teachers and piano-tuners."

"Piano-tuners can be useful."

The cards were on the table—or was this just a joke? In any case, Gabriel was an old hand at this game. He had been familiar with codes, secret signs, pass-words, revolution, conspiracy ever since he could remember. A fellow like Gus was sure to be in on something.

"Better begin at the top," said Gabriel, "if you're dealing with old masters. I'll take you to see Ruskin."

If there were anything in this, Bill with his Board of Trade connection could be trusted to follow a clue.

Gabriel let his chin sink forward. Then he started, as if suddenly aware of his surroundings.

"Can't sleep here—or can I? Had I better go home and come back later? But he'll be worn out to-night, after his lecture. Hardly worth sitting an hour with twenty people and the Bayswater medium for a message from great-grandmamma's pet tabby—or is it? Better than nothing, you'll say, and it's fun watching the others. But," Gabriel pulled himself, as with difficulty, to his feet, "you said Ely wouldn't see me again, for a private sitting. Who are you, anyway, Gus?"

"I've just told you. I'm Dr. Ely's secretary. I make arrangements."

"Oh, I thought you were the tambourines or Rain-in-the-face or whatever he calls himself in Bayswater."

"We don't have tambourines here—"

"Come, come, Gus, don't put on airs. It's your job, you just said so—but about those other irons in the fire. Browning's in Paris—or was—on the way to Florence." Gabriel pulled his cape about him. "*Faut de* Browning, will Ruskin do as understudy? He's a cad and a sneak but he knows everybody. Called me Ressetti this evening, before dinner. How about coming out for a sandwich and a drink?"

"I told you I had to wait and see that they don't stay too long, after the group's over."

"Good-night, till soon—" said Gabriel. He walked half way to the door before he turned round. "Oh, by the way, arrange a sitting for me—when old Ely is not too tired."

. . . . . .

Norton Ely did not look up from his table. He was apparently writing letters. He looked more like a clerk in a counting-house, now that Gabriel saw him seated in his own room. The shaded lamp cast a half-circle of light on the thin hand that held the pen. Dr. Ely held the pen like a schoolmaster, not like a creative writer. Gabriel noticed these things. He noticed everything. You could see from the way Dr. Ely sat at his desk that he was a man with a conscience. He would sit up half the night, correcting exercise books, sums or Latin. That reminded Gabriel, he must not forget to bait Ely about languages. He would forget, once Ely turned round.

You can't judge a man only by his eyes. The man was sitting at a desk, after school-hours, correcting papers, or he was going over the books after office-hours, because someone had been ill in the estimable but second-rate firm he worked for—or there was two farthings missing. He was not forging a cheque.

He might be forty-ish from the back of his head.

The cloth was good, he wasn't a parson, new cloth, cut, old-fashioned. Gabriel forgot, for a moment, that Norton Ely was from America. Must remember to mention his great country. Gabriel had been directed to Dr. Ely's private office. Maybe this wasn't actually for a sitting.

Scratch—scratch—"His is not the pen of a ready writer," thought Gabriel.

Norton Ely turned round. "Don't look at his eyes," said Gabriel to himself. Gabriel bowed, "do not let me disturb you." Dr. Ely passed his hand over his forehead. He laid down his pen.

He said, "pray, be seated. I leave the arrangement of the groups to the desk. But I require a personal interview before I engage a new medium. My secretary sent you?"

Gabriel said, "yes."

"Ours is, you understand, a personal dedication. But already the movement is growing, perhaps growing too fast. There are new, unforeseen developments. Now, as to that congress in Cleveland; they are already arranging for branch societies and supervision of group-centres. It appears, all this is necessary but it is really beyond my power to control the more popular and sensational aspects of our work. I don't know. They say we must have some sort of hold over meetings and demonstrations. They say, how else control but by committees and supervision? I don't know. I say, let control come from within—guidance will best serve and personal devotion. It was at the suggestion of Miss Fox, the elder of the sisters, that I came here to help establish this London centre."

Gabriel saw from the shadow that Norton Ely now had his back to the light. He looked up.

Norton Ely's eyes were half-closed; "dead tired," thought Gabriel.

"But I need not interview you," said Dr. Ely, "you are a seeker. They will tell you, at the desk downstairs, your duties if you wish to work here."

Dr. Ely coughed. He turned back to his table, a polite intimation that the interview was over. "Good-night, sir."

"I'm sorry," said Gabriel, "I am not a medium."

"It's Miss Mary," said Dr. Ely, "I do not frankly approve of Miss Mary, a sensitive, delicate lady, appearing at public meetings."

("Those Fox sisters," thought Gabriel. He had heard Mrs. Howitt speak of them.)

"But I see you are too tired to-night," said Gabriel, "for a sitting."

"Mr. Manuel does not send clients to my private office."

"It was a special arrangement."

"You are a friend of Manuel?"

"You do not remember me?" said Gabriel.

Norton Ely turned. The phosphorescence was burnt out. He had probably been working earlier in the evening. Gabriel had especially wanted to see Dr. Ely when he was not tired.

"Manuel, like myself, is not wholly English. My name is Rossetti."

"I think I remember seeing you. I think I remember your face."

"I have attended your lectures and sat with your mediums at the séances. But I am grateful to say, you gave me two private sittings."

"I am all gone this evening," said Dr. Ely. "It's thinking of Miss Mary. Pray—did you receive guidance from my Guardian?"

"Guidance and consolation," said Rossetti.

"Then I will ask your guidance now," said Dr. Ely. "I am not in two minds about it. But they argue round me." He lowered the lamp. "They say if you have a message, you must give it. We in America are a divided people. We do not pretend to see the future, but war is coming. What can we do to stop war? Nothing. But we can do this. We can leave the door open."

"Je dis que le tombeau. . . .
     Ouvre le firmament,"

said Gabriel.

"I do not understand," said Ely.

"You do not speak French?"

"I know no foreign language."

"It is a line of Hugo."

"Hugo?"

"Victor Hugo, a French poet. I learn he is in Jersey."

"Jersey?"

"One of the Channel islands. I am told that he, too, communicates with the Spirits."

"This is a message from the Spirits?"

"You asked me for my guidance and I thought of this poem." Gabriel remembered how Mary Howitt had brought the poem to him and asked him to translate it for *The People's Journal*. He was back in their good graces at the Hermitage. "The translation is,

The tomb, I declare it. . . .
Opens the star-gate,

but star-gate is not literal, *firmament* he says, firmament or heaven."

"I take it for an answer. We must go on. My personal predilection is for—secrecy. But secrecy is not quite what I mean. I would have more selection and smaller gatherings. It is not so much persecution from outside that I dread, but actual submergence. I cannot interview everyone who enters these doors. It is a tide-wave. I am told that Italy, Belgium, Holland, Sweden, Spain—the whole world has been swept into this current. There are undesirable write-ups and sensations about the movement. Is it the Lord's doing?"

Gabriel was silent.

"In confidence, Mr.—"

"Rossetti."

"You know languages. You are French?"

"Italian," said Rossetti.

"Mr. Manuel is conversant with foreign languages. In confidence, I have not yet signed this."

Dr. Ely turned to the table. He handed Gabriel a letter.

Gabriel leaned forward to the half-circle of the light. It was unquestionably, Manuel's writing, dashing and ornate.

Ely said, "It is a French princess."

"Well—not a Bourbon," said Rossetti.

"It is difficult for me to follow things in Europe—the Continent, Manuel calls it."

Gabriel handed back the letter. "What did you tell Manuel to say?"

"I asked him to explain in a few words our predicament. We have funds. Chiefly, how communicate?"

"I see. This Madame de Fontenelle does not, I gather, expect you to lecture to her group or circle?"

"No, she specified a favour—one or more private sessions. It got about I might take a trip to Europe. The International Society, as it now calls itself, sends out a monthly bulletin. I guess this Lady Fontenelle talks English."

"It is possible," said Gabriel.

"It is different with lectures and discussions. That is, someone at hand to prompt you or them, or to explain or interpret generally, doesn't put you out. Foreign people call here. Generally they are diplomatic or connected with the Foreign Office and talk English, but there are times when they bring a distinguished visitor."

Gabriel, with no visual effort, saw the visitor. He had seen so many in his time, that is while old Gabriele (as he called his father) was still living.

What was it Ely wanted to know? Didn't he trust Manuel? But Gus was, as Gabriel had already admitted, no fool.

"Manuel simply says what you say," repeated Gabriel, "that for a private sitting, you don't want interpreters. But Manuel says it, of course, as if dictated by you. Perhaps he is a little—well, gushing at the end, but felicitations and all that, is the French way of writing."

Dr. Ely handed him back the letter, "Read out what he says."

"Dear Princess—"

"But you just said she was no princess."

Had Gabriel come here to elucidate the mysteries of the French aristocracy? Or had he come for his own (as Ely would say) guidance?

"Well, it's difficult to explain."

Had Ely never heard of Louis and Eugènie?

"The present Emperor is the third Napoleon. There was the French Revolution before Bonaparte. The aristocrats who escaped, still hold to their old titles."

"Some came to America," said Dr. Ely. So he had heard of the French Revolution.

"It's a matter of taste—or etiquette—"

"That," said Dr. Ely surprisingly, "is just what I meant. There's a sort of boudoir air about this letter."

"It's only French, it's only—elegance. In any case, Manuel makes it quite clear; you will know or she will know, immediately on meeting, whether or not a private session is desirable."

"You're keeping something back, Mr. Rossetti."

"No," said Gabriel.

Gabriel had read between the lines; Manuel knew what he knew—Norton Ely did not realize that his trance communications were sometimes delivered in foreign languages of which he himself knew not one word.

And Gabriel wondered what ordering of fate had caused him casually to ask his neighbour, one evening at one of the lectures, to come out afterwards for a drink.

"Has Manuel always been your secretary?"

"I never had a private secretary till recently. I needed someone for these foreign letters."

There was honour among thieves, whichever way you look at it. Gabriel gathered that whatever else Gus was up to, there was some sort of tacit agreement, that to let Dr. Ely know what happened in his trance-state was to break the charm, or the power, as Ely would have called it.

There was honour among thieves.

"I assure you, Dr. Ely," said Gabriel, "that this is the sort of letter that passes merely for ordinary politeness in France. It is a difficult language, untranslatable.

Je dis que le tombeau. . . .
      Ouvre le firmament;

when I gave you my English words for those lines, it was stones for bread, or stones for star-dust."

"It's what in a way I have been saying to myself. But you couldn't call anybody swine, even in the Scriptural sense. It's those pearls."

Dr. Ely was tired certainly, but Gabriel believed there would be no difficulty now. Gabriel felt he could help Ely, without cutting across Manuel. He had only to find out what evening or evenings Ely put aside for letters. He was a methodical man.

"Miss Mary is only a girl, but her devotion to her father compels her to vow not to marry. Miss Cathy won't leave her sister. They are really up-state people, but Mr. Fox had, out of sentiment, kept on their Connecticut farm."

Now Gabriel was listening to a foreign language.

"Connecticut?"

"Pretty with golden-rod up to the door, and asters drifting to the stone-walls. They wouldn't let the hired man mow down the field that September. It was the first year they were alone there. I didn't know what took it into Miss Mary's head to leave the golden-rod and asters growing in their front-yard."

"They lived there?" Gabriel felt that Ely was retreating into his reverie. "But I must not keep you from your letters."

"Pray, Mr. Rossetti, forgive my being absent. I was there in that farm. Not a large place, counting in acres, but containing an edge of woodland. The spring rose beyond the wood, from a hollow dip. There was fern there, may-flower and violets. Miss Cathy was child-like in her ways and would always set the violets in one of her grandmother's old mugs. She had notions. The barns were empty though there had been cattle, in the old days. There were, of course, blackberry tangles, the run of the stone walls. The sumac made red splashes there; Indian paint-brush, some call it."

"Paint-brush?"

"The Indians painted themselves."

"Were there many Indians?"

"Mr. Rossetti, you will forgive me, but here you are singularly ignorant about our country. The Indians, but for the Far West, have all gone."

"I am ignorant, I grant you—Con-net-ti-cut? Is it a town?"

"One of our New England States."

Ruskin was planning to send pictures to some exhibition in America. But America to Gabriel was chiefly associated with talks at home in the old days, Ida de St. Elme and discussions of a certain Louisiana Purchase.

"I confess to ignorance. There was talk at one time, at my father's home, about Louisiana."

"French and Spanish," said Dr. Ely, "far away but near at hand, too. It concerned Miss Cathy when Miss Mary said they would move out of New York State altogether and live there, at the farm, all the year round, not only in the summer. They were working for the run-aways."

"Run-aways?"

"The slaves, Mr. Rossetti. The Friends in Philadelphia had the tunnels. The slaves got across from Maryland, even from the deep south, and worked their way up. The Abolitionists in Boston and the Friends in Philadelphia, it was being reported being said from Virginia, would land the country in war."

"War?"

"Secession, they call it—the right to what the plantation-owners call their own property; some of the States already plan breaking away. I told you our country was divided. It is a grave problem, but it is no problem. It was worry about the slaves got Miss Mary thinking of the Indians. Hiram the man, was son of old Hiram who was head of the farm in grandfather Fox's day. He was loyal. But he stopped my buggy on the road. He stated there was talk from people driving down that way to the rocks to watch the sunset, summer evenings. But Thanksgiving Day was near, and Miss Mary and Miss Cathy had just told Hiram they would stay the winter. Hiram didn't want to be seen coming to my office. I had heard some rumour, a doctor must be pleasant, and you can't always keep a patient quiet. Hiram suggested I look in some day, just for an excuse in passing. I made the excuse that I heard they were staying for Thanksgiving, would they spend it at our house. We always had what strangers there were about, for Thanksgiving. Not that Miss Mary and Miss Cathy were strangers. My wife is a good woman."

"Is Mrs. Ely with you here in London?"

"No. It is partly on her account that I contemplate the trip to Europe."

Norton Ely went on, "They wouldn't come for Thanksgiving. Miss Mary said they were keeping it with the Indians.

"Miss Cathy took me to the door. 'Dr. Ely,' she said, 'it's getting about that Mary is touched. You know our father. I would consider it charitable of you if you would contradict any rumours.' She supposed I had heard what people said about them. She went with me to the fence. 'Mary keeps the garden this way for the Indians.' I confess I wondered if Miss Cathy was touched, too.

"They were not exclusive and they knew people. They had been to Philadelphia. They read what Mr. Hawthorne wrote on evil that had been done by early settlers. Indian villages were burnt out and Indian mothers and the children smoked out and destroyed, like you smoke out a hornet's nest and with no more feeling, for they were heathen. Miss Mary had been writing to Mr. Hawthorne; he was on consul or diplomatic business. Perhaps it was Mr. Hawthorne talking of coming to England that first put it into Miss Mary's head that I might come here. But she said it was the voices."

Dr. Ely placed his two hands flat on his knees. He sat upright.

There was a tension in the atmosphere. Gabriel recognised what he called the "symptoms." His own hackles, he felt, were rising. Or like a cat watching a mouse-hole, his whiskers felt the stir beneath the boards where there was no stir. Gabriel was reputed to be the most selfish man in London. He was the last to defend his reputation. But Gabriel Rossetti had his moments.

"Dr. Ely," he tried to be casual, "I've taken enough of your time. Some evening, when you are disengaged, perhaps you will let me come again to see you."

"You are yourself engaged this evening?"

"If I were, I would gladly cancel any previous arrangement for the sake of talking with you."

"I will tell you then, what I have told no-one," said Norton Ely.

But still he sat there, erect, as he did when the trance took him.

"I was kept for lying-in cases and the dying sometimes, half the night, on my circuit. I could not confide in Mrs. Ely. But I could make occasion to pass the Fox farm, hitch up the buggy, sometimes even unharness, for Hiram helped me and kept grain ready in the feed-box. In conscience, I could say I was helping the Fox sisters, for who was there to help them? It had begun in the old grandmother's time and she had talked about it, but grandfather Fox forbade mention of irreligious subjects, as he called the tales of hauntings, ghosts and—rappings. It was wind in the pine trees, the wood was closer to the house then, even it might be wind from the sea, or old boards creaking. Grandmother was what in the old days, they called a wise-woman, what in the older days, they burnt for witches.

"It never had taken Miss Mary until she went to Philadelphia. Some said unmarried women and girls should not know things, but Mary was with the plain Friends, working for the cause—the run-aways. Some had marks of chains and marks burnt on them of their masters. Miss Mary attended meeting and though not a Friend, the Spirit moved her to stand up and witness. She was afraid after that, Miss Cathy told me. Mary said she had lost conscience of her surroundings, when she spoke. What did she speak of? Cathy told her. When they got here, it was as it had always been, with pansies by the door-stoop. 'We'll leave them this time,' said Mary, 'then, we'll get pansy-violets from behind the spring-house and put them in, and let what's wild stay.' Cathy said she liked the crow-foot and the pansy-violets, but Gran always had the pansies. Mary said, 'Gran tells me, let it run wild.'

"It was Cathy I got to be afraid for, Mary was away on her trances but Cathy was there all the time. It is a letter to Miss Catharine Fox there, lying at my elbow."

Gabriel could think of nothing to say. Dr. Ely was waiting for him to speak.

The Fox sisters—he had thought of a music-hall turn, the first time he heard of the Fox sisters.

Now there was Cathy with crow-foot . . . "What is crow-foot, Dr. Ely?"

"It's a violet, bigger than field-violets. It's because of the leaf, Cathy told me, that it's called crow-foot. I asked that very question."

"I see . . . and a spring-house?"

"It's usually of stone, with slabs over the stream or spring; this was a stream flowing out of the spring in the hollow. The slabs or slates hold the cold, and butter is laid there and raspberries on plates or in leaves. My mother pulled grape-leaves."

"I should think raspberries would look very well on vine—I mean, on grape-leaves," Gabriel spoke at random.

"Nothing tasted the same iced; they got to storing ice in ice-pits, to last all summer."

"The summers are hot there?"

"Very hot and the winters are very cold."

But Gabriel knew that they were marking time. He must ask a question or Norton Ely would not tell him what he had told no-one.

"And the voices?" said Gabriel Rossetti.

"It was Indians speaking. Gran, Cathy said, brought them. Gran at first talked for them. Afterwards, they came by themselves. Mary talked with Indian voices."

"And you understood her?"

"This is out of St. Paul. There are tongues and the interpretation of tongues. Cathy interpreted."

"She understood the language?"

"This is what we are trying to find out—there is a new word, telepathy. She understood the thought back of the language."

"But Miss Mary understood the language, I gather?"

"Miss Mary was in trance. She did not know she spoke with tongues. Cathy said, Gran said that the Indians would not come, if Mary (or any but us) knew. It would go, the gift, if Mary knew about it."

"I see," said Gabriel Rossetti.

"What happened, we thought, was summer-people. Cathy said she felt Mary might break up. She would sing or intone, at times. That too, worried us—for I was, as it were, Mary's left hand now, Cathy being her right, like Paul again and the Body Spiritual. We were a whole Body, though only three. But there were moonlight picnics and summer-people loitering in their wood, that second summer, and down by the shore. Cathy remembered her Gran's little table. It would be quieter and the three of us would take the power together. Their Gran had made a secret of the table for them when they were children. But there was always grandfather Fox who might break in on them, and their own father had been sympathetic but he was taken up with Swedenborg. Cathy got out the little table.

"It might have been Mary and Cathy sitting alone with the table, in the summer with the door open or (Hiram's wife was away with a sick mother) the new girl in, part time from the Bridgefield farm. She was only supposed to be there mornings, but she would stop in evenings with the breakfast eggs, or she got curious. Anyway, it was in his wife's absence that Hiram thought it started. They had the same foreman's cottage beyond the barns, where Hiram had been born. There would be no way to convey how Hiram said, *summer-people*.

"It was the summer-people. Some out-of-town journalist got hold of the story, rappings and voices at Haunted Hollow.

"It came to be known in less time than you can think that Miss Mary and Miss Cathy were in communication. They called them the Fox sisters, and try as I would to avoid them, anybody, at any time, in town or on my rounds, would hand me a newspaper. 'You will be interested, Dr. Ely, in happenings on your circuit.' And head-lines, local re-prints of articles from New York and Chicago and worst of all, the Hollow besieged by visitors, ladies from Albany or even from New York, 'we hear you tell fortunes here, Miss Fox,' showing them, Mary and Cathy, pieces from home newspapers, brought along in their handbags.

"It was beyond all reason.

"Mrs. Ely is a loyal woman. She listened to no gossip.

"As a matter of fact, it didn't actually come out."

Gabriel thought it time to put in a word, "Your sitting with them at the table?"

"Well that—that was a recreation, you might say, a rest from the other."

"From Miss Mary's trances?"

"Yes—and from mine.

"Cathy was the go-between, between us.

"Of course, Cathy gave me to understand that my states were on a different level, stronger maybe, but Mary was nearer the Spirit. Mary said we were the same, but Mary didn't know what Cathy and I knew, that she (Mary) spoke with tongues, in trance state. It was somehow agreed between us, without too much talk, that I was to leave town."

"It is fortunate for us, Dr. Ely," said Gabriel, "that you came here."

"A professor from Harvard, interested in what they call metaphysics, came to our help. We got the thing under some sort of control, after the summer visitors cleared out, and Mrs. Hiram took in a group from Boston, over Christmas. I need not tell you that we would, as I said, have worked together in secret, if it were possible. But it was no longer possible. The table helped us, you might almost say Gran's table saved us. Miss Mary and Miss Cathy gave good-will messages from the table to the Christmas people. The folks from Boston said they would see that the two were sheltered. Miss Mary and Miss Cathy agreed to spend the summer visiting in Vermont and Massachusetts. That was last summer. There was a distinguished set in Boston, abolitionists and writers. It was your speaking of this French poet and my remembering Mr. Hawthorne, that confirmed me. I did not want to go on with the work. But I will try to do what I can in Europe; there are others already arranged for, to go on with the Academy, here in London. I would rather go home to Connecticut. I am a simple man, a doctor."

"You are not a simple man, Dr. Ely." Gabriel remembered Gus speaking of simple-Simon health-cures. "Do you do health-treatments?"

"I talk to people. Doctors always talk to people."

"But the table—why do you say it saved you?"

"We could talk about the table. We had to cover rumours. And there had always been talk of mystery at the Hollow. It was old tales from the past, we could say honestly. But the table started other tables. There was a mushroom growth of talking-tables, right across the country, and they say the same of Europe. All this sprang up because of Miss Mary and Miss Cathy and myself. I feel responsible. And I think of how we sat together, winter evenings, and I think of the clear water of the spring from the Hollows, and I fear as I said earlier, that clear rivulet being lost in these dark waters."

And why had Dr. Ely told him all this? Gabriel knew the answer. It was the message he had had the second time, the last time, *war* and *inheritors*.

There had always been war, Ely had said earlier, but we could leave the door open.

"We cannot stop war," Dr. Ely had said.

"We cannot stop inheritance," said Gabriel.

Dr. Ely reached forward to adjust the lamp.

"I will finish my letter," he said. "I will tell Miss Cathy that I will go on."

IV

What is happening to Lizzie in Paris, they asked in London. She wrote to Ruskin, deprecating her talent, but Ruskin brushed aside her objections and said this year, at any rate, was settled. "I cannot have you going to Paris or near Ida," Ruskin writes Gabriel, ordering him to finish certain drawings, commissioned for one of his art patrons in the North. But seeing a fresh picture of Gabriel's, at Chatham Place, Ruskin buys it on the spot for thirty-five pounds, and Gabriel is off to Paris.

Lizzie had already been six weeks in Paris.

She looked stronger, better; Gabriel perceived a certain poise and elegance.

"What have you done to yourself, Lizzie?"

She rose gracefully from the faded brocade *tabouret* where she was sitting, and in the small salon of the modest hotel where she and Mrs. Kincaid were staying, she swayed to the door and stood before the curtain. She might have been Miss Louise Herbert, in the green-room.

"Well, I asked you, what have you done to yourself, Lizzie?" Gabriel repeated. It was perhaps perversity on her part that she stood so still, that she turned her head, so that the chin and throat took the line, "Your chin, your chin—you've spoilt that line." It seemed that she would tilt her head back and laugh. She did laugh. It was not, however, the green-room laughter of Miss Herbert. It was too tense, "her flighty giggle," William had called her laughter, and "she is flighty," William Rossetti had said (it was reported to her) on more than one occasion. Gabriel's outlandish pranks and ridiculous and not always funny parodies, were acclaimed as expression (even the most trivial) of genius should be. It was never put on record that William Rossetti called his brother flighty.

"What is the matter with you, Liz?"

"What is the matter with you, Gabriel? I hardly ever remember, except for the first few times I sat for the *Damozel*, your asking me to talk."

"You've been here six weeks, Lizzie, something's happened to you."

"Something's happened to you, Gabriel."

"*Tu quoque* was always forbidden in our family."

"Ah—your family." (Ah—Miss Herbert!)

"Something stiffish about you, Lizzie."

"That's what you said of Spenser and Wykeham Deverell."

"My God—what a memory you have."

"That's what you said when I remembered after three months (at Red Lion Square) that you hadn't thanked me for the *Damozel*."

"But I think I said it wasn't finished."

"And you said, why should you thank me, 'it's you,' you said, 'who should thank me, for making you immortal.'"

She swayed over to the window. Outside was a walled garden. She looked down on the wall; above it, there was placed for her exact requirement a roof slanting at a probable angle to meet gables, and above and beyond, uneven planes, roofs set at impossible angles, broken now and again by dormer-windows. Beyond them, was the pinnacle of the lesser *Saint Germain*. There were bells, no sweeter but more personal somehow, than the chimes of Bridewell.

"I thought Scotus would come over with Monro, but only Monro turned up."

"You have already seen him?"

"We crossed together."

"What are you planning to do first?" From an immense height, from an immeasurable distance, Elizabeth Siddall, for the first time in the erratic, surcharged years, spoke with gentle patronage to Gabriel Rossetti.

"Do? Well, we'll barge into the Louvre, I suppose, first."

"You won't like the way they've been cleaning up the Claudes. There is too much of Rubens but you'll like the *Marriage*."

"Marriage?"

"Veronese's *Marriage in Cana*."

It had been reported in London that the Sid was getting out of hand. Scotus had remarked to one of them, William, Boyce or Stevens, that she actually thought herself a genius, with her "small, quaint, quasi-poetical imitations of his works." It was Scott who had looked in at Chatham Place last summer to retrieve some books he had lent Gabriel and found the Sid in charge "sleeping there—well—in Gabriel's absence." William Bell Scott had also run across her, at the Hermitage. It was during the time that the girl was sleeping in Gabriel's studio. Where wasn't she? True, Gabriel was staying at the Queen's Head to be near Brown and to finish the *Bridge*.

"I was trying to find Gabriel. That caretaker told me he was out at Highgate, but I just pushed upstairs. Imagine my feelings. It was damn' hot. I would go out the next evening to Brown's. No, Emma said, he wasn't there. No help from Emma. He might be sitting with them in the Hermitage garden. No, the maid informed me, the family was away. I just took a look round. You know the summer-house? Mary called it the studio—romantic, rustic and all that. There was Gabriel and—the lady. She slid off. No, I hadn't seen anything. Gabriel walked back with me to Brown's."

Romantic but hardly rustic, Miss Siddall continued, "John Hancock has an *épergne* at the Exhibition."

Gabriel with difficulty recalled Hancock, a fellow he and Monro had known in the early days.

"Whoever mentioned that I knew John Hancock?"

"Mrs. Kincaid."

"Why should Mrs. Kincaid speak of John Hancock to you?"

"She remembered him, she met him at your mother's; she saw his name written on the card in the show-case at the Exhibition."

"What's an *épergne*, Lizzie?"

"It's knights chasing each other in a circle, and pages between, with holders."

"Holders—what for?"

"For putting flowers in."

"Lizzie—are you dotty?"

"I thought it would interest you."

"Are you coming out to dinner?"

"Is it time for dinner?" Dinner was any time, in London, as she well knew. "Are you hungry, Gabriel?"

"No, we had a snack and the crossing was rough. I thought you might like to come out."

"I thought we could go out to-morrow."

She did not want to spoil this perfect moment. She wanted to prolong it. She wanted to be alone afterwards, to think about it. She wanted to re-assemble her impressions; herself, it seemed for the first time in her life, needed no assembling. She wanted to savour this moment and recall the moment, less than a half-hour ago, when Madame Bonnard had announced

Gabriel. She wanted to remember Gabriel's voice, behind the curtain, the voice of a new Gabriel, his French voice. It did not abash and shut her out, as his Italian did when he and William got excited about something (usually some criticism of their father's Dante) and "disappeared" in a mysterious manner; strangers. They were fluent, vituperative in a new way, not that they weren't talkative and dramatic enough in English. But the French Gabriel was different.

"Funny, your not knowing what an *épergne* was," said Lizzie. "I heard you talking real French with Madame Bonnard in the hall, before you came in.

"That *épergne*, as you described it, wasn't really anything. And why a damned Exhibition?"

"It's cheap," said Lizzie, "cheaper than the Crystal Palace and easy to get to. I mean, we can't walk around the shops all day looking, though we did buy, in the beginning." She had turned from the window. Now, again, she swayed forward and seated herself, this time on the gilded settee. The room was growing darker. Her hands seemed to be resting at her sides, but she was fingering the folds of her skirt, then as if at a sudden "damn—your hands, Lizzie," she drew them forward and they rested on her lap. Still, her fingers felt within them the sheen of the deep-rose taffeta she had chosen that first week, with such care and so extravagantly, with Mrs. Kincaid. She had worn the dress to get the "feel" of it, so that she wouldn't be shy in it when Gabriel saw her. It (or something) had gone to her head.

It was *taffetas de soie* but it wasn't silk exactly. It had the lustre of shot-silk but it wasn't stiff like taffeta.

"It was the stuffs; they have rooms and show-cases and costumes made up, and you couldn't buy anything, not outright, at the Exhibition, even if you wanted. So you look around, without embarrassment, at what they call the *dentelles*, lace, every kind of stitch-work, Flemish, Spanish and of course, French embroideries—and tapestries."

"Old tapestries?"

"I—I don't know."

"You mean you wasted six weeks pottering about the Exhibition?"

"Oh—no, Gabriel."

"You think the time wasn't wasted? Why the protestation?"

"I wasn't protesting. It was a way of—forgetting."

"Forgetting what, Lizzie?"

Gabriel, strangely contrite, thought of bleak London periods, his neglect, her illness. He wished he had not asked her what she had forgotten.

He saw the face, a shadowed cameo. There was the throat and the hands, in the darkness.

"It was a story I made up while you were out at Highgate, out of what you called the Lasinio book, peeled off from the walls at Pisa.

"It was a story as real as if I'd lived it.

"It was those coffins on the ground and the Kings, meant to be portrayed horrible, in the coffins.

"I knew it was a picture (you all talked about it) of a painting from a wall in a grave-yard, what you called the *campo santo*.

"It was going to Chartres. That's why I wouldn't leave Paris."

The face, the throat, the hands—the rest had faded away.

"*Lizzie—*"

"What's the matter, Gabriel?"

"O, I suppose the crossing. I felt funny."

"There's matches, Gabriel, always in the saucer."

"Well—damn—where's the saucer?"

He did not believe, even now, that there was more to her than a face, a throat and two hands, folded upon darkness.

"It was Mrs. Browning saying it was that way with her—or it had been—not knowing whether a book or a picture was more real than the un-real world she lived in."

He did not even know she had met the Brownings. He heard the rustle of her skirt as she rose from the settee. It was silk of some kind. She was not clothed in impalpable darkness. He saw through his eyelids and through his hands, clasped over the flaming bar of Angelo, that there was light. She had found the matches.

He did not open his eyes.

"Sitting there in the Cathedral, it was as if one of the Queens had stepped off from the wall and was lying in a coffin. The Queen it seemed, belonged to one of the Kings in the picture—but this was just the opposite of that grave-yard painting. It was mixed up with my being afraid of cholera."

"You never spoke of cholera."

"One fear joins to another fear—one fear reminds one of another. But in that Cathedral picture—or—dream—it was as if the Queen might have come out of a Missal, like the ones Mr. Ruskin showed us at Denmark Hill. And I thought of other Cathedrals—or rather it seemed this might be the very place where Héloise and Abélard might most fittingly have worshipped. It seems from what Mrs. Browning told me, there was mystery about them.

I had read about Abélard in one of those pamphlets sent to your father, that William used to bring in. It was *Forerunners of Dante* by a Professor in America, mostly about Abélard."

He opened his eyes. He saw Lizzie standing by the curtain.

"It was connecting terror of that far past, the wrong they did Abélard (and actually in a French Cathedral) that reminded me of others, and Harry lunging at me with a knife and Walter Deverell dying and Mr. Greenacre."

The story had horrified Gabriel, but he should have made Lizzie talk more about Mr. Greenacre.

"Then, I was afraid, remembering the guillotine in Paris."

"How could you remember, Lizzie?"

"I mean (maybe I didn't tell you) Mr. Tozer (whose name was Toussier) told me how his father's master had been killed and I was afraid of Paris."

"I thought you wanted to come to Paris."

"I was afraid. But Mrs. Kincaid took me to the shops and sights, and Madame Bonnard said we must go to Chartres.

"I went alone sometimes. I even spent the night there with a cousin of Madame Bonnard's." Now Elizabeth Siddall remembered the story, herself and the embroidered falcon on the saddle-cloth, the cord twisted in the reins. She fell from the awkward saddle as if into the abyss . . . the gentlemen in the forest were led by her own companion. His sleeves were caught in at the wrist and at first she had wondered why that should be, as apparently he was one of their hawking party. But he turned off into the forest and the gentlemen, for the most part, followed him. Her companion in the picture was not Gabriel. But she had worked that out; her own fever of anxiety lest he and Fanny were together . . . had projected this other for her. She could not then think of Gabriel without some compensating hope for herself; but here in Paris, Gabriel was different.

"It was suddenly knowing that the story had its real side and wasn't what you just now called dotty, that made everything seem different. It was her telling me she got 'lost' sometimes like that. That is she got 'lost,' as she called it, alone there in her father's house, before she was married, and she experienced the same terrors, things thought being true, and the washstand and the dressing-table and everything on it being—'hallucination' was her word. She was happier when she had Flush."

"Who's Flush, Lizzie? And who is this who had hallucinations?" He did not know his own voice, but he recognised unfamiliar smothered sobbing in it. He had never cried, not even when Gabriele left him.

"Flush was the little dog she had, when he first came to see her."

"Lizzie dear, who came to see who, and whose was the little dog called Flush?"

Was Lizzie really going dotty?

"Why *he* came to see *her*, Gabriel."

His hands dropped to his sides. He wanted something to eat—a drink, badly. But he couldn't leave her in this mood.

"Get on your mantle and come out, Lizzie."

"You see, it doesn't matter, but it was always that way, when I started talking. You always said, 'come out, Lizzie.'"

"It does matter, Lizzie."

"She went to the circles sometimes, but I never saw her. He called it 'slumming,' and she loved him so she stopped going. But she wanted to hear about the circles. There was a doctor who had helped her, talking to her; he didn't call it 'healing.'

"She said Robert didn't understand. She was so happy."

"Damn it—Browning is a rich man."

"I asked her if she still had the fancies; she said, yes, but now everything is different. She is so happy about us, Gabriel."

"What did you tell her about us?"

"Only that we are happy."

"We aren't happy, Lizzie, not as we could be. We could cut everything and get out, go to Florence—"

Florence?

"She talked about Florence and Venice."

Venice? "I suppose that's Ruskin."

"Why Ruskin, Gabriel?"

"Who ever heard of Venice, before Ruskin went there?"

He was only marking time. He was thinking of Veronese. He was thinking of Carpaccio. He was thinking of Titian and of Tintoretto.

"Do you remember that first time you saw me, Gabriel? If I think of Venice, I think of that first time at Walter's studio in the garden at Kew."

Kew. It was bog and fog and water sucking under the wharves, and the gnawing of rats in the old partitions. The *Bridge*.

"There's a bridge there; she called it the *Bridge of Sighs*." Lizzie was taking the very thoughts out of his mind.

"Well, Byron really started it," he said. "Why did I drag in Ruskin?"

"Yes, Byron and Shelley and Keats and Mr. Landor—all of them, she told me, went away, went out of England."

"You mean, we'll get married at once and never go back to England?"

She moved over to the settee. She spread her skirts about her.

"Yes, it was England. It was that Mr. Greenacre, and Lyddy having the same fancies. Lyddy and I knew that if Harry was really touched, it was a family failing. But then, I put it all together, Mr. Greenacre cutting her up and her head caught in the weir (which had a gate that pulled up, like Mr. Toussier described the guillotine) and then Abélard and the wrong they did him, that I read about in the folder that William had left. I even remembered how I had looked over the folders and was about to put them back, as they were mostly Italian and German, and then I found that one in English and I read it. There was the story of Abélard and Héloïse, for the first time, and the studio and everything in it, less clear than the stones of that Cathedral in France, and her being put away as a nun, till I looked up and saw what was equally real with Abélard, your picture, unfinished on the easel—"

"They're always unfinished, Lizzie."

"You wrote you finished one for Mr. Ruskin."

"I wanted to come to Paris. I could finish things—and anyway, Ruskin more or less offered to see us through—that was in the beginning, if we wanted to get married. I have only to write Ruskin."

"They're older than we are. We can wait, Gabriel."

She thought of Aunt Polidori and the family and the times the rent was not paid, and her own feelings about taking Ruskin's money. But nothing, somehow, could spoil her rapture over her first extravagance.

"Then at Chartres, I fancied the Queen in the coffin had a book. And I recalled her—she said, I must call her by my own name, Elizabeth. It was talking to myself, talking to her. I even told her about the Queen from the wall, and the book. She said, yes, it was really a poem."

"When are you going, Lizzie?"

"Mrs. Kincaid arranged to get to Nice for Christmas."

"Christmas is a long way off."

"There will be orange-trees and snow, only on the high mountains."

"I thought you liked the snow, Lizzie. You were always leaning out of the window when it snowed, and watching."

She did not answer him. "Before you go, Gabriel, you must tell me, why you asked me, 'What have you done to yourself,' when you first came."

She straightened her shoulders. He saw the long throat rising from the shot-silk.

"It's a new dress, Lizzie."

"It's *the* new dress, Gabriel." She stood before the curtain again, but this time she faced him, forgetting "your chin, your chin—you've spoiled that line." It was not a line that she wanted him to notice; it was the billowing folds of a great rose that fell to her feet.

"And what else did you talk about with Mrs. Browning?"

"It's what I'm trying to tell you, she likes the new frame. We discussed all the latest fashions."

Now he saw her.

"I see, I'm hardly fine enough to escort you, Lizzie."

"We'll go out to-morrow, I have the old mantle to go over it. I kept this till you came, though I wore it in the house a few times, to get the sway of it. It's like walking on air—being a sort of cloud—but fashionable."

"Oh—fashionable—"

"It's the way they walk. It's their seeing me somehow, different. No-one ever seemed to think I was a scarecrow, even in the beginning."

"Whoever thought you were a scarecrow?"

"The girls at Mrs. Tozer's—not Ellen and Jenny, but the others—and, oh, Gabriel, lots of London people."

"We'll never go back to London. We can talk about that later—why Lizzie, you look like an empress."

"It's what it's called—the bell-flower."

"Bell-flower?" asked Gabriel.

"Bell-flower *Impératrice*," said Lizzie.

V

"If we hadn't had that champagne, you could have stayed a day longer." Lizzie had been horrified, reckoning the francs back into shillings. It was almost a week at Mrs. Tozer's. Why did Gabriel run his eye down the list and pick the most expensive? They had had champagne at Madame Bonnard's, now and again. Mrs. Kincaid said it was expected, the day the Emperor opened the new Boulevard, and then, Mrs. Kincaid had her husband's solicitor friend in, and they discussed the prices, and Mr. Barrington knew what he called the "vintage" years and seasons.

Mrs. Kincaid said, the first time, "We won't take the cheapest, it looks mean, but the next." It was the other way round with Gabriel, only he didn't take the "next," he took the most expensive.

Was it necessary?

"No heel-taps, Lizzie."

"But I haven't finished this glass."

"You don't finish, it just keeps re-filling, like the Holy Grail."

"But that's the old name for the Communion."

"This is the new name," and he read out the French, the date, the place, *Château* something, from the label on the bottle.

"We'd better have another."

"Oh—Gabriel—"

"It simply evaporates; it's like you, there's no body to it."

He called the waiter and though Lizzie could not follow what Gabriel was saying, she understood enough to know that he was scolding the waiter. Gabriel waved his hand toward her and the waiter bowed, *"Parfaitement."*

"What did you say, Gabriel?"

"I said that while I was looking at the lady, half a bottle had evaporated and it was up to the house to bring me a new one."

"I don't understand, Gabriel."

"I said, unless he hurried, the lady might likewise vanish. She was wearing, I told him, under the table, a cloud *Impératrice* that would, in a minute, waft her away to heaven."

But "Gad," Gabriel said, "*quelle politesse.*"

A gentleman had risen from the next table and was making his way to the door. There was music playing somewhere.

"*Ancien régime,*" said Gabriel, "wears his broadcloth like brocade, a little like Allingham."

Gabriel had turned round in his chair.

Lizzie said, "Why did you say *quelle politesse*, Gabriel?"

"He didn't look at you, Lizzie."

"Is that politeness?"

"The essence. You were in his line of vision. Of course, he wouldn't turn round, but he never saw you."

"He must have seen me, Gabriel, he was sitting just opposite."

"So you've been looking at him?"

"Not to notice, not till you said he looked like Mr. Allingham, and he does, a little."

"He's faithful—but he didn't stare at you. That's why I'm suspicious. He treated you exactly as he would her, not a *soupçon* of recognition."

The waiter had placed a fresh bottle on the table; Gabriel hadn't even noticed his drawing the cork and re-filling the glasses.

But Gabriel lifted his glass, not looking at Lizzie.

"*Madame, la Princesse.*"

A lady followed by a gentleman was standing in the doorway. As if by accident, their former neighbour paused for the two to enter; surprised, he lifted the lady's hand to his lips, bowed stiffly to the gentleman and passed out.

"Good timing," said Gabriel, "that's the husband."

"Well, you're not, according to what you just said, being polite, Gabriel."

"Lizzie, you share her with me."

That was quite true.

Her skirt was not too full to be awkward, Lizzie noticed that, first thing. Her own bell-flower was moderate by the latest standards, but Lizzie had noticed that the most extravagant creations were not seen in public. The lady's creation belonged to eternity. It was what Gabriel was saying, "she's walked out of a Velasquez."

"You shouldn't stare, Gabriel."

"They are curiously tolerant in Paris, to what are known as artists. The lady—and even her husband—would know if they saw me staring, that I am no common pleb, nor even your excellent Mr. Barrington, run across on business. My clothes aren't right but your cavalier (her *inamorato*) would recognize a fellow-spirit. And if not for myself, he, she, or even the husband, would know me for what I am, because of you, Lizzie. In spite of insular opinion to the contrary, the French have far more respect for women than they have in England."

"It's what I felt, Gabriel."

"I have a faint suspicion," said Gabriel, "that your cavalier has not consummated the *liaison*."

"I thought a *liaison* was lovers being together."

"There can be *liaisons* without lovers being together."

This did not sound like Gabriel.

The gentleman was arguing with the head-waiter.

"It's all been a mistake, on purpose," said Gabriel, "*commedia dell' arte*. There never was a table *à part*, upstairs in the balcony. They'll go on somewhere else."

"And pass him in the lobby again?"

"No, it will be something different—but *mon mari* is indignant. Ah, the manager, in person."

But Gabriel talking, was still looking at the lady.

"Now, who was Madame la Princesse, before she married de Fontenelle?" said Gabriel.

The manager was motioning to a waiter to find a table, but the gentleman stepped back and the lady brushed past him. Not acknowledging the head-waiter's profuse apology, the gentleman swept out.

"God save the King," said Gabriel.

"Why do you say that?" said Lizzie.

"His high-and-mightiness does not, for all of Baron Haussmann, accept our new Paris. The other fellow is more of a gentleman."

"What do you mean, Gabriel?"

"It's just *je ne sais quoi*. They both belong to the old world, but there's that difference in them. This fellow, *mon mari*, would have had a good look at you, if he had been sitting where your cavalier was."

"The other was waiting, you said so, for your Princess. He just didn't see me."

"*Ma foi*, Lizzie."

"And in any case, Gabriel, you saw the lady."

"I saw, I have seen . . . the lady."

"You know her? You knew her name?"

"I like to think that I might have heard her name in London."

Lizzie remembered discussions of gatherings, before Mr. Rossetti died, and Mrs. Kincaid had talked too, but Mrs. Kincaid did not go to the soirées, as she called them. They were mixed, they were foreign, Mrs. Rossetti was a cousin of her mother's, Mrs. Kincaid had explained carefully. Her mother had been a Miss Pierce.

"Do you think we ought to go, Gabriel? It's very crowded and there seem to be people waiting for our table."

"Let them wait. What did I order this champagne for? Which reminds me—" He re-filled his glass.

"Places like this, that's what they're for, to keep people waiting. Who's waiting? Oh those, they'll find places in a minute. It's Velasquez and della Guardia. Let me entreat you, Madame, the gondola is waiting. You never were a girl to grudge a fellow exaltation—and you exult, too. It is better to talk about her and to have you talk about him, than for us to dilute our sacred raptures—no, not dilute, Lizzie. What is the word for what I mean?"

"What do you mean, Gabriel?"

"I mean—should fill your—your glass, shouldn't I?"

"I don't think you can, Gabriel."

"No, Lizzie, it's not that makes me tremble; it's the Elixir of Life, the Transmutation of Base Metal. Ever hear of Caliostro?"

"Who's Caliostro?"

"He was a chap in Venice . . . in Paris . . . or perhaps it was Versailles. It was all the rage of the Trianon. She was one of them. But French, unlike her royal mistress who came, didn't she, from Austria?"

"Who came from Austria, Gabriel?"

"This one had more distinction, much more *je ne sais quoi* than that one. If she carried a crook, she did not tie ribbons round it, nor even primroses— do they have primroses in France, Lizzie?"

"I don't know what you're talking about, Gabriel."

"I don't know myself, Lizzie. I can't see her pretending to make hay, but she had to do what Marie did, I suppose, *noblesse oblige*."

"Marie?"

"Antoinette—but it doesn't ring true, somehow. No more than he does. I mean, no more than he would, tricked up like a royal lackey to follow the Grand Soleil. But it isn't my world. Perhaps you were there, Lizzie."

She did not know what Gabriel was talking about, but "Mr. Allingham would never look like a lackey," she said.

"All right, all right; you were always partial to that cad, Allingham. But he knew his Paris—this one. He didn't show his breeding. He didn't look at you, Lizzie. It's a fancy of mine—what you would call a fancy—that Madame de Fontenelle and her *inamorato* were no more at home in Versailles than I myself would have been, had I been there. But I wasn't."

"All right, all right, Gabriel; but how do you know she is Madame de Fontenelle?"

"I don't know that she is Madame de Fontenelle, I just like to think she might be, because I heard a chap in London talk about Madame de Fontenelle. He didn't like Caliostro."

"Caliostro?"

"Well, imagine it yourself, Lizzie; it was a harmless little outing. And easy to arrange things. We were discussing the *fiesta*, always a crowd in the Piazza, and easy to get lost, and in a dark mantle like she wore—"

"She didn't have a mantle—"

"She left it in the foyer. That's how I knew that de Fontenelle had ordered a table *à part.*"

"It's so mixed, Gabriel."

"It was mixed, certainly, imagine it for yourself. You know Longhi?"

Lizzie had never heard of Longhi?

"But Caliostro—" Now she remembered. She had heard of Caliostro.

"Not a bad chap, really; he was making a living by it, but the gold rubbed off the brass. It would last, however, for the time it took him to get out of Paris. He had other irons in the fire—I mean alchemy, retorts, *retorts*—'I have affairs in Venice with the Grand Master.' Ah, Venice! They would all go to Venice. So they all went to Venice."

It seemed an anti-climax; the story was evaporating like the champagne.

Lizzie saw mirrors on mirrors and candles reflected in them.

They had found tables for the group that had seemed pressing down upon her, obstructing her vision.

"Music—not, Lizzie, unlike this music."

"It's the new waltz."

"Lizzie, you know everything."

It was at Kew that she had heard of Caliostro; it was Mr. Allingham talking about Dante.

"Did you ever read *Zanoni*?"

"Who ever has?"

"Mrs. Deverell said something once about it, at Kew; there was someone in the book, a Count it was, the same sort of thing as Caliostro, I should imagine."

"St. Germain? I must have heard the story—that's it, this is the same story."

"I don't think so, Gabriel."

"Well, the French Revolution came in, and counter-plots were going on, in the name of talking-spirits—and—conjurations—"

"Did she—get back to Paris?"

"How do you know they tried to keep her there in Venice?"

"You said something about Mr. Allingham going to her rescue, from Vienna."

"I said nothing of the kind, Lizzie." But to her, everything was quite clear. There were mirrors that reflected double candles and then reflected them again, going backward and going forward. "They say the new waltz is from Vienna."

"Allingham knows Vienna?"

"You said so."

She had stepped from the marble pavement (it was mosaic pattern) onto the polished dance floor. Her heels were lifting her, like a ladder, to God, and someone whispered, "Ah—Mozart."

"Was it Mozart invented the waltz?"

"You're thinking of the minuet, Lizzie."

"Did we dance in Venice?"

Everything was so clear. You could see where the wall began or the wall ended, and count rows and rows of candles, reflecting each other in the double mirrors.

"This is what you meant, Gabriel, when you said, that first time, 'those circles, you know. I never did pretend I understood them, though I have explained them to you often enough in my lucid Bacchic moments.' You were talking to Walter Deverell."

So she swayed to the ground. It was a white rose, this time. But she was not broken. The violins lifted her to her feet and she crossed hands to another partner.

"What do you mean—Allingham?"

"Ere she was born
That vow was sworn;
And we must lose into the ground
Her face we knew."

"Is that Allingham?"

"Well—from a private letter."

"To you, Lizzie?"

"No, Gabriel."

"But Allingham—you know all this about him?"

"It was you started it; you said he didn't show his breeding. What a funny thing to say, Gabriel, but I knew what you meant."

"Oh—that fellow."

"My shroud of white, stuck all with yew
O prepare it!
My part of death, no one so true
Did share it!"

"Oh—that Swan—"

"You said you didn't like the Elizabethans, Gabriel."

"I always say things like that, Lizzie."

"Yes, it was like that. Pretending. She didn't know anything about them."

"Who didn't know anything, about who?"

"Versailles. It went on in three circles. When you came to Hastings and told Mary, 'I am not engaged to Lizzie,' there were still two circles left me, Mum and our family was one, and Scalands was another and Mary Howitt who wouldn't speak to you. I thought I would see clearly, two circles, and that would be enough for my whole life. They would be clear circles; I would help Mrs. Howitt with her girls' foundation, patterned on the Working Men's College in Bloomsbury. But I had committed myself to Mum and Lyddy, half pretending, so I said to Mary, 'I will marry Gabriel.'"

"So you married Gabriel?"

"No, I was already promised."

The circles did not interfere with one another. But it was not a three-ringed circus. They spiralled upward, it was the violins. One violin repeated what another violin had whispered, "Ah—Mozart."

"But who is Longhi?"

"He is Venice, the crowd in the Piazzetta, the cloaks, the tricorns, the sword and dagger."

"But they're dancing."

"That's what I mean, Lizzie. It did not affect them. They just went on dancing."

"What did not affect them, Gabriel?"

"Oh, the usual things . . . Venetians! They were a plague on God's earth, they were more effete, more decadent even than Paris. What does decadent mean, Lizzie?"

"I don't know. What does it?"

"It's a thing that's come from Paris, they've begun to talk about in London, or it would come if we weren't such manly fellows with Sebastopol and all that."

"First time he kissed me he but only kissed
The fingers of this hand wherewith I write.

But I don't think she writes," said Lizzie.

"She writes letters," said Gabriel, "and signs them, adding her estimable but comparatively bourgeois *née*—but let us be discreet. Suffice, she might have been a princess if she hadn't married a Valois—only the princess was Napoleonic pinchbeck."

"You mean, she isn't a real one?"

"I mean, she is more real than a real one."

"*And ever since* something *grows more bright* . . . I wish I could remember it."

"Is it *bouts rimés*? 'And ever since the candles throw more light.' Will that do, Lizzie? Well, it's your turn now."

"But I'm not making it up; I'm trying to remember it."

"What is it, Lizzie, that you're trying to remember?"

"One of the *Sonnets from the Portuguese*."

"Translations?"

"But you've surely read them?"

"I don't remember; what is it all about?"

"I wish I could tell you, I wish I could tell you. He kissed her and it was God and she walked."

"That's scriptural, took up her bed and—"

"No, no, this happened and in London. But it was no laughing matter not knowing where the wall began and the sonnet left off. But I saw just now, where the wall ended and the candles began, I mean, the candles (do you see them?) in the mirror that reflect the candles in the mirror—and reflect the candles in the mirror. And each set of candles lights a separate room, and you can't prove it but you can see it. We are in separate rooms, dancing. A minuet you say, one was?"

"I couldn't say; it was catch-as-catch-can, after midnight on the Piazzetta."

"But the wall doesn't end now, the doors are all open, Velasquez, Versailles, Venice. The sun through the glass throws different colours on the pavement, like it might be violets, but it was the same pavement."

"You're drunk, Lizzie," said Gabriel.

"That's what I've been trying to tell you. You said to Walter Deverell, that first time at Kew, that you didn't understand Mr. Rossetti's Dante's circles, but you could explain them, in 'lucid Bacchic moments.' This is a lucid Bacchic moment and I'm trying to explain things."

"There's only one cure," said Gabriel, "a hair of the dog."

"A—hair—of the dog?"

"A hair of the dog that bit you; I mean, another bottle." He snapped his fingers, but the waiters were all busy.

"No, no, Gabriel. Please, Gabriel. I only want to explain the Dante circles, then we'll go."

"They stay open all night."

"But I only wanted to ask you, why did he cut her up, Gabriel?"

"They're doing it all the time, that was only an isolated instance. *Addition garçon*. We'll go immediately. There's a chap splashed blood, I mean paint, all over the walls of *Les Invalides*. But he didn't paint the pieces. He left all that out, in his glory-of-battle pictures. They always do leave all that out—a beastly little frontier question."

"What are you talking about, Gabriel?"

"I was saying to a chap in London, or he was saying to me, that you couldn't stop war. They'll start soon in America."

"America—about what?"

"About—about the *Moor of Venice*. Don't let's talk about it, Lizzie."

"That's what you said, 'Madame,' you said, 'it was a night on the Rialto—but it wasn't Shakespeare.'"

"No, it wasn't Shakespeare," said Gabriel.

VI

Of course, she knew she couldn't stay in Paris. Mrs. Kincaid had it all mapped out. Gabriel wondered why Mrs. Kincaid wanted to go to Nice. Probably Mrs. Barrington or one of that set, suggested it. There had been talk of Mentone. They were going by slow stages. Well, they were off. He and Monro tucked their travelling-rugs about them in their first-class carriage and waited till the train pulled out. The next day, they were back in London.

What would Lizzie do? Sit about and play cards with solicitors' wives and army widows? He didn't see her in Nice. Nor did Ruskin. "If she would only get out of Nice," Ruskin grumbled to Gabriel. Well, after Christmas, they left the *Hotel des Princes*, that was something. But the new address conveyed nothing to either Gabriel or Ruskin. "It's lodgings anyway," said Gabriel, "and she says they're outside the town, on a slope above some olive-orchards." He remembered how Lizzie had spoken of orange-trees and snow, only on the high mountains.

"They had trouble with their passports," Gabriel told Ruskin. He read part of the letter to him.

"Well, at least she's out of England," said Ruskin, "with this new epidemic about."

Ruskin was actually sitting on the edge of the table, with his great-coat wrapped about him.

"I'll tell Miss Heaton then, that you'll do a replica of *Paolo and Francesca*, in place of *Beatrice*."

Gabriel said, "you were always ragging me about copying my own pictures and selling them twice over."

"Well," said Ruskin, "you needn't copy it; do a variation of the same subject."

"But she ordered *Beatrice*," said Gabriel, "why not copy the *Beatrice*?"

"Because I do not want you to copy the *Beatrice*," said Ruskin.

All right. Gabriel wasn't quarrelling with his bread and butter. He was wilful and usually shouted down Ruskin's pronouncements, "take out the green there. I don't like your shadows. You must have some line somewhere." Gabriel was looking through stained-glass. It didn't really matter what Ruskin said.

"You roughed out some arched windows one day at Denmark Hill. Did you do anything about them?"

"I was sketching? A comment on my *Lamps*, was it? I don't remember."

"We were talking in Paris. Lizzie got me thinking of stained-glass. She went moping alone around Chartres, having fancies."

"What sort of fancies?"

"Oh, Queens in coffins, and Abélard."

"Why don't you do an Abélard?"

"I've got no model for him. Anyway, I've started Gus as Hamlet."

"Gus?"

"The fellow I sent out to see you. Is he a fake?"

"He knew something about Turner."

"His father was a copyist, he told me, and there are two more chaps who say they want to meet you. You may have heard of their *Oxford and Cambridge* venture. Inspired by our *Germ*, they told me. They've already mapped out their rag for a whole year—but then, Morris has money. Jones and Morris, they're called. They almost made me feel that England mattered. I was for cutting it all. Lizzie talked about the Brownings—Oh, no—"

Gabriel felt that Ruskin was about to suggest putting his life on a secure foundation again, so that he could go away.

"It would be nothing to me, Gabriel. You owe it to your art, to all of us, to Ida." He looked round the room. "But it's—inspiring. What shall I say, Gabriel? Not all the fellows could carry off this affected carelessness—"

"It's not affected," said Gabriel. "The Birrells turned the place out, as they called it, in my absence—never again—"

"I was thinking of Cellini, you are like those chaps, Gabriel. You are a great Italian living in the Inferno of England. Must you stay here?"

What did he know of England? He had money. Then Gabriel remembered Effie.

"But about those fellows," said Gabriel. "It was, Morris said, your *Nature of Gothic* and seeing a Cathedral in Beauvais (I think it was) on a summer holiday, that made him chuck up Oxford. Well, he's still there, but in an architect's office, at the moment. But Gad, they were both intended for the cloth. Fancy two budding parsons, hearing High Mass at Beauvais (they were on a walking-tour) and swearing, before they left Havre, that they would dedicate themselves to art—in place of, or because of God. But why come to me about it?" asked Gabriel and with no affectation.

"Who else would they go to, Gabriel?"

"You started them. It was the *Nature of Gothic* and your description of the Guilds, artist and craftsman all submerged in the Cathedral—so this Morris told me. I never read *The Stones of Venice* and I never thanked you for the copy that you sent me."

"My *Venice* can teach you nothing."

Gabriel did not know himself. He had always on principle quarrelled with "that sneak, Ruskin."

"This Morris thinks if he can get in with the architects, he might in time, stop some of these restorations."

"Venice," said John Ruskin.

"What about Venice?" asked Gabriel.

"They're talking about taking up the old mosaic and laying a new floor in St. Mark's Cathedral."

"What can we do about it?"

"I'm starting a petition. Gladstone might help," said Ruskin.

"Well, Gladstone's some use then. I should have thought he was too busy with the Powers—France, Austria, Prussia! But Austria and Prussia got out of the alliance, didn't they? I don't know. What's it all about, anyway? And Louis Napoleon got out of it, too. That meant only us—only England was left. But I suppose Louis has come back or there wouldn't be talk of a Conference in Paris."

"Is there talk of a Conference in Paris?"

"Well, I heard something—probably confidential—from Gus. He has a finger in every pie. Looks like a Spanish grandee sometimes, like an organ-grinder with a monkey, others. Which reminds me, did you ever hear of *Sonnets from the Portuguese*? Lizzie was a bit foggy over dinner, the first night she wore her bell-flower, and quoted something that she called a sonnet, saying she didn't know where the wall left off and the sonnet began."

"Ida—foggy?"

"Your Ida was illuminated and dead drunk."

Ruskin got off the table. "You're lunching with me, Gabriel."

"I'd like to. But I want first to talk of Lizzie. If you would sit down—Oh, throw those things on the floor. This isn't equal to Ruskin something-or-other Domecq, and it isn't sherry, but Monro smuggled it back from Paris under his Inverness. I didn't even know he had it, till he left it on the table. I swore to myself, I wouldn't have a drop without Lizzie—without Lizzie being in it, somehow." Gabriel placed the bottle on the table. "The glasses are clean, too."

"I see you've opened it. You had a drop then?"

"When I came back, trying to remember. I think the damned stuff's Russian."

Ruskin studied the label on the bottle, "Curious—maybe Turkish." He lifted his glass, "The bouquet is Greek."

"Damn you, John Ruskin, how did you know that? You are a curious fellow. Someone called you a spiteful saint, I don't know who. Gus said you were the best mannered fellow he ever met, and one of the best dressed. I forgive you everything."

"What have you to forgive me, Gabriel?"

"Your damned professorial attitude, your pseudo-superiority, your way of drawing leaves under a microscope; your way of teaching the fellows at the College to draw, 'line is everything, colour will come afterwards.' Was there any line in the firmament when heaven and earth created He them? There was colour first. Let them have their fun with colour."

"Line's fun, too," said John Ruskin.

"You see everything reflected and you see it all so damn' clearly that he makes me sick."

Ruskin went on savouring the bouquet.

"Don't you like it? Oh, I see, you are waiting for your host to prove the stuff isn't poison. Ah, Lizzie—" Gabriel raised his glass.

"And when I say Lizzie, John Ruskin, I mean another Lizzie than your frowsty Ida. I mean Lizzie in a bell-flower and Lizzie talking about Chartres and Lizzie in a room, stuck round with mirrors and candles reflected backward and forward (as she said) in them, and Lizzie with a waltz playing—anyway, she said it was a waltz and from Vienna."

"And the bell-flower?"

"That's what I mean—why don't *you* marry Lizzie?"

"Is this what you meant, when you said you wanted to talk first of Lizzie?" Ruskin placed his glass back on the table.

"Yes, you've never seen her."

Ruskin did not say, "I have seen *Beatrice.*"

"You've run across her, here in these digs—she needs a setting. She was happy there in Paris. She talked about the Brownings—damn, of course, Elizabeth Barrett must have written that sonnet, I mean the Portuguese Lizzie quoted,

First time he kissed me, he but only kissed
The fingers of this hand wherewith I write,

Lizzie said she couldn't remember the rest, she wanted to remember because 'he kissed her and it was God and she walked.' I wanted to ask someone what it was all about."

"Why didn't you ask Ida?"

"I have—well, Lizzie and I have been about together but we're not lovers. I have kissed Lizzie, but it was not the kiss she wanted. I knew she wanted something else or someone else when she said 'he kissed her and it was God and she walked.' We were making up a story too, over the champagne and the music. The hero wasn't Gabriel, she was promised to another."

Gabriel refilled the glasses.

"She liked Allingham—you know old Allingham? But somehow, it wasn't Allingham. It was something rugged, though polished if you will. It was something with eyes from which there is no escaping. It was something less suave than Allingham—I say nothing against his—his charm. It's just something Lizzie wanted. Does Lizzie love you, Ruskin?"

"No, Gabriel," said John Ruskin.

"You're hypnotic, Ruskin. You could make her love you."

"Women don't love line. They want colour."

"What she wants—she as good as said so—is a rock."

"What is a mere mountain when you have the firmament? I always told you, Gabriel, when I didn't like your pictures."

"Why do you buy the damn' things, then—to keep Lizzie?"

"I buy them, as I buy Turner for the colour. I don't like the mediaeval."

"What of your glass windows, your seven lamps, your Byzantine mosaic, your Carpaccio? Lizzie looks Byzantine; you said yourself at Denmark Hill, she was like those elongated figures in your Missals—yes, you did see her once, in a proper setting. She liked your room, your mother showed her your room—horrible, no curtains, those beastly windows. But Lizzie liked it. She liked the shells you showed her and the rose-quartz or whatever it was in chunks, blasted out of your beastly mountain. You can't say she doesn't like you."

"I didn't say she didn't like me. You're volcanic, like the fire in the mountain."

"But she likes snow," said Gabriel.

. . . . . .

He saw him now. Gabriel had been trying to "see" John Ruskin. He was the father-superior of some learned order, who had served inheritance.

"They even discussed seriously, they told me, at one time, a plan for a monastic foundation. They are good chaps, really. Jones is the more sensitive and the less gifted. I mean, the other fellow whom Jones calls Top, has the verve or the nerve. And there's another blighter I haven't seen yet, a sort of golden goblin or dwarf Sebastian, I gather from their description. Top writes too, but he says the other fellow writes better."

"Who is the other fellow?" asked Ruskin.

"They call him Algernon. They promised to bring him along one day, and later I'll shepherd them all out to Denmark Hill for your inspection. That's what you're for. Top went on about your guilds and the subservice in the Cathedral, of all to one objective—the loss of self. They're selfless fellows. I think I said, a moment ago, that you said (Top said) the artist in the middle-ages was submerged in the Cathedral—drowned in it. It was a word used by another, a religious fellow, I ran across with Gus. More of a mystic, less of a fanatic, this other, but he was afraid his work would be submerged, as he put it, in a tide-wave of dark waters. He himself was following, he said, a clear rivulet from a hollow—a hollow-dip, he called it. Fact, he's an American. Hollow-dip. This place where he had his illumination was near what he called a spring-house, an old farm called Hollows. There's no connection."

Gabriel said, "That was before they saw the real thing at Chartres, I mean Beauvais. They couldn't do anything after that, about the Church of England; they had, Jones said, 'looked behind the veil.' Well, now their dedication is toward saving an old foundation, rather than establishing a new one. That's where you come in. Superior, yes, I have said I hated your damned didacticism. But it's your inheritance. This chap I spoke of (of the Hollows' illumination) was afraid his clear rivulet would be lost in the dark waters— or these dark waters, as he put it. Here in England, he meant and on the Continent. Not that he had any illusions about America and a war that he said was coming. But the idea came to me just now. They'll never be a foundation, not in the old sense. It's one here, one there. But somehow, they find their way through the dark waters."

VII

Gabriel sent Lizzie a story, she said she hadn't read it. It had been printed in the *Germ*, their early Pre-Raphaelite paper. He sent it to her, as the setting was Pisa and she had spoken of the Lasinio reproductions, and told him about the story that she had lived or "seen" last summer. They were sitting on one of the benches in the Louvre. She had been frightened in London, she had told him, by the story or the vision. Probably, she said, when he mentioned his own tale of Pisa, she had heard them discussing it. Anyhow, engrossed in the *campo santo* reproductions, it was natural that they should both choose Pisa. She told him about the falcon and the embroidered saddle-cloth and he laughed and said,

"One of my rival families in the Pisa story, bore the falcon."

"Then I really must have heard you talk about it," she said. She was reconciled to his going back to London. She had so much to think about, to work out, she said.

She said she had lived her story. Well, he had lived his, too; what was imagination but a heightened perception of life?

Gabriel called his story *Hand and Soul*.

"What do you call your story, Lizzie?" he asked.

She hadn't a name for her story, she said. The girl got her bird's cord tangled, she told him; she was carrying a falcon on her wrist. She was alone. Her companion in the story had taken most of the gentlemen into the forest. Her party had cantered on ahead down the sea-road.

"It was Barbara asking me to ride at Scalands, made me remember the saddle. It was worry about the cholera in London, made me think of those dead bodies."

"I speak too, of cholera or of leprosy," he said, "in *Hand and Soul*. And there are plenty of dead bodies."

Lizzie read *Hand and Soul*, and she remembered how Gabriel had asked her what she called her story. She did not know why she did not tell him that she called it the *Gold Cord*. But then, it was really not about Gabriel, though Gabriel might have painted or helped paint the frescoes. He was a painter. In her thought, she made no apology. In her thought, she knew that Gabriel would never have headed the company nor have led the gentlemen into the forest to hunt. In her thought, she no longer contrived to deceive herself, she had loved walking with Annie and Mum and Dad sometimes, swinging along—and Gabriel at Scalands had slept late, even in the country. He had accompanied her to the woods, but he was not caught in it, like she was, like being at Chartres in the dim light and violets showing like those rainbow-blue and green splashes on the floor of the Cathedral. She was glad that she had been alone at Chartres, almost she had resented Gabriel in the forest.

It wouldn't be like that with her outrider, in the feather-cap. He would see everything, not just because he was a hunter. Gabriel had proposed to her actually, in Scalands forest, and he wrote a poem about it, but he did not see the curl-over of a fern, he did not notice the speckled leaves with the new leaves growing on the same stem of the groundsel, nor feel that certain feeling that a beech tree gives you, whose leaves seem always spring leaves till they turn in autumn and even so, when they are turning, they take colour, as of fresh-opening leaves. Gabriel would stack pot-plants back of her to make a forest of it, for a picture, but it was an indoor forest. He was indoors, in the forest. He would throw himself down on the old sofa in the studio, so he threw himself down there at her feet under the beech trees.

But it was important that she loved Gabriel. Or that she had loved Gabriel. It came to her after he proposed, and Barbara's Aunt Julia was so kind about it,

> I cannot give to thee the love
> I gave so long ago—
> The love that turned and struck me down
> Amid the blinding snow.

It came to her, that is, that the Gabriel she had first known had denied her, saying he was not engaged, at Hastings. And he might deny her again. He would deny her again. But she had stepped into the circle of Gabriel's inspiration. Without Gabriel, she would have remained unrecognized—or

would she? There were the others, there was Mr. Allingham; Walter Deverell had drawn away, only after Gabriel came into the studio. But the out-
rider in the feather-cap wasn't Mr. Allingham. Perhaps she remembered too
clearly, when she thought of the figure by the lamp-post, that curious feeling of loyalty to Ellen and Jeannet; she was one of them, that "girl from the
bonnet-shop." She was just a girl from a shop until Gabriel began to paint
her, for she was still compromising, still delaying her decision while she was
with Walter Deverell; he himself had agreed to her working part-time.

There was no part-time with Gabriel, he would never have let her go back
to the shop and yet he kept her sitting to him, with the windows closed and
his cigar-smoke, and he took her late to little upstairs restaurants where it
was crowded and hot, so that she couldn't eat anything and only wanted
to get away. She only wanted to get away; she wanted to gallop across the
fields with Barbara but she refused even to consider the offer of Aunt Julia's
habit.

She didn't want to quarrel with or about painters. Chiaro dell'Erma was
a painter and no matter how often she read the story of his leaving Arezzo
and his princely habitation to come and be a poor painter with a famous
master, she couldn't associate herself (the girl that is, with the falcon on her
wrist) with the painter, shut in his rooms, with his dreams, by the Church of
San Rocco. In the story, she was riding out toward the forest, and the leader
of the cavalcade that met hers, at the turning below the outer fortress, wore
her hawk-plume in his cap. And this was like Verona, but the gentleman
was more like Mercutio than Romeo; Gabriel said the rival faction had the
hawk for heraldry. She was one of the falcons and when they fought outside
the church, along the arcades that were lined with Gabriel's—with Chiaro's
painting, the blood splashed the pictures and they were pictures depicting
peace, so it said in this *Hand and Soul* of Gabriel's.

She cared for peace, as much as Gabriel, though she didn't like his calling
her the dove; no, she was not the dove. Perhaps a hawk does not belong to
peace, nor a falcon.

He wore her falcon-feather stuck in his cap and he met her, as by accident, below the outer turrets.

He must have been killed.

But why did she blame Gabriel? He was not in the story really, her story,
the *Gold Cord*.

Those Lasinio frescoes were fourteenth-century and she had wondered
if Dante were the same time. She wrote Gabriel about it. He said, yes, Dante
was thirteenth and fourteenth century. The dates did not matter, of course,

but she was, Gabriel said "fussy" about numbers; perhaps she got that from Dad having praised her for keeping the accounts right. You had to be fussy about numbers and she had done a good deal of explaining to tradespeople that Mr. Rossetti was busy on a painting and couldn't be troubled but she would work out the overdue bills, check up on the last month's and promise to get things in order. Yes, Mr. Rossetti was paid considerable sums for his pictures, sometimes. Money just melted away with Gabriel.

Gabriel gave an exact date in *Hand and Soul* to the painting, 1239. Perhaps the modern artist who really tells the story, did see a picture with that date, in Florence.

But Chiaro quoted Dante, or something that sounded like the translation of the Dante, Gabriel read her, and Dante must have been later if he went on into the fourteenth century.

It was things like this that made her tiresome, she knew that. It was her worry about the bills and wanting to see that Gabriel wasn't cheated when he did hand her over a sum to settle things with, that annoyed him. Well, she couldn't help it.

She had to laugh to herself, sitting by her table in the pension, in the half-dark, thinking out how the outrider in the feather-cap would know just how many arrows there were in his own quiver and knowing just how many more arrows in the company could be relied on, knowing just how many and which were likely to fall short, and how many, if any were likely to snap off or how many, if any, were undependable, provided there were a row.

Now she had come back to Hastings and her wonder about who would and would not stand by her. She did not actually count her friends or number her adversaries, but again she thought, "It's like what Gabriel called Mr. Rossetti's Dante's three-ringed circus."

In the third ring or the middle-ring, there was Gabriel. And because he had already betrayed her and because he would, she knew, betray her again, she conjured up an enchanted forest, an outrider who wore dangerously her falcon-feather in his cap, a face that was more rugged than Gabriel's, with hard bones showing, hands perhaps not so beautiful nor so eloquent in gesture, but reining a horse, notching an arrow, drawing a bow, had a peculiar meaning for her, at the moment, when she laid down *Hand and Soul*, because the light was going and she wanted to think about the arrows. No, she did not (any more than Gabriel) believe in all that . . . murder. But the isolated instance, as Gabriel had called Mr. Greenacre, as compared with the dead and wounded at Sebastopol was countered or was checked or was check-mated by another isolated instance. Gabriel was not isolated. He drew her into the whirlpool of his enthusiasms and the plots and counter-plots of Pre-Raphaelite quarrels and intrigue. She was, Mrs. Gabriele Rossetti was right about that, "Gabriel's model."

And Gabriel's model might gain immortality as *Beatrice* or as the more personal presentation of Beatrice, the *Damozel*, but there is something, thought Elizabeth Siddall, that must not be washed into the inner sea (she did not call it the Sargasso sea) of Gabriel's circle. It was all right, there was fire there and she had been stiff and frozen, that is inwardly (she thought) frozen and stiff, sitting those hours and staying those extra hours at Mrs. Tozer's. She did not realize her state of spiritual and almost at times physical paralysis, until she got out of Mrs. Tozer's. And sitting there at Kew was pleasant, and what did an hour mean, in pleasant company and no-one to jeer at you, but the strange opposite, being thought beautiful.

She went back to Gabriel's story. The story had really given back the early Gabriel to her. Yes, he was a painter, he was the painter in the *Hand and Soul* who dedicates himself "in the ecstasy of prayer to his mystical lady now barely in her ninth year." But that was numbers, Dante's numbers, the mystical nine that Gabriel had explained to her. But why did Gabriel make Chiaro say, "the lady he had won on earth had been dead an hundred years?" No doubt, it was symbolical like Dante, as Gabriel explained but you had to hold on to something. She was ashamed, almost, as she remembered how she had borrowed Mrs. Kincaid's travel-book and searched through it for some dates. She had found in fine print at the back, a list of painters and writers and famous people, and she found Dante: Dante Alighieri, 1265–1321. Then the picture in 1239 was painted before Dante was born. Then the mystical lady and the "band of whom he was one . . . permitted to gather round the blessed maiden, and to worship with her through all ages," was all before Dante, yet it was out of Dante. She wondered if Dante came into her story. She wanted the *Gold Cord* to follow on after Gabriel's *Hand and Soul*, but she would have to think up some way of getting round those dates.

Might she say it was Abélard and another, or the same lady? Was Beatrice, Héloise really? Was it the same story? Would Gabriel's "the lady he had won on earth had been dead an hundred years," refer back to a former lady? Would a hundred years from the time the picture was painted bring the story back to the time of Abélard and Héloise? She believed, roughly it would. She had remembered noting that Abélard was born after 1066, but she didn't recall the exact date. This was important to her. It was important in this sense, she did not believe that Gabriel himself was aware of what he meant there. It was something taking hold of Gabriel like it did sometimes that made him another person, or that made him, you might say, the flame burning. Or as it happened sometimes that something he said was like light shining through ruby glass.

Hand and Soul was published in January, 1850.

Then Gabriel must have written it before that, say in 1849.

It was just about then that she met Gabriel.

It seemed to have been written for her, to give her back her faith, so that she could go on.

In the basket-chair in Chatham Place, her thoughts had been a fever. She had suspected Gabriel of making love to Fanny, his *Bridge* model for the girl who had gone on the town. Elizabeth had been almost as unhappy before that, about Annie Miller. But Fanny Hughes and Annie Miller and her agony about unpaid bills and the rent overdue, no longer mattered.

She would write her story.

Moreover, she would go into Nice, the first thing in the morning and find some drawing-paper suitable for illuminated lettering. She would get out her paints and brushes.

She would sketch in the *small consecrated image of St. Mary Virgin that Chiaro dell'Erma had in his room, before which stood always in summer-time, a glass containing a lily and a rose.*

PART II

Gabriel did not trouble to shout "come in." They had the run of the place, he had told them, when they came up, week-ends. Jones usually turned up Saturday. This was Saturday. He had said, last time, he would be busy in the afternoon. It was Denmark Hill and the matter of those drawings, but he had expected the fellow to walk in, long before this. They would be getting out of Oxford, Jones said last time, as soon as they could manage. They wanted rooms of their own, somewhere in this neighbourhood or not too far off. Furnished rooms were expensive for what you got out of them. Gabriel wondered if Deverell's old studio at Red Lion Square was vacant. He had never been there since—

Well, let them stay away, then. He realized suddenly his disappointment. It might be Freddy Stephens or old Boyce, but then he remembered that he had told Boyce and Stevens he was busy—not that that would have made any difference, in the old days. He knew the fellows thought him surly, since he got back from Paris. He had said he was staying with Brown.

"It is a cold winter," Mrs. Birrell told him. "We are still at war," he heard frequently.

If Mrs. Birrell were there with coals, remarking, "it is a cold winter—and the rats are gnawing something fearful in the basement," he knew he would not be responsible for ungentlemanly expletive. But coals?

"Well, now you speak of it, Mrs. Birrell, the place is a bit draughty." Gabriel pushed aside his easel.

"Now you speak of it, Mrs. Birrell—" Gabriel opened the door.

"Hell—I expected Mrs. B—"

"I'm sorry. I'll push off."

"Gad—no. I thought I told you fellows not to knock but to come straight in. I told the other fellows I was out at Highgate."

"But—ah—Mrs. B—"

"Mrs. B is the lady wot does for me. She lives in the basement. We want coals, or don't we? Come in."

"But you're busy."

"I can go on painting, and anyway what's that got to do with it?"

Gabriel realized that this was the first time he had seen this fellow without the other fellow.

"Where's the other fellow?"

"He went round to the College. He said you had suggested he go round the next evening he was in town."

"I? When did I ever suggest to anybody, teaching the Working Man anything?"

"It was there Ted said he met you. He said the chaps like what you teach."

"What the Hell do I teach? I go round there to take the taste of Ruskin out of their mouths. 'Line, line, line,' says Professor Ruskin. I say, 'Don't you chaps like colour?' 'The Professor hid the paints after your last lecture,' they said."

Gabriel said, "You've got to bang the door shut or it will blow open." The door banged shut. "I didn't tell you to knock the house down," said Gabriel. "You'd better take off your coat—unless it's too cold. I can't tell your length from your breadth. It's got snowed on? I didn't know it was snowing outside."

"It is a cold winter," said William Morris.

"I think I've heard that remark before," said Gabriel, "but you say it differently. Where have you hailed from? Just down from the bridge?"

"The bridge?" said William Morris.

"Isn't that what they call the thing the captain hails from? You look like a sea-rover. Hate the elements myself, but there's no accounting for taste. There was a peg on the door, before you banged it," said Gabriel, "hang up your coat, if the peg's still standing."

William Morris found the peg on the door.

"And stop walking round, you make me nervous. There was a chair once. This isn't the bridge and anyway, three or six or eight bells sounded, sometime since. It's not the black-watch, or is it? Those hooters on the river—is it the snow? And what is the black-watch, anyway? But don't tell me. You're a literal sort of a fellow and you'll say, 'we are still at war,' next."

"The war is over."

"How do you know that? Did Gus tell you, in confidence?"

"Who's Gus?" said William Morris.

"Gus? He's sitting there, on my easel. I was touching up his cuff. Is it the hand of Hamlet? I don't think so. Why did I paint Gus as Hamlet? And Hamlet wouldn't have that sort of cuff, would he? Anyway, I'm painting it out. I have my moments, but I don't pretend to be Velasquez. He might have done Gus. Gus is a cheat and a forger but Ruskin liked him. I don't mean Gus cheats at cards. Why do I call him a forger? He makes an honest living, or tries to, making copies of old pictures—well, so do I, but I copy my own pictures. Difficult getting models, men—and I knew I could sell *Hamlet*. Whoever would want to do your mug, and what as?"

The owner of the mug met the blazing eyes of Gabriel Rossetti. His own eyes stared back.

"If you want a model, you might do me as—as a sea-captain, as you suggested."

"Heaven forbid. I don't want you as a model," said Gabriel, "I don't like Vikings. But what I was thinking, just before you came in, was that there might be empty rooms for you later, at Red Lion Square, where I once had a studio with Deverell."

"Where is Red Lion Square?" said William Morris.

"Holborn way, past Lincoln's Inn, set back in its own garden. You might find rooms or put your names down for the next vacancy. It's cheap, too. There was a north light. It's worth looking into and it's worth waiting for."

William Morris said he would tell Ted about it.

"Ask for number seventeen," said Gabriel.

Gabriel was looking at the portrait.

"Could Hamlet wear a lace cuff? Come, look at this damn' thing. Where are you off to, now?"

"I was wondering," said Morris, "about the river—"

"Damn-blast, don't touch that curtain. If you must look at the river, go into the other room. There's this room, the next we call the long-room, then the corridor with the books (there are candles somewhere, if you want to explore the place) and the bedroom if you want to sleep here."

"I just thought I'd take a look at the river."

"Nor'–nor'–west?" asked Gabriel. "Have it your own way. To tell you the truth, I took the place myself because of the river, because of the bridge, rather. But I found a better wall for my *Bridge*, out at Highgate. You've opened that door."

"How could I get into the long-room, as you call it, without opening the door?"

"Must you watch the weather? You remind me of Lizzie. She always hung out of the window or plastered her mug against the window-pane, if there was a beastly snow-flake in the offing."

What was Morris doing?

There was something in the offing.

Gabriel did not turn round, he leaned forward as if to scrutinize the canvas, in case Morris was looking at the back of his head.

The fellow had whiskers—those cat-whiskers or dog-hackles, but he didn't show it.

He was more like a great St. Bernard than a cat, though—heavy but soft in his tread like a young lion.

Was he still standing there?

Had he sneaked into the next room without a candle?

"What I mean is, that cuff is a bit van Dyk—still, van Dyk might have painted Hamlet, in his own way. But it's not my idea. To paint or not to paint, that is the question. Deverell wanted to be an actor. Could act, too. Family stiffish, about the stage. Took up painting to please his father and painted to please the Academy—that's not painting. You paint because you have to, and for no other reason—unless you're a cheat and a forger and are making a sort of living by it, like this Hamlet. To paint or not to paint—"

Was the fellow listening?

"Called me Ressetti, did Professor Ruskin, said I was chaotic. Della Guardia is my name really. Rossetti, Hamlet told me, was he'd wager, from me 'scutcheon, a rose. Deverell was Romeo, troubadourship. That's what we all thought. We drew lots for the parts, then we let Deverell cast us. We did out whole plays; *casa Rossetti* killed Walter Deverell, they said. Excitement, fever, inspiration, a mixed lot, Italians, shady kings and princes, revolutionaries, piano-tuners—no place for Walter. But we loved him. We would have pushed him on the stage somehow, but *casa Rossetti* killed him, they said. I say it was Kew and Bloomsbury killed Walter Deverell.

"It's being in two minds kills people," Gabriel went on. "I kept away; they didn't like me. If he'd made up his mind, after his father's death, to look after his mother and his sisters, it would be too painful for him to see outside people. What they called outside people. Someone said, Margaretta was at a dance the night before he died; I don't know; his mother hadn't been dead long, either. Of course, I might have done something. But Lizzie saw him, walking across Blackfriars Bridge in the snow, the exact moment (we ascertained afterwards) that he died. Do you believe in *revenants*? Lizzie saw him. She said he was coming here to say good-bye. It was February, in the morning. Don't look out of the window, you might see something."

Gabriel turned round. The fellow was still there.

"Did you see something?"

"No, I was only listening."

"Did you hear something?"

"The hooters on the river."

"I mean—"

"No. I don't see things."

The fellow was a liar.

"What I mean is, Lizzie is not consumptive. Ruskin sent her to Doctor Ackland at Oxford. Ackland said (a profound diagnosis) her ill-health was caused by mental power long pent-up and lately overtaxed. That's what I do, overtax people. But Lizzie is out of London."

"Where is—"

"Siddall her name is, Sudal really, came in with the Conqueror like Deverell, D'Evrolles."

"I'm plain Morris."

"I can see that. I'm not worried about you. But the other chap might get *exalté*. It's what they said of Deverell, that *casa* Rossetti was a bad influence. Well, this isn't like the Old Antique days—Antique is the mater. She gave up the *casa* gatherings after the death of Gabriele, my father."

"What could you do to Ted but inspire him?"

"That's just what I mean, inspiration, they say, takes it out of one."

"They say?"

"I'm told so."

"Then you—ah—know nothing first-hand of inspiration?"

"It's just routine—inspiration was our daily bread, while old Gabriele was living. But you damn' English are so suspicious of inspiration."

"I don't know," said William Morris, "there's Browning."

"I'm glad you didn't say Tennyson. And I don't mean you."

What was it Lizzie had said? There would be snow only on the high mountains. Was there snow in the *Hollow Land*?

"You have your feet on the ground."

"Well, Ted's practical."

"Who got religion, first of you two?"

"Religion?"

"You know what I mean, exultation, ecstasy."

"I should say Ted."

"Gad—it's worse when you stand still, than when you walk round. But you're not as broad as you look. How's architecture? You can't stay forever in that Oxford office, you know. What are you thinking of—

> Ships sail through the Heaven
>> With red banners dress'd?

I like your poetry. It's heraldic."

"You know that I like yours."

"*Tu quoque* was always forbidden in our family, as I had occasion to remark to Miss Siddall in Paris. I ran over with Monro, one of the fellows, to see her off to the South. What's an *épergne*? But don't tell me. Lizzie said a chap I knew designed one for the Exhibition.

> All day long and every day,
> From Christmas Eve to Whit Sunday,
> Within that Chapel-aisle I lay,
>> And no man came anear.

Of course, I don't really know you fellows, but I think Jones is a sort of streamer on a lance or banner-pole. He might get ripped off in a fight."

Gabriel did not add, but nothing could break the banner-pole.

> Naked to the waist was I,
> And deep within my breast did lie,
> Though no man any blood could spy,
>> The truncheon of a spear.

So you saw yourself? Lizzie had something of the same experience. A Queen stepped down from the wall, and lay in a coffin, clasping a book. That was at Chartres. Lizzie was happy about it, because Mrs. Browning said it was a poem. Lizzie does little jingles herself.

> Many a time I tried to shout;
> But as in dream or battle-rout,
> My frozen speech would not well out;
>> I could not even weep.

But sit down in the Professor's chair—here's where he sat the last time—and tell me how, by the sweat of your brow, you came to write poetry?"

"If that's poetry, it's easy to write."

"So you don't get into a fever, inspiration doesn't burn you out?"

"Not if that's inspiration."

"All in the day's work—eh?"

"If you call it work—I suppose so."

"Can't you sit comfortably? I told you you were hearing things."

"I'm not hearing things, I was thinking."

"Well, even Professor Ruskin lounged with almost undergraduate abandon, in that chair, the last time he was here, but perhaps, he wasn't thinking."

"I've left Oxford, I mean the College."

"You mean Ruskin hasn't? Perhaps you're right. And what, if I am not intruding, are you thinking?"

"I was thinking about *The Hollow Land*."

"That thing of yours?"

"I was thinking, it wasn't mine."

"Whose was it?"

"I got the idea of going back in time, half in a dream, from your *Hand and Soul*."

"It's hardly my idea."

"I got the idea from you, anyway, and the *Oxford and Cambridge* too, from the *Germ*. You don't know what we owe you."

"God bless my soul."

"I had an idea that *Hand and Soul* should be copied out in Canterbury Missal script—or I suppose you'd choose Venetian."

"Are you *en rapport* with Lizzie? Or are you mind-reading? I had a letter from Lizzie only to-day, saying she had bought drawing-paper and was making illuminated letters for some of the Chiaro story."

"Perhaps I am *en rapport* with Miss Siddall. Only, I don't know her . . . *like one just come out of a dusk, hollow country, bewildered with echoes, where he has lost himself.*"

"I don't remember your *Hollow Land*, not to that extent. I remember the 'Ships sail through the Heaven' and

'Christ keep the Hollow Land
Through the sweet spring-tide—'"

"It's not my *Hollow Land*, I'm quoting, it's your *Hand and Soul*."

Gabriel's nonchalance abandoned him. He did not know why. He remembered how he had seen Lizzie's face, that first evening, like a cameo rising from the shadows and her hands resting upon darkness.

"Come, come, my dear fellow—" What would he say, what would he say next?

Jones was bad enough but you could cope with Jones' charming affectations. This fellow wasn't affected. He meant everything he said. Jones had been in, frequently. He had brought Morris once or twice. Gabriel had considered Morris awkward and shy.

But William Morris was not shy.

"Tumpty-ti-tum—might have some grog or something. Rather go to the pub on the corner, or stay in?"

"I'd rather stay in."

"Well, I've only the Elixir of Life to offer you."

"I don't need a drink."

"I'll just scrape out this cuff, while you go on thinking."

"There was snow," said William Morris, "and a walled city. That is why I wanted to look out of the window. I did *The Hollow Land* in what I called Fyttes. I mean, there were three Fyttes, after I died. I called myself Florian, ours was the House of Lilies, so I was Florian de Liliis. There was a feud between the Lilies and Red Harald. That was when they went out into the snow."

"A good fight," said Gabriel, "I remember—crash, bang, lashing with swords; picturesque but realistic, soldiers and monks fighting together on your side, battle-axes, trumpets, long spears—"

"Her hair was not light yellow, but dusky golden, when he saw her."

"Eh—what? Reciting poetry?"

"It's a line from *The Hollow Land*."

If only he could explain to Gabriel Rossetti, but how could he?

"Ted said, it was a bit confusing, going on with the story after Florian was dead. Perhaps you remember that Fytte the First, Second and Third were Florian's experience in *The Hollow Land*. He meets Margaret and loses her and finds her again."

William Morris had seen the face of Margaret from *The Hollow Land*.

He was standing behind Rossetti.

Rossetti said, "Damn-blast, don't touch that curtain."

But William Morris had seen the picture before he dropped the curtain.

It was an unfinished picture, in a wooden frame, set against the wall under the window.

There were other canvases.

Should he ask Rossetti if he could have a look round, at his pictures?

He sank back in the chair. Rossetti was right, "did you see something?" he had said.

He had seen something.

Christ keep the Hollow Land.

It was Margaret as she would have been, if he had seen her before he left the world.

"O brave heart," she had said.

She should have been Margaret de Liliis. She bore the sign of their house, three fleur-de-lis, a single blade of iris with three flowers.

She had three lilies in her hand. William Morris remembered the *Blessed Damozel* of Gabriel Rossetti.

She had three lilies in her hand
And the stars in her hair were seven.

They had borrowed robes from the Abbot, the monk's habit slipped easily over armour. The prior had supplied them with ladders and Florian and his men scaled the walls and opened the gates to the others.

"It was nearly three o'clock," he remembered he had written, "and the moon began to clear."

The moon began to clear. A pale disc showed above Thames' tide-way.

William Morris had walked over the bridge to Whitefriars.

Florian de Liliis came slowly back. The snow had blown off the parapet and drifted against the stone ledge of the pavement. The tide was rising, washing against the triangular buttresses of the bridge foundation.

Their party had been supplied with white garments, priestly vestments from the priory.

So they stood together on the inner wall, invisible against the snow, about to pass the castle guard-house and descend to open the gate.

There had been a voice singing from one of the inner turrets.

Ships sail through the Heaven
   With red banners dress'd;
Carrying the planets seven
   To see the white breast

  Mariae Virginis.

Whitefriars, Blackfriars, St. Bride's Well.

He had longed to be out of the place, to battle with the wind, to plough through drifts, to shout, to exult openly.

But he had wanted to stay.

Rossetti had placed two glasses on the table. "Here is the Elixir of Life," he had said. It was a quaint, squat bottle with a label that Rossetti said, "the Professor calls Greek. I think it's a magic-brew of some sort. There's only this left, but I'm getting Gus to bring me some more, if he can find it again in Paris. Monro dug this out of some pub or other—curious. I called the abracadabra Russian—or Turk. What do you think?"

"I wouldn't know. I'd say Coptic."

"Well, Ruskin is in sherry, you know Ruskin and Domecq. He said the bouquet was Greek. How did he know that?"

"Maybe a touch of resin, that pine-stuff they sometimes put in."

"Do you notice any resin?"

"I couldn't say so."

"What do you notice?"

"Taste—smell—or see?"

"All together—does it taste of Malaga?"

"Shouldn't say so."

"Colour—port-ish?"

"A stain of rose—lighter than port."

"Not attar of rose—that's Persian."

"You were speaking of the colour."

"Well—what the Professor calls the bouquet, then? Inland or island?"

"I should say island."

"*Lily on lily that o'er lace the sea*—eh? Which island?"

"Not Cos."

"Why not Cos?"

"I should say theirs was a white wine."

"Can't you have both?"

"Not both—if you're speaking of the Elixir of Life."

"It is the Elixir of Life, then?"

"Certainly."

"I spoke of Lizzie's champagne as the Holy Grail, in Paris. It didn't seem to shock her."

"I should say this is the Elixir of Life, rather than the Holy Grail."

William Morris was nearly back in Blackfriars. He looked up at the river-window of number fourteen Chatham Place. There was a faint gleam of muffled light above the first window, where Rossetti was probably still sitting at his easel.

Snow had transformed the walls. The Victorian bay with the balcony that opened out from what Morris supposed was Rossetti's bedroom, looked like a mediaeval turret.

The ugly house and the hideous surroundings were transformed by winter-magic.

Magic?

The fellow was a magician.

"I'll pretend it's the Holy Grail," Rossetti had said, "at that, very few are fit to sample this Elixir. I'll get Gus to bring over those bottles, if he can find them, and pretend it's all out of the fabulous original."

"What did Ted make of it?"

"Ted?"

William Morris remembered the way the shadow fell on the forehead and how the wide-spaced grey eyes were black with their dilated pupils.

"Yes, Ted."

"What made you think that Ted was qualified to sample the Elixir?"

"What made you think that I was?"

"Sea-dogs like grog."

It was the way he said it, tenderness mixed with mockery. William Morris had never heard a voice so beautiful.

"It's all very simple," said William Morris. He stopped above the water-steps to stare at the river.

He drew the fragile image closer to him and tucked the frail hand into his great-coat pocket.

"But you are Margaret de Liliis," he said, "you like snow."

. . . . . .

"You ask me to explain it to you? Let's stay a moment, looking at the river. But your hands are ice, put on my gloves." He laughed at her and stooped to pick up the heavy leather glove she dropped in the snow.

"I don't know what to do about it," he said, "you left your gloves upstairs? Shall I run back and get them?"

She said he mustn't leave her.

"Shall we go back together?"

She said, no, she liked to be out of doors, and he might want to finish the picture.

"But he's working on Gus."

That was, she said, only because she had been away.

"But he wouldn't have you sitting in a cold room, and so late?"

She said, he never noticed the cold, that is, not when he was painting and that he never knew what time it was.

But, she said, he was kind about her hair and said he would convince people in time that she was beautiful.

"Well, really darling, aren't you a little morbid?"

She said, she wasn't any more morbid than he was, he was always thinking about chapel-aisles and tombs.

"But he said, *tu quoque* was forbidden, you remember, in his family."

She said that this was not his family.

"You're a little stubborn, and stop staring at the river."

She said, it was he who suggested that they wait above the water-steps and look at the river.

"Darling, must we be always quarrelling?"

. . . . . .

They walked almost as far as the law courts.

"St. Bride's should be here somewhere," he said.

She reminded him that, apart from being late, the city churches didn't stay open like the churches in France.

But there was a gleam of light from a window, and in a side street where he dragged her, blinded with snow, there was a church door.

"I thought it had stopped snowing," he said.

She said, it was the wind that was blowing the dry snow in their faces.

"I suppose we can wait here, in the porch, out of the wind," said Florian.

. . . . . .

"But the door's locked," said Florian.

She said that she had already told him that the city churches were always locked.

"There was a light in the window."

She said it was moonlight reflected.

She wondered what he had expected. This is only Fytte the First, she reminded him. It was not until the end, when he had lost her and found her again that she said, *come now and look for it, love, a hollow city in the Hollow Land.*

William Morris, huddled in his great-coat, sat down on the stone step. "I'll call it St. Bride's," he said to himself, "it might be. As long as I'm broad, am I? Oh, Margaret, for the *brotherhood of the golden dwellings.*"

The wind swirled the snow, a transparent mist, the veil before the altar.

"Fancy her having that idea of illuminated lettering," mused William Morris.

"Can't take her into a pub to get warm, can I? I suppose that was some

Avenue de l'Opéra place they went to. Was she really happy or was she just pretending? He seemed to want to talk about her. There was some gossip at one time, that he was indifferent to her, but Ted ran across that fellow Monro, the chap who was in Paris, and Ted said, Monro said that Rossetti was mad about her. I told him didn't I, that you can't have two Elixirs?

"A stain or rose, I said, did I, for colour when he asked me? Rossetti—roses.

"And he called her Liz; I suppose it's his *quatro cento* way of pronouncing Lis.

"Lizzie—Lily.

"He knew I'd seen something.

"So she sees things?

"What will she be doing with *Hand and Soul*?

"She wrote (he read out that part of the letter) that she started an illumination of St. Mary Virgin with Chiaro's lily and rose in a glass. And she was worried about a date; Rossetti himself was a bit dim about it; he quoted something that she said sounded like his Dante. Had he confused the date on purpose, she had asked him. And who was Chiaro quoting if not Dante? Was it Abélard?" He did not think Elizabeth Siddall was superior; she just wanted to know the date, for some point in her own story, which she said (did Gabriel like the title?) she was calling the *Gold Cord*.

What was this cord that bound them?

"I don't mean you," William Morris spoke now to St. Bride beside him. "I understand perfectly how she feels about him. I am a hearty person, as long as I'm broad, he told me. He doesn't like Vikings. I was talking to Algernon about a Nordic Saga. Algernon wants to work this Saga into a play. The Albigenses—I suppose you know about them—had a Church once, in France. I told Algernon, it seemed a long way from the fiords of Iceland to the orchards of Provence. Lizzie is happy, he told me, in Provence, by some stone steps, above the olive orchards. There are blossoms on the south wall, while we sit here in the snow. I should say this; St. Bride is that Virgin of the *illuminati* of *The Albigenses*, as Algernon calls his play.

"It's a big subject but perhaps little Algernon can do it." William Morris struggled to his feet; he shook the snow from his great-coat. "But I can't keep you any longer . . ." He pressed his flaming forehead against the pillar of the doorway, "Good-night, St. Bride."

William Morris turned down the Strand.

III

He pushed aside the drawing-board. He was working in G. E. Street's Oxford office, making tracings of the designs for the restoration of St. Albans.

There was nothing to be done about it; they had begun work there and who was he to stop it? He was an apprentice, a clerk in Street's office, learning his trade. But he could not go on with this trade of desecration.

He would stick it here till Ted finished at Exeter, then they would leave Oxford together.

There had been the traditional scenes and incriminations, when he had announced to his mother on their return from France last summer, that he could not go into the Church, and must leave Exeter. He had compromised, however; he had agreed to stay at the college until arrangements could be made for some alternative profession.

He knew better than to mention art, outright. He had studied manuscript and missals, old reproductions, modern photographs at the Bodleian, as well as in the Marlborough College library, before he went to Oxford. His mother knew from his letters how he spent his half-holidays, exploring ruins and old churches. "Fitting for a lad, destined for the Church," was her inevitable comment to the boy's grandmother, after reading out his last letter to the Water House, at Walthamstow, where they had moved from Woodford Hall, soon after the death of William Morris, his father.

But William Morris, the son, was not destined for the Church, not in the sense implied in the words of Mrs. William Morris his mother, to Mrs. William Morris, his grandmother.

"I am plain Morris," he had said to Gabriel Rossetti, now more than a month ago, that night in London.

He had already had a preliminary tussle with his mother, about leaving

Street's office. "But you have only just taken up architecture. After our disappointment about the Church—what will you want next? I need not point out to you that we have always been reliable business people, professional people, law and the Church. Your father had implicit faith in you."

William Morris had left his son William a not inconsiderable fortune.

He did not mention his own writing to his mother, or their plans for a magazine, when he stayed with them. He would be busy in Oxford, he assured her, and then to ease the tension he said, that if Mr. Street could find a place for him in his London office, he would go on working there, after he and Ted left Oxford.

For how long?

He had realized when Fulford, Ted, Dixon, Crom and the rest of them first broached the matter of the magazine, that they could not meet preliminary expenses and the risk of failure. But it was to be a gesture, a sort of continuation of those already rare copies of the *Germ*, they swore by. William Morris was glad enough to take financial responsibility.

Ted must have lent or given Rossetti one of the proof copies of *The Hollow Land*.

Or he may have asked Fulford to enclose it with the January copy of the *Oxford and Cambridge*. Fortunately, Fulford was now settled in London and saw to the printing and distribution of the paper.

Ted had told him that Rossetti had asked about that "new poet fellow, Morris," at their first meeting and quoted poems of his. William Morris hadn't then published anything. He had copied out poems (everyone did that) and even sent originals in letters. Who had received what? And to whom had it gone next? The rumour of a new poem or picture spread like wild-fire in that set. Had Ruskin passed on the poem or poems to Rossetti? And who, if anyone, had sent the poems to Ruskin? They were a mad lot.

Gabriel Rossetti had read poems of his before he had published anything, so Ted had told him. Deliberately, William Morris returned to his drawing-board.

He had been over the ground before, but never with such dreary discipline.

He was as his mother had pointed out, trustworthy, reliable, honest, honourable—or he should be. There was no streak or freak of discernible madness in her family. How well he knew that. "I shall be master of a useful trade," he had written her. His mother's father was a certain Joseph Shelton of Worcester. But he could no longer be implicated in the generations; his mother had reminded him of her two brothers, both canons, but Worcester Cathedral and Westminster Abbey had another message for him now. Bishop, canon or dean, they were all rapacious, smug as earth-worms—and now these restorations. But he must be honest—it was hardly the fault of the many good church folk that he knew, that a fortune was being squandered on a disgraceful restoration of St. Albans, while Thames-side stank like Babylon to heaven.

Line upon line. He lifted the tracing paper. Hack-work, any journeyman apprentice could do this and do it better. No, not do it better. There was grim irony in the thought that he had done this vile copy as well as the least of them.

Well, at the worst, if he were a copy, it was a copy of a good original; a faithful copy? It was possible. After all, there were the tradesmen. His mother called them professional people but law, business and the Church were hardly to be distinguished now from one another. It was his mother's harping on the Church and law side of her family, that had led him to pry deeper. What is a mercer but a merchant? There, he was happy in the discovery of one Henry Shelton, a mercer of Birmingham, in the reign of Henry VII. It was as far as he went, as far as he wanted to go.

"I am plain Morris," he had said to Gabriel Rossetti.

He carefully spread a new sheet of transparent paper over the arch and vault of the next in the series of the neo-Gothic restorations.

Sudal, D'Evrolles—did the fellow say his name was della Guardia?

It was affectation.

"I am plain Morris," he must hold on to something, till he got out of this job.

The mercer would do.

They could have their Conquest.

An English fellow, Henry Shelton.

Rossetti called his mother Old Antique, more suitable for a grandmother. Well, he had a grandmother as well as a mother, both Mrs. William Morris.

"I am plain Morris."

His grandmother's father had been a navy man from Nottingham. That would account for the Dane or the Viking in him.

This was the Church temporal; he went on outlining a false trefoil pattern around the base of a capitol. The Church Spiritual must wait.

The other chaps had already got the March number of the magazine into some sort of shape. There was his *Dream* in that. They had intended to open with his *Hollow Land* but after the proofs were set up, Crom found it would have to be spread over two numbers and he had taken *The Story of the Unknown Church* instead. But he must not think about his writing.

It was the spirit of the thing. Even if this trefoil were introduced at or about the time of St. Albans, anyone could see that it wasn't in the spirit of St. Albans.

If this artificial scroll were beautiful, it would not matter that it was historically incorrect. It was neither beautiful nor correct. This was clay. There would never be light reflected from these surfaces. It was Walter in *The Unknown Church* who carved the marble "all about with many flowers and histories." His sister was Margaret; Amyot his friend loved Margaret; his face was "the most beautiful among all the faces of men and women I have ever seen." Amyot was wounded in the wars, and Margaret, on his return, died with him.

"Margaret and Amyot did go, and left me very lonely and sad."

That was the January number, so Rossetti must have read *The Unknown Church* as well as *The Hollow Land*. "I must ask Ted if he sent Rossetti *The Hollow Land*."

But William Morris knew that he would not ask Ted anything about Gabriel Rossetti.

Rossetti—rose.

And of course, there were two of them.

Who was the second Margaret? Perhaps a cousin of Florian's, not a sister.

He had Margaret. He would always have Margaret, but he had never had her in his heart and his head, at one and the same time, until he saw the picture.

Granted that the picture had been painted by Rossetti, granted that the girl in the picture was Rossetti's rose—that did not alter the fact that she was Florian's lily, de Liliis, Lis.

It was as he had told her on Blackfriars Bridge, all very simple.

But Gabriel Rossetti's Elixir of Life was a potent solvent; it would dissolve William Morris before he had really come to man's estate and claimed his inheritance.

He must establish, fortify himself before he gave way.

This alternative career or profession, as his mother called it, was outrageous cheating. But he was determined to give it a chance.

Were all professions the cheat that this was?

Walter lived as a monk in the Abbey for twenty years, in order to construct the tomb and carve the figures of Amyot and Margaret, "lying with clasped hands like husband and wife." Walter lived till he had finished "the last lily of the tomb."

William Morris followed the involutions of what he called the copy-book trefoil, with cynical detachment.

"You damn' English are so suspicious of inspiration," Gabriel Rossetti had said. One had every reason to be suspicious.

"But I gave him my swashing blow," thought William Morris, "I said, there's Browning."

If he thought of Robert Browning, he was drawn inward (still tracing neo-Gothic) to the vast chaotic depth of weathered masonry. It was dark, no exotic incense, no flare of candles. The Cathedral was empty but it had been thronged, and processions would pass again, orderly, Benedictine, Dominican, stout fellows with tradition and learning, good living and sensible political affiliations. There was no stuff of tattered pennants hanging on these walls. Ordered, dim outline of religious story was copied in good Bruges or Brussels or Chipping Campden wool-thread. It was a warm interior. "Like the belly of a whale," thought William Morris.

"One can get one's swashing blow at these neo-Gothic fellows inside their own sham fortress," thought William Morris.

"This is clay. It will crumble, flake off. It won't last forever. Why worry, then, about it? Learn their technique, their tactic before you leave their crumbling citadel."

It was one thing to splash on colour. You must have line, too; Ruskin was right there. Not this rule-of-thumb deadening and uninspired traditional reconstruction—but other reconstructions. He thought of Hans Memling and the van Eycks and visualised ordered water-ways. The east houses of Kent and Sussex always suggested Dutch landscape to him. There were streams in London, water-ways that had been paved over; they ran underground; once silver rivulets wandering through fields of buttercups in Kensington and Chelsea, had been clamped under iron gratings to mingle with the filth of the sewers. The whole of Thames bank, both sides of the river, could be reconverted. His right hand continued in grim irony to trace imitation Gothic oak-leaf. He remembered his great moment. He had discovered Gerard's *Herbal*, just before he was sent away to his first school.

That was his first great moment. Every leaf, every hedge-rose, every bluebell stalk took form. A cluster of blossom detached itself from the maze of the thorn and became stylized, a theme for decoration. There were stone flowers in some of their northern Cathedrals, not yet "discovered." He wondered if Ruskin knew about the fern, the dandelion. They'd be sure to call the latter, romanesque acanthus. He felt sure that this particular trefoil was a later innovation. The stone flowered of itself, if you let it alone.

That is, the living stone.

The living stone had gone from most of their Cathedrals, and what was left, was being smothered, killed . . . but he must not go on rebelling. He knew that beads of sweat were forming on his forehead, "but if I stop now, even to mop my fevered brow," he thought, "I will give up hope forever. I must just go on here, till this job is finished." He was thinking how a group of them went down (in spite of college prohibition) to the slums of Marylebone that first year, to help with the cholera carts.

Gabriel Rossetti's least remark was a flare in the darkness. But you need not follow every flare, even if you are lost. Rossetti's remark about Ted for instance—did it ring true? But he knocked me breathless by reciting *All day long and every day* and then he went on before I had time to defend Ted, with

Naked to the waist was I
And deep within my breast did lie,
Though no man any blood could spy,
    The truncheon of a spear.

And then on and on, talking about Lizzie and Chartres, of all places.

It was the first time he went to France that he saw Chartres. He had wanted to take Ted back there. The miracle really happened the second time, last summer with Ted and Fulford; it had happened at Beauvais, not Chartres.

So Ted was a sort of streamer on a lance that might get ripped off?

Hardly.

Even if he were a streamer on a lance, they were none of them alone, flaunting solitary pennants. There was Harry MacDonald, Ted's oldest friend, the brother of little Georgie whom Ted hoped to marry. The King Edward School, Birmingham, had sent up most of their set. Dixon and Crom were both King Edward's, as well as Harry and Ted.

He must fortify himself, get his bearings. To think of them, re-established him, set him back again on his own orbit. The voice of Rossetti pulled him side-ways. He must tow the line, at least till he got this job done.

He summoned his retainers, Ted, Dixon, Harry and Crom from King Edward's. The Exeter crowd had proved utterly uninspiring. Pembroke was their headquarters. Godfrey Lushington joined them from Balliol. There were eight of them at Oxford, though Fulford, a little older, had just left for London. They met chiefly in Faulkner's rooms in Pembroke. Then there was the outpost, Trinity College, Cambridge with Wilfred Heely and Vernon Lushington.

That was their Brotherhood.

The Pre-Raphaelite chaps were older, established in the world or already disestablished. Gabriel Rossetti was the core and fire of a Catherine-wheel that seemed momentarily to have burnt out. That is, burnt out (from what they told him) as a whole, a Brotherhood. They had more or less dropped Millais, out of loyalty to Ruskin. Holy Hunt, as Rossetti called him, was off on various expeditions, painting religious subjects in the Near East, set pictures, Rossetti called them, ordered by Rabbis or City Corporations. No, they had not quarrelled, Rossetti had insisted, none of them had quarrelled; they had merely separated, lost touch, for the most part, with one another.

Rossetti had insisted that he and Ted had brought back life and renewed his faith in the work.

There was Madox Brown of course, but Ruskin didn't like him. There were lesser members of the original group, Stevens, Boyce and a fellow they called Scotus, writers or painters. William Rossetti was now well established as a critic and there was William Allingham whom they had invited to contribute to the magazine. The only outstanding writer *and* painter was Gabriel Rossetti; could one do both?

There were, of course, Rossetti's sisters and Ruskin said Miss Siddall had talent.

What did Christina Rossetti make of Elizabeth Siddall, he wondered?

Algernon will be joining us soon.

They have lost Walter Deverell.

. . . . . .

But they had not really lost Walter Deverell. Perhaps he was their greatest asset. His own Walter in *The Unknown Church* became identified with this other Walter. There were three of them in *The Unknown Church*, Walter, Margaret and Amyot. There were three of them that night he had seen the picture, Walter, Margaret and Gabriel. Was he (William Morris) another Walter, a *revenant* on Blackfriars Bridge? Rossetti was talking of Walter Deverell, just before he spoke of Ted; "Who got religion first of you two?" he had asked.

Those hours alone with Rossetti had gone so quickly, though compressed with endless thought, measureless emotion. They were a distillation, an essence, like that attar of rose, he spoke of. Like his own knight,

Fast to the stone,
The grim walls,

he had doled out to himself, grain by grain or drop by drop, the precious essence of the memory of that evening. A drug, an elixir, if you will, that might with care, last a life-time, this life-time in Street's office, waiting for Ted to get on to his finals at Exeter.

I V

It was not disloyalty to the others that had led him of late, to seek out God-frey Lushington at Balliol. Their intimacy had really come about because of Faulkner and the table. After one of their hectic evening discussions at Pembroke last winter, Faulkner had asked for volunteers for his new experiments. There was a good deal of it going around, but Faulkner was taking the matter of the new *tables parlants* seriously. If it had been anyone else but Faulkner, he himself would have been inclined to consider the whole business trivial or a bit sensational—a new fashion or after-dinner pastime.

Faulkner was admittedly the most brainy of the whole lot, and out-wardly the most athletic. He was a great oarsman and there was already talk of keeping him on at Oxford; he was one of those freak mathematical geniuses. Faulkner talked in terms of planes and parallels, which none of them could follow. There were, he said, serious experiments being done at the Sorbonne, and Dixon remembered having heard that the Brownings were interested.

William Morris didn't know what it was that had put off Ted and Dixon. Last winter, they were the most enthusiastic of the whole lot. There had not been any remarkable messages, but Faulkner was taking the thing seriously and was interested in checking up on what he called thought-transference. He didn't want a crowd. Usually Ted and Dixon stayed on after the others left, and he and Lushington took it easy in the armchairs smoking. There were the three of them at the table. Ted and Dixon said they didn't know any Vernon, nor did Faulkner, but V-e-r-n-o-n kept coming back. Lushington let it go on, for two evenings. The third time he said that Vernon was his brother.

They didn't know that Godfrey had a brother at Trinity, Cambridge.

You could not actually say that the table had suggested their enlarging their group, but Vernon and his friend Heeley eventually became the Cambridge of *The Oxford and Cambridge Magazine.*

He and Godfrey laughed of course—what else was there for them to do? They agreed with Ted and Dixon that they had gone far enough with the table. "Don't tell old Faulkner." Of course, they wouldn't tell him. But the next time Faulkner called for volunteers, Godfrey tactfully said he thought it would be more convincing and more interesting if some other chaps took over the table, for a change. Didn't one, perhaps, get into a sort of groove? It was all right with Faulkner. Ted and Dixon had already dismissed the whole thing (in confidence to Godfrey and himself) as boring; they were glad to get out of it. Godfrey Lushington (William Morris was certain) was himself deeply interested. But they had dropped the table altogether, after Ted and Dixon told them that they themselves, to liven things up, had pushed Faulkner's table about and made it spell the words they wanted—not all of them, they admitted. "It was slow and more than a little futile," Ted said. They had been interested enough in the beginning.

Perhaps it was the latest report about Browning that had put off Ted and Dixon. It was now said that Browning was trying to get Mrs. Browning to give up communication. Had the same thing happened to Robert Browning that had happened to Ted and Dixon? They had followed so far, then for no perceivable reason, had made a joke of the whole business. He'd warrant Mrs. Browning hadn't turned back when her circle or her messages became "futile," as Ted put it. It was a way of saying that they couldn't or wouldn't follow the clue, that they hadn't the patience to seek out the Grail.

There were halts, deserts, moors, swamps, impenetrable wastes and unsurpassable mountains in every Malory story.

Faulkner had plenty of friends for his experiments and it had seemed wiser to avoid speaking of the table, after Ted and Dixon backed out. He himself and Lushington, he knew, had followed Faulkner and would have gone on with the work. But he rarely saw Faulkner alone and then talk was as a rule along the usual philosophic, sociological, college gossip and literary lines.

"I like coming here," said William Morris. "It's all very well but Dixon with his church-warden's pipe, doesn't really understand my feeling about St. Albans."

Godfrey was a fellow who could go on and on about nothing, in an easy conversational manner. He could turn a slightly serious accent into pleasing laughter, the moment he saw the seriousness was not acceptable. He was witty in a subtle way; he lacked, Ted said, humanitarian virtues. He didn't seem to care what became of the Church and State, he had no sociological bee in his bonnet, he might never have heard of Keble or Newman, he listened politely when Harry MacDonald held forth on social reform. He occasionally proffered a noncommittal comment when the names of Kingsley, Carlyle or Ruskin came into the conversation. He liked *The Stones of Venice.* He liked Tennyson. He could not say that Browning was the greater poet. He liked Browning. He preferred, however, Elizabeth Barrett Browning. He preferred Shelley to Keats. He agreed that Pope's influence was regrettable, but that Pope and Dryden were the inevitable reaction, after the extravagances of the later Elizabethans. He liked sitting up till all hours talking. He liked being alone.

Godfrey didn't think that Ted and Dixon had really pushed the table, not seriously, a little ragging at the end, perhaps. They wanted to get out of it and that was their way of saying so.

"Why couldn't they come out with it? We discuss everything," said Morris.

"They might have thought it ungracious to old Faulkner."

"Dixon can shout down anyone in an argument, he doesn't mind what he says."

"Perhaps Dixon was afraid to shout about it and so retreated to the Englishman's final refuge, the practical joke."

"Can't say it's funny, there's a sort of—sort of spiritual discourtesy about it." William Morris was speaking in what they called his husky whisper; his usual terse brusque utterances seemed to be shouted from a battlefield, but in moments of emotion, his husky whisper carried echoes through dim corridors.

Godfrey Lushington realized that Morris was disappointed in his friend Jones.

"Jones is a sensitive chap," said Godfrey, "the tappings may have taken it out of him. He wouldn't like to say so."

"There were three of them at the table."

"Jones being more sensitive than the others, may have got more of his share of what I believe they call the power."

"Don't think so. I think he and Dix talked it over in the vestry."

"I thought Jones was getting out of the Church."

"Well, we wanted to get *in* to a Church, we vowed to be positive whatever happened. We couldn't go back to Rome, though we even talked of that too. We found the Anglo-Catholic ritual lacked the guts of Amiens and

Beauvais. We wanted colour and direction, we didn't just want to mark time with *Pater Nosters* done in English. We wanted the *rose* of Rome, the *rose* of England, not a plaster rosette."

"Well, there's the old circle."

"Circle?"

"They called it the Rose, didn't they?"

"You mean the Round Table?"

"In general—but didn't those old Rounds always have an inner circle and so on and so on, till you got to the inmost?"

"Can't say I know much about it."

"I thought it was you started them all on Malory."

"Can't say I remember Malory going on about the Round Table as—what you call a circle."

"I may be wrong. I always thought it was what it was all about."

"A circle in the sense of—"

"Well, not always talking-tables but meetings; that *Chapel Perilous* was the last, I gathered, test before the Rose."

"Interesting—ah—theory—"

"Jones and Dixon and perhaps old Browning (don't you think) couldn't keep vigil all night."

"All night?"

"The night of doubt, depression, of hope lost."

Who is Lushington? William Morris had heard the question asked on a number of occasions. The answer was always the same, that's the frightfully good-looking fellow from Balliol with the pleasant manner. He looked at Godfrey stretched out in his chair. Godfrey looked like a greyhound. Yes, he was handsome enough, in that sort of devil-may-care aristocratic manner. But he did care. But who could imagine Godfrey Lushington knowing anything of hope lost? He would win every battle. He was the not important actor who appears in the last scene, like Richmond in Richard III.

"Can you unite the red rose and the white?" asked William Morris. He knocked out his pipe on Godfrey's fender. The wood had burnt out but there was still a glow in the embers. Are white roses, red roses burnt out? But what would Godfrey know of these things?

"The white rose is red," said Godfrey.

"Ah," said William Morris, he went on tapping his pipe-bowl on the fender, "you mean those York-and-Lancasters. We had them in the rose-garden at home." But he was not thinking of the Water House at Walthamstow. He returned to Woodford Hall, for his roses. They had left Woodford

Hall, before he came back from Marlborough, on his first holiday. He was only fourteen but he felt that they should have consulted him about giving up the Hall. He must take his father's place, they had insisted, there were the younger children. Relatives were deferential, they kept repeating that he looked more than his age. There were, to be sure, the two older sisters, but he was the first son and there was the battalion of youngsters after him, four brothers and two little sisters, nine of them altogether. He had taken his father's place, and they had not consulted him.

"Youngsters have funny notions," William Morris remarked solemnly, standing before the fireplace.

"Such as?"

"Bashing around with wooden swords and rescuing the fair from dragons."

"You mean Malory?"

"Yes, and—children. Ghost stories and roasted chestnuts, dressing up for charades, guessing-games, split-proverbs, anagram letters spilled out on the table, card-houses—playing cards. I was thinking, there was always a rickety round-table in every nursery and they drag out card-tables from the hall or under the stairs when there's company after dinner. This sitting around a table suggests sociability and games. I don't say the thing is futile, as Ted does, but isn't it—well, childish?"

William Morris did not want to know why Godfrey Lushington said, "The white rose is red."

But Godfrey said, almost as if he hadn't heard him, "There was always the tradition."

Godfrey said, "I ran through a lot of stuff at the *Bibliothèque Nationale* when I was last in Paris—some loose pages, difficult to follow in the old script. A chap I know is collecting Chrétien de Troyes; dates are difficult but he said they had pretty well cleared and catalogued Marie de France."

William Morris had never heard of Chrétien de Troyes nor Marie de France.

Morris said, "Ah, yes—about the Wolfram von Eschenbach Minnesinger period."

"Troubadours—Minnesingers—I suppose it's the same thing?"

Godfrey Lushington seemed to take an immense time, getting to his feet. He couldn't lose a battle. He would stroll in when all hope was over; the Saracens in full panoply, had already announced victory. William Morris saw them caught in a noose and the rope drawn tighter. But it wasn't a miracle. There was something almost apologetic in Godfrey's manner, as the host turned. But any chap could have done this, he seemed to say, I came in at the last minute. He was as polished as his blade and as unbreakable. Godfrey said, "They're afraid of the unspoken question."

Godfrey Lushington placed the decanter and the glasses on the table.

"I haven't a crusader in my family," said William Morris, "only a fellow in wool, in the north of England. But what question?"

"The question they daren't ask," said Godfrey as he filled the glasses.

"To the question," said Godfrey, as he raised his glass, "I don't mean just the spoken question."

"Are you talking of those planes and waves and thought-transferences that Faulkner was trying to check up on?"

Godfrey said, "Vernon and I started it with this chap from Paris. His sister or his *belle-soeur* rather, had a group there. As you say, there are always tables, usually the one you want is in the servants' hall, but we found one in the attic. Vernon suddenly discovered that he wanted to do some sketching and got out his easel; he set it up in the summer-house; they would have chucked the table out of the library or carted it off to be varnished, if we had had it in one of our rooms. Funny how you start with intrigue; the whole story starts with how and where you find the table, and how you can disguise it. Vernon became suddenly temperamental—you know—a fellow has to be alone sometimes. Poetry? they asked him and he said, no, his brother was the poet. They talked about Byron at the house, one had the answers."

So his brother was the poet.

"Mind if I take your chair," said William Morris. "Um—what sort of poetry?"

"I was trying my hand at translation—the old French things—with Roland."

"Any ready for—"

"I must see my way first, thanks all the same. I like your *Unknown Church*. It's like that; a sort of screen of secrecy is thrown around a situation that brings it into the realm of intrigue. You have all the trappings of a situation—Byronic, if you will—and you are planning all day, your way to the *rendezvous* and all night, thinking about it. It's true, we overdid it. But Rolando had to get back to Paris."

"Um—rather difficult—"

"Of course, there are always difficulties, that's part of it."

"I mean, I shouldn't think a summer-house was quite the place for that sort of secrecy."

"It's one of those octagonal tower-rooms, really, with a door and seven windows. We called it the summer-house."

"Up and away through the drifting rain!
Let us ride to the Little Tower again,"

said William Morris.

"You note in any of the early stories, the lady is inevitably likened to a rose."

"Traditional."

"That's what I was saying, there was always the tradition about the meeting, the love-affair. The troubadour or the poet meets with thorny hedges. The *rendezvous* is secret. There is always danger. There is always a husband, another lover or some false friend at hand to betray their meetings—also traditional. Those are the world, the church, the misunderstandings and inevitable falling off of old friends—who won't or who can't follow. The rose *is* the lady—"

"Though our arms are wet with the slanting rain,
There is joy to ride to my love again,"

said William Morris.

"Faulkner's table was all right," said Godfrey Lushington, "I was asking it questions, myself."

"But you didn't do any talking."

"You don't have to ask the question out loud—just so the question is clear in your own mind—"

"Um—"

"Don't you like this port?"

William Morris raised his glass. It was all there, the light through the ruby glass at Chartres.

"I like looking at it."

William Morris was no greyhound, he was (Rossetti was right) a great St. Bernard or a young lion.

He must pad carefully through the jungle.

"Funny fellow, Ruskin—did you know his people were in sherry?"

"Hadn't heard so."

"Good stuff, I believe, Ruskin and Domecq. Um—it was Rossetti told me."

He had said Rossetti.

"That painter fellow?"

"Um—"

"What I mean is, the whole of the *Roman de la Rose* tales are symbolic. The Rose is the table."

"Weren't they—curious at the house?"

"Suspicious, you mean? Naturally. It was all the young French gentleman of course, leading our young gentlemen into God-knows-what lecherous company—none of the young ladies at the Hall, mind you."

"This—Rolando's a good fellow."

"It didn't matter what they said about him, he said; he was going back to Paris, but we all agreed it might be diplomatic if occasionally Vernon and I spent an evening out of his company, so we rode off to Quarles, but we made a *détour* and met Roland at the Tower (Rolando called it the Tower). It only came out afterwards that we'd never been to Quarles. But by that time, Roland had gone and it didn't matter. Nothing really mattered."

The lion had made a *détour*, he padded into the open.

"Ah—what sort of questions did you ask Faulkner's table?"

"Faulkner had put a question, rather vague, I don't remember—I cut across it. The answer to Faulkner's question, or to mine rather, was Vernon."

"I remember."

"It might have been one of those—well, thought-transferences. I asked the same question the next evening."

"They didn't know any Vernon."

"I asked it a third time."

"And the question?"

"I asked if the fellow, sitting there beside me, was in on this."

"Yes, thank you," said William Morris, "the port is excellent."

"They spelt Vernon a third time."

"And the fellow?"

"Enjoys his port?"

William Morris put down his glass.

How mark time?

"No furlong farther for us to-night,
The Little Tower draweth in sight.

There are a lot of things I must ask you."

"Not always disembodied, from what Roland said, and did it matter if it were a form of dual-personality?"

"I don't quite follow."

"The question that you ask the table—the Lady answers—or as with the *belle-soeur*, the Knight or the *preux chevalier*."

"And—ah—Vernon?"

"My brother," said Godfrey Lushington.

V

"I seem to have been gone a long time," said William Morris, "but I wanted to think things over."

"You haven't been gone at all," said Godfrey, "that outside time is non-existent—well, I don't know. I've been busy myself."

"With other things?"

"Plenty of other things."

It didn't do to ask a chap like Godfrey, what his people expected him to do when he left Oxford; diplomatic, William Morris presumed.

Godfrey said, "It was like that, I mean, the shock of losing Roland after Vernon went off to Scotland. I thought, I was clamped back in time, forever. I thought, I had lost the table."

"I finished my *Little Tower*," said William Morris. "I tried to put rhyming away, until I got out of Street's office. Then after I last saw you, I found that I could do their beastly copy, and rhyme at the same time. She doesn't get burnt as a witch.

The grim king fumes at the council-board;
Three more days, and then the sword—"

"Go on shouting."

"No. I only wanted to say that I know those seven windows. They look out on lake, forest, field, sky, each different. Don't tell me there is no lake there. But even if you did, I wouldn't believe you. I go there."

Godfrey was sitting on the window-seat. He turned and drew the curtain.

"I hear the wind. I know all your trees, Godfrey *sans peur et sans reproche*."

Godfrey was lighting the candles.

"Wearily, wearily,
Half the day long,
Flap the great banners
High over the stone,

but that was when I was in prison. You got me out."

"Rolando got you out. Or Rolando got you in, rather."

"In—"

"In the summer-house, the tower-room, the Tower."

"There were curtains?"

"Curtains?"

"The way you drew the curtains, put me back there. No, don't say there are no curtains or that there are, or that the place was once neatly shuttered but now some of the shutters sag and here and there, there is a row of slats missing. Don't tell me you unbarred or unlatched only one shutter and opened only one window—the one that brought the sandy shelf of the lake (to the left) in focus. Don't tell me of your precautions to keep the right side or the right sides free from prying cottagers, your own gardeners or a stray poacher. Don't tell me that a storm came up and you didn't get back till morning. Don't tell me—"

"How the second gardener came in and said the table would do nicely for the potting-shed?"

"That's an invitation—but—what happened to the table?"

"I should have thought it amiable on your part to ask what happened to me."

"Well, you survived the—test, or whatever you call it, you're here to tell the tale."

"I can see that you're wondering about the spiders."

"I hadn't given the spiders a thought."

"You should have thought about the spiders."

"It's too clear-cut for spiders. I'll wager spiders don't like octagons."

"I wouldn't be too sure of that. What of their spinning?"

"You're an observant fellow. There were blackberry bushes?"

"A few."

"The webs always seem to come clearer on a thorn-bush, the dew of course, brings out the pattern."

"You're an early bird."

"You saw the silver threads, strung with brilliants, when you came forth, staggering into the dawn—you saw them, then, for the first time."

"Yes."

"I don't mean that you hadn't seen them before. I mean, you saw them—"

"Differently."

"I don't know what charm or enchantment you used."

"It was very simple. Vernon went first. Roland remembered what he called his manners, at the end—he seemed contrite, the *châtelaine*, my beautiful mother, what had she thought of him? It was all right, I assured him, she approved of my polishing off my French and working on old French in the summer-house, all useful—well, you never know, you have to show an intelligent interest, in my job. Roland was worried, he said, he wanted to make the separation easier. 'It's so painful breaking away suddenly,' he said, '*mon Godefroy*, what it was to find you and Vernon.' He entreated me, 'don't make it too hard—it will be easier for us both to give up the table, if we don't go to the Tower, the last days. And if the two of us were alone, it might prove disappointing. How much better to leave it,' he argued, 'rather than be disappointed.' He must himself have experienced some bitter disappointment. 'Of course, we won't go back,' I said, 'I've never really shown you to our neighbours. We must ride over to Quarles.'

"They brought Vernon's horse for Roland. 'I see,' he said, 'this is a compliment. I am then, not so out of favour. Your people consider me, after all, one of the family.' I had not thought he realized that the servants had been talking. He was wary and sensitive. 'But my mother loves you,' I said, 'and says you have improved my manners.' '*Your* manners,' he flung at me, '*mon Godefroy*.' We turned off toward the Ayton valley and followed the bridle-path. 'We'll cut across by Barnfield and Bolton,' I said, 'and I'll show you the old Carew Place before we reach Quarles.' But we didn't reach Quarles."

"Where are we?" said William Morris.

"I have told you, on the bridle-path, along Ayton."

"You haven't told me what you saw and what you talked about."

"I'm coming to what we talked about."

"But I want to know everything."

"Well—then you tell the story."

William Morris said, "There is or there was a charming sister in the nursery. Roland loves her, he will wait till she grows up."

"You are wrong there—and if there had been, Roland was, as I told you, sensitive. Well, they were de Fontenelle, they had lost everything."

"There is the pretty cousin, rather distant, at Quarles."

No doubt, Morris thought, Godfrey like Ted, is thinking of getting married.

"Emilia and Olive are both lovely creatures. They are not my cousins."

So Godfrey check-mated him.

"You thought the other one would do for Roland?"

Godfrey did not answer.

"Or does the other one belong to Vernon?"

"What an incorrigible match-maker you are. You want everyone to be happy—like yourself, eh?"

"I am not in that sense happy, but Ted is and I like to think that others may be."

("So he was wary, the other chap, Rolando," thought William Morris, "and what of this one?")

William Morris said, "I am happy, but in another sense."

"So was Roland happy."

"You just said he knew bitter disappointment."

"Well, to continue—or will you tell the story?"

With some vague feeling of insecurity, William Morris thought of Quarles and Carew—and of Roland. These crusader fellows!

"I don't know the story."

"*Mon ami*, I think you do."

"You were on the bridle-path along Ayton?"

"We were. Roland seemed thoughtful. I ambled ahead through the ford. I thought I had found a rhyme that had eluded me for some days. I reached in my pocket for my notebook. When I looked up, I saw we had turned below Barnfield, but Roland wouldn't notice. This was where Vernon and I broke into a gallop. Sure enough, Vernon's horse was following after. The last time I had followed Ayton, I had been with Vernon, and the four or five times before that. The horses were cantering back, but to the King's Wood. We called it the King's Wood, there was the usual legend. Henry VIII had hunted there, stayed at the Hall and so on."

"And so on?"

"I said the usual legend—you are a romantic fellow, work that out for yourself. You did not ask what Vernon and I did with our mounts, when we rode over to the Tower. Didn't you wonder where we stabled them?"

"I did wonder. I did not see them grazing."

"There were no spiders, the Tower was or had been by way of a hunting-lodge. The forester kept it. The door was merely bolted from the outside.

We had no poachers. There was a row of bridle-rings in the old wall of what was once the outriders' stables. Part of it was still roofed over, in old tile. I see you did not look out of all the windows. We had tethered our ponies there as children."

Children? How many had there been, Morris wondered, and he thought of his own first pony.

"My sister was killed in the King's Wood," said Godfrey Lushington.

William Morris cursed himself for the clumsy, tactless fellow that they said he was.

"She would go her own way. We would meet in the Tower. They blamed us, afterwards. She wasn't in the summer-house; 'She must be playing the Bold Baron,' said Vernon. That meant, according to the old ritual, that we must collect our retinue and seek out the Baron. It is a deer-park, really."

"You hunted there—" Morris couldn't think of anything to say. He presumed the girl had been thrown. He must say something, "You—you found her?"

Godfrey said, "Vernon said, 'we'd better light the candles,' but 'it's still light enough to see by,' I said. Vernon said, 'we'd better light up anyway, you remember our old signal—just to show her that we give up and that she's won. Do you remember,' Vernon said, 'the time she almost got drowned on the lake and we thought she was cheating when she shouted?' I remembered. 'Maybe, she's lost now,' I said. But they had already found her. It was Giles—the forester."

It was something woven, it was tapestry. It was not true to life; it had no perspective; it was flat. The pony followed after, like the dead King's charger.

It was as if the wind fluttered the green and brown and stitched blue of the lake, the carefully embroidered stone and sedge. The figures were not really moving.

"I—I'm sorry, Godfrey. I don't know how to say it. This—has shocked me profoundly."

"It didn't shock me at the time. It just hadn't happened. There was work to do, then the next holidays, work again and so on. Fortunately, the holidays were work, too. It was a narrow path. It took all one's surplus thought and energy, just to keep one's feet from slipping. One could manage to keep on, provided one didn't stop and look over the edge. There was the night of doubt, of depression, of hope lost."

This was Godfrey Lushington, the charming rather superficial fellow from Balliol.

"It—it came back—the memory?" asked Morris.

Godfrey said, "It was Roland brought it, talking about his *belle-soeur*. He had told us of her group or circle in Fontainebleau, when he first explained the table to us, but he didn't talk about the *belle-soeur* personally, when the three of us were together. He said Henri, his brother, was worried; he didn't actually forbid the circle, *tables parlants* were the rage of fashionable Paris, and as Faulkner explained to Ted and Dixon, the Sorbonne and various scientists were taking the matter seriously. Coming through the King's Wood, I explained to Roland, that it was absent-mindedness on my part; I had been thinking of one of those translations, crossing the ford. I hadn't been anywhere for the past fortnight, except with Vernon when we had made off, as for Quarles and turned back after the crossing. Roland said he was glad to see the King's Wood, it was like Fontainebleau where there was the rustic summer-house, a cottage really in the Petit Trianon style, above the river. A cousin of Valérie's had it and they met there, for boating-parties and for picnics. It was there they had their circle. Roland said, 'Henri knew all about it, but he didn't know that I loved Valérie.'"

Godfrey went on, "Roland said, Valérie said that he had betrayed them. Roland could not explain to her. 'How could I betray my *belle-soeur*?' Roland had asked. And when he said *belle-soeur*, by the first oak-coppice, I knew that it had happened."

What had happened? William Morris tried to keep his hands still. He remembered the hammocks he had woven at school. His mind would be clearer if his hands were busy. No wonder women seemed indifferent to controversy and to policy. Their hands did the thinking for them.

Something had happened by the first oak-coppice. Was it there that Giles found her? What wonderful names they had, Vernon, Vivien and now Valérie. Everything was commonplace about him—William. But Godfrey's name was sociable and familiar, it went with Geffrey, old Chaucer. He, William, did not go back to their crusaders, but as far as home was concerned, he felt he went back further than they did. Giles might go with him. They were not out of the King's Wood but the wilderness.

It was a wilderness. Fontainebleau and the King's Wood had their keepers, their Little Trianon cottages and their hunting-lodges. William Morris said, "it was by the first oak-coppice that Giles found her?"

"It was there that I found her," said Godfrey.

Godfrey said, "it was the way he said *belle-soeur*. I said, 'if you don't mind, we'll dismount and walk part way through the forest.' But I sat down on an oak-log where Vivien and I had often talked together. Roland stood with the bridle over his arm. He seemed restless. 'We must not do the table alone,' Roland said again. I seemed to feel what he was thinking. He said, 'Valérie said she would work alone, if I broke up their circle. It was not that she did not love Henri, but she was getting *exalté*, more intense each time we had the table. There were only three of us, at the end. Valérie thought that I was getting fond of her cousin, Aurélie. "Henri thinks we are meeting here, because of you and Aurélie," Valérie said. Then she turned on me, "Aurélie is almost as good a *parti* as I was." The marriage had been arranged, as is usual with us in France. It is true that Valérie's dot would help reestablish de Fontenelle, if the rest of us agreed to give everything to Henri. "All Henri thinks of, is a son," said Valérie. I said, "Henri loves you." "He loves de Fontenelle." "But you are one of us," I said, "Valérie." I was thinking of her mother. Valérie was indeed one of us, frail as moonlight ... .'

Godfrey said, "Roland was afraid Valérie would call him back to the table in Fontainebleau. She had not come to the table when the three of us were together. Roland said, 'if Valérie comes to the table, it means that she is dead or will soon die. It was not only Henri's son that the table was taking from us, it was Valérie. She was burning out like a white candle. You cannot work alone,' he said. Aurélie had told him that the two of them together had had no answers."

Godfrey said, "I asked Roland 'why do you fear the summer-house now we have agreed about the table?' Roland said, 'it is surcharged with memories.'"

Godfrey repeated, "it was surcharged with memories. But we went back."

Now William Morris left the oak-coppice; oak was *drus*—Druid, wasn't it? The forest had taken its sacrifice.

There was Valérie like a white candle or a camellia with its petals folded round it. There was Vivien in green.

Godfrey said, "Roland and I sat talking in the tower-room, till dusk. He had managed to break the circle before Valérie burnt out. But Valérie turned on him, he was not a gentleman. He had used Aurélie badly. Even Henri blamed him. He could not tell Henri that he was fighting, not only for him but for Valérie and his son. Valérie was ill, she said it was all his fault. Aurélie with an older sister, went on with the boating-parties. Roland did not think that Aurélie continued with the table. Aurélie was, he said, *oeillet*, fragrant and—worldly. He had not disturbed her equanimity. She would find a new circle in the *faubourg*, if she wanted to go on with the work. *Tables parlants* were all the fashion. If it had been just fashionable—

but Valérie was different. Roland said he had left home, under a cloud. The table curiously (though the woods and the tower-room reminded him of Fontainebleau) had freed him. 'When we three were together,' Roland said, 'it was cool, it was comforting; it was England.'"

Godfrey said, "I asked him, 'can we two not be England, in the tower-room?' 'We have talked too much,' said Roland, '*mon ami*, that moonlight and the *fleur-de-lis* might claim you.' It was then," Godfrey said, "that I lighted the candles for the first time—remembering. I said to Roland, 'England has already claimed me.'"

Godfrey went on, "you know how unselfishness takes some people? Roland changed utterly, 'ah, *mon ami*, but you never told me.' 'How could I tell you what I have only just found out for myself,' I answered."

Godfrey had found out that the white rose was red.

Was sacrifice always necessary?

William Morris knew that it was.

The white rose was stained with the blood of the heart.

But the heart drained of blood, renewed its heartbeat, and that throbbing was almost unbearable. So no doubt, Roland had found it, after his sacrifice. But Roland, William knew, embraced his thorns, he would not be without them. The thorns, it had been long established, were part of the Rose.

William Morris said, "did Valérie—finally—"

"Love Henri? I don't know but the quarrel with Roland led to their coming together on at least one issue—Roland had behaved badly. It was Valérie's distress, Henri told him, that had been responsible for her illness. Valérie had thought of Aurélie as a sister, really a sister. Roland did not of course, allude to it, but we may presume that Aurélie would have strengthened the material position of the family. Roland had given up everything to Henri on his marriage, but he would not give up—"

"His thorns," said William Morris.

"The final family verdict was that Roland's action toward Aurélie had been unpardonable. This verdict had shielded Valérie. Her reputation was irreproachable."

Godfrey went on, "now having spoken (and he said for the first time) about Valérie, Roland became distant. We blew out the candles and bolted the door. We rode back. 'What shall I tell them about Quarles?' said Roland, on the way home. It no longer mattered. 'Say that we turned round—say anything—it doesn't matter.' I knew that I spoke abruptly. I had been killed recently by the oak-coppice. I lived it. My forehead struck the stone. I was dead instantly. Then I was whispering to Godfrey, my beloved brother, 'I am here. It's Ven, Frey.' I heard, Frey-Ven, Ven-Frey—then Venfrey. We were the same person."

What was there to say?

Godfrey said it, "I haven't a brain like—Faulkner. But I have a superficial way with people. It's chaps like me they want for ticklish situations. If I shouldn't come back—"

"Come back?"

"From the East, you'll know where I've gone. You're the only one who knows this."

It came from somewhere. The husky whisper found words for what could never be said.

"The Little Tower will stand well here
Many a year when we are dead,
And over it our green and red,
Barred with the Lady's golden head;
From here old age when we are dead.

But you're not going yet, Godfrey?"

"I'm not going till I've told you the whole story," said Godfrey Lushington.

VI

He would come to no conclusion until he had heard more from Godfrey. He kept away for a week. He ran across Godfrey in the library but avoided strolling around with him afterwards, as he usually did, if they met casually. He drew in his horns and retired to his shell, or, rather, he curled up on his bed of leaves and hibernated, when he would get away from the mere routine of living. Dreaming was no sharp sword, his withdrawal from life was as automatic and as necessary as sleep. He had found that his hands could actually continue the Gothic tracing and leave his mind free. He would rather have done something useful, as he put it; nets for hammocks or fish. Perhaps this was old Shelton in him, perhaps Henry Shelton was a weaver; Paul was a tent maker. Yes, they could have their conquest, he had concluded, that day in Street's office, when he had first (painfully awake in daylight) gone over the Rossetti visit. Those hours, he had considered, were a distillation, an essence, a drug to be doled out carefully. But William Morris had found a new distillation, a new essence.

This white rose, stained red, was not like the others. Lis was a snow-flower. In memory, he was again whirled with the stinging snow-dust round a corner into a little courtyard. He tried the church door. It was fastened. But the creature beside him was tangible, though a mist of fine drifting snow veiled her occasionally. She was a white rose, certainly.

But he had already found her, before he walked across Blackfriars Bridge with her in the snow. She was Margaret, Walter's sister in the *Unknown Church*. And she was Margaret again, a cousin perhaps, the lover who had waited for him in *The Hollow Land*.

His heaven characteristically, was no infinite vault; it was the lap of earth, the bed of leaves, the beech-wood by the stream, *into which I let myself down carefully, by the jutting rocks and bushes and strange trailing flowers, and there lay down and fell asleep.*

But the strange flowers were really his familiars, he knew the foam of meadow-sweet, the flat pads of the elderberry, the briar-blossom, the various low-growing pulse and the blue bergamot, as the bee knows them. From these, there was the sustenance of no heady dream. Rossetti had asked him by what sweat of the brow he wrote poetry. If this is poetry, he had explained to the fellows from the beginning, it has no affiliation with the midnight oil or Shelley's *Skylark*. There were no whirling spirals lifting him to heaven. If this is poetry, it is easy to write, he had told Rossetti, and Rossetti had said, "you don't get into a fever, inspiration doesn't burn you out?" But inspiration of some sort was burning out Godfrey; he was like the *belle-soeur* Roland loved, he was another white candle.

They were all of them in the same *impasse*. William Morris had re-read Rossetti's *Hand and Soul*. Himself, the modern Rossetti (the artist narrator of the story) had fallen in love with the picture which by inference, he had painted in a former life, in Pisa. The Image in the picture was his own soul. So he, William, had fallen in love with a picture but he knew the frail image to be a living woman. But as his way was, he abstracted her from the frame, even as he called to companion William the Englishman, Margaret or the Lady Alys from his own romances.

He had told Rossetti that he got the idea of going back in time, half in a dream, from *Hand and Soul*, but he had always lived in the dream. *Hand and Soul* had merely fortified his resolution not to let the dream go. There were others in that world. But to William the Englishman and to Gabriel Rossetti the Italian, there was no real danger. He had kept away from Godfrey. There was danger in Godfrey saying, "I was dead instantly. I had been killed recently by the oak-coppice." It is true that Florian watched his own death in *The Hollow Land* and that he, William the Englishman had stood and looked down on himself within the chapel aisle, where

> Naked to the waist was I,
> And deep within my breast did lie,
> Though no man any blood did spy,
>   The truncheon of a spear.

But something threatened Godfrey.

Roland had seen the same threat in the case of the *belle-soeur*—but how could clumsy William deal with the so subtle and lovely wraith that might endanger Godfrey's reason? *La Belle Dame sans Merci.*

. . . . . .

But Godfrey forestalled him, "How's single-stick?"

"Oh, we hang round as usual, at Maclaren's."

"A pity he turned me out."

"Well, it was pleasant having you drop in occasionally, but old Archibald said it would give no good name to his gymnasium, if he allowed the best fencer from the school, to be bashed about by his chaps. I've been thinking a lot since I was here last. It's about a lady—I've—seen."

William the Englishman, fearful as he had been lest he should find Godfrey ecstatic and eager to go on with his story, was now in a panic lest Godfrey withhold the story. No doubt, Godfrey wondered why he hadn't come sooner. He'd better tell his own story, as much of it as he could assemble.

"That—that *belle-soeur*. I was working round the situation from de Fontenelle's point of view. I don't know that this lady that I speak of, goes in for tables or anything of that sort. (I call her Lis from the Margaret de Liliis of my *Hollow Land*.) But she sees things."

He would have thought that Godfrey looked as usual, if he hadn't now the clue to Godfrey's appearance and behaviour. He was the same polished blade—but was the blade unbreakable? Certainly, nothing in this world could break it.

"This girl is like the Valérie of Roland's story. Well, the fact is they say she's not consumptive, but why say that if the question had never come up? And thinking of this, I was reminded of Robert Browning. He's a curious fellow. Lis knows Mrs. Browning. I can't say that Mrs. Browning actually encouraged her in her—her trances—I don't know actually how the dream takes her. But she saw herself, a Queen in a coffin, with a book in her hand, at Chartres. Is it possible that old Robertus made a renunciation like de Fontenelle, to keep Elizabeth Barrett out of it? Another candle, Elizabeth Barrett Browning, don't you think so? You were saying, I remember, that old Browning couldn't keep vigil all night."

"I remember mentioning Browning, in connection with Ted and Dixon."

"I think Ted and Dix are on a different level. Ted is going to be married, and Dix has minor canon writ large already on his bland, inexpressive countenance. Not that marriage in itself—" but William Morris did not know what to say of marriage.

"You mean, that you yourself want to keep out of—well, the night of vigil—because of this lady and that you, like Robert Browning with Elizabeth, want to save Lis?"

"I want to save Lis." Godfrey had unwittingly expressed what he, William, had only half-admitted. Lis was in danger.

"Well," Godfrey said, easy and affable, the Godfrey who had looked in those few evenings, at Maclaren's, "then all you have to do is to set about and save her. You're a substantial fellow like old Browning, just whisk her off to Italy or the South."

"She is in the South."

Godfrey turned as if looking for something, "Ah—you have your matches."

But William had not yet taken his pipe out of his pocket.

"Look, Godfrey—you've got this all wrong. The lady—"

It was not like Godfrey to let a pause lie, painful and patent for all to see, between them.

"Dash it, Godfrey—the lady's to be married to the man I love best in the whole world—except—"

Tell Godfrey that you loved him?

Said William the Englishman, "with the single exception of Godfrey—"

"*Sans peur* but not *sans reproche*, you're thinking."

"Godfrey *sans peur et sans reproche* is, perhaps, as I am, in danger."

Godfrey said, "there is only one danger."

"Perhaps ultimately. You mean death?"

"I mean separation."

"From the Lady?"

"From the self."

"Well, if you look on it that way. It's what in a way I've been thinking, why (heroically) I stayed away, just as I've stayed away from London."

"You said, the lady was not in London."

"Dash it, Godfrey, have you no imagination? I could talk about her with—with—"

"This other fellow? Can't you talk about her with me?"

"You don't know her, Godfrey."

"Then, you can explain her to me."

It was William the Englishman who had come, confident and comparatively cool, to minister to Godfrey. But this was a new Godfrey, detached as William never could be, indifferent almost.

"We walked across Blackfriars Bridge in the snow together. Her hands were cold. I offered her my gloves. She slipped one on. Of course, it wouldn't stay on. It fell in the snow. I picked it up. I put her hand in my great-coat pocket. We got across the Bridge. She would stand staring. It might have been St. Bride's, a small church off a turning. The wind blew us down there. She is Margaret de Liliis. Rossetti called her Liz, a mispronunciation or his *quattrocento* for Lis. He read part of her letter to me. She was doing some manuscript illumination for his *Hand and Soul*. I read and re-read *Hand and Soul* when I got back to Oxford. Rossetti said, he burnt out people; what he said was 'I over-tax people.' That was after he told me that Ruskin sent her to Doctor Ackland, Oxford's Ackland. I didn't even know she'd been to Oxford. I know nothing at all about her. I have never met her. I saw a picture, unfinished, in a plain wood frame, set up on the floor. I was lifting the curtain to look out at the snow. The face was the face of Margaret de Liliis and of the Lady Alys, out of *My Golden Wings*. I did not—"

William the Englishman paused to draw breath.

He said, "I stayed away because I thought you would burn out. Ackland said her ill-health was caused by mental power long pent-up and lately over-taxed. I am that plain, blunt man—is he out of Shakespeare? But I am nearer Chaucer. I am clumsy. I never saw this lady, only a picture of her. We never walked across Blackfriars Bridge in the snow together.

"Here, values are reversed, or the situation. I thought it all out. But I am no good with a set speech. This is not what I meant to say. *Alone and palely loitering*, I said to myself, but I was thinking of you. *And no birds sing*, but how do I know what is singing in your reverie?

"*And her eyes were wild*, so I saw Vivien, *La Belle Dame sans Merci*."

Godfrey said, "she is all *merci*, merciful, pitiful."

"Then, the sedge isn't withered from the lake and the birds do sing? I felt that you, like Lis, had been pent up. You did not tell me exactly when—it happened?"

Godfrey said, "it happened three years ago, but it was only last summer that I realized it had happened."

William said, "she saw a *revenant*, an artist, Rossetti told me, who should have been an actor. She saw him in the snow, he said. This Deverell was walking across Blackfriars Bridge in the snow, and she saw him at the exact moment of his death. Rossetti said, she said, this Walter Deverell had come to say good-bye. My name is Walter in *The Unknown Church*. So she became my sister, Walter's sister. But it was Walter who died and she saw him—did you see your sister?"

"I imagined I saw my sister, but I really heard her talking."

"Outside? You mean a voice outside?"

"Inside myself. It was in the summer-house while Roland was telling me about Valérie and Aurélie and the others."

"They must have found water-lilies in some of the reedy inlets. Or doesn't the Seine have inlets? I seem to imagine a sort of sandy island in wide shallow water, and some reedy islets or eyots, I believe they are called. But that is de Fontenelle's story. I thought of de Fontenelle because I was trying to think of you. How do you mean, that you heard your sister talking?"

"We went back to the tower-room or the Tower, as Rolando called it. We didn't talk about Valérie. I did not tell him about Vivien. We were working on translations. After he left, I used the Tower for my study. We had spread out our books and papers on the centre table. But I did not go back to the centre table. I did not unfasten all the shutters. I left the door open. Half-sheltered or screened behind the door, I made a nook for myself. The round-table had been there the whole time. It is easy enough according to Faraday, to explain the table by unconscious or half-conscious muscular reactions. Of course, she spelt Ven. It is what I would have spelt if I had been in her place. Perhaps, I was in her place, perhaps she was a projection of myself; they say we have some sort of double. Well, so be it, I said. It wasn't alarming but I confess I was astonished. If it was myself tapping out the letters, then I was drawing on forgotten memories, and if I could make myself remember other memories, the shock of the most recent memory would be modified. Do I speak clearly?"

Godfrey went on, "how do we know what Bacon or Newton, for the matter of all that, were up to in their tower-rooms?"

"Do you think Roger Bacon or Isaac Newton had a—a try at it?"

"A try at what?" said Godfrey.

"Oh—to turn the tide—the black wave of their so-called civilizations?"

"I'm sure they had a try at something."

"And failed? As probably we'll fail. I have a feeling that Rossetti is, as you said of me, in on this. He didn't say anything to make me think it—it's a feeling, rather. In fact, I thought he took Miss Siddall's over-taxed and long pent-up state of nerves too casually. But there is Rossetti. There is Rossetti the Italian, William the Englishman and Godfrey the Crusader. But that's nonsense about your going out East. You must stay here."

"And turn the tide?"

"If we can turn it. Probably we can't. Then someone will come along in a hundred years, pent up—like we are. By that time, if things go on at this rate, civilization will be smashed entirely. Not that we're not civilized at Oxford."

"Are you thinking of Oporto?"

"It's not a bad idea," said William Morris.

. . . . . .

"What I thought, when Rossetti asked me the colour of that wine or brew he offered me, was—it's Rossetti-colour. He had asked 'colour—port-ish?' I said there was a stain of rose, lighter than port. He is the red flame in the spectrum, the ruby glass in the window. I am almost colourless. I have the quality of a snow-cloud. He said I was a Viking. I don't mean drifted white snow, but snow blown about—or I'm the froth of elderberry or of hawthorn. I am that sort of cotton-wadding in the chestnut-buds or the chestnut-flowers. I know what I am.

"Some say my poetry is nursery-jingle. I don't draw people up to heaven or force them off the earth. I get people back to earth, or I try to, if they're in danger of sliding off it. I want to get you back. I don't know that I can do anything about Miss Siddall. How could I cut in and marry her? Anyway, who would look at William after Gabriel? It isn't that he's so striking to look at. It's his voice, his manner. His eyes are fine, he has a high forehead, his walk is careless, slouching; he doesn't, he says, care for fresh air. He hates the snow. She loves it. I feel that he has drawn a magic-circle round her. I felt it about to enclose me. That's why I stayed away from London. But I will go back. I expect she will come back sometime—how could she keep away from Gabriel Rossetti?"

"Poor moth—she has seen the flame."

"Have you noticed? You can't really rescue a moth."

"I wonder," said Godfrey, "if there's only a—a sort of pane of glass between us and them. When you leave the window open and the light burning, do *they* singe their wings?"

"Coming in from outside? Oh, I see, you mean—Vivien."

"In a way—Vivien."

"You could blow out the candle."

"You can't, once it starts burning."

"Have you tried it?"

"Have you ever tried to stop breathing? You can't stop it for long. She is such a comfort to me, *Merci, la Belle Dame.*"

"Now you make me see it. It isn't my illumination—I mean, illuminations. I mean both, really. Mine are Canterbury, yours are Persian. I don't know how you got there. I was trying to find a colour for you and all I could think of was crystal. Mine is, I told you, clouded or cloud. You can't see through my window; you turn back indoors to the loom or you fling yourself right out, harvest or winter, into the fields. I see the East in you, not just the Paladin who gets there from England or from France, but I see the

cypress-avenue, the flat painted plum-tree in flower. It is *Merci*, the Goddess of Mercy, you mean—perhaps she was Tibetan. I am out of my depth,
really.

"But perhaps I think of Persia, because when I said his cordial—the Elixir
of Life, he called it—was a stain of rose, he said, 'not attar of rose, that's Persian.' Every word he spoke is there to draw on. I called it an attar or essence,
rather, and doled myself out drops or grains."

"Can you use up memory?"

"You can overdo it, intoxicate yourself, drug yourself."

"You're a strange fellow—what do you know about it?"

"I only know a magic-circle when I see one. I stepped free of the *piège*
in the case of Gabriel. I walked around it. He didn't put the picture there
to trap me. He didn't know I saw it. Perhaps I shouldn't have dodged the
entrance to his Aladdin's cave, if I hadn't seen the picture. I wanted to get
her out. Yours is another sort of circle. I've been walking round it. Do you
think it was easy to deny myself your story? But you're not going out East. I
had to see that first and say it honestly, before I heard your story."

"But they want me to go to India."

"Who—these diplomatic fellows?"

"Yes, and I judge—the others."

William lifted his glass with assumed *bonhomie*. "Well—to the others."
He had padded round the circle. It was no cave entrance this time, but a
sheet of crystal water that enticed and warned him. Godfrey's story was
about to take shape above the mirror of the lake, but William Morris was no
crystal-gazer. He must meet the other, head on, bash at his gleam and glitter
with his single-stick. He must entice the crusader from the Sepulchre, or
lure him into his own wilderness.

He said, "I like shaggy things, block Canterbury missal-script, ragged-
robins or corn-flowers, flat common daisies, untidy, uncleared forests. You
and de Fontenelle go plunging in such perfect form, to—death."

"You're thinking of the Brigade?"

"Who is not? But they'll soon forget the Brigade."

"That's what I want to prevent. I knew some of the fellows, they took
disproportionate toll from the Ayton hunting families. I fenced with the last
Ayton Carew, at St. James's."

I see, I see, mused William Morris, better leave that port, for the moment. Better do something, say something. "What became of those matches
you were looking for?" This is tactless, clumsy William, always put my foot
in it. Well, what of it? "Lancers?" "The Light." It would be.

William the Englishman had taken the charge of the Light, as all England took it. But distinction, chivalry had no chance in modern warfare. Why go blind or dazzled? "Wouldn't it have been better if one of the chaps had mutinied? I don't know the word for it—"

"There is no word for it," said Godfrey.

Steady William, don't lose your head, "there should be," said William Morris, "after all, isn't that why the new Victoria Cross has been introduced—for independent thinking? Why couldn't your Carew have shouted to the fellows that it was all damned nonsense?"

"You didn't know Carew."

"I've seen certain of his sort, changing guard before the palace. Don't think I wasn't dazzled."

"There's plenty of romantic fighting in your tales."

"That was before the Czar moved up his cannon. The Brigade wrote *finis.*"

"That's what they tell me."

So they told him things? Go easy, William.

"Vivien was really too young to come out. But she had her first season. It wasn't merely that it was suitable, the two together—"

"I can see them. I can see them dancing." Don't listen to the music, William, it puts you off, and you don't like dancing, you're too clumsy. Music makes you dizzy, stick to plain-song. "But I don't like music," said William, "it distracts me."

So—candles—glitter—romance. Don't get dragged into their hypnotic circling, the new waltz, better a romp on the green round the maypole. Vivien should never have gone to London. "Did she meet him in the King's Wood?"

"Vernon and I would never have asked her."

More damned nonsense. "She rode with the groom usually?"

"Always."

So it went to her head, Vivien in a green habit, she was lost, she was *exalté.*

"You say it wasn't dark when she came back?"

"It was getting dark, but light enough to see by."

"Did she ride in the evening?"

"Never."

She was blinded, dazzled. They never should have left her.

"I know," said Godfrey, "I know that I killed Vivien."

"What nonsense—"

"It's what you're thinking. That's why you stayed away. I said, I was God-frey *sans peur* but not *sans reproche*, you remember."

"But you may remember that I contradicted you."

"You said I was in danger. I was, until Vivien brought Carew."

Carew, some damned Elizabethan or Lovelace fellow. William claimed only superficial knowledge of the counties but he wondered if this Ayton Carew was descended from the poet. Better go easy—cup-bearer to King Charles, damned Royalist.

Circles upon circles of enchantment. I go back to Chaucer.

"It was Byronic nonsense. We've got to be realistic. We've got to face it."

"That's what I'm trying to do," said Godfrey.

Said Morris, "we've got to go back to Chaucer. There's about two hun-dred years between him and Shakespeare."

"What exactly," said Godfrey, "has that got to do with it?"

"For two hundred years, the country was wasted by—Roses."

"The wars?"

"The wars of the Roses."

"Historically, you're a bit out."

"I'm not speaking altogether historically. All wars are wars of Roses."

"My dear fellow—"

"For two hundred years, we had no poets. Then one William Shakespeare dug his roots in, dragged up the sap of the field, the orchard, the garden into his Tree of Life. He completed England forever. We've got to circle round his Prospero, go back to older magic, the magic of the Saxon sea, the Saxon wilderness. *Into the breach, my friends* but not—" go easy William, he loved Carew.

"It's got to stop, it's got to stop," said William Morris. "I didn't know your Carew, nor one of them. I'm thinking of the horses."

Was he being brutal? "Forgive me, Godfrey."

"There's nothing to forgive, really," the words sounded automatic, con-ventional, and William sensed through the sudden weariness of his friend's voice, Godfrey's solution. He had renounced pain and pleasure. He no longer felt the shock; "I was dead instantly," he had said, but he no longer remembered his death. He was removed like Prospero, apart on a magic is-land, shut up in his own crystal. William knew now that he dared not smash the crystal.

"Don't think that I don't feel it," said William Morris, "the beauty of their sacrifice. But there's two hundred years missing, the wars broke the conti-nuity. You may say that Shakespeare more than made up, that he filled the gap with his Historical Plays, so he did, really, and then, late in life, he went back to early Britain and the Rome that made our civilization. But I tell you there are gaps somewhere, we're uneven, unbalanced. We haven't caught up to Shakespeare."

What was Godfrey thinking?

"You're thinking I'm an oaf, Godfrey. I glory in it. If I have a part in your play, I'm Giles the forester."

"My play?"

"Your story then. You said you wouldn't go East till you told me the whole story—so I would delay the telling and keep you here forever."

"It's not my story, really, it's Carew's."

William said, "I'm very angry about Carew and the others. My rage, the last years, threatened my sanity. My sanity was only saved by my dreams— my stories. They are the anodyne that saved me. I might hope that they'll save others—I mean, if I go on writing. But it's too easy. I simply talk. I simply tell a story—it's all improvised. I don't myself know what will happen. I go on writing to see what will happen. They don't shout at me, they crop up. You pass a field one day, it's brown, the next, pale green, green, then gold. So you know the seasons. It's that way with my stories. I wonder why Shakespeare didn't have Chaucer walk into one of his plays? Do you know why? Chaucer didn't."

"Chaucer didn't?"

"Don't you notice? I listen and wait for Chaucer. *The Tempest* is an artificial storm, a device, an invention to get Naples to Bermuda (was it Bermuda?) There is wind on the moors, the heath, *Lear* and *Macbeth*. There is only one forest, Arden. Don't you see, Godfrey, having Shakespeare makes us too important. They didn't know, perhaps not one of them had read through a whole play, but *wish not a man from England* was the reason for it.

"But it wasn't Agincourt, and they'll go on making Agincourt of it till the world's ruined.

"Do you think it was easy for me to keep away from that flame? I don't know how I did it. But I'll tell you. I faced England.

"I faced the glory with a single-stick.

"My eyes were not dazzled.

"I remembered that first year, before you came up, how we dodged authority here in Oxford. We've got to dodge authority."

Godfrey said, "I don't remember."

"It was before you came up. We managed to get to London."

"But they let us go to London."

"Not to help with the cholera carts," said William Morris.

. . . . . .

When Godfrey finished speaking, William said, "I knew you'd cut down all my arguments. But I will go on arguing. Your table and your voices are to you, what my romances are to me. I am afraid to name Florence Nightingale—that is, I have no power against my overwhelming feelings. If I were a devout Catholic, I would cross myself and be done with it. As to the others—I died with them. I met my death before the massed spears of *The Hollow Land*. That is why I say, all wars are wars of Roses. But perhaps I evaded the end. Red Harald did not get me with his axe. I was holding on to a tuft of yellow broom. The long spears had crowded me off the cliff edge. I had sheathed my sword and I heard their laughter. The broom gave before Red Harald's axe reached me. I fell down into *The Hollow Land*."

VII

He hadn't been altogether honest the last time, or he had been too honest, he didn't know which. He had tried to suggest that there was danger and had dragged in the Brownings, to bolster up his argument. But would Robert Browning make a renunciation if his curiosity were thoroughly roused? William Morris didn't really think so. He wondered if Browning had been clumsy, cruel, thoughtless in regard to Elizabeth (her own name, Lis). He knew now that he himself had kept faith with Godfrey. Godfrey had had the answer, whether it was dictated by his dead sister or his unconscious self, his "double" as he called it, didn't really matter. The "double" might be the soul or conscience.

That is what Gabriel Rossetti had formulated in *Hand and Soul*—call the "double" the muse or inspiration, in his case. Gabriel Rossetti was apparently in sympathy with Elizabeth Siddall's dream or vision, though William so far, had taken the line that there was danger of Rossetti over-taxing her. Rossetti confessed it himself when he said, "that's what I do, over-tax people."

But Robert Browning had really rescued Elizabeth Barrett from semi-obscurity and possibly death. Was it the same with Gabriel Rossetti and Elizabeth Siddall? You could hardly compare the two men, though he admired them both unconditionally. But the two women seemed to have much in common. In his own mind, that is—for what did he know of either?

He believed that Gabriel Rossetti was self-centred, indifferent to his surroundings. Browning was like a well-fed abbot or friar. "Materially, I am like Robert Browning," thought Morris, "though the dream is different." Browning might be unaware of the need for spiritual comfort, communion or "communication," as Godfrey called it. Rossetti was aware of the need, though he hadn't said so.

Godfrey had understood his reservations, William had gone back to Godfrey the evening after the talk about Shakespeare and the Roses.

It wasn't on the whole, much different from the work they had done with Faulkner, that is, the technique was the same, only Godfrey was working alone. William had asked Godfrey if de Fontenelle had worked alone, been disappointed or overdone the thing, and so tried to put him off. Godfrey didn't think so. He believed the inspiration or the impulse came when the time was ready; to force an issue was to court disappointment, but Godfrey was sure that Roland had not rushed in heedlessly; the time and place were ready. "Place is as important as time," Godfrey had said. "But once having established your time and place, can you work afterwards—anywhere?" William asked him. Godfrey didn't know. He believed these things were timed and to continue aimlessly, after the impact of the original contact was over, he thought was also to court trouble—as Roland had himself foreseen in the case of Valérie. Godfrey believed that his own contact was almost at an end, that is why he wanted to talk about it and to someone who might be to him, what he and Vernon had been to Roland. "Is it the same table?" William asked him. Yes, Godfrey had specified certain old pieces that he wanted sent on to him, he had said to furnish his man's room, though he only had the house valet; he wanted to be alone. They had sent the chairs and the table he had asked for. They had varnished and waxed the table. "I keep it in my bedroom," Godfrey told him.

William did not ask him what message he and Vernon had had, when de Fontenelle was with them. He supposed they were routine, experimental as the work they had done with Faulkner. Godfrey believed if you held back the message, it died somehow. It reached out like a plant growing. You could lop off the awkward growth, but something in you would die with it. Not die entirely but perhaps wait for another hundred years or so, to put out a new shoot. William thought of the vine, its root and branches. Toward him, almost visibly, as from Godfrey, the frail tendrils reached out; would they strangle him or parasitically endanger his own strength? The vine and the branches. Odd that the revelation should come from Godfrey and in his comfortable armchair, not sweating with ecstasy (as he phrased it to Ted and Fulford) kneeling on the stones at Beauvais. Coming too, with no under-tone of tidal music, incense and flaming banners. But there were candles on Godfrey's table, and the decanter and the glasses. But the table and the curtained room had, William knew, fulfilled his need for communion more fully and more precisely than High Mass at Chartres or Beauvais. It was the literal revelation, in time.

The frail tendril from Godfrey's Tree of Life reached out to him. Oxford had been a hot bed of religious altercation, Christian Socialists, humanitarians, Keble, Newman, Pusey and the rest of them. But the fire of the combat was no longer heartening, by the time he and Ted had settled at Exeter. They had their own plan for a monastic foundation, the Order or Brotherhood of Sir Galahad. They had talked endlessly, round the subject, but somehow, it had come to nothing. It was, however, his discovery of Malory that had first inspired them. William had humbly chosen for himself Sir Palomydes, the Knight unloved.

Godfrey had said, in their first serious talk together, after Ted and Dixon gave up Faulkner's table, that there was always the tradition. Godfrey said he needed no proof of this, but his own thoughts outran him. He could ask Vivien or Carew questions. The answers were prompt, authoritative.

"Is this part of Arthurian legend?" Yes.

"Did Bacon experiment?" Yes.

"Did Newton?" Yes—no.

"How did they say yes-no?" William asked him. "There was one tap," said Godfrey, "a distinct pause, then two taps. We used the one-tap, two-tap signal with Roland, as we did with Faulkner. There were some questions that I didn't care to ask them, and occasionally Carew wouldn't answer."

"Perhaps he couldn't," said William, but he did not like to ask what questions were unanswered.

"It was mercy they were after; you were right about *Merci*. And you were right about the East. Carew kept coming back to it, e-a-s-t."

"Is that why you thought they wanted you to go there?"

"Yes."

"It doesn't follow. I went over some of the older Arthurian texts. There was one with Latin annotations. For once, I found my Latin useful. Didn't those paladin fellows pick up some mystery? There was a suggestion that when the fighting died down, they got together somehow, The Cross and Crescent."

"Do you think it likely?" Godfrey asked him. "I'm asking you to ask Carew," said William and when he said that, he knew that he had entered Godfrey's circle.

"We'll ask now," said Godfrey.

Godfrey brought out the table and said in a matter-of-fact way, "would you like to share it with me?" But William said, if the table talked alone to

Godfrey, it was better if he sat back and let Godfrey do the asking. "But you can ask it mental questions," Godfrey told him, "if you want to."

"I would rather ask out loud," said William.

Godfrey laid his hands on the table. "Well, ask then," he said.

William laid down his pipe. "This is all very friendly," he said. "I confess, I was afraid of some transcendental business. It's warm here. I thought, I'd feel cold shivers. They're friendly people."

Said William Morris, "did the Cross and Crescent get together?"

"Yes," said the table.

"All these mad new inventions," said William Morris, "I suppose something will come of it, in time?"

"Yes," said the table.

Godfrey said, "they call it the *télégraph de Dieu*." He took his hands off the table.

"I'll wait for your next question," said Godfrey.

William said, "thank you. I'll think this over." When would these wars stop? He must formulate his question. But why waste time, talking about war? He had already found the answer in *The Hollow Land*. Harald was his enemy that time, they met again after they were dead. That was after he met Margaret, in Fytte the First. This would be Fytte the First, for Vivien and Carew. But was it Carew answering? Better leave that question, for the moment, thought William. In Fytte the Second, Florian loses Margaret and finds desolation—and his enemy. He could not go on to Fytte the Third and last, until he (or until Florian) was reconciled with Harald. They renew their quarrel, hand and fist as serfs do, then with barbaric weapons, till Wulf kills Swerker; Florian and Red Harald had lost their names with their identities, at least, they lost the names that they had died with. It was when Wulf (or Florian) remembers and calls "Harald," that they regain identity. Florian finds armour for himself and then for Harald, and Harald then (William remembered he had written) "looked a good knight." Until you have un-armed your enemy and re-armed him, you cannot go on. Until you see that he looks a good knight, you cannot go on.

But that was afterwards.

Need we wait till afterwards?

Better not ask questions like that. "I must find the right question, Godfrey," said William, "if I want the right answer."

Godfrey had not seemed altogether sympathetic to the Cross and Crescent idea, so that if there had been involuntary muscular reaction on his part, it would be reasonable to suppose that the table would have said no, to William's first question. But perhaps Godfrey was sympathetic. "Let's ask the question again," said William Morris. Godfrey laid his hands back on the table. "Were Cross and Crescent reconciled?" asked William. The table spelt, t-e-m-p.

"Is that a whole word?" asked Godfrey.

The table spelt l-u-m.

It stopped.

"Is there more?" asked Godfrey.

The table spelt, i-n.

"Is there more?" asked Godfrey.

The table spelt, t-e-m-p.

"You'd better write it down," said Godfrey.

"T-e-m-p, l-u-m, i-n, t-e-m-p. It's telegraph all right," said William. "What do you make of it?"

"I should say it's something about light coming in time," said Godfrey, "*lumen* light anyway and temp for *tempus*. It wants us to think about it. It's good to have you here. This is a new departure."

"It's Templars," said William.

William Morris remembered Rossetti speaking of roses on his 'scutcheon—Della Guardia, he had thought, what affectation.

"I expect it's a family motto of Carew's."

"Carew's motto was old French," said Godfrey.

"Well, I'll wager it's about the Templars, the Knights of Malta, both (according to that annotated old text) were inheritors of the Round Table. Or all of them were inheritors of—of—Better ask the fellow."

William felt, in spite of himself, a curious reticence. He tried to be bluff and hearty, "if it is a fellow."

"Are you asking mental questions?"

"How can I help asking?"

"Well, it's spelling something, but I can't follow as I don't know your question, o-m-n—now, u-n. But it's stopped. O-m-n-u-m, it might be *omnium*. I think it's a mistake. Will you spell this again?" said Godfrey.

The table spelt o-m-n, paused and then spelt u-n. William wrote down the letters. "It's another telegraph, omn. un. for *omnes unum*. But why not ask?" said William.

"Is that right?" asked Godfrey. The table said, yes.

"It's almost too much," said William. He got out of his chair, presumably, to tap out his ashes on the fender.

William said, "I notice you said, it wants us to think about it. Hadn't we better think about it? And when you said 'it,' I wondered. You said Vivien came, then Carew—don't they—ah—come any longer?"

"They're part of it. I don't understand it myself. But after the first exultation, I'm afraid I overdid things. I lived with them. I was with them. I went over and over our life, our lives. Then, it seemed to me that if they had found each other—how shall I put it? It's what I mean by the candle burning by the open window—perhaps they singe their wings. This doesn't quite express it, but you see what I mean. After the proof, the fulfilment, surely they want to rest or go on? And I went on and on with them, asking . . . 'of course, it wasn't your fault, how could it be?' she answered. I was getting myself entangled."

William knew that Godfrey had found *The Hollow Land*.

Godfrey said, "then, I understood Rolando. He had asked me not to go back to the table, not alone—and not the two of us together. He had said that the table was cool, it was comforting—our table, that is, as if he had been seared in the flame of some earlier experience. Later, I understood what he meant. He had wanted to spare me. He had over-insisted that two people could not work together, therefore, by implication, how could one go on alone? It is the one alone who meets the flame. I know now that Rolando knew this, he wanted to spare me. He had said it was cool, it was comforting, it was England, the three of us together. He would have saved me. But as you said, it is impossible to rescue a moth."

"So your Rolando knew all about it. He knew that Valérie could and would go on alone, unless he stopped her. He knew that it would destroy her or drive her mad. I confess that I was worried about you, alone and palely loitering."

"I was not exactly worried about myself. I was determined to get out to the East—"

"And never come back? When did you stop working alone?"

"I stopped after Faulkner's table, spelt Vernon. Vernon knew nothing of Valérie nor of Vivien. I went back over our old meetings in the tower-room and again remembered Rolando saying, 'it was cool, it was comforting, it was England.' I asked a second time, a third time about you. You speak of your memories, your talks with Rossetti as being opiate or attar—"

"I had only one talk with Rossetti. I went in with Ted several times but that was different."

"I knew that I had tasted of Eternity or of Lethe. It might be Lethe. Not deadly night-shade, no not deadly night-shade—

My heart aches, and a drowsy numbness pains
  My sense, as though of hemlock I had drunk,
Or emptied some dull opiate to the drains
  One minute past, and Lethe-wards had sunk—

but I would get out of England and I would work for England."

"You can work better for England by staying in England."

"You're a stout fellow, reliable, dependable and almost as mad as I am. This is the first time I've touched the table since that night at Faulkner's when, after asking the mental question about you, I got Vernon for an answer. Of course, I don't write Rolando of these things, but I see now how he renewed faith or kept faith, by introducing Vernon and myself to his *table parlant*. We English chaps might so easily have shouted him down—"

"Dash it, Godfrey, you and Vernon are no English chaps."

William the Englishman was surprised at his own intensity.

"You've been talking about England, about my staying in England—what do you mean by saying that Vernon and I aren't English?"

"Dashed if I know."

"You must mean something."

Godfrey pushed aside the table and deliberately sat down in the chair that William had just left.

"You've finished with the table?"

"Well, you just said, hadn't we better think about it? I asked too many questions, at the end. One word or part of a word sets up a ripple like a pebble thrown into a pool. That is, if one has a stout, reliable fellow like yourself about, to put the brakes on. It's that old Icarus story—"

"Clipping the wings of inspiration? I would like to go on."

"To-morrow or any evening, you'll come in. This is to me, what we were to Roland—only, more so, I feel. I had no Latin."

"Do you call that Latin?"

"Sign-post Latin—I mean, I see it carved on old stones—"

"Tomb-stones?"

"Mile-stones."

Godfrey sat down on the window-seat. "But before you go, you must answer my question, as my table or our table answered yours. What do you mean about Vernon and myself not being English?"

"Why does an Englishman take offence at being told he's not English?"

"I wasn't offended; I'm afraid I was rather flattered."

"Will it wait—the table?"

"It will wait forever."

"Perhaps I meant—well, I thought of you and Vernon, Vivien and Carew in some—damn it, you're out of Shakespeare, the house or the Tower is Belmont."

"Belmont?"

"*The Merchant*, you remember—and there it is. That's what I meant by saying we must go further back than Shakespeare. He mapped out all enchantment. I lose my clue—then, I say Belmont. It's the Renaissance, we all know. Shakespeare re-oriented Italy. You're not English, that's the worst of it—you should be. Do you want me to go home?"

"I don't want to tire you. I don't want you to get into the state that I did. There is time for it all, in time, *in tempora*, isn't that what they said? And we're all together, OMNES UNUM—so why rail at Shakespeare?"

"They said, as I remember, TEMP. LUM. IN. TEMP; it's the lum, *lumen* that's the important thing; you've left that out."

"I said, there is time for it all; I meant the candles."

"And I refuse to discuss *The School of Night* with you."

"*The School of Night?*"

"It's all there, all this, everything—The Templars, Shakespeare, Raleigh."

PART   III

I

Elizabeth Siddall might never have been away. She had fortunately kept on her room at Weymouth Street. They had always been pleasant to her. There was only one change. The basket-chair that Gabriel disliked so, had been sent around. She had annoyed Mr. Ruskin by not going on to Switzerland, and he had made Gabriel promise that she was not to sit for him or work at Chatham Place, for the present. It was very cold there. Gabriel had new interests. There was a young Mr. Jones; Gabriel had written her of his weekends in London. Mr. Jones was at Oxford. Gabriel had met him at the College, he said, and talked with him afterwards, at Vernon Lushington's rooms. Mr. Lushington was at Cambridge. Mr. Jones and a friend whom Gabriel said they called Top, were at Oxford, but Ted and Top, or Mr. Jones and Mr. Morris, Gabriel hoped, were soon coming to live in London. In spite of being draughty and cold, Gabriel was seldom alone at Chatham Place. But he had wanted her to come back. It was his Valentine that brought her. "Come back, dear Liz . . ."

She was only too glad to come back. Mrs. Kincaid was getting restless, as their plans for February were spoiled by a sudden change of weather. The gardens lining the stone steps that led down to Nice, were a mass of spongy green and yellow-green mimosa. The rose-cloud of almond-blossom was swept away in the leaden downpour. The paths through the olive orchards were rivulets of icy water. Her hands were too cold to manage pen or brush; at least, she could work here. There was so much that she wanted to do. She felt for the moment that she would like to reassemble herself, before sitting again for Gabriel. It is true that he sketched her here in the room, as he had always done, but she wanted to order her thoughts and emotions before being swept away again, in the hectic maelstrom of Chatham Place. Gabriel had suddenly regained his old enthusiasm and was finishing a number of neglected pictures. He said that he had founded a School of his own, with these younger painters—or writers. Elizabeth Siddall had met the two most important members of Gabriel's new School. Mr. Jones was conservative in appearance. Mr. Morris was intentionally abrupt.

Mr. Morris had asked her if she had seen their magazine. When she said she had not, he said he would send the first copy to her. There was a story of his, called *The Unknown Church*, and he enclosed what he called the proofs of another story, *The Hollow Land*. He sent her a poem, as well. He said he had written it for her and Gabriel. It was called *Two Red Roses*.

She knew the poem almost by heart, but she reached over to her work-basket and unfolded the sheet of paper.

> There was a lady lived in a hall,
> Large in the eyes and slim and tall;
> And ever she sung from noon to noon,
> *Two red roses across the moon.*

Mr. Morris said that he particularly wanted her to read his stories, as she would find his Margaret there. Mr. Jones had just announced his engagement to the sister of his oldest friend, and Mr. Morris said that they were both so happy that she and Gabriel were going to be married. She supposed that Mr. Morris was engaged too, as he said, "my Margaret is a lily, not a rose." They were having tea in the long-room, but Gabriel was back and forth, showing Mr. Jones his paintings. He was explaining to Mr. Jones how he had cut up his large canvas, *Pippa Passes*, though he had saved *Hist! said Kate the Queen*. There was only one other fragment of the picture. Gabriel said, "this was part of the *Kate* sequence. I'll have to call it something else. How about *Rossovestita*?" Mr. Jones looked puzzled and said, "did you hear that, Top?" Mr. Morris said, "is this part of your 'scutcheon, Gabriel?" Gabriel said, "I said *rosso* not *rosa*, but *Hesterna Rosa* is a good name for this one. These are only sketches," he said, "but I'm really finishing up some work, now." Elizabeth Siddall said, "what is that about the 'scutcheon?" Mr. Jones and Gabriel had gone back to the studio for some pictures. Mr. Morris said, "I was referring to Gabriel's coat—he told me last winter, one evening when I came here, that Rossetti (the name) was probably derived from roses, a rose or rosette, his family bearings." Elizabeth Siddall said, "he never told me." "But that is why," said Mr. Morris, "I just said that my Margaret is a lily, not a rose. I have a poem in mind, about Rossetti, roses. I mean, about you and Gabriel."

It seemed a very long time ago that she had first talked to Gabriel about Sudal and de Hope.

There was a knight came riding by
In early spring, when the roads were dry;
And he heard that lady sing at noon,
Two red roses across the moon.

She read the stories and thought of her own *Gold Cord*, which she had not finished. Mr. Morris said that his stories were patterned on *Hand and Soul*; she remembered Chiaro and the glass before the Lady; it held a lily and a rose. She had made a sketch of it but it needed colour. Mr. Morris had asked to see her drawings. He said, Gabriel had told him that she was doing some illuminated lettering for *Hand and Soul*. He hoped she would understand *The Hollow Land*. The last part was the most important, he said, as Margaret comes in then, but it is after they are both dead. Margaret dies too, in *The Unknown Church* but there, she is his sister. Perhaps it was all symbolic and he had been unhappy in an attachment. It didn't seem a natural way to write about a girl he was engaged to.

She didn't think that Mr. Jones did any writing. They talked about Chartres and Beauvais. She told Mr. Morris, she had never been to Beauvais, but if she went back to France, she would rather spend all her time at Chartres.

"A dream?" he asked her. She did not know what he meant. "Gabriel told me," he said, "that you were a Queen there."

"I don't remember," she said. "Oh—you mean the picture! I called it a poem."

What else had they said about her? He must have felt what she was thinking, for he said, "Gabriel had just had a letter from you. He read part of it to me. But I was very busy at Oxford and I did not see him again, until Ted brought me in last week. I am coming up every week-end now, until we move from Oxford." She had seen him only once, last Sunday. Gabriel had asked her to go in to tea, again to-morrow. She read:

Yet none the more he stopp'd at all,
But he rode a-gallop past the hall;
And left that lady singing at noon,
Two red roses across the moon.

Gabriel and Mr. Jones came back and Gabriel flung down a roll of sketches.

"You should be more careful," said Mr. Jones. "Now what is this?"

"You may well ask," said Gabriel, "it isn't finished. It is an early drawing for a Borgia group. This one is *Guardami ben, ben son, ben son Beatrice.*"

"Dash it, those words are beautiful," said Mr. Morris. "You're a weird chap, Gabriel. Is it old French or Italian?"

"It's Dante," said Gabriel, "this is the meeting of Dante and Beatrice in Paradise."

So *The Hollow Land* was the meeting-place of two lovers, and the lover sees himself in Margaret, as Chiaro saw himself in the Lady or the Image, in *Hand and Soul*. Did Mr. Morris mean that Margaret was his own soul?

> Because, forsooth, the battle was set,
> And the scarlet and blue had got to be met,
> He rode on the spur till the next warm noon:—
> *Two red roses across the moon.*

She would tell Mr. Morris that she liked the snow scene, in the first part of *The Hollow Land*.

She had missed the snow, this winter. Gabriel said the river had been blotted out, the worst storm they had had, since that February when she had seen Walter Deverell on Blackfriars Bridge, after he was dead. She wondered why Gabriel wrote to her about that; he had never spoken of it. Soon after, he told her that he had regained something—faith in his own work. It began by meeting Mr. Jones at Vernon Lushington's. Mr. Lushington was another enthusiastic fellow, and then Morris turned up. The old crowd evaporated, somehow. Though Brown was dependable enough, he had quarrelled again with Hunt; he couldn't see Millais (or Millais wouldn't see him) because of the so-called scandal about Ruskin. Ruskin was right when he said Woolner was negligible, and Collins was still flirting with Rome. Who was left, really? He had frozen off Freddie Stevens, for the moment, as he liked seeing the younger fellows alone. "Top blew in out of the snow. He is an awkward, ungainly fellow, with a good forehead and the eyes of a sea-king. His eyes are odd, they look at you, wide open but with a sort of hooded gaze, like a vulture. You would probably not agree about the vulture and would see *an Eagle displayed*. Perhaps. But he has a straight nose, not aquiline. I called him a Viking. He walks like a sailor. No, he is not really ungainly, he moves with the lumbering grace of a bear. I wonder if you will like him."

> But the battle was scatter'd from hill to hill,
> From the wind-mill to the water-mill;

And he said to himself, as it neared the noon,
Two red roses across the moon.

They were talking and laughing in the other room. Mr. Morris turned his head, as if he were listening to them.

Elizabeth Siddall said, "perhaps you would like to join them."

William Morris said, "no—but I have never heard a voice so beautiful as that of Gabriel Rossetti."

Gabriel came back, carrying a framed picture. He said, "do you remember this, Liz?" It was the unfinished *Blessed Damozel* that he had begun so many years ago, in Red Lion Square.

You scarce could see for the scarlet and blue,
A golden helm or a golden shoe;
So he cried, as the fight grew thick at the noon,
Two red roses across the moon.

She had almost forgotten the picture and now Gabriel said, "I'm glad you've got the promise of number seventeen, Ted, when the present tenants move out."

"Number seventeen?" she asked.

"Red Lion," said Gabriel, so he was remembering too. "The fellows have got our old place, or the promise of it."

But it wasn't "our" place, it belonged to Walter Deverell. Walter Deverell had finished his first picture of her. He had begun it, it is true, before he saw her, but she liked to think of things begun, being finished. There was Mr. Hunt's *Silvia*, and he had done a second *Viola*. There was Mr. Millais' *Ophelia*. She had been happy about the *Ophelia* until he did the floating draperies. She didn't see why she had to be submerged with them. But she had so admired his work that she wanted to be helpful. It wasn't so much lying in the water as the thoughts (Ophelia's thoughts) that turned afterwards to a fever. They blamed John Everett Millais for the cough she had that winter. But it was probably her own fault. She liked being with Mr. Millais, and his mother was kind and it was a happy family. She remembered *The Carpenter's Shop* or *Christ in the House of his Parents*, as it was now called. She was glad to hear from Mary Howitt that Effie and John Everett Millais were happy. Mary wrote, "we are sorry for Mr. Ruskin but it is said, it was no true marriage." Elizabeth was now, she thought, more married to Gabriel than Effie had ever been to Mr. Ruskin. She had avoided discussion about her "coming marriage," she wished William Rossetti and her family wouldn't talk about it. Really, she was very happy now. "I am happy as things are," she thought.

> Verily then the gold bore through
> The huddled spears of the scarlet and blue;
> And they cried, as they cut them down at the noon,
> *Two red roses across the moon.*

There seemed something symbolic about Gabriel always putting away the *Damozel*, and then forgetting it. She wondered where it had been, all this time.

"I was looking for a frame," said Gabriel. He started blowing the dust off, but Mr. Morris jerked out a handkerchief. "Phew, Tops—looks like a flag of truce."

"Flag of truce?"

"I never saw such a huge, immaculate hanky. Don't spoil it." But while Gabriel was looking for a paint-rag, Mr. Morris went on with the frame. "I wondered where that frame had got to," said Gabriel.

She began to cough and Mr. Morris said, "sorry" and stopped dusting. She pushed back her chair. She said,

"Stand it in the corner, we can dust it afterwards," but Mr. Morris had rested the frame on the table and was loosening the fasteners at the back of the picture.

"Hide this," he said, and handed the canvas to her. He walked to the door of the studio and called out, "Hi, Gabriel—here's your frame."

> I trow he stopp'd when he rode again
> By the hall, though draggled sore with the rain;
> And his lips were pinch'd to kiss at the noon
> *Two red roses across the moon.*

It was not a very large picture. She slipped the canvas into her own portfolio. It was there on her dressing-table, propped up before the mirror.

It wasn't finished, there was something ghost-like in the blue drapery. She remembered how Gabriel had folded it about her; one hand was finished, the other was only sketched in, a ghost-hand. It was the left hand; the right was holding the flower-stem. Gabriel had carefully painted the green stalk and blade-like leaves and the three flowers. He had tinted her eyes the same blue as the iris. Her hair was smoothed back, not looped or tumbled as he so often did it. She had placed the canvas beside her, on the dressing-table and looked at both faces in the glass. They were the same size and proportion.

Now she glanced at the dressing-table and her painted face looked back at her, from the mirror-frame.

After the wear and tear of travel and the lack of privacy in the pension, her room drew about her, enfolded her. It was sanctuary.

She thought backward, of the other painted faces. It was painful to think of *Ophelia* because of the blame they put on Everett Millais for the cough she had that winter. Dr. Ackland had said, when she saw him in Oxford, that the cough was partly a nervous affectation, there was nothing wrong really. She was glad now, that she had had that time in Oxford. People were kind, really. She was shy and unsure of herself; she did not like their assumption of superiority. She was "received" because of Mr. Ruskin who had sent her to Dr. Ackland. She had been annoyed by references to *Ophelia*; had her father brought an action against Mr. Millais? Mrs. Combe had referred to her father as an auctioneer. She refused to discuss her family.

But she liked Mr. Pusey. She was taken to see his sisters in the big house in Christ Church. His mother, Lady Lucy told her that Edward was Father Confessor to half the ladies in the county. Edward Bouverie Pusey had taken her into his study and talked to her about his dead wife. She went with him to the Cathedral. She had not been to Chartres then, but since talking to Mr. Morris, she could look back differently to Oxford.

She had heard that Dr. Ackland had considered her, "a kindly, gentle person—not beautiful."

She had heard that Miss Ackland wondered at her manners, "brought up within a street or two of *Elephant and Castle*."

Mr. Ruskin had arranged for her in George Street, so that she could be alone, and Gabriel had escorted her down and seemed proud of her.

But Oxford had sent her back with a seared soul.

It wasn't just their voices.

Mrs. Ackland said she would be welcome in their house in Broad Street at any hour of the day. Mrs. Ackland took her about, to teas and lectures. There were various invitations and Oxford spoke respectfully of the P.R.B. activities. It was a mouse gnawing at her entrails, something she couldn't give a name to. Miss Pusey took her away, in June, to Clevedon. Gabriel came down to fetch her back to London. She had little to say about Oxford, except that everyone was so kind. In fact, they were. That is why the curious feeling of a mouse, or a sudden sinking in the pit of her stomach, actually dismayed her. Oxford! "Did you enjoy your stay at Oxford?" "Oh yes—everyone was so kind." They wanted her to settle there. She did not know why she loathed it.

She hated herself for her stiffness, her want of manners. But it came back to her (in the way these things get round) that Oxford had not criticised her manners.

She felt dispossessed—but of what?

It was chiefly the Cathedral. She belonged there. But she had not lost herself in the dim mystery, until she got to Chartres.

When Mr. Morris spoke of France and the Cathedrals, he gave back Oxford to her.

Under the may she stoop't to the crown,
All was gold, there was nothing of brown;
And the horns blew up in the hall at noon,
Two red roses across the moon.

II

Gabriel said, "blast, they've heard us shouting. You'll have to stand by, Ted, while I freeze them off. It must be Monro or Freddie or even Scotus. Emma must have told Scotus that I was back in Chatham, when he didn't find me at Highgate—where I said I was."

Gabriel shut the door of the long-room. Evidently he didn't freeze them off, for there was a growing murmur of genial voices in the next room.

Elizabeth Siddall started to clear the table, then decided to leave things. "I'm fussy," she said, "it's hard for me to see things so untidy, but there's no place to stack the dishes. I leave them outside the door sometimes, for Mrs. Birrell or Katy to wash up. It all seems so—unnatural, but Gabriel doesn't like to see me washing up or dusting." She stood by the table and her glance round the room was eloquent. "It's funny—it makes me more tired to see things untidy than it does to clear up. I'm not, in that way, artistic."

"It's friendly and delightful," said Mr. Morris, "all this."

"If I touch the books in the hall, he says I have disturbed the sequence. I don't know what sequence. He says he has his own method and can find things best when they're lost."

"He doesn't always find them."

"That doesn't make any difference. If he's looking for an old photograph of Florence for a Dante background and can't lay his hands on it, he turns up something else in the search and says that it will do for his *Carillon* or for another of the sequence he planned, after his trip with Mr. Hunt to Belgium."

"I didn't know that Gabriel had been to Belgium."

"It was a long time ago, after he sold *The Girlhood of the Virgin*."

Mr. Morris said, did she mind his smoking? She said, "of course not. He sold *The Girlhood* for eighty guineas."

Now she could have bitten out her tongue, "but it's sordid, isn't it," she said, "to speak of money?"

Mr. Morris said, "I will make up in some other way, but I want you to give me the picture."

"What picture?" she said.

"The one I asked you to hide."

"Oh—but it isn't finished."

"I want it as it is, unfinished."

"It's always like that, everything's unfinished," she said. "Oh, don't tell me all Gabriel's done, I know that," she added quickly.

"And done," she went on, still standing at the table, "not only for art, writing, translating—look at his Dante—painting, teaching and generally inspiring people—I should say *inflaming* people—"

Mr. Morris did not answer.

"He fairly brought me alive—and other people. Don't think I don't know what Gabriel's done for me and other people."

"He has done a great deal for me," said William Morris.

"You haven't known Gabriel very long," said Elizabeth Siddall. "At first, he set me in a flame. I called it a magic-circle."

"I understand that," said Mr. Morris.

"But it burnt away everything outside the circle."

"I understand that," said William Morris.

"You can't understand it," she said. She noted and tried to check the stammer that always threatened her when she was nervous or excited. That is why she spoke so carefully, when she was embarrassed. But as she considered the bent head of William Morris, her fear of stammering left her.

"It's funny, you sitting there," she said.

He did not answer her, he was fully occupied stuffing tobacco into the bowl of his pipe.

"Friendly, like you said. Only the kitchen at home doesn't look like this."

Mr. Morris felt in his pocket for his matches. His gesture was slow, deliberate, over-controlled.

"What I mean is, if I had been at Oxford, one of the gentlemen would have jumped to his feet and pretended he could help me, when I started to clear the table."

What he said, he felt was irrelevant, "you know Oxford?"

"I was sent there by Mr. Ruskin, to be looked over by Dr. Ackland. I was looked over by a great many people. It was last summer, before I went to France. Various people sent for me. Mrs. Ffoulkes in St. Giles, the Warden of New. I couldn't tell you half the people I met." She added her invariable formula, "everyone was very kind at Oxford."

She said, "when I got home last Sunday, I was wondering where that frame could have got to."

She walked round the table and drew out a chair, facing William Morris. She sat upright in the straight-backed chair. She did not feel as tired as usual. Perhaps the trip to the South had really helped her.

"There wasn't anything wrong, really. Dr. Ackland said I had been overtaxed. I am always overtaxed with Gabriel. That is what I mean by a magic-circle. He makes everything come true. Only, I had no time to get accustomed to it. It would be better if we never married. But there is Lyddy, my younger sister and Mum has set her heart upon it. Dad never wanted my leaving home and getting engaged to Gabriel. My father's people came from near Sheffield, they were once affluent, of Hope Hall. Gabriel made me think it was important."

He waited for her to go on.

"I mean," she said, "*Per Bend Vert and Gules*. I never knew, I don't yet know what *Gules* are."

"*Gules* is a colour, really," said William Morris, "if you're speaking of a coat of arms; it's the *Bend* or band drawn across the shield, *Vert and Gules*, green and red."

"That was the Greaves quartering and *an Eagle displayed*. I tried to write a story that was a sort of vision. It was here, I had it, before I went to France, sitting here in an old basket-chair that's in my room now, in Weymouth Street. I called the story *Gold Cord* because the girl in the story had a hunting-falcon and the cord got tangled when she fell off her horse. She had the falcon embroidered on her saddle-cloth."

"I would like to see the story," said William Morris.

"It's the same style as you and Gabriel, romantic but it isn't finished. You make me want to finish *Gold Cord*. It got mixed up with those old drawings from the wall in Pisa, that Gabriel was speaking about last time. The book is in the hall. Would you like to see it?"

"We can wait till they come back," said William Morris.

"It got mixed up with my being frightened of the cholera."

"Cholera is frightening," said William Morris.

"I was here alone. Gabriel was out at Brown's, for they kept the cart and the calf there for his *Drover* picture. He called it *The Bridge* sometimes. Like everything else in our lives, it isn't finished. But I shouldn't say that, either. People finished pictures of me. But it's like that, I mean the magic-circle. I was Ophelia and I was Viola and Silvia and some half-sketched Beatrice and the Damozel, that never will be finished. But I was the freak at Mrs. Tozer's, or the scarecrow."

"Mrs. Tozer?" asked William Morris, preoccupied with matches.

"Where I worked. I was a shop-girl. I had twenty-four pounds a year."

Mr. Morris dropped the match in a saucer.

They were still laughing and talking in the next room.

"You see what I mean by the magic-circle. Inside it, I am Viola, Ophelia, Beatrice or the Damozel. Outside it, I am afraid people will laugh. They didn't laugh at Oxford."

His heart was breaking.

"Do you think I'm funny?" she said.

"Why—ah—yes, to speak in that way."

"It wasn't just my clothes. But Gabriel likes this dress."

"It's very beautiful," he said.

He saw only the long oval of the pale face, the heavy weight of the carefully braided hair, the fragile hands resting on the grey silk.

"But in Paris, I was fashionable."

Would Ophelia ever be fashionable?

"Ah—you ladies—"

"You see, it having been my profession, I knew how people should look. It wasn't just bonnets; we had model gowns to copy."

Almost William Morris wished the others would come back.

"What it was, was my hair."

Her hair was, as he had written . . . dusky golden.

"What they called the civet-cat," she said.

Her face was, as he had written . . . not fair in white and red, being rather pale. He said, "I think that frame was stuck behind a curtain. I saw the picture last winter, the first time I saw Gabriel alone, when he told me about the 'scutcheon and read me part of a letter from you."

"Was it the blocked-up window?"

He said, "I don't know. I wanted to look out at the snow. I lifted a curtain. Gabriel told me not to touch it."

"It's the draught there," she said. "He works in the other corner, and anyway, he said, he didn't want the cross-light. Perhaps Mr. Jones pulled the curtain back, like you did. All the curtains should be pulled down and shaken. I wanted to do it, while he was away, but I couldn't get a ladder. I knew he would be angry if Mrs. Birrell came in."

"Then, you'll keep the picture for me?"

"I wonder why you want it."

He said, "I'll be perfectly frank with you. It resembles, in some way, the lady that I spoke of, the Margaret of my stories."

So he was going to be married.

"I hope you will be happy," she said, "with—Margaret."

"I don't know when—or if—" he said, "but I will ask you to think of me as happy, with this lady I call Lis."

"Lis?" she questioned.

"It's from the story, he is de Liliis. I told you, I think, that my rose was a lily. That is what I meant, her name, I mean, being Lis."

She did not know what had happened to her. She felt like a stone being dropped down a deep well.

It was not a new sensation, but she had not had it for some time.

It wasn't that she resented people being happy.

"Friends tell me that Mr. Millais and Mrs. Ruskin—I mean, Mrs. Millais are very happy."

"Ruskin—" he did not really want to talk about them.

"He was very kind, Mr. Ruskin, I mean; he offered me one hundred and fifty pounds a year, for all my drawings. I can't go on taking it. It's almost seven times as much as I got a year at Mrs. Tozer's."

He wished she wouldn't talk about it, but she might think he was indifferent, "ah—how long ago—when—"

"When I left? Didn't you know about it?"

"How should I know about it?"

"I thought someone might have told Mr. Jones about it."

"I don't think Ted would have mentioned it to me, if they had."

"You see, that's what I mean. My home is Kent Place," she spoke deliberately, "a street or two off *Elephant and Castle*."

"I am always delighted with the theory that *Elephant and Castle* is a derivative of Infanta of Castile."

"Is it?" she said, "You mean like Charing Cross."

"*Chère Reine*?" he said, "yes."

"It's a small house," she said, "but we have some nice pieces, what Mum said they thought was Chippendale, two chairs, and we have a Flemish cabinet."

Why did she tell him these things?

"They were given to Mum—"

"Listen," said William Morris, "I must know everything about you. They'll come back in a minute. But before I hear the story of the Flemish cabinet, you must promise to meet me somewhere. I'm coming up on Saturday. I'm in an office, an architect's office, and I've got to finish up some detail drawings and tracings, before I leave Oxford."

She was looking at him from far way; her eyes were not as blue as the blue eyes in the picture. They were greenish-blue or grey, depending on what light she was sitting in and on what she wore. Even as William Morris looked at her, the colour disappeared and he was staring into the dark wells of the over-luminous pupils.

He was shocked suddenly.

Her expression had not changed, perhaps her face was paler. Was she suffering?

"I've tired you," he said, "frankly, I'm selfish."

Would he lose her now?

"I want to talk, I want to talk to you and of you. But understand, it is because of Lis that I must see you. We have been separated, such a long time. Have you—have you—" he turned his head. "I mean, I wonder if you have a bowl or something—I can't tap out my ashes."

"There's that tray, Gabriel uses," she said.

He did not see the tray, though it was at his elbow.

"It's there, on the window-sill," she said.

William Morris laid his pipe down on the ash-tray. He stood with his hands on the back of the chair. He stared at the darkening window.

She must have moved away, for there was light and shadow, where there had been gathering darkness.

"I like candles," she said.

She had come back to the chair.

He thought of Godfrey and his room in Balliol.

He thought of *The Little Tower*.

"You will come," he said, "it's just an idea, a sentiment, but I would like to meet you, just inside the station waiting-room."

She said, "at what time and what station?"

William Morris said, "at four-fifteen exactly—*chère reine*."

William Morris said,

"No furlong further for us to-night,
The Little Tower draweth in sight."

PART IV

I

"What I mean," said Elizabeth Siddall, "it is sweeping across in the wind out there. It isn't like other poetry, it sweeps across with rain and flowers in it.

"I mean, first reading your poem *The Wind*, I saw the banners and King Olaf and the shields.

"I could make up the *vert* or *gules* or *azure* from the herald-book you brought me. And there seemed power in the banner-patterns, like the old symbols from the star-book that Mr. Manuel brought in, explaining some influence, as he called it, to Gabriel, out of Dante.

"I don't like to think about the future, only everyone talking about the Bis-sextile year and explaining about a comet due next summer, got me thinking that those old lions and the different attitudes of them in the herald-book, have meaning like the star Lion, in what they call different aspects. Gabriel told me that *Leo* is August. And this is funny," she said, "not that it's against Mum and Dad, but they never were sure what day I was born. It wouldn't be a thing you'd forget, would it? But there was Annie, then Charlie who died in Sheffield. I was between Charlie and Lydia but they put both Lyddy and me down, born 1832—but we're not twins. I was half-ashamed when Mr. Manuel and Gabriel were working out the star-dates, that I didn't know my birthday.

"I said, when Mr. Manuel asked me, that he could guess what he thought might be my birthday, as he was boasting to Gabriel that he could tell the other sign (he called the rising-sign) from what people looked like. Some people even know the hour they're born and that's the rising-sign and as important, they were saying, sometimes as the original. It got me thinking in those patterns, but thinking more from the *rampant, guardant* or *couch-ant* lions in the herald-book, rather than from the *Leo* in the star-book."

William Morris was sitting with his back to the window. He saw as if reflected in dim silver, the oval of the face, though his eyes were focussed on the irregular, worn, wooden lozenges of the floor-boards. "They should get to work on this place," he thought, "even the best inlay gets warped without an occasional coat of beeswax." He didn't want to interrupt her reverie. She was thinking out loud. Even his thoughts might interrupt her.

"What would a sign be that had wind and rain and flowers in it? You could hardly draw it."

William Morris did not answer.

"It wouldn't be lions, *rampant* or *passant* or anything like that. Perhaps what they call *wayy* or *undy*. Funny, me remembering those words. All of them seem to have poems in them, like your poetry. I mean, it must make a difference to you, if you can take guidance from the star-patterns. But now knowing the day—not even the month—makes you—" she laughed, "*wayy* or *undy*."

"Undine," he said, under his breath, "was a mermaid."

He didn't know if she had heard him.

"It seemed I could write a whole book of poems, just looking at those words and the pictures that went with them. Taking a word, any word would make a poem. I was looking up bird-pictures because of the *Three Birds*. I don't know what sort of birds they were, though we had *per bend vert and gules* stamped on a china plaque, so I did find *Eagle displayed*. I had thought displayed meant just shown, but it means with spread wings. And an eagle, it said, is one of the most noble bearings. But you know all this, it's from the book you brought me."

William Morris was counting the squares of the boards. He was making a mental calculation, there are four here to the right and four to the left of the one I stand on, or add one more and count five feet each way—how many five-foot spaces from here to the closed door on my left, how many back of me to the window . . . "but it doesn't interest you," she said.

"It interests me profoundly," he said. "I was listening."

"Not to what I was saying."

"I was listening to get an answer to your question."

"I didn't ask you any question."

"Not directly." He looked at her now.

"You're tired of sitting here," she said, "you want to go back, even if it is raining."

"I never minded the rain, but I don't ever want to go back."

"Did I ask you a question?"

"In a way, a number."

"Perhaps, I asked you before. I meant to ask you that first day in Chatham Place, when you told me what *gules* meant. I wanted to ask you then, what kind of birds would *Three Birds* be on a coat."

"I thought it was *Eagle displayed*."

"That was one—"

"Quartering."

"I couldn't find any *Three Birds* in the book, there were eagles and *volant* meant a bird flying and *close* with its wings folded and there was *martlet*, a bird—"

"The fourth son," said William Morris.

"That is a story that is written somewhere," she said, "about the nine sons and why one has a rose, another a ring and that star—"

"If you mean *mullet*, it's a spur," he said.

"I don't remember their names nor the order of them, but they are charms or gifts and they all mean something. How else did the nine sons in that list (at the beginning of the book) of what they call differences, get star-symbols? It's old—old—"

"I was saying that to a chap in Oxford—or something along those lines, about a related problem. My idea was, it went back to—well, the crusaders of course, but before that—"

"That's what I mean," she said, "take *escallop*, the pilgrim-shell we all know. But when you see it on a coat, you feel that journey to—"

"Palestine," he said.

"—and you have a story. You can see everything. It's so hard and central. I seem to float off sometimes, or to be driven off into myself, when I hear them talking and can't follow. But I think the heraldic signs are like the *Leo* and *Scales* in Mr. Manuel's book. They simplify some vast plan or state or dream or idea. And if you could get how they first came about, you could understand everything. Like the *Ram*, the first sign in the star-chart, being from shepherds—so it seemed to me—watching in the night and Biblical. I wrote down the animals from Mr. Manuel's book and checked up, where I could, in your book, and I found the *Ram* or the *Lamb* rather, but only for the Knight Templars—no other rams and lambs, as there are various lions and not a few eagles. Was it part of the Knight Templars, all the heraldry?"

"Is that the question that you wanted to ask me?"

"It came while we were talking."

Elizabeth Siddall was seated on a bench, covered with frayed rose-brocade. His was a low rush-bottomed chair that the caretaker had brought

in. It was not by any means Godfrey's arm-chair at Balliol, but he was reminded of Godfrey and the table. He had been asking mental questions as
Godfrey called them, but the table was not needed for the answers. William
Morris had seen Elizabeth Siddall now, on a half-dozen occasions. He had
discovered, even the first time, with a gate-legged Buszard tea-table between them, that she answered his mental questions—that is, if he led her
along and when her reverie had entered the proper channel, managed to
keep himself detached, without altogether "disappearing."

It was, he presumed, what Faulkner had been working on, thought-transference, but it didn't need the table. Yet without his own experience and
Godfrey's illumination, he would never, he felt, have found the clue to her
apparently vague yet somehow palpable dream-realities. He himself knew
the *King of Arms*, the manual of heraldry that his father had given him on
his tenth birthday, by heart. That and Gerard's *Herbal* had remained his
most precious possessions. He had been inspired, literally, by the words and
the heraldic emblems, when he wrote *Two Red Roses*, *Crecy* and *The Wind*.
He had written *The Blue Closet* for Gabriel's picture, "a stunning poem,"
Gabriel had called it, and *The Seven Towers* came to him that very evening
when he went home, after his first talk with Elizabeth Siddall at Chatham
Place, being assured in his heart, that she would not fail him. That was the
first occasion and direct in a cab, to Buszard's for tea.

"You'll be thinking of tea," he said.

"I was wondering," she said, "about—"

"Therefore, said fair Yoland of the flowers,
This is the tune of the Seven Towers—

is that what you meant by saying that my poetry sweeps across, with rain
and flowers in it? Were you thinking of the *Little Tower*?"

"*Up and away through the drifting rain*—yes," she said.

"And I was wondering," she said, "how we got in here. The last time, you
said the porter told you, it was being done over or rearranged, preparatory
for the public."

"The sun was shining last time," he said.

"And the time before that. It's the *Seven Towers*," she said.

He was thinking of Godfrey and Vernon and Roland. He had called himself Oliver in the *Seven Towers*.

This was like Godfrey and the Lady whom Godfrey said, answered his
questions. Godfrey said, the Lady might be one's unconscious thought or
reverie, one's double or one's soul. But here was Elizabeth Siddall, Lis, Yo-

land of the flowers, herself a flower, sitting opposite him, on a brocade-covered bench, drawn up against the wall of the small ante-room that led on the left, through the corridor to William's Orangery, and on the right, into the main hall of the Palace.

It did not do to appear to be involved in this. He cast his net and waited.

He must not be too far withdrawn, yet he must not let his shadow fall on the surface of the still water.

He must appear to be detached, yet he must be communicative.

William Morris had admired Godfrey's diplomacy, his own was far more subtle. It dealt, however, with a different set of values, fluttering of wing or flash of fin. He had occupied his nervous, thwarted fingers weaving nets at school. He watched and waited. He knew, though he did not know he knew it, the give and stretch, the resilience and spacing of the squares or woven triangles of the intricate mesh of his brain-net. He watched behind himself, himself watching. Yet it was no question of disassociation. With her, it might be different. He could lure her far out, but could he lure her back, once her spirit or soul had broken bounds?

Would her spirit break bounds?

He thought of Vivien.

"I used to talk things over, symbols and Rounds with a chap at Oxford."

"Rounds?"

"Well, he put it all down to the Round Table and Arthur and the Knights. He did tell me that he had read somewhere, in some old French chronicle he was at work on, that there were originally twelve of them."

"Like I said—Biblical."

"Yes and no. He argued it with me, the Cross and Crescent. They said—I mean, it occurred to me that the Crusaders or the Templars reconciled the two religions—or all religions."

"Like Mr. Rossetti's Dante."

"*Mr.* Rossetti?"

"Gabriel's father."

"I don't know anything about Dante."

"I mean, those circles."

"Ah—"

Should he say it or should he let her say it?

He said, "I don't care for astronomy."

"But you have planets in your *Hollow Land*," she said.

"I don't think so."

"Ships sail through the Heaven
  With red banners dress'd,
Carrying the planets seven—

isn't that the same as Mr. Manuel talked of? Different signs or houses, as he
called them, being ruled by different planets?"

"I didn't associate—"

Could he let the pause lie, eloquent between them?

"Perhaps," he said, "the seven planets are the seven towers. But I like to
keep down to earth, my heaven is hollow, the lap of earth."

"Isn't that just the bowl of heaven, turned round?"

He said, "yes."

But he must not let her go on like this. He noted how her eyes dilated, her
face grew paler when she became *exalté*—the word that Gabriel had used
of Ted.

He said, "it's a game really. Children love animals and make fairy-tales,
as simple wood-folk and fisher-people do—"

"And those shepherds."

He said, "yes. It's nothing to be frightened of."

"Why do you say that? Do you think I'm frightened?"

"No," he said. He pushed back his chair and strode over to the window.
"These boards need waxing," he said. "I told the gate-keeper that I was in
an architect's office and wanted to look over the place. That's true, anyway.
I said, I had been discussing the re-arrangement of the galleries with an art
expert. That's not untrue. I said the lady must get out of the rain, somewhere."

"You're tired, waiting. The rain's almost stopped," she said.

"I shouldn't bring you out here, so often."

"Oh, but I live it all over, in between times. I go over all our talks and the
flowers in the garden."

"I want to show you the water-lilies later. I used to row down from Oxford with old Faulkner, and my father brought me here once. I looked in that
very mirror. I remember how funny I looked. I wouldn't look in it now, for
a king's ransom."

She turned her head. The mirror was set flat into the wall.

"It must always have been there," she said.

The mirror was in two parts; the green-silver surface was uneven and
flawed.

"It must be a very old mirror."

"Don't look in it," he said.

Now he turned his back to the window, and the room seemed darker.

She said, "I didn't mean to—but why? Do you think I'll see ghosts?"

He thought, "the *Seven Towers*. I called it *The Tune of the Seven Towers*. I was thinking of Godfrey's tower-room and the seven windows. I was thinking of Vivien and Carew. I was thinking of England. I was thinking of that sneak Godfrey, as Gabriel would call him. I was thinking—but he's not lost—he can't be—yet. No, he must not be lost. Carew, Vivien. If I give her a clue, she will give me the answer, like asking the table questions. But she doesn't know she has the—gift. No-one knows it. She must be protected. I must not tempt—the—I must not ask, *will Godfrey come back from India*?"

He said abruptly, "we'd better go now. I won't send you any more of my poems, if they make you talk about ghosts."

II

"I was surprised to find gillyflower, in your book," she said, "is for carnation or pink."

He said, "yes, it is sometimes confused with the *quatre foil* or *set foil* or even with the *double quatrefoil*."

"A real pink would be more like the rose-pattern," she said, "the rose usually has (like the pink) those other smaller petals."

"In heraldry, they are leaves," he said, "or symbolic leaves—*barbed*."

"Thorns, I should say."

"I don't think so."

He wished she hadn't spoken of carnation. He was trying not to think of Godfrey and the tower-room. She brought Godfrey back with her carnation, an awkward word really—it was Roland saying that Aurélie, the girl they wanted him to marry, was *oeillet*, carnation or pink. "How and when, do you suppose they came to call our garden-pink, carnation?" he said. "Was it the colour? It seems Persian somehow . . ." He must go on talking or she would become entranced again. "So you like Dutch William's sunken-garden?" he went on at random and before she could answer, "but the ghosts are common-place. Even the porter is sure to have run across them. There is Anne Boleyn—or is it Katherine Howard?—running down the long gallery. We must take a tour round the whole place sometime—don't you like muffins?"

"I was thinking how pretty this room is with those china dogs on the mantelpiece and that old clock ticking and everything so polished. It's funny to see it almost empty. Last time, we couldn't get in, do you remember?"

"And the time before that, they laid a table for us under the apple-trees."

"It was almost too much, those apple-blossoms. I wonder where we'll be next year?"

Next year. Dear Lord, she had said it, she had said it.

"Why—why—next year?"

"I think it's Gabriel and Mr. Manuel talking about a comet, due next summer and trying to explain it, in terms of recurrent happenings. I mean, they were explaining a comet that is woven on the Bayeux tapestry, as for William conquering England, and one (the same one) earlier for Caesar, and later for something else important."

"It's theoretical."

"They say it's proved fact, with numbers—the Fall of Constantinople, that's what the other was. And Mr. Manuel worked round from the table of numbers, and said next time it will come back, is in the next century—"

"You said, next year."

"I was talking of the smaller comet. The important one should come back about 1910, in—well—"

"About fifty years time."

"It's '56 now," she said, "the Peace Year. Yes, it would be fifty-four years from now. Why—" she laughed, "we even, might be living. We wouldn't yet be eighty."

"You think quickly, or did you work it out with Gabriel?"

"Dad always said that I was good at numbers."

"But why did you think of—all this?"

There was no use, the question was hovering between them. He had had the letter yesterday. Godfrey had left it with Vernon to be posted after he left. And now she said, gillyflower and pink and that brought back Roland and his *oeillet* and the tower-room . . . and she said next year.

"Do you get geography from flowers?" she said.

"Well, not exactly—yes, sometimes, places and periods."

"Why did you say pinks are Persian?"

"I don't quite know." He did know; he had been thinking back over those last hours or sessions with Godfrey and he remembered telling him that his first talk with Gabriel was an essence, an attar, a distillation to be treasured, to be doled out carefully. "Can you use up memory?" Godfrey had asked him. He had lain awake all night, going over the talks that he and Godfrey had had, in his room at Balliol. He was consoled only by this plan, their arranged meeting, after the pattern of the others, at Hampton Court. Spring was early this year and unusually fine for England. This was the first rainy day they had had.

He was glad for the quiet and the rest around them, the crackling of the fire in the fender, the occasional fall of a log, the splash of raindrops on the window-ledge, the drip-drip from the eaves, the clock ticking. It was impossible to think of India.

"Well, to be frank with you, I am thinking of what you call geography, because I had rather unexpected news yesterday from a friend. He's gone East."

"That's what we were talking about, travel and Palestine."

"Well, in a way, I suppose it's a sort of pilgrimage. I don't know. I was thinking that the talks with my friend were condensed, as you said of the star-pictures or the heraldry. Or my—well, rather overwhelming feeling and memory of the last few intimate talks we had at Oxford are a distillation, an essence. When we say essence, we think of attar, of attar-of-rose—that's Persian. But what I mean is, the essence of the talks seems to follow a concise pattern—can fragrance have a pattern? I am talking at random. I would like some more tea."

He went on, "you said what I am trying to say, the heraldic symbols pin down or weight down or simplify—what was it you said? *They simplify some vast plan or state or dream or idea.*"

"I thought I said that about the star-pictures."

"But you said, didn't you, that you felt that the heraldic symbols were derived from the star-pictures?"

"I said, I thought the Lion *rampant, couchant* was, it might be, different aspects of *Leo.*"

"We have it all there," said William Morris, "but you forget, I take sugar in my tea."

"What do you mean, we have it all?" asked Elizabeth Siddall.

"All that we are looking for."

She did not answer.

"We have it all here. I thought I had—well, persuaded Godfrey (that is, the friend I speak of) not to go out to India."

"Why—why did he go?"

"He had had an experience. How can I explain it? His sister—"

"The one you call Lis?"

She had never mentioned Lis or Margaret to him. He had, after his first explanation at Chatham Place, made no further reference to the hypothetical Lis, or excused their meetings on the ground of another lady. There had seemed no need for excuse or explanation.

"Lis?"

"You have forgotten her—already?"

"I have never forgotten her—for a moment."

He noted how carefully she set down her cup.

But she did not really love him or she would have given him the picture he had asked for.

She was keeping it—and Lis for Gabriel.

It would embarrass her and perhaps she would no longer meet him, if he told her that Yoland of the flowers, Margaret and the Lady Alys were all Lis.

"I expect you think I'm ill-mannered," she said, "but you said you wanted to meet me to talk about Lis."

"I do not know that I want to talk about her now—that is almost impossible."

"You write about her?"

He said, "yes."

"You send the poems to me, so I will talk about the poems and talk about her, talking about the poems."

He said, "yes."

"You make it out sad," she said, "that Yoland. I don't know if I can remember, *The white ghosts walk in a row*, you said, and *The graves stand grey in a row. This is the Tune of the Seven Towers*, you said."

He said, "This is the tune of the Seven Towers."

"I know I shouldn't ask, but it's like—like as if you had known disappointment, as regards this lady."

"I have known no disappointment."

"I mean, like—Oh, I don't know, I don't know. I remember a blue owl on a shield or pennant in one poem, and a dragon in *The Wind*, and Margaret and the lilies, and there is Marguerite in the gillyflower poem, and there is a mood like I said, wind sweeping rain with flowers in it, like it must be outside—though the cherry and the apple-blossoms are now over. I mean, I hold on to something, flapping on a banner, a blue owl, not knowing whether it is friends or enemies—but it is *toward* something."

"This is the Tune of the Seven Towers," said William Morris. He spoke in his husky whisper.

"So a vast state or distance or a character, unknown till now, comes clear in a picture or an image, like one of those lions I speak of, *Leo* being, they said, the heart, and for kings."

"My friend thought that he had killed his sister."

"*Killed his sister?*"

"She was thrown, riding alone in what they called the King's Wood. Henry VIII had stayed there; it was a romantic notion of mine that Godfrey was a direct descendant. No—" he interrupted her unspoken question, "he is a modest, subtle, well-bred, intellectual, diplomatic fellow. He makes no claim, other than the usual family connection. He thought that he should not have let his sister ride off alone in the evening, to the King's Wood, to—"

"Lis is dead, then," she said.

He did not answer.

Would she think him callous, if he did not make some suitable reply? He felt hypocritical, sitting silent, with bowed head. Even a shadow of a dishonest gesture was repellent to him.

"Well," he spoke brusquely, "she isn't quite lost. I mean—let me be frank, though I should in other circumstance, feel it a betrayal of confidence. But Godfrey betrayed my confidence, my hope—well, no. He meant to spare me. But it seemed assumed between us, after some rather heated argument—I mean, he had led me to understand that he was working in England—well, for England. He may not have said in so many words, that he was staying, but I had the impression that he was and he didn't contradict it—the impression—"

"Can you contradict an impression?"

"Yes."

He was not only hurt, he was angry that Godfrey had out-witted him.

Should he contradict the impression about Lis—that is, as far as it concerned Godfrey and Vivien?

"It's far off—India."

"Very far," he said.

"It's like—I see—" she said, "you feel he isn't near to talk to about—his sister."

"And other things; there was a group, a circle. A friend of his in Paris was working with him on the old legends."

"The Rounds," she said, "of Arthur that you spoke of, was that Mr. Rossetti's Dante-circles?"

"I don't know. You must ask Gabriel. But Godfrey was hoping to find more people for his own Round or circle. He didn't expect to find twelve but we discussed it, though we didn't actually associate the twelve with what you call the star-signs. I am disappointed, I feel I have lost so much, now Godfrey has gone. And I had just now, a special, personal pang or panic that he wasn't here in England, so that I could show him to you and so that he would rejoice in your—your overwhelming discovery of heraldic lions and *Leo* and the star-rounds."

"It can't be my discovery."

"Well, you bring it into consciousness—how shall I say? You make me feel as you said just now of my own banners, it is *toward* something."

"Wasn't Mr.—wasn't Godfrey's circle toward something?"

"Yes, it was toward this, but he hadn't begun to fill out the—the—what do you call the thing the stars go by? Zenith or Zodiac or something. It's ridiculous how obvious it all is."

"Like you said, your *Hollow Land* is heaven."

"It was you who said it was the bowl of heaven turned round."

"Then Arthur's people and—and Godfrey's, *in* the bowl, would make a pattern round the rim or in a belt or band inside the bowl-hollow."

"*Per bend or,*" he said.

"And their Lion, Dragon, Owl—all the symbols on their banners—would each have its original or likeness or substitute in star-signs."

"Arms," he said, "of Sovereignity, of Pretension, of Concession, of Community—I knew the list by heart, before my next birthday."

"Your next birthday?"

"My father gave me *King of Arms* on my tenth birthday."

She sensed that he was comforted about the loss of his friend, when she spoke in terms of the *King of Arms.*

It didn't matter what she said to William Morris. He never criticised, argued or broke her off in the middle of a sentence, with "you *are* quaint and dotty, Lizzie."

"Then, Godfrey is *King of Arms.*"

His useful pipe—he abstracted himself in the usual ceremony, making much of re-filling the bowl and getting the thing going.

Yes, Godfrey was *King of Arms.*

"It was more than—than a game with Godfrey? I don't mean a game, exactly. It was more than Gabriel draping me for Guenevere?"

Guenevere.

"I won't ask Gabriel about the star-circles being the same as Dante. That is, I won't ask him in connection with the herald-book or the Rounds. There might be other circles outside, going on and on, each larger, with more people. One wouldn't know how to place them. Gabriel and Mr. Manuel are interested in the higher teaching. But it isn't the same as Godfrey and his friend and those old parchments. I see them as old parchments with Missal-like saint-pictures of knights and ladies and . . . But look, the room is empty. It's getting dark. We must go back."

"I've ordered an omelette or something to be brought in later. They're drying your mantle in the kitchen. It's dark because it's coming on to rain again."

"It doesn't really matter," she said, "I might be at Kent Place or out at the Browns', at Highgate."

"You—you—"

"No, I don't tell any lies about it. I always did go off, now and again, to Emma—Emma Brown, that is—or home to see Mum."

She went on, "Mum isn't worried any longer, about Gabriel. I mean, I was thinking that story of mine being in Pisa, wasn't quite right, though I come back to frescoes peeling off walls. It might be the *Gold Cord* is *per bend or*, like you say. One could imagine castles on the mountains, that hem or ring round your *Hollow Land*. Each castle has the banner or sign of some star-house or its likeness or substitute. Mr. Manuel explained the twelve divisions (the twelve months) were called houses in the star-chart. I go in and out of the rooms here, I mean the Palace rooms, but I don't think it is actually this Palace, I go exploring in, for my *Gold Cord*. One would want to visit all the palaces or the houses. There were deer in the forest for my *Gold Cord*, and I found many deer or stags in the herald-pictures. I work it out, the stag is maybe the goat in the star-map, and the hunter is the Archer. There are arrows tied round with a cord or separate, on some of the shields or banners."

He said, "*three arrows paleways, points in chief sable, feathered proper.*"

"Could you use a hawk-feather for an arrow?"

"What a poem you are making."

"The gentleman in my story wore a hawk-feather in his cap, from my hawk and that was dangerous as he was the rival faction. We had the hawk on our coat. That's what I meant, when I said, seeing the banners, you didn't know friends from enemies. But I didn't quite mean that. I feel one must work through the—aspects, Mr. Manuel called them."

"Aspects?"

"The seven. He explained, for example, how maybe Venus in relation to Jupiter might be good but at the same time, Venus might be badly, or dangerously aspected in relation to Mars. We wouldn't know—at least, I wouldn't know, not knowing my birthday, not even the month. It would help to know one's birthday."

He felt almost ashamed to have a birthday, in spring, just passed. He felt she expected him to tell her the date, but he went on, "there is another arrow or knot of them, *three arrows proper, banded gules.* And any number of stags."

"I looked through them," she said. "It might even be the Goat, *Capricorn* was the Unicorn."

She was wondering what his sign was. He wasn't sure of it himself. She wouldn't ask him. Oh, well—

"I was born at the end of March," he said.

"That's the Ram then, or Templars' Paschal Lamb," she said.

"I wanted to convince Godfrey that the East that he was set on, was here in England because of the influence brought in by the Crusaders, who had possibly been themselves—well, descendants of the tradition that Arthur symbolizes. I did find some reference-notes suggesting that Arthur's Round Table had descended from other Rounds—but the continuity was broken."

"Perhaps, it wasn't broken. Perhaps, it went on, well, with private people, like you and Godfrey and his friend in Paris."

"Roland," said William Morris.

"Godfrey and Roland and—William doesn't sound right."

"I called myself Oliver in the *Seven Towers.*"

"Names make a difference—now Lis."

Now Lis—he tried to circumvent her. "I like the idea of the *Hollow Land* ringed or ridged with mountains," he said.

And before she could return to Lis, "how odd. I must have seen the Signs of the Zodiac, they always have them worked into the Book of Hours calendar, as decorative motive in the full-leaf pages of the months and seasons. But I am afraid I thought of the Signs as casual design; there would be a Ram or Lamb naturally, in a spring picture; I suppose the Scales would indicate the harvest. I don't even know their order."

"The Scales are October, I think," she said. "The Girl is September; they call her the Maiden, sometimes she has wings. They had various sets of the pictures to illustrate. Gabriel said it was Greek or Roman, going back earlier in ancient times. Is it against Scripture?"

"Scripture?"

"Well, Old Testament—star-worship."

"The Pope in his infallibility, must have encouraged, at least not have discouraged the idea of the star-signs. Otherwise, they wouldn't have found their way into the Book of Hours, which is, isn't it, a sort of Prayer Book, a collection of prayers and Saints' days?"

"I think so," she said, "Mr. Ruskin showed me a Missal and an old Book of Hours he had. But I didn't then, especially notice the signs or star-pictures. In fact, I only think of them now you mention it. Each month has a half-circle of blue star-sky, like a stained-glass window at the top of the picture. There is an outline of star-figures but dim and sometimes, I seem to remember, calendar-numbers in a band round the outside or over the sun-space. I can't quite see it."

"See it?"

"Remember it, I mean."

"There would be bee-hives on a bench for February," he said, "with little mounds or domes of snow."

"The same snow made the hay-stack look like a huge bee-hive. There were four bee-hives."

Desperately, he tried to recall some detail of the snow-scene in the Bodleian Book of Hours. He had discovered that the pictures were traditional, so that the same scene would be shown, with slight variations, in other calendars. Yes, she was remembering pages that Ruskin had shown her and no doubt explained in detail. "Did Mr. Ruskin speak of the—the blue-glass oval windows?"

"It's as if you look out of a huge wide door left open. You see outside—the picture, the season's scene. You don't look up at the stained-blue oval of glass, set in above the door."

"I—I must make some excuse to get out of the office one afternoon next week and try to lay my hands on a Book of Hours. I—I should think possibly the British Museum—"

"That patch of snow, melted on the lathes or lattice of the sheep-fold, is realistic."

"Ah—yes—and—" he would risk it, "the tower in the snow-scene, the birds in the snow, the little thicket of wood and the boy with the faggots on his cart or sledge—"

"It isn't a cart or sledge. It's a donkey with a pannier, one of those baskets that fit on."

"Those details vary slightly."

"Only for the castles; they painted their private castles in the background. But," she said, "I don't know why I say that. I don't know what—what Book of Hours you have seen."

"To be frank, only the Bodleian—not of the best period, though I found a comprehensive essay or thesis, descriptive of the earlier French and Flemish artists."

"My Book of Hours is French," she said. "That's what made me say each of the twelve star-signs should have a castle on or near the mountains. There are castle scenes in each of the twelve pictures in the Book of Hours."

. . . . . .

William Morris did not think that Jones admired Elizabeth Siddall. Nor had he any desire to discuss her with Ted. It was only the realization of Godfrey's leaving England that had made him conscious of a sudden void. He had just realised that he had really unconsciously, been looking forward to talking over these meetings with Godfrey, for it was Godfrey who had drawn out his confession in the first place, the story of Blackfriars Bridge and Lis in the snow, before he himself had met her.

She had been, although the realisation of it had only come to him to-day, part of their spiritual life, their meetings and sessions with the little table, in Godfrey's room in Oxford. He had wondered why Godfrey even from the first, had insisted on limiting their questions, though he was open to endless discussions afterwards. Godfrey had argued that the table wanted them to think about things; a single word or part of a word was enough to start things, but either he like Roland, in the first instance, was afraid the parting would be more painful if they went into things too deeply, or else Godfrey knew instinctively, that the questions, the answers or the table in some way, might give away what he so sedulously was hiding, the fact that he had from the beginning, made up his mind irrevocably, to go to India. And he, William, had had the temerity to challenge this flickering rapier with a single-stick. But perhaps William the Englishman had not even succeeded in challenging this *King of Arms*.

He had said if he had a part in Godfrey's story, he was Giles the forester. Godfrey might have been plotting in secret, the whole time with his real cronies, what was left of his old St. James's fencing-partners and the younger Carews.

"What would a chap like Godfrey want to do in India?" he asked Elizabeth Siddall. For the moment, he was done with subtlety and double-answers. He had known that Godfrey kept half of Godfrey hidden, or almost all of him. But he had felt that Godfrey had given something of himself to William the Englishman that he had withheld even from his devoted Roland. But Godfrey, *King of Arms*, he felt suddenly, had probably withheld nothing from the old remnant of the Light, and the younger men who had taken the places of those who had gone. Suddenly, William the Englishman felt that he had never known Godfrey, though he had been so deeply moved by his story and the fact that Godfrey had said, "you'll know where I've gone. You're the only one who knows this."

Elizabeth Siddall said, "but I do not know—Godfrey."

"You feel things, you know things," William was fretting now, impatient. Anyhow, he didn't want a subtle answer.

"You make me feel like—like I was Aunt Day."

Her sudden laughter startled him. He pushed back his chair. He said, "you're tired of talking. Do you want me to get your mantle and come out for a stroll before dinner? It's blowing and darker, but the rain seems to have stopped. They'll want to clear the things here." He suddenly felt that he could not face the answer to the question he had just asked.

"They'll come in when they want to clear the table," she said, "and isn't this the nicest time, sitting and talking after tea is over? Was it rude, laughing? I couldn't help but laugh, suddenly thinking of Aunt Day by the fire in the room back of the shop, and how people would come in while we were sitting over tea, with just such a question as you asked me, and then arguing, 'just this once Mrs. Day—*you feel things, you know things.*'"

She laughed again, and in presumably a fair imitation of Aunt Day, she said, "cut three times with your left hand—I said your *left* hand . . . but I haven't the cards and anyway, I never told them except sometimes for Lyddy. Can you tell fortunes without cards?" she said.

"Well—yes—" said William Morris.

Her laughter had brought some light into his darkness. Her first reaction to his question had been an unexpected burst of laughter. It was happy laughter; sometimes her voice was too high-pitched, her laughter, taut and nervous. She was happy with him; she was not unhappy about Godfrey. "Well, I haven't the cards," she went on, "you must give me some indication, if you want me to tell your fortune. I can't help laughing," she concluded, "thinking of Aunt Day."

Then, she set her plate and cup to one side and cleared the space before her on the table. "Have you cut carefully," she said, "or shall I shuffle them again?"

He had never seen her eyes slant upward with amusement. So this was Aunt Day. "Thank you, Mrs. Day," said William Morris.

"I even did this for Lyddy."

"Telling the cards?"

"Telling the cards, without them," she said.

His eyes focussed on the slender hand, the fall of the wide sleeve. "Ah—"

he must play his part apparently. He laid down his pipe and carefully assembled the cut pack. He opened his hand and his broad palm roofed the narrow hand, held out above the cleared space on the table. He did not touch her fingers. "Thank you," she said, "my advice always is, do not look at the cards I lay out. Different people learn from experience different methods, and sometimes self-interpretation can make interference." There was a lilt in her voice though she spoke so precisely. Was this Aunt Day speaking?

"Specific questions sometimes have specific answers, but not always. But don't waste our time and *their* time, asking about your Uncle Timothy's will, though maybe some inference might come through about that or about your favourite nephew—it was India that he sailed for?"

Was he to answer Aunt Day, in character? William Morris cleared his throat. "Hm-mm, that scoundrel—" he growled, playing his part in the charade.

"Not that I would call the young gentleman a scoundrel. There are plans and portents and a diamond. The Queen wears more jewels than she can carry. But the Empress of India looks toward the sea-city. Is it the Queen or the Empress that will win the gambit? The servant of the Queen is Crusader by profession. No man wins to the Sepulchre before the Ancient Lady. Sceptre and Crown are indicated but—" she stopped suddenly.

"Actually, it's funny," said Elizabeth Siddall. "Lyddy used to say I ought to go on the stage, after my doing Aunt Day for her. I never really tried to do other people. Aunt Day is Welsh really, she was a Miss Evans like Mum."

"But they're going to interrupt us," said William Morris as one of the *Tudor Rose* waitresses began drawing the chintz curtains. The girl said,

"But I'd better light up first, and about that omelette that you ordered, Sir—"

"We're in no hurry," said William Morris.

"And Madame's mantle's hung behind the door, now, it's dried out."

"Thank you," said William Morris.

"Your fire's going nicely, but I'll fetch some more logs."

"She didn't interrupt," said Elizabeth Siddall, "I almost felt I was doing my own fortune while you were talking to her. That is, I was Aunt Day, doing her dear Lizzie; the worst that could happen was Aunt Day sending me out when she had a client, to answer the shop-bell. Nothing can stop it really, once you get started. It almost seemed, it was Aunt Day doing for all of us. King. Double-king. He comes back."

"Godfrey comes back?"

She did not answer.

"What I mean," she said, "the door opens. Being Crusader, gave him the pass-word to them. Wings and a hawk displayed—or some bird out of your book." She was speaking naturally. "Funny, just now, I see that mysterious fight about the Sepulchre. It always seemed a far-away, unrelated cause to fight for. It's a door in a mountain. Wasn't Our Lord laid in a new cave, hewed out? If it was His Body they removed, it was a contradiction, for Our Lord had the Resurrection. Then why the Sepulchre? Was it a symbol? They were fighting for a door or an entrance through a mountain. It couldn't have been actual. It was the way through the mountain to—"

The candles drew the old-gold from her hair. Although she was speaking conversationally, she was still "holding the cards."

"Why double-king?" she said. "I would take it to Aunt Day but she wouldn't do my cards after I went to Mrs. Tozer's. Lyddy said Aunt Day was jealous. Mrs. Tozer was a friend out of Mum's Euston Road days. My—just speaking of Euston Road, makes me think of Constantinople. I do mix things up. It's Constantinople that's in ruins. Biblical. Why, I could transpose even such things as—as round St. Paul's, for ruins of Byzantium. I never thought St. Paul's, Byzantium, but maybe it is with that dome—spires and churches all down, but by spires, I really mean those minarets or campanile. But there's no gold and glitter, like Byzantium. It was talking of that comet. Double-king? I can't remember what Aunt Day meant by that—or maybe it wasn't Aunt Day. But it went on?"

She was asking him a question.

"It went on?" he echoed.

"I'm asking you. It went on long after it was conquered. But it's not exactly conquered. But there's no colour, it's washed out—the gold. Double-king? In two elements? Does he get through the mountain?"

Must he answer?

"Ah—you mean—"

"I tell you, I've mixed things. He got into the dark city. It may be Jerusalem."

"*In England's green and pleasant land*," said William Morris.

"That's it—it will be—" she laid down a card.

"Three—double-three—a feather—two wings—could it be eagles fighting?"

"Symbols from banners? There's Russia, Prussia, Austria, eagles and double-eagles . . . some—distant—war?"

"Very distant," she said, "all in my imagination. Didn't I tell you, I was *wayy* or *undy*?"

III

She could live completely now, in two circles. She didn't need the cholera scare or concern about Gabriel's infidelities to drive her through the darkness. It was, as she had said the last time she saw William Morris, all imagination. The day-dream could be directed, she was writing.

Gabriel was busy, there was always a crowd now at Chatham Place and Mr. Manuel seemed practically to live there. Elizabeth Siddall was grateful to him, however. He talked to her about his star-charts when she dropped in sometimes.

He had told her more about the various Houses. She had more or less memorized them now, with their planets. The House of Death *Scorpio*, was the only one with more than one symbol, or the same symbol with different meanings. There were three of them, the Scorpion, the Serpent and the Eagle. Her eagle fancies drew her to the House of Death, but the Eagle was, Mr. Manuel said, the higher vibration of the Scorpion or Serpent, or their resurrection; it was in a sense, worm and butterfly.

Now Elizabeth Siddall could look back with a certain detachment. She remembered how Harry had plagued them, darting out, choosing her especially, for his pranks. It was scorpion-like, she thought, his pouncing from behind the kitchen door, and threatening her with the "very knife he did it with." At last, she had the answer. The scorpion-sting, "the very knife" had been associated with a bride, the murdered woman. She had thought she would die if she married Gabriel. But she still hoped that the magic, as she had called it, of his fame and influence might counteract the lurking terror. It hadn't, altogether.

She had written poems for Gabriel, after his first repudiation at Hastings, "I am not engaged to Lizzie," and afterwards, when they actually were engaged at Scalands. The poems were wistful, resigned and hardly lover-like.

I cannot give to thee the love
I gave so long ago—
The love that turned and struck me down
Amid the blinding snow.

But the blinding snow was from the old winter-drama of Kent Place. It was not really Gabriel who had struck her down, it was the adolescent nightmare of Mr. Greenacre that she had shared with Lyddy.

But Gabriel or Gabriel's circle bordered on the nightmare. It is true, he had drawn her away from it but he had not vanquished it. Elizabeth Siddall remembered how she had said, last Saturday at the *Tudor Rose*, "names make a difference—now, Lis." She thought, "it started with my saying that William didn't sound right, with Godfrey and Roland." She could not think of William Morris as William. But it was only now, with her note-book on her lap and her pencil in her hand, that she remembered that Mr. Greenacre's name was William.

"Well," she said to herself, "so is Mr. Allingham, William. And as far as that goes, there is Gabriel's brother."

Nevertheless, she had found a fresh clue.

"You might just as well go back and say the Conqueror's name is William," she thought.

The clue was the Conqueror, a Conqueror, a Crusader who had manifested.

She needed this image for her story, the *Gold Cord*. So far, the story hadn't really come true. She would be able to destroy the rambling, disjointed first sketch, once she started on this new one.

It wasn't really Pisa, to begin with. It wasn't William Morris that she waited for in the clearing, with the falcon perched on her shoulder. She had tried to sketch Mr. Morris into it, as she needed—well, a model for her picture. But neither he nor Mr. Allingham, the only two whom she could at all consider, would do for the finished picture.

Sand drifted through the moss, there was a forest and a sea-road, but it wasn't Pisa. True, there might be Kings in coffins and a grave-yard, for this was the House of Death.

She remembered how happy she had been at the *Tudor Rose*, to find at last, the King who fitted in the picture—and a King actually. Hadn't Mr. Morris said that Henry VIII had stayed at King's Wood? Mr. Morris had said, "it was a romantic notion of mine that Godfrey was a direct descendant." Lis was Godfrey's sister and Mr. Morris had said that she was like Lis.

It wasn't a thing in the old days, she would have laughed at. But it came over her; she was free of the old nightmare. In the place of the knife and the murderous scorpion, there was the Hunter with his arrows and her hawk-feather in his cap, or the Crusader with *Eagle displayed* upon his banner.

When she was doing the fortune-telling cards for fun, for Mr. Morris, the pictures were mixed up. She couldn't tell him that she knew, from the pictures, that Godfrey wouldn't come back from India.

It is true that the pictures were too confused with things she had read about or seen or even remembered, to be true vision or Aunt Day's second-sight. She knew the images from Aunt Day's talks over the tea-table in the room back of the shop, in the Roman Road in Pentonville. But with William Morris, she had told the cards as with Lyddy, when she "did" Aunt Day to amuse her or to keep her from fretting sometimes, when the shared terror seemed about to descend upon them. She had known that Mr. Morris was worried and she had given her imagination full rein partly to amuse him, so she had lost track of what was Aunt Day and what she made up. She could remember now how she had said at the *Tudor Rose*, "three—double-three—a feather—two wings."

By that time, as she said to Mr. Morris, it seemed that Aunt Day was telling the cards for all of them. That is, she felt though she did not explain it to him, that the cards were in answer to Mr. Morris having talked about the Round Table and the group that Godfrey and his friend Roland wanted to assemble. She thought, "there is Roland, Godfrey and—Mr. Morris said he called himself Oliver in the *Seven Towers*, but he pronounced it *Olivier* the French way." There was Olivier, there was Lis, both French names; L-i-s, Mr. Morris had spelt out, that first time when she asked him, "it is the French for lily."

Mr. Morris said she reminded him of Lis and in that picture, he had asked for, she did hold that iris-stalk in her hand. But that was only five out of the twelve to be collected, besides that—well, they would be two and two, wouldn't they, Knights and Ladies? There was Mr. Morris or Olivier and Lis, Roland she would imagine would have a Lady in France. And then there was—this was her own imagination or a reflex of Aunt Day's second-sight—herself and Godfrey. But that would make only three out of the twelve couples. Was that the double-three she spoke of at the *Tudor Rose*?

In any case, that would do for the story, for her reassembling. She had assembled herself before, but only in a sort of fever. But this time, for the first time, she recalled herself, clear-sightedly, seeing the Scorpion, the child nightmare, as the dark giant emerging from behind one of the sheds in the tan-yards or stalking her at dusk as she hurried home from a late winter afternoon walk to see the ships at Wapping. He would smother her. The scream was stifled as in a nightmare. She had waked up, out of a bad dream.

Mr. Allingham had rescued her from Mrs. Tozer's. Gabriel had, for a time, numbed the terror with his charm and irreverence. Mr. Ruskin had showed her the way to what he called his gentians, but she had felt that the snowy mountain views and the Alpine pastures would only exaggerate by contrast, the black, lurking terror. Mr. Morris had taken her right out of it, but from the first, he had made it clear that his dedication was to Lis, this Lily, the sister as she had learned last Saturday, of his friend, Godfrey. Devotion to the dead and dedication, was final.

Not that she had wanted, in any case, to claim him altogether. He had been the most understanding, the most friendly, the most kindly, the most sympathetic of them all. And she had, she admitted frankly, used him for a model; there was no harm or disloyalty in sharing him with a living woman. But when she realized that Lis or Lily was dead, she knew that she could no longer claim him, even for a model.

But by some law of spiritual compensation, as soon as she realized and accepted his dedication to this dead girl, the other, stricken brother appeared. This had happened at almost the exact moment that she had let go all spiritual rivalry with the sister. It was a story she could never have invented. Granted of course, her part in it was imagination, yet it was imagination she could never have imagined.

She could do no harm to Godfrey, that is, the Godfrey in the story, by knowing (in the story) that he would not come back from India. It would be next year that would unite them—that is, in the story. Mr. Morris had realized that she connected next summer's comet with Godfrey and with India, though she had tried to pretend that she did not notice the start he gave when she spoke of next year. Lyddy had told her of Mr. Wheeler's confidence—and Mr. Wheeler knew that he could trust Lyddy (she was in that relation, almost another Lyddy.) Mr. Wheeler had said that there was certain danger and frightful problems about India and he wished the East India Company had never been established or that they would get out quickly, before it was too late. There would be divided loyalties, he had said, and dissension enough about India.

It made a straight track to somewhere, her knowing that Godfrey wouldn't come back from India—in the story.

He must have a name of his own, of her own, that is. Names made all the difference; they projected people or concentrated or consecrated them, as the symbols on the banners represented some virtue or abstraction. She wanted Godfrey in the story, to belong to England. She wanted an English name that yet had a French sound in it, like the Olivier that Mr. Morris said was the Oliver of his *Seven Towers*. She must find something that was both French and English. Many even of the English names would have been pronounced French when the Conqueror came in, and she held on to the Conqueror because of her *per bend vert* and Gabriel having made her feel set apart, almost dedicated with it. He had not told her his own coat, except that they were della Guardia and from Italy.

It was Mr. Morris who told her that *Red Roses*, the first poem he sent her was for Rossetti being roses, and when she asked Gabriel about it, he made some joke about his grandfather being a blacksmith. It was just another idea of old Gus, he said. Mr. Manuel used, for the most part, another name in London, his English grandfather's (so Gabriel told her) but Gabriel said, "I don't want to be reminded of his frowsty English family, Charles Augustus has got to be Manuel if he comes here, with orange-trees and castles in Spain—in Portugal I should say."

Yes, names made all the difference. She wanted a name for Godfrey that would go with London or recall or conjure up London. She began lightly writing down names as they came to her. She would erase them later. She would not spoil the first page of the note-book that she had selected with such care and pleasure for her new *Book of Hours*.

"Bedford, Russell," she wrote, "both Bloomsbury; Curzon, West End, is better but it's not quite right; Gloucester, Gloucester Square, that's over by Regents Park, it's some present Duke, I think and anyway, not suitable." She thought out and around Hampstead and Highgate, but she could find nothing. "It's for England's green and pleasant land," she said to herself, "and to recall Olivier for Mr. Morris. When you say it in French, it's living and a tree and green like England's pleasant land—and it was for honour and peace, wasn't it, in the old days, so Mr. Ruskin had said."

John Ruskin. She did not want a name like John or George or Henry—but there was that king. Henry VIII had made her feel that Godfrey was *King of Arms* of their Round. But the name wasn't Henry. It must be English, as English as *Tudor Rose* where she had first heard of Godfrey and where in the flickering firelight and the glow of candles, her nightmare had suddenly been exorcised. It happened in a second; all those hours and nights of anguish were as if they never had been. But it wasn't enough to banish a nightmare, something must take its place. It wasn't just the horror of his murdering her. It was the way he died, cursed by the horrible people watching him at Newgate. As if the curse of the multitude hadn't been dissolved with that mangled body in the prison lime pit . . . she could think about it.

But it was waste of time, that's all that thinking was. She had a pilgrim-shell now, her own journey to take.

Hampton—that was a name surely? Hampton would bring back the apple-trees and the crocuses that had been as if the earth had cracked with very abundance of beauty—those crowded, uneven blue, white and gold fissures of crocus-colour in the fresh grass. Hampton might do but it was a little unfamiliar and stiff. They had explored Bushey Park and twice walked along the river to Richmond. *Richmond*? He was Richmond.

And with Richmond, Oliver or Olivier (whichever you choose to call him), came into a new perspective. They had talked about the pilgrim-shell and Palestine. Oliver, England's green and pleasant land—was that Jerusalem and the Mount of Olives? They had talked about the Crusades and the Holy Sepulchre and she had said the cave, fresh hewn, might be a door into a mountain—the Mount of Olives? But she believed that the mountains around Jerusalem were low-lying and the mountain she visualized was like one of the great Alpine peaks that Mr. Ruskin had talked about when he showed the sketches to her. It was the Holy Mountain. She had found it. It was part of her story, or it was her story. She had called her story the *Gold Cord*, but was the name of the story, *Holy Mountain*? In any case, there would be as well, a collection of poems and prayers. She could just call it, *Book of Hours*.

She was not anticipating, in the story, the death of Richmond. How explain it? It was too difficult to explain but it would be simpler for the story, to say he had been killed in India. He might live, but it would confuse the story. It was not right, but how could she get around it, to contemplate the death of a living person and that person so near to Mr. Morris who had himself opened the door, just with that human kindness and the way of thinking whether her mantle needed to be dried and her having her tea, and supper to follow it. That was the magic that had exorcised the Scorpion, the presence always lurking in Kent Place. At Aunt Day's, it was different and you felt Aunt Day was exorcising things too, with her cards. Did it need the death of good men, dedicated and crusaders to exorcise the evil? It took her too far.

She could not talk of these problems but with Mr. Morris and she did not want him to know her thoughts were concerned with India. Put it that Godfrey didn't die but stayed in India and she never saw him; it would make the same pattern but not so—heraldic or dedicated as the other. Richmond might be separate from Godfrey, even if Godfrey were still living. Richmond would be what Mr. Manuel and Gabriel spoke of as a double. But Richmond would be the same person as Godfrey, only more so. In any case, Richmond belonged to her in the Round, whatever else his life was.

But in the story, she could not have Richmond go to India, for you must think of someone reading a story if you want to get reality in it, and the only person she wanted to read her *Gold Cord* was Mr. Morris. Richmond would go East as on a pilgrim journey, but now she didn't want to set her story in the old time, as Gabriel had done in *Hand and Soul* and Mr. Morris in the *Hollow Land*. Yet there was Constantinople; Byzantium came into the story. It would be old and new, both together, a sort of fairy-tale, she supposed, but with prayers.

She wanted to get the story under way before Saturday, as she wanted to talk to Mr. Morris and find out all she could about Godfrey, and what he told her might influence or even contradict the story as she planned it. Richmond was to go away as a soldier, but in the back of his mind, was the search for the Mountain. She couldn't call it India. Persia that Mr. Morris spoke of, might do. She didn't quite know. Mr. Morris said he got geography from flowers and there were small bay-roses along the parapet, after she came out of the first hall-corridor.

The land seemed endlessly far below her. She did not dare lean out and look over. An eagle was swaying, but far down; she could only explore a little at a time, inside the mountain.

You would never know the rough ledge covered with the thorn-bush, hid the entrance. The goat-path branched off and even the goat-path was difficult enough scrambling. No one would think of turning off that narrow rough way, to the thorny ledge above it.

Once inside, after the first threshold, it was roomy enough. To her right, the wall curved like the inside of a dome and there were inset, oval windows. The windows could never be seen from outside, as it was jagged and rugged and too high up. The other side dropped sheer like a wall, though those rose-bay bushes had found foothold.

The inset windows had a square-ledge really, with the oval inset at the top like the pages of the *Book of Hours* that they had talked of, but the oval was not set with glass, it was simply the round of blue sky. The ledge of the windows to her right was about on a level with her head. There seemed no special reason for trying to look out that side, she could judge the shape and rocks and thicket-growth from the outside of the mountain, before you got to the entrance.

The entrance slanted and looked too narrow but she had slipped in easily. From the inside, it threw a beam of light, lighter as your eyes readjusted. She went over these things to prove to herself that she had been there; it was not a dream.

She couldn't say quite how she had got up that goat-path. She crept along the pillared corridor at first, fearful lest someone should find her. It was a secret place. There must be the wide door-entrance like a door to a great Cathedral far, far down, below where the eagle had been circling. It had that feeling like Chartres might have if she had found her way to the upper turrets. It might be it was Chartres. Here, there was no glass. She could remember the blue and green patches of colour on the stone floor and— *gules*. Yes, it was as it might be, the upper level of some mysterious Cathedral. There would be rooms (she knew) leading off corridors, and stores of song and missal-books. There should be an old brocaded chair, put away, discarded somewhere, that she could drag out. She could find these things in time and maybe, people. She would find Olivier in time, he would come here and of course, it was because of Richmond that she had come here at all.

Mr. Morris would talk about cathedrals and there was his *Unknown Church*. Was this the *Unknown Church* of Mr. Morris? But she knew it, and it was because of him telling her about Lis and Roland and their Round that she knew it. There would be time to explore the corridors; the stairs would be narrow, winding at first. What did Our Lord say about the sheepfold? There was the proper barn-door and there was a way for thieves and robbers. Was she a thief and robber, stealing into sanctuary?

There was Our Lord, the slain Lamb and he talked about goats being cast out. But she thought Our Lord would phrase something suitable for our times. It was, Mr. Morris had said, the convention of the Church now to spend money on bad restorations; it seemed to make him so unhappy that she did not ask him more about it. It was London, he wanted to restore, make pathways all along the river in the city, like the way from Hampton Court to Richmond. He would, he said, decentralize London; it was a new word and a new idea to her. So it must be people with wild-will and stubborn intent now who would find their way to the *Unknown Church*.

It wasn't that she didn't believe in prayers any longer, but just thinking in terms of the star-maps was heaven to her. They were the Ram or Templar's Lamb segment of the sky-map. Others might fill up other spaces or chapels (it might be) but it seemed their Round belonged to Richmond, *King of Arms* and the first or the Ram segment. There was time for all that. They called the Houses, stalls, Mr. Manuel had said, in the old Chinese or maybe it was Indian charts; wasn't that like the Nativity with Ram or Lamb and Bull, with the sheepdogs for Lion and with Mary Virgin, Virgo, the Maiden? She need not let go the old enchantment of Nativity and loaves and fishes. Well, there were those fishes too for the Last House, called the Fishes, and Crab as well might have been dragged up in that draw-net.

It couldn't be the Church of England and you couldn't go back to Rome, it would be like St. Mark's in Mr. Ruskin's *Stones of Venice*.

The wind blew her cloak about her when she stood and looked out from the parapet, beyond the row of pillars. The pillars had apparently been hewn out of the solid rock, or the rock had been cut away from them, for they were part of the floor. She could not judge of the ceiling but they must be one with the rock-roof as well. The wall opposite the pillars was smoothed off but not polished. There was no colour.

The pillars divided the hall-corridor. They were set about two-thirds over toward the windows. The doors were opposite the oval windows, they were rock doorways without doors. Godfrey was on his way to India. It would take a long time to get there.

There were saint-pictures in the Missal books that Mr. Ruskin showed her. He had given her a little volume so that she could identify saints from pictures. She had only glanced at it, but since that last talk at the *Tudor Rose*, it occurred to her that the saint-symbols might correspond to the coat and banner-pictures. In fact, when she looked over them again, they recalled the star-patterns as well, arrow, crown, sceptre, tower, hawks and eagles.

There was the familiar Fleur de Lys for St. Louis of France and a Swan for Hugh of Lincoln.

She had intended to finish the illuminated lettering for the sketches of *Hand and Soul* she had begun last winter in Nice. But now she wanted to study the symbols, to know more about them, and anyway, there was this story. She had so much to think about, the *King of Arms* manual, the star-maps and signs, and the heraldic bearings and properties of the Saints in the book that Mr. Ruskin had given her.

She carefully erased the lightly written London street and square names. She had found what she had been searching for, Godfrey's name was Richmond. But there was so much else that she must find out, before she explored the mountain, and she could not begin her story until she had explored it.

She had sat for three days with the note-book open on her lap and not a word of her *Book of Hours* was written.

She turned the page for she had already written down and erased an earlier list of the star-symbols. On the second clear page, she started a new list, remembered attributes from the book of Saints. There was the Eagle of the Apostle. There was a Falcon and a Feather. There was Lis, of course, but they spelt it Lys in the Saint book. There were palm and olive-branches. There were arrows. "Unicorn, Tower, Sword, Stag," she wrote down. She wanted a symbol to answer a word or to correspond to a mood. But wasn't that what the painters were striving for in their pictures and the poets in their poetry?

Unicorn, Tower, Sword, Stag. She looked at the words. They were heraldic, saint, banner and star-words, all together.

She felt suddenly elated, excited as Mr. Morris had been when they were talking of the star and herald symbols and he said, "we have everything." She had been telling him that she wanted to write a whole book of poems from herald signs, but she had not then, connected the armorial bearings with the Saints. Mr. Morris was right, "we have everything." It was not herself only, it was Mr. Morris—Olivier.

It was Lis and that other French Lis or Lys; it was Roland and Oliver, Lys and Lily and there was herself and Richmond.

Perhaps she should have a name, too?

She was living the story, but she was not alone in the story. There was Mr. Morris and Godfrey, and others would come in later. She thought of Lydia Siddall, but she did not see Mr. Joseph Wheeler in the story. She was glad now that Gabriel had seen Lydia those few times, at the studio. But after Gabriel had finished Lydia's arms for a Queen of Cyprus, he was doing, she arranged carefully not to be at Chatham Place, afternoons when Lyddy was free. Gabriel admired Lyddy's "classic features" and he named her "the Roman."

But Lyddy was engaged now, and happy with Mr. Wheeler.

Perhaps Lyddy might come later. But she could not yet admit Gabriel to their circle. There was Roland and Oliver, Lys and Lily, Richmond, King of Arms and—

"They called me so many things," she thought. "Certainly, I am not Mr. Ruskin's Ida in this Round, nor the Cid, nor Gabriel's Dove, nor any of the picture-characters, I had with Gabriel and Mr. Millais and the others."

But it all started with a picture; it had started with Shakespeare and with Viola. Viola was a flower-name but she wanted something that included or suggested her first meeting Mr. Morris. *She had three lilies in her hand*, it was that picture, the preliminary *Damozel* picture, just the head; Gabriel had planned doing a large picture later, and with angels. But *she had three lilies in her hand*, though Gabriel had not painted *the stars in her hair*. There were seven, those planets and out of Mr. Morris too, as she had reminded him in his own *Ships sail through the Heaven* from the *Hollow Land*.

She was not the *Damozel* in her story, nor any of the picture characters. But there must be three lilies. There was Lis or Lily and there was Lys and the three lilies in her hand were heraldic iris, the fleur-de-lis or Fleur de Lys, as they wrote it in the Saint book. Fleur would be a nice name.

She could not be Lily or Lys. She printed very carefully, under her list of Saints' attributes, FLEUR DE LIS. What she wrote now, she would leave. It even seemed in itself, a sort of poem, the words written that way.

IV

"How did we get here?" she said.

He had already told her.

"Last time was the water-lilies," she said, "the time before that, you took me on the river. How many times were there between the island—you called it eyot—and the last time it rained?"

He must answer her.

She had been telling him at last, the story of her story, *Gold Cord.*

"There were—"

She said, "I remember—there was the summer-house and honeysuckle; there was elderberry over the hedge and you said it was the first time you remembered elderberry-flower and honeysuckle-fragrance blended. That was before the island. Before that, was the new tea-garden but we didn't like it as much as the *Tudor Rose.*"

"I liked it. I didn't like old Faulkner turning up, that's all."

"Mr. Faulkner was very pleasant, really. Before that, was the yellow tea-roses and your showing me ribbon-roses, as you said your grandmother called them."

"Mrs. William Morris," said William Morris.

"Mrs. William Morris?"

He pretended not to notice her sudden start of surprise. "My grand-mother," he said.

"But this is funny, counting things by roses."

"It isn't at all funny," he said.

He said, "I told you, the last time it rained, that I had made friends with the porter. A half-crown goes a long way."

"But—"

"Well, it's true, I had gone out of my way to drag in the office and my art-critic associates. I did not call them artists. I told him I wanted to see the pictures before the galleries were open to the public. But you may still wonder how we got here—out of a dream."

"Well, in a dream—or nightmare. I told you about Lyddy's and my nightmare. That bed might be part of it."

"I don't think—"

"Not like *Othello*."

Everything recalled something. She was thinking of Gabriel and the *Moor of Venice*.

"I'm looking forward to your coming to Red Lion Square," said William Morris.

Elizabeth Siddall said, "but I'm not coming to Red Lion Square."

She had spoken of *Othello*. Gabriel had told him that Walter Deverell had wanted to be an actor. "Because of—was Deverell, Walter Deverell part of your story?" he said.

She said, "yes."

How get her back to the story? Perhaps a clean break would be best. "You are right, it might be a stage-scene," he said. "Well—before or after the act. *Romeo and Juliet*, maybe."

"I don't fancy lovers in that bed," said Elizabeth Siddall.

"It will look better when they hang the curtains. But I like it this way, with the carpenter's bench across the window in the other room. It's like a studio or stage-set, back-stage or between the acts. Must we always come back to Shakespeare? I was saying to Godfrey that Shakespeare—"

What had he said to Godfrey?

"You wouldn't hear," said Elizabeth Siddall, "not yet. Mr. Wheeler made inquiries for Lyddy."

William Morris walked over to the window. The box-trees in the garden showed the W and M, outlined clearly, as you looked down on them from the upper gallery of the palace. Without turning, he said, "did I tell you about the box-trees?"

"Those initials," she said, "yes. But what is important to me is that Fleur, as I told you her name was, is Flor really. Now, why did that make a difference?"

He said, speaking over his shoulder, "I am Florian in *The Hollow Land*."

"It isn't hollow," she said, "that is, it is a mountain with the galleries cut out and those rough support-pillars. But perhaps it is hollow, but *in* the mountain. I called it the Holy Mountain."

"Mount—"

"Don't name it," she said.

He came back and sat down on the brocaded stool that he had found in the anteroom. She was perched higher in a chair he had dragged out from the small retiring-room, to the right of the great bed. She said, "you make me think I read it somewhere. You know all about it." He said, "no." If only she would go on.

"I try not to think too much about your *Hollow Land*, lest I should seem to be influenced," she said, "but in the end, they came to a City and a great Cathedral, you remember."

He remembered.

"It's like I thought. The Cathedral is far below the gallery that I found from the other side. He thought they couldn't get out. He thought he had blocked them with his boulders, in the cave-vault at the back. The Cathedral was twice an eagle-flight down."

William Morris looked at Elizabeth Siddall, "an eagle-flight?"

"They measured things that way. Didn't you say so in the *Hollow Land*?" He said, "no."

"It was concerned with Goldwings."

"I did write the story, *Golden Wings*," he said.

"That's what I mean. But maybe, it was someone else who wrote it— *Roma* being *Amor*, I mean."

Now, what did she mean? He could have knelt and prayed her for the answer, but he knew he wouldn't get it that way. With an effort, he unclasped the hands that were resting with white knuckles, on his knees. He sat up and bent back his head. "This restoration might be a damn sight worse," he said. "I wonder who could have done it. Some period-chap, not fussy."

"Period-chap? You mean out of the Elizabethans? Or earlier? It was Henry VIII, all this, wasn't it? But Richmond must have been here too. You said he was Henry VII, didn't you? But it confused me, calling him Richmond—"

"I fancy Deverell would make a good Richmond."

"Deverell?"

"Didn't you say your—your partner in the story was called Richmond?"

"Yes," she said. "I don't feel I ought to sit in this museum-piece, this chair—but it's like I told you. I wanted a chair (funny) in that gallery and I imagined just some such faded-brocade chair to sit in. It didn't go with the rock-gallery. But did they, maybe, before he burnt them out, furnish the gallery? They must have had food up there. But it wasn't far to the coast. Perhaps, they went right out. From the other side, the City side, it was said there was no track through the mountain. It was rock-wall. How could they cut through that way, with the galleries?"

"It might have been Phoenicians."

"Phoenicians? From long past, you mean?"

"Possibly. There are old wells and mine-shafts in Cornwall, said to have been the work of the early Phoenicians. They had some secret like the Egyptians, apparently, for tunnelling. My father had—had mining interests in Cornwall, and they used to talk about it. I never heard of galleries high up, but obviously you could tunnel in or through the high slopes, as well as underground. But—*Roma*—"

"He swore he'd exterminate the last living remnant."

No, he hadn't spoken to Elizabeth Siddall about the Albigenses. It was only to Lis in the snow, that first night after he left Gabriel. "You must talk to Algernon about this. I must bring him along to see you."

"I can talk to no one but to you and—Godfrey, if he was here. Or if Lyddy wasn't being married, I could talk to Lyddy. But Lyddy's happy."

"Must they all be unhappy?"

"No. But how explain it? They are—what they called illuminated."

"The *illuminati*," he said. He had read of the *illuminati* and the *credentes* (the believers) in the book that Algernon had lent him.

"You must see Algernon. He was the first to bring the poetry of Provence actually, to my notice. It is the Grail story, but history. I knew it was real, but real in another sense—that is, legendary, symbolic. But apparently, it is both history and legend. The Inquisition destroyed their books and literature."

"O—no—" she said.

"Well, there was an echo, a reflection in certain of the *lai* poems and *virelai*, even in the *villanelle*, the shepherd songs. Algernon is collecting them from various sources. It began in Provence and worked its way up to North France. But it was only a reflection of Provence. De Montfort destroyed the Circle when he destroyed the City."

"Did—did Algernon tell you?"

"It's in the book he lent me."

"And who is—Algernon?"

"He's hardly grown up yet. He was in Oxford with his tutor. His name is Swinburne, Swinburne of Capheaton. I shouldn't say, he isn't grown up. He has a more mature mind, even than Rossetti—than Gabriel. It is impossible to compare him, even with Rossetti. You can only think of Shelley. But he's—how shall I say? He told us—well, it's a sordid story. His head grew but his body didn't. He's a—"

"You need not say it. I can see him. But why did Gabriel not tell me of—of—"

"I don't think Gabriel's met Algernon. He's Balliol—next year—but—"

She remembered how he had spoken of talks in Godfrey's room, and when she told his fortune the last time it rained, how he started when she said "next year," as if it were the answer to an unspoken question.

"Algernon—he has hair like yours. His is one of five Northumbrian families who were in England before the Conquest. He should be as tall as Aucassan. He should be Aucassan to your Nicolette."

"But he's younger."

She was marking time. The golden page was leaning too far out. He had crawled like a lizard to the edge of the rock. There was the crushed fragrance of the bay-leaf. He disappeared over the ledge. But he had not fallen. "You caught him," she said to William Morris.

She said, "he was as slender as an eel, a stripling but all muscle. He lashed out at you, like a whip-snake. Blood dripped where his fangs caught your wrist. You dropped him and he rolled over to the ledge again, but you shouted, 'no one cares about your carcass but it will catch in the bushes and the vultures will show them where we are.'"

It was very quiet in the royal bed-chamber. There was no clock ticking.

"Yes, we might be related," she said, "they called him the fox, like they called me the civet-cat. Judas had red hair and they threw stones at Swinburne of Capheaton in Northumbria."

She said, "his name is Florence."

William Morris said, "there is Florence, the son of Amis or Amile, I don't remember which, in an old French story, called *Amis and Amile* that he brought me."

Elizabeth Siddall said, "odd, my noticing the dust on his jacket when he turned over. It was such clean dust as if from chiselling. It was your saying Goldwings, that made him crouch over and fall back, instead of tearing or biting through your hose as you stood straddling him. Or—it fell from his hand. It was a blade as thin as only—Toledo it was—could temper. We were on the edge, weren't we? Not Spain, but the dividing mountains. I knew the knife and I stooped down. He let me take it. It was written on the haft, the name of him who gave it. It was understood, if we were torn asunder, the one left could follow. It was understood, the door was open, if the chain snapped. But it was of so fine welding, it might have been a silk cord. He brought it to me when he brought the dagger—the *Gold Cord*, he called it.

"He was to protect the Circle and I was to maintain it. The *Gold Cord* was the Circle.

"Funny me remembering how gently you dusted his jacket, after he stood up.

"Yes, he was as tall, maybe a fraction taller than I was. Goldwings, you called us."

He was somewhere else. If only there were a clock ticking. He was writing *Golden Wings*. William Morris said, "*then one thrust me through the breast with a spear and then I heard my darling shriek.*"

She said, "it wasn't this time. He had gathered us together in the robe-room behind the altar. We knew of the stone stairway. Don Gregor said, 'you cannot risk that stone,' but Father Magnus said it was no risk. The Knights Credentes were at hand, obedient. Father Magnus would have taken some of the Credentes, but they refused to separate.

"Father Magnus had drilled us but only in the alleys of the crypt. He told us there would be dangers and terrors on the dark stairs and winding corridors. Don Gregor would be the last to go. He was powerful enough to support the stone from within, while from above, the Knights lowered it. It was a key-stone with degrees marked upon it and a fraction of a degree out would give away the passage. The Spaniards would be looking for key-stones and secret markings around the altar and the inner pavement. The Knights would wait by the altar, within the great Cathedral."

Said William Morris, "*unchanged, unchangeable were its walls, whatever else changed about it.*"

"It was hard breathing in the passages and the fear of fainting took me. We had no light. I pressed my hands to my heart and felt the clasp of the gold cord. It was two wings, fashioned after hawk-wings. It was he wore my hawk feather in his cap, out of that story of Pisa that I told you—but it wasn't Pisa. The sea-road where we cantered was below the fortress and that was blocked off by—what did you say his name was?"

"Whose name?" he asked her.

"Him—who burnt the City—blocking it off from the sea. He had burnt our boats. There was no way through the rock-wall that backed the great Cathedral. But Father Magnus had known through Don Gregor, what might happen. Don Gregor was fighting the Inquisition. It would wait at night at the inaccessible (so thought) rock-bay—Don Gregor's ship.

"It was sheer down, but if the goats could reach it, Don Gregor said, we could. Didn't you say there were songs, sung by the goat-boys?"

"*Villanelles*, the shepherd-songs," said William Morris. "It was Simon de Montfort at the time of our Henry III in England, who destroyed the Kathars."

"Kathars?"

"So called from a Greek word meaning to cleanse, to purify. They even called them Puritans, at one time."

"Not like our Puritans, here in England."

"No," said William Morris.

She said, "I must go on and not die, suffocated in the dark. It was, he told me when he gave it to me, the *Gold Cord* of birth, of re-birth, regeneration. The goldwings was the inspiration that went with it. It was inspiration and the same on the haft of the dagger, gold wings chased on that steel. I looked at his dagger, like a cross. I unclasped my wings and laid the chain about his shoulders. I said, 'let me keep the dagger till he comes back.' I said, 'he said, the incantation and the litany would bring him.' Florence was troubadour or poet. We would work together."

"Gold wings across the sea!
Grey light from tree to tree,
Gold hair beside my knee,
I pray thee come to me,
Gold wings!"

She said, "I said to Florence that Gregor might be coming—but there was already, acrid fumes even at that height. They must have got brushwood and poured oil on it. It wasn't the smell of wood—it was—"

William Morris saw the golden head sway forward. She would fall from her chair. He should not have let her go on with the story.

William Morris knelt at her feet. He took the pale face in his hands. "Margaret," he said.

She opened her eyes. She smiled her wan smile. "You are always thinking of Lis."

He said, "yes. You must not tell me any more of the story."

"There's only one thing," she said, "they called those songs *villanelles*, in honour of the goat-boys who showed them the way down."

V

"But it will be easier to tell the story," she said.

He had with difficulty unlatched the lower window. The air was fragrant with the untrimmed climbing roses. He was seated on the window-ledge, his arms about her waist, his head bowed forward. He felt her heart under his burning forehead. It was the first time that he had touched her. He remembered how he had first talked to her on Blackfriars Bridge in the snow. He remembered how he had first heard of this same *Gold Cord* from the letter Gabriel read him, that first time he saw him alone. He remembered that he had talked to her outside St. Bride's, about the Church of Provence, and of a play, *The Albigenses* that Algernon was writing. "St. Bride," he had said, "is that Virgin of the illuminati." It was not the last time he had talked to Lis in the snow.

She was a snow-flower, he had concluded, and she is a white-rose.

"Actually, it was Richmond in *Richard III* who said, 'we will unite the white rose and the red,'" said William Morris. With an effort he lifted his head.

"That Richmond—"

"He might have built this place or started building it. I don't know. I can't remember a thing about Henry VII, except the poet Skelton. But Richmond, I remember. Perhaps because romantically, I associate him with Godfrey. One can't associate Henry VIII with Romance though he was a handsome fellow and may have hunted in the King's Wood, while his brother was still living. In any case, Henry VII or Richmond would be the first king to unite the roses. And—"

She had taken her hands from his shoulders and placed them on his head. "Now, looking like that," she said, "you look like the sketch that Gabriel did of you for Launcelot. Only in the sketch, you're looking down in the boat at Elaine the lily-maid—"

He said, "I am looking up at—" he dared not say it. She would not see him again—or would she? In any case, the story would be lost.

"You must not stand there," he said, "it's cold for mid-summer." He had only, this moment, felt an icy finger.

"In any case," he became brusque, though he could not raise his voice above the husky whisper, "they'll be locking the place soon. We'd better clear out."

"It's not late," she said, "it's the rain makes it dark in here. So you called Godfrey, Richmond?"

He said, "yes. I thought I told you. It seemed odd, our both having a Richmond in the story."

"But my Richmond isn't Walter Deverell," she said, "like you thought. And anyway, only just now, sitting in that chair, I found he was Don Gregor."

"I thought you had worked all that out, before you came here."

"No," she said, "only the goat-path and the rock-hall came true. I wrote down other things, but only that came true. My first story was part true, but I didn't have a name for my out-rider in the forest, nor did I know where it was. It was asking you if you knew geography from flowers made me realise somehow, that it wasn't Pisa." He fastened the window back into its warped frame. He wondered if he dared listen to what she was about to tell him.

She said, "finding I was Flor, helped me more than you can imagine."

He did not dare imagine.

"Well, they got off?" he tried to make it sound like a holiday excursion on the river. She was too tense, altogether. "It's a beautiful story," he said casually. It was all imagination. It was her story, even if he was in it. She didn't know Godfrey. Godfrey was standing before the altar. "This—this Gregor," he said, "reminds me a bit of Godfrey."

"You must think of him then, as Godfrey," she said.

"We'd better look at those pictures," he said, but she was seated again in the old-brocade chair. She said, "there's time for the pictures."

"And time for the story—"

"Yes. You think it's tired me but I get more tired when I get stuck somewhere."

"You mean when you can't find a name for one of your characters? I know that feeling."

"Yes, and just now I said halberd to myself. I think you have it in your poems—or in any case, you mention many times, yourself being killed—just now you mentioned it."

"*Then one thrust me through the breast with a spear.*"

"Yes, almost as if it was—how shall I say? Almost as if the act of being killed with a spear was part of you, like Lyddy and me with Mr. Greenacre and that knife."

"But—but—" It was a long way in time, in space to the Knights Credentes and Godfrey before the altar, and Kent Place off Elephant and Castle in the year of—the year of—"It is August," he said, "it is 1856. It is England. It is Hampton Court. We are sitting in the upper gallery. Don't think of what happened in—whenever it was—"

"You mean Mr. Greenacre. It's part of me. But for the 'very knife he did it with' (poor Harry rushing at me), I might never have picked up, off the stone-floor, the Toledo dagger with the wings, gold on the steel."

"It's what Aristotle said of Greek Tragedy."

She did not pretend to follow him.

"He used the same word, *katharsis*, for the cleansing of the soul; pity and terror were induced by watching the tragedies. Or living them. Watching a play, reading a book or hearing an old mystery-story is living it, if one has the artist's passion. I'm living your story with you."

"You are in the story. That's what I meant by halberd—but would it be different in French?"

"It is a French word," said William Morris, "if I am not mistaken, it's the same word, *hallebarde*. It's a lance or spear." But was it? He thought of single-stick. "I think of a wooden shaft with the metal-point fixed on it. I'm not sure. The point snaps off sometimes, in a fight. But—it's so familiar—"

"It should be," she said, "Halberd—it's your name."

"*Hallebarde*?"

"It was he held the rock to give light on those first dangerous steps. To fall, would be it seemed, to drop down to endless darkness. That's what I meant when I said it tired me more when I got stuck somewhere. It seemed it would crush me across the shoulders—that stone. But why, I wondered, couldn't they have held it from above and lowered it, after he got through?"

"This is pure symbolism, all this."

"But it happened."

"Things are more real in a story than in history."

"But you said it was history, out of a book about *Roma*—"

"*Roma*? The Kathars were the opposite of Rome (the Inquisition), they were the heretics."

"They burnt them, down there." Her voice was colourless, toneless as if it no longer mattered. "It was history, something that happened out of a book, like we read of—" she looked round the room—"well, that first girl—"

"Katherine of Aragon was the first girl," he said.

"I think of her older—wasn't she older and already married? It's confusing, but it doesn't matter. It's just history."

"It is confusing," he said. "I remember that first time I met you, speaking of the Infanta of Castile. But that happened here too, Spain, the Inquisition, *Roma*."

"It happened here too," she said.

"It was Rome, *Roma*," he said, "that really set us against this makeshift Anglo-Catholicism. After hearing High Mass at Beauvais, Ted and I really talked seriously for a time, of going over to Rome. But we couldn't do that. But the other, the Oxford High Church offered (I remember saying to Godfrey) only a plaster rosette after the Rose. We wanted the Rose of Rome (I remember saying), the Rose of England, not a plaster rosette."

"But that's what I'm telling you. He would be after us anywhere, that—"

"Simon de Montfort," said William Morris.

"So it was decided between Donna Anna and Father Magnus, to disguise the worship. We didn't want to fight Rome. It was they who would exterminate us—heretics. I think it was Donna Anna speaking Spanish. Many of our words were similar and there was the scholar's Latin. It was Donna Anna, I like to think, discovered *Roma*. Magnus called her Ma Donna. He would without betrayal, blend with Manfred's circle. But Sicily was far off."

So they got to Sicily.

"I'm not sure about Manfred," he said.

She answered, "nor I—the name came to me, maybe remembering Byron. To save time, sometimes, I take a name, any name that just comes. It was you who held open the door, after Gregor told you he wasn't coming. You would have stayed with them but it meant, the secret might die out, Gregor said, and the sacrifice of the Credentes be in vain. It was to save the Credentes that you consented to follow Magnus. He had chosen you as disciple."

"But I thought we were all disciples."

"Not in the same sense, not in the sense of Magister or Magnus."

"Master—of what?"

"I wouldn't know, I wouldn't know," she raised her hands in a helpless gesture. "They were so mixed down there."

It was what he had told Godfrey. "Saracens," he said, "beside the Greek foundation and the later Romans—and any number of lesser colonies from—well, the Phoenicians to begin with."

"I don't know. I don't know the words—but it was *romantic*—"

"Romance—the Rose."

"Donna Anna said, 'you have only to spell it backwards.'"

He looked at her with the unspoken question.

"*Roma*, I mean," she said, "*Amor*—Love to reverse politics, hate and ambition, the thing the power of Rome had come to stand for. It was not Christ, surely? To reverse ambition but to be more sly than they were, more cautious, more diplomatic. It meant letting the Church go, in its outward semblance. Magnus said we must never be gathered together, all of us together, in one place for public worship. The Credentes had been sacrificed for our illumination. Now, our illumination must save them for eternity. They would be in all tales of chivalry, now in our day, and always."

William Morris walked over to the window. "Gold wings across the sea," he said under his breath, "Grey light from tree to tree," so the mist clung about the box-trees, set out in the W M, William and Mary pattern. "Gold hair beside my knee." He had only to draw her down, down from the dais (so he thought of the old-brocade chair where she sat above him.) "I pray thee come to me." He would bend over like Launcelot in the sketch that Gabriel had done of him. Her white hands were almost pleading, a mermaid. He had called her Undine. She said she was dreamy, *wayy* was her word, out of the herald manual. "Gold wings."

He drummed on the window-pane to discourage her from talking. She had told him too much.

Gold wings across the sea. He beat out the measure on the flawed glass. There was a stain along the window-ledge where rain-water had dripped through. "But this is a good job, this restoration," he thought to himself. "I must ask Street or Philip Webb at the office, who has done it."

He had noted the floor-boards last time. He turned round. "It's a pity this inlay is so warped," he said. He had said that before. She answered as she had done the last time, "but you're not interested."

He crossed the room again and stood before her. He said, "I don't understand, you're bewitched and you've bewitched me. It's like one of these new translations—you've read them? It's that story of Briar-rose in the Sleeping

Palace." He remembered that the Prince had wakened her with a kiss. He turned again, restless, "prowling" as Ted called it. He looked into the other room. "This is only a continuation," he said, "the whole length is one room. I suppose they slung curtains across—just about here, there would be curtains." He seemed to be shouting at her to drown the husky whisper of his thoughts, speaking names out of old chronicles and nearer at hand, here in this very room, Katherine, Anne, Catherine again, Jane, Anne of Cleeves, Catherine—Elizabeth.

He was like the rest of them. He was railing at Rossetti. *Bocca Baciata*? Foolishly, he had asked Ted about it. While the place at Red Lion Square was being done up, Gabriel had asked if he could "make free of the garden." Did she know about it? Ted said it was one of Gabriel's best pictures, so far. A gold head against gold—marigolds. If only Gabriel would re-name the portrait, before she heard about it. Or had she heard about it? A strand of the ragged rose was tapping at the window. Or did he dream it? He would not wake her—no, not Gabriel.

He was indeed Halberd, halberdier, or a young lion as others, as well as Gabriel had called him. You cannot call a picture *Bocca Baciata*, the kissed mouth.

It was one of those occasions that they teased him about at Oxford. He exaggerated to amuse the fellows. When there was no answer to an argument, he would bang his head against the wall and astonish them with simple circus-feats like letting Maclaren's youngest hang on to his hair, while he slowly lifted his great head with the child clinging to what Ted called his lion-locks. Unlike Sampson, he had the locks shorn frequently. He thought it yesterday or the day before that he had been "sheared" as Ted called it. But as he pressed his hands against his forehead, he felt the thick curls heavy on his head. The pelt grew overnight. He would have flung it from him. Now was the moment to bang out his thoughts—but he couldn't do that here. "It's pressing down on my head."

She said, "it's that stone. I was wrong to talk about it. But we got out, following the winding corridors. *We got out.*"

What had she done to him? He was staring at her with those eyes that Gabriel had first written her, were hooded like an eagle. They were slightly uneven, one eyelid drooped lower than the other and that gave him, what Gabriel called, his "veiled look." His look as he stared at her now, was not veiled.

"When do you marry Gabriel?"

She had heard that question before.

She had heard it frequently. She had been officially engaged for—for—actually, Gabriel had asked her formally, courteously and—romantically to marry him, soon after the death of his father. Two years was not so long for an engagement.

"I promised to wait five years." Who had she promised? Answers to this question came automatically, she had given the answer in various ways and to so many people, Mr. Wheeler, Aunt Day (to say nothing of the family), William Rossetti, even trades-people and Mr. Keates, the chemist on the stairway. She knew that Mrs. Birrell would explain that the lady who stayed in Mr. Rossetti's rooms in his absence, was the one he was to marry.

"But you have known Gabriel for almost seven years."

"We have been engaged for two years." She knew this was no answer. "My father does not approve of the engagement."

How fend him off? She had heard that he was given to sudden bouts of anger. Mr. Jones said sometimes, he smashed furniture, to amuse the fellows. It would be awkward if he started on this place—museum-pieces like the chair she sat in. He did it to amuse them, Mr. Jones said. Yes, she had wanted to be an actress. Maybe, he was acting. She was thinking of those queens, here in this very bed and two of them—her head caught in the weir. It was perfectly true, she believed in it explicitly, her theory that terror drove her through the darkness. But the first talk about Godfrey and the ones that followed, had given her a fresh clue. Godfrey was a fencer. She had not made that up. And she judged he was a soldier, though only associated with the Light, as William Morris called the Brigade. Mr. Wheeler had told Lyddy, they were keeping the news back.

She said, "I must confide in you, for your confidence to me, about Lis."

He said, "*Lis*? I tell you, there is no magic needed."

What was he going to tell her?

She had decided to step graciously forward, to stand a moment, surveying the royal bedroom, to remark that the rain was over, to suggest his finding her mantle for her, she had flung it on the work-bench by the far door. They would trail through the orangery, past the sunken-gardens, remarking on the flowers in their seasons. She had marked time by the flowers. *Flor*? Had she made it all up?

She could not get out of her chair.

William Morris said, "*Guenevere* and *The Defence*—what is that? A poem I wrote, hearing a lady maligned by vicious gossip. Did you read *The Defence of Guenevere*, I sent you?"

She did not answer.

"You usually—you always thank me for the poems I send you."

"*The knight who came was Launcelot at good need,*" she said, "but I don't need anybody."

"You—no—you have a host of friends, people who admire you, who admire—"

"Mr. Ruskin wanted to help me because of Gabriel. It's Gabriel who charmed him."

"There's Allingham and the people you told me of at Mrs. Howitt's, Garth Wilkinson, and the others at Oxford, the Acklands—"

"There are plenty of people, now you bring them to my notice. There is also, Barbara Leigh-Smith and Bessie Parkes, besides, I know the Brownings."

The colour had come back to her face.

"That's what I mean, the Brownings." He remembered Godfrey, "you're a substantial fellow like old Browning, just whisk her off to Italy or the South."

"Anyway," she flared back at him, "I was trying to work out that poem. It was confusing."

"It's very clearly stated."

"I don't call that clear."

"*Nevertheless, you, O Sir Gauwain, lie—*"

"I don't mean that part. I mean those pennants—"

"*One of these cloths is heaven, and one hell,*
Now choose one cloth forever."

There were spots of flaming colour in her cheeks now.

"She had no choice," said Elizabeth Siddall.

"There is choice between—Flor and magic."

"Do you mean between Halberd and—"

"You said he set you in a magic-circle, that he burnt out everything outside the circle."

"I said, I was Ophelia, Viola, Sylvia inside the circle. It wasn't only Gabriel. There was Mr. Hunt and Mr. Millais."

"I just said that you had a host of friends."

"I said, outside the circle, I was the scarecrow. I told you, that first time at Chatham Place, that I was the freak at Mrs. Tozer's—"

"I do not have to believe everything you tell me. You see things in a distorting mirror, like the flawed glass in the room downstairs, where we talked the first time—"

"Ghosts, you said ghosts were in the Palace. Why don't you take me out, then?"

"It is what I am saying to you. I said, there was no magic needed. The red-rose is red-and-white in the hedges. You don't need those artificial York-and-Lancasters. The bramble-rose is the red and white united, the faint colour of the berry. The briar-rose that runs wild in our English lanes, is more—"

"Heraldic—yes. That rose we spoke of, in what you called the differences—"

"The seventh son."

"—is a single wild-rose. Must we go on about it? I told you it was a fairy-tale. You said, that wild-rose was barbed, meaning with small leaves. I said, it was thorns, didn't I?"

He said, "yes."

"Why are we waiting, if you want to leave here?"

"You told me you had something to tell me in confidence, in return for my—Lis."

"I have been trying to tell you. It's that story. It was being in love—"

So she was in love.

He walked slowly down the long room. He picked up her mantle and came slowly back. She was standing now, dismissing an audience or waiting for the executioner.

V I

He said, "don't talk about it."

She said, "it's no matter, only I can't lie about it, not to convince myself, that is, and if you can't convince yourself, you can't convince others. It was part of our religion. There was love and—illumination. It was after I found I loved him, that the story really came true. I could imagine Mr. Allingham in the forest, I could imagine you in the forest, but it wasn't you or Mr. Allingham. I could imagine Dr. Wilkinson (even though he was married) but it wasn't Garth Wilkinson, though he was so kind when the Howitts took me to him and he was, as Mr. Howitt first described him, tall and upright as a spear.

"You can see him for yourself—Gregor. Could I be in love with a person I had never seen? I fell in love with him and the terror that Dr. Wilkinson wanted me to talk of, dropped from me. I talked to Dr. Wilkinson about— but I won't ever speak of it again—just the knife, because I can say, when I fell in love with Gregor, the knife that threatened me, turned to the sword that saved me.

"I have tired you out with talking. I'm not tired. I could go on and on talking. To talk about him, makes me forget the other. I wasn't made for a King's mistress nor was I made for a Saint, like Mary Howitt. I like simple things and nice curtains, as much as you do."

He had not lost her. In a way, she was nearer to him than ever.

"Here's a funny thing," he said, "I felt an icy-finger and a rose-spray tapped on the window. I was foolish enough to think it was tapping me a message. You will forgive me? I was thinking of Briar-rose, the Sleeping Princess and I wanted the Prince to wake her. How charming those tales are. Here, it's warm and the clock is ticking and we're just as we always have been, for weeks now, with the tea-cups and the muffins. And it's not an anti-climax. It's a sort of reward."

She was crying, crouched low in her chair, her wide sleeves fallen back from her white arms, while she tried to smother her sobs in the handkerchief that her hands clutched.

He had never seen her cry, nor dreamed of sobs so pitiful.

"You think I made it all up," she said.

"No, but there's a new idea—there are stories waiting. The *Little Mermaid* was simply waiting for one of the Grimm brothers—"

"It's Hans Andersen," she said. He had trapped her neatly.

"There always were these stories. They're in the saga of the north, as well as in the Greek tales of Nereids—or are mermaids Syrens? They're the same stories. I said your story was symbolic. They're all symbolic."

"The worst of it is," she said, "I couldn't say what I did make up. I must have read some of it from one of the Dante books that Gabriel has, or maybe it was a pamphlet that William Rossetti brought in; books and papers kept coming to Mr. Rossetti after his death. There was one called *Forerunners of Dante*. It was in that, I first read of Abélard. There might have been more of the story in that. It was about the group around Dante and how they developed from the Provence poets. Maybe, even Gabriel has a note on it, in the *Vita Nuova*."

Had he really wounded her when he said, "I do not have to believe everything you tell me"? Or had he delivered a more vital blow when he spoke of having heard a lady maligned by vicious gossip? Was she trying to conceal that injury by reference to the story?

"I was not speaking of the story," he said, "when I said that I did not have to believe everything you told me. Faulkner remembered having heard of you in Oxford from one of the fellows who had been to Miss Cardwell's readings. He said they asked you to read the *Blessed Damozel* but that you refused. He said they were wild about you."

"Gabriel made many sketches for the *Blessed Damozel*. He did finish a small picture of me sometimes, because Mr. Ruskin bought them. It was symbolic, I thought, his not finishing that picture that you wanted. He did finish a Saint George and the Princess Sabra. Gregor is a sort of Saint George."

"And you are the Princess Flora in that story."

"I could make out I was a Princess."

She had stopped crying.

"Your tea's cold," he said. He reached over and emptied the cup into the china basin. "These forget-me-nots are funny, aren't they? I am almost certain that we had this very tea-set in our nursery."

"You were a happy family."

"It did not prevent my looking for the Princess in the wild-wood and the hornbeam forest."

"And I suppose I was looking for the Prince too, always watching the ships at Wapping. It was pretty, before they built it over."

That terrible weeping! He knew the desolation, only he took it out in anger.

So she watched the ships at Wapping.

And Gregor was Saint George.

He said, "Godfrey was a bit overwhelming, at times. But I thought of him as Richmond, turning the battle. I didn't go as far back as Saint George."

"Well, I don't mean—Gregor wasn't in that sense, a saintly person. Not a Saint, really. I mean, you could not help but wonder at him. But that's what it does to you, if you are in love with someone. But—"

He was afraid she would start crying again.

"It makes me sad to think how happy I was with Gabriel in Paris. That sounds funny. We made up a story in a place where we sat late, with mirrors and music playing. There was a lady with a gentleman and another sitting near me, who left when he saw them coming. Gabriel even had names for them. He called the lady—she was frail-looking and in white—a Velasquez. He called her a Princess—and then he spoke her name, Madame de Fontenelle."

"*De Fontenelle*?"

"The gentleman was sitting near me. He got up as if to leave, and kissed her hand as he passed through the doorway. Gabriel admired his manners. It is odd how Gabriel sees things. He thought the gentleman whom he called the lover, was a little like Mr. Allingham. I remember how Gabriel said, 'he wears his broadcloth like brocade.' Gabriel can make you see things."

"You love Gabriel?"

"It's like I said. There is love, but being in love is different. They were lovers, those two."

"Did Gabriel know them?"

"He said he had heard mention of a Princess—but I couldn't follow. He went on talking about Venice. But—"

William Morris pushed back his chair, jolting the table with his sudden movement.

He said, "it was Roland and Henri and the *belle-soeur* that you saw in Paris."

"What is the matter?" she said.

He was staring at her as he had done in the Palace.

"That rose-spray tapping on the window."

"It was windy," she said.

"There was no wind. I thought it was a message."

"Messages can come," she said. "Mrs. Howitt had tapping messages when Mr. Howitt was on that voyage to the Gold Coast."

So Godfrey was dead.

(She thought, "Dr. Wilkinson said, one shock begets another, one fear is sometimes displaced on another. Godfrey's sister was Lis. The shock of Lis being thrown in the forest would come back. He said he was looking for a Princess in the forest.")

She said, "I haven't sat with the Howitts for some time. There was quite a group and there was talk too, of what they called comparative religions." She tried to reassemble herself, as she was wont to call it. She had been stricken in the King's bed-chamber. William Morris said, "you see things in a distorting mirror," but what was worse, he had said, "*The Defence*—a poem I wrote, hearing a lady maligned by vicious gossip." That started with Mr. Scott finding her at night, in the arbour with Gabriel while the Howitts were away. It was better to say anything, rather than have him think of Godfrey in India.

She said, "you were upset in the Palace, thinking of that lady that you spoke of being maligned by gossip. She would be glad, I think, to know your defence of her. But there is hardly any use taking an attitude, once people begin talking. It upset Mary Howitt—some gossip about me and Gabriel, being found after dark in their summer-house, while they were away. It would be worse, I told Mary, to try to explain things. I got careless, sitting at odd times for Gabriel. He would want to finish something and I'd stay on, in the studio." She was speaking almost indifferently.

William Morris said, "don't try to minimise my brutality. I was heartless in the same way with Godfrey."

What was it Godfrey had said? It was Godfrey who had first expressed what he, William had only half admitted, Lis was in danger. Was Godfrey saying it again with the rose-spray on the window? And was his own response to chivalry, the challenge,

One of these cloths is heaven, and one hell,
Now choose one cloth for ever.

"People call me clumsy," he said. There was only one thing he could do now.

He did it, as only he could do it.

"That sort of thing does happen," he said. "Drink up your tea, that's right. But you pour, this time."

"There's an old superstition that only one pours," she said. He refilled her cup and managed the milk and sugar. "It's one of Mum's sayings."

"I'm partly Welsh too," he said.

"Yes," said Elizabeth Siddall, "it's like you said, sitting here is a sort of reward. I can't think of anything I'd like better, if I had a wish-ring. I might wish to finish my story, properly that is, with insets of verses."

"Like Aucassan and Nicolette," he said. "It's the same story, the forest and the bower—or summer-house."

"I thought I would die, remembering," she said, "till you remarked in that summer-house (the time before the island) on elderberry-flower and honeysuckle fragrance blended."

"Godfrey heard the same story from Roland."

"You think then, that was Roland that I saw in Paris?"

"I know that it was Roland."

"I don't think Gabriel knew his name."

"But his name is de Fontenelle."

"I don't follow."

"It was his *belle-soeur*, his sister-in-law. She was married to his brother, Henri. They were all de Fontenelles."

"I can't get over Gabriel knowing of them. I don't think he knew them."

"There was a summer-house or boat-house on the river, and I even remember thinking there might be a sandy island, an eyot, when Godfrey told the story to me. They met there, Roland and Valérie, his *belle-soeur*, and a friend of hers, Aurélie, whom she wanted Roland to marry."

"Just those three?"

"There had been others. It was a sort of circle. Rather like our Brotherhood. But like our Brotherhood, the original group had dwindled down or concentrated out (like the jewel in the matrix) to just three. There were eight of us, in the beginning, well—the fellows are all there but Godfrey and I renewed the Brotherhood or re-created it, or crystallized out. Though I didn't know Roland and Valérie, they were a part of it."

"And the other—the girl you speak of?"

"Godfrey didn't say so and obviously, Roland wouldn't. But Valérie must have been desperate. She wanted Roland to marry Aurélie, so that they could all go about together. Godfrey said that Roland said, Valérie was burning out like a white candle. Obviously, Valérie was in love with Roland."

"*Is* in love with him, from what I could see from that glimpse of her—burnt out but lighted inside. But what became of Aurelia?"

"Godfrey said that Roland said, she had friends in the *Faubourg*—the—the fashionable quarter and that *tables parlants* were all the rage in Paris. She would find another circle. She was, Roland had told Godfrey, *oeillet*, carnation, fragrant and worldly."

"And did he have a flower for Valérie?"

"He said she was a white camellia." William Morris had forgotten that it was he himself who said it.

"It's like her. But their being in that summer-house is hardly the same as me and Gabriel in the Hermitage arbour-room at night, with the family away."

"Well, I don't know how often or when they went there—"

"You mean there was gossip?"

"Roland only—well, one had to get the story from the things he didn't tell me—or tell Godfrey rather. And Godfrey may not have told me the whole story."

"I see."

"It's this way," said William Morris, "these circles go on, dimming at the edges, dispersing or growing fainter—"

"Like a pebble in a pond."

"—and the centre crystallizes like the pebble—only it's a jewel."

Mercifully, he had only to get out his pipe now. The worst was over.

"Do you think those people noticed, who just left?" she said.

"It wouldn't matter," he said, "but they didn't notice."

"You had your back to them. You wouldn't see them."

"And they wouldn't see you, crouched in the corner."

She was afraid—she was afraid of people.

"But nothing matters," he said, "because—"

"Being in love makes people careless."

"No," he said, "when love crystallizes out or contracts—how shall I say it?—to its single flame, one is no longer careless. But there are other dangers. As you said, Valérie was burnt out but lighted inside. Godfrey was a flame in crystal. One could not get him away, without smashing the crystal."

"Get him away?"

"He had messages from a table. It was Roland introduced him to what he called the *télégraph de Dieu* or talking table."

"Your—your Galahad Order had the talking table?"

"Only for experiment in old Faulkner's rooms at Pembroke. Ted and Dix—one of the fellows, Dixon—began rapping, so we stopped it. But Godfrey and I continued alone. Godfrey and his brother Vernon had apparently taken the matter seriously when Roland introduced them to the table."

"Then, there was Vernon, as well as you and Godfrey?"

"No. Vernon is at Cambridge. He was helping with the magazine. But anyway, Roland only confided in Godfrey after Vernon had left. It was the summer when I was with Ted at Beauvais. Roland was staying with them at Ayton—"

"That was the King's Wood?"

William Morris said, "yes." He remembered how Godfrey had said the message would die somehow, unless you shared it.

But Roland was convinced that Valérie would die if she went on alone. And Roland had tried to dissuade Godfrey.

He said, "in the old chronicles, they say that Martyrdom is a Sacrament."

"Why do you say that?"

The cloud was lifting, the heavy weight on his head—that symbolic stone before the altar.

"I was thinking of your story. You needn't make a Saint George of your Gregor. He is the hero in the legend; the Greeks worshipped heroes. But there is no need of worship. It's a Sacrament that should be remembered."

VII

He wouldn't hear, not yet, she had told him. But he thought he knew as much as Mr. Joseph Wheeler, and maybe a little more about communications with the East India Company. Godfrey had a way of disappearing in mid-term, William had thought nothing of it. There was no date on the letter, forwarded by Vernon Lushington from Cambridge. There was no indication of where the letter had been written. The original letter to Vernon, enclosing his own note, might even have come from Marseilles. At that, Vernon might have been asked to hold it over. News would leak through, in any case, if it were bad news. India! He almost envied Godfrey. He thought of rugs, the shawl his mother cherished, one of the early imported cashmeres. He remembered his silk-worms.

Why think of India in terms of disaster? And hadn't Godfrey said of the messages or the senders of them, "not always disembodied, from what Roland said." That was the first talk in Godfrey's room. There was no use asking at Balliol, what has become of Lushington? If Godfrey had covered his tracks, there must be a reason for it. In any case, he William had his story. It was her story.

He doubted if she were, as she said, "in love." That is, he doubted if her love or inspiration or illumination burnt her out like Valérie, like Godfrey. Well, there was still Roland, balanced and logical (he saw him), impetuous, romantic, devoted, devout, loyal. He was, if you will, a survivor of a vanished France. France, however you look at it, had been destroyed by revolution and by conquest. But there were a few left.

Roland—wasn't the other chap, Oliver?

William had called himself Oliver, sometimes Olivier. But he felt now, it might have been an unconscious association. He must have known from the beginning, that Godfrey would leave him.

Was it Charlemagne? There was a narrow defile or valley—Ronceveau, Roncevalle?—the name eluded him. Did it matter? There was a trumpet sounding. But his story had Sicily for its setting and Count Robert for its champion.

Why Robert? She had said Manfred.

It was an island-story, and however he might try, he could not get away from Shakespeare. There was a Duke of Sicily or Count, in one of the plays, wasn't there? He couldn't remember. But he saw Algernon and Lis, or Florence and Flor in the old *Twelfth Night* character. They were of a size, they were of an age; she would crop off her over-abundant length of mermaid tresses. She had (her own story) taken his dagger and flung her chain, in the traditional Rosalind gesture, round his neck, "wear this for me." If Shakespeare hadn't written her story, who had? It was, as he had said, one of those stories, waiting to be written. Viola was her first part or character, and Deverell who chose it for her, had wanted to be an actor. It was natural to see the thing, in retrospect, in the form of a play.

She couldn't write it. She hadn't the detachment, the drive. Her dream might take her deeper, further, as a mermaid might dive down. But he was the helmsman, the mariner aware of danger. She would slide off or around jagged reefs that would rip open his keel. She was not aware of the treasure that she gathered from the depth. Viola—it was a flower really, one of her many Flor names.

Or he was a fisherman, wading deeper, deeper with the thick or fine mesh, woven by his own hands.

The Fisher King—that was another of the Grail stories, with threats of devastation, war and famine.

They called this the Peace year, and however he might try to steel himself against these vagrant rumours, he could not help remembering half-whispered confidences in their drawing-room after dinner. He had a "safe place" with a book, on the sofa in the corner. His father and Mr. Worthington or Mr. Ellis from the city, would inevitably move over from the fireplace, with their coffee-cups and cigars, and talk of "India and the Company."

It was part of adventure, Drake, Hawkins, Raleigh. William Morris had derided what he called the out-moded Byronic gesture of Carew and his fellows. It was no good. He didn't know what intrigue was on foot, what danger to the East India Company. But there had always been whispered danger.

He had muttered to himself, while Godfrey in the candlelight, lifted the decanter to re-fill their glasses, "Carew, some damned Elizabethan or Love-lace fellow." So was Godfrey! You couldn't break their Brotherhood, "cup-bearer to King Charles, damned Royalist."

But there was another Brotherhood and Godfrey was of it, with his lyric translations of de Fontenelle's findings at the *Bibliothèque*. You might say that every cavalier, every King's gentleman was a rhymester, as he was a swordsman by profession. There was one gentleman—hardly of their com-pany—whose game was only one remove from single-stick. He was an ar-cher, like every stable-boy on the common.

He was a vagrant, a gypsy, a strolling-player.

William Morris never talked of William Shakespeare except to challenge him, as he had challenged Godfrey.

You would die of worship if you let yourself go.

You would never write another line.

He had said to Godfrey, if he was anybody, he was Giles the forester, in his play.

He had said that Shakespeare had mapped out all enchantment.

But there was a gap, those years between. Chaucer belonged to the mid-dle-ages; there was a tradition that Chaucer had met Petrarch at Padua. Dante—Petrarch—Chaucer. Before Dante, the troubadours.

Yes, they went to Sicily.

It was, he told himself, a walled city. She had not spoken of the bay-blossom but the crushed fragrance of the bay-leaf. It was winter. Algernon had spoken of Nordic runes for his Provence play. It had seemed a contra-diction. But the Vikings were sea-rovers. Ruskin had spoken of a stone lion in Venice, scratched with the names of Sea-kings.

He had thought of Vikings and the singers of Provence as widely sepa-rated in time and in space.

But were they? What did he know of either? And nearer home, the Nor-mans were Norsemen. Duke Robert was a Norman.

You could get (in Algernon's play) a migrant Norse Chief meeting his counterpart in Robert of Sicily. But this was not Algernon's play, though Algernon had first inspired him with his talk of Vikings influencing or being influenced by the singers of Provence.

There were both Southern French and Northern French in Sicily—Franks.

There were the earlier settlements of Greeks and Romans. Sicily was con-quered by Duke Robert. Who conquered England?

The story was later than Duke William. He had told her (Flor) that Simon de Montfort was a contemporary of the Plantagenet Henry III. Henry II was the father of Richard Lion-heart. They were still sea-rovers.

But Eleanor, Richard's mother, if he was not mistaken, was of the province (Provence). They met even here in England, the Viking and the troubadour. One did not have to go to Sicily to find the School of Love challenged by the Conqueror.

But it was the School that challenged the Conqueror, Robert in Sicily.

He himself was Hallebarde. Even in Provence, you may have a Viking forebear. He was Hal; he was of the Knights Credentes, Halberd or Hallebarde.

He was of the School, as they had already come to call the Church in England. He was Hal the Bard, with the *illuminati*.

Had they ever forgotten? He did not think so. He had said to Godfrey (almost his last words to him), "it's all there, all this, everything—the Templars, Shakespeare, Raleigh."

It was in answer to Godfrey's question, "The School of Night?"

They went by contradiction, *renversé*. It must have been the School of Light.

Its law was preserved in the set metres of *lai* and *chanson*. No doubt, to the initiate, there were still further inner readings in the *vers* or *verset*.

Runic—divinatory.

But we need not spoil the texture of the *verset* to understand the message, any more than it is necessary to pull a rose to pieces to get at its secret.

Flor—adore—before—door—floret—verset.

Ships sail through the Heaven
    With red banners dress'd,
Carrying the planets seven
    To see the white breast
    Mariae Virginis.

His were nursery-rhymes. He had been the first to say so. But sometimes,

Two red roses across the moon,

he could equally say that the words were an invocation.

Bay strengthens our bastion
    The bay-branch in leaf,
Bearing the seed to leaven
Sorrow and all grief,
    Flor Amoris.

The rock-way is open
    Through rock-cleft and cave,
The dark stone is broken
That covered the grave,
    Flor Amoris.

She had said, "you make it sad, that Yoland, *The graves stand grey in a row.*" And when they were speaking of the messages, that last time in Godfrey's room, Godfrey had said he imagined their Latin carved on old stones. "Tomb-stones?" was William's inevitable rejoinder but Godfrey had said, "milestones." Their few abbreviated words might almost have been clock-numbers or a motto on a sun-dial,

TEMP. LUM. IN.   TEMP. OMN. U   N   .

Well, there was the School of Night, of Light, *Lumen.*

He believed the old Temple, near the Law Courts was originally octagonal, like Godfrey's tower-room. The Templars were dispersed and disbanded by the Inquisition. He had spoken of them and the Knights of Malta with Godfrey. The Knights of Malta were the Knights Credentes.

Godfrey had communicated with his friend Carew. No doubt, the Knights had established some form of communication. William believed that was their secret and their Brotherhood.

It was again, a far cry from the Knights Credentes in Malta and Provence, to the new vulgar elegance of Paris. But oddly, it was from Paris that the *table parlant* had come to Godfrey. There were three grades, degrees or divisions. There were the merely mondaine, carrying social intercourse into a vague, unreliable dream-world. There were the new investigators, Faraday and other serious technical experimentors in the higher vibrations, telepathy and so on. There was a final group, if group it could be called, so far, he had found only two—individuals of outstanding distinction, de Fontenelle and Godfrey.

The *lai*, the *villanelle* and *roundel* had something to do with it. She had said, names make a difference. How well he knew that! There was an inevitability about rhyme and assonance that he sometimes felt could not be wholly accidental. It was inevitable that seven should rhyme with heaven. *This is the tune of the Seven Towers,* he had written and *Therefore, said fair Yoland of the flowers.* Flowers, towers, bowers. He was glad he had remembered Aucassan and Nicolette and the wattled flower-arbour in the woods. It was Aucassan and Nicolette? He had been surprised when he got back to his rooms, after their last meeting, to find he had been mistaken about *Amis and Amile.* There were two stories of the period. Florence was in *The Tale of King Florus and the Fair Jehane.* He had referred to himself as Florian, when she first spoke of Flor.

Florence was the son of King Floris and Floria was his daughter.

There was Jehane too. Perhaps it was because of Jehane that he had confused the stories. He wanted a different ending for his *Golden Wings.*

I cannot stay here all alone,
Or meet their happy faces here,
And wretchedly I have no fear;
A little while, and I am gone.

But she had fear. She was still wretchedly obsessed.

Why has she a broken sword?
  Mary! She is slain outright—

that was the end of *Tall Jehane of Castel-beau.*

He had called her Jehane in *Golden Wings.*

But Jehane was someone else now. He did not know who.

Jehane was the friend or companion of Hallebarde in the story. In the original tale, she was the wife of the King. In this story, she might be the sister of Florus.

She was not Margaret, not de Liliis, not Alys.

It was through no lack of understanding her nightmare. He understood only too well. He could not lure her out of her magic circle, he must not be dragged into it. He had been warned by a rose-spray tapping on the window of a notoriously haunted Palace, in its very Bluebeard chamber. It was her way of telling fortunes.

He had flung wide his nets. If only she were a mermaid. Her humanity was at war with the fiction woven round her. Perhaps, he had helped weave this fiction but he had at the same time (ruthlessly if you will), offered the sword that would have severed the fatal Gordian knot.

He would have saved her. He had said, "when do you marry Gabriel?"

He had written poems to her and although the stories were for the most part, written before he met her, she was in the stories.

But "one thrust me through the breast with a spear," in *Golden Wings*, and though "before them lay a great space of flowers" in *The Hollow Land*, it was after his death, her death. He would find "a great space of flowers" for the Fair Jehane and Hallebarde, before death.

In *Svend*, he had written of ghastly wounds and streets red with blood. There was *Gertha* in the field of battle, "something very horrible to gaze at, to pass over." Olaf the King finds her when she enters the circle of trees, but Olaf is a ghost and after embracing Olaf, Gertha dies. "The blue speedwell kissed her white cheek." Hallebarde and the Fair Jehane must meet, this side of the grave.

A Dream ends with "the moon shining on the tomb, throwing fair colours on it from the painted glass," and Walter in the *Unknown Church*, dies, having dedicated twenty years of his life, to chiselling the stone-lilies on the tomb of Margaret and Amyot.

Lis. He might have saved her.

They were mile-stones, not tomb-stones, Godfrey had said.

PART V

I

"I see you have succumbed at last," said Gabriel.

"A fellow must rest sometimes."

"I don't mean that."

"You mean my blue shirt?"

"Partly. I was thinking of your brushes."

"Brushes?"

"You've found a use at last, for your white ties."

"That was Ted's idea."

"I doubt it. Ted is not eccentric nor does he encourage eccentricity in others. He works like a *vernisseur*. He'd never hang his brushes in the window on a white tie. It's not done. He's not a rebel. There's no rebellion in him. He's a disciple, a follower, an imitator—"

"I thought you liked Ted's work."

"So I do. But he would never order a cupboard or a sideboard or a settle or whatever you call this thing, until he'd taken the measurements of the door it was to come in by. This will never be forgotten."

"No," said William Morris.

"It will always be held against you, this—"

"It was my first essay at designing furniture."

"It's not furniture, it's a luggage van. It's like you. It's as long as it's broad. It's clumsy. It's unusual. I ask myself, is it a barn? Is it an Ark? What made you think of it, anyway?"

"We had to have furniture. You admired the table."

"That's sheer refectory. Perhaps you're right. Perhaps it's all monastic. But I prefer the stuffiness of the Bishop's palace, heavy velvets, brocades— Bill calls me a *brocanteur*—candelabra—"

"Why do you waste your good paint then, on those doors?"

"They're not my paints, they're Ted's."

"I've heard you called an indolent fellow. Do you never stop work?"

"My salutation," said Gabriel Rossetti.

Gabriel had chosen to paint the *Salutation of Beatrice*, on one of the doors of the already famous settle that had had to be dismantled before it could enter the door of No. 17, Red Lion Square. It had three shutters over the seat. Gabriel Rossetti remembered Walter Deverell. He might even now be standing behind his shoulder. "I'm sorry Gabriel, but I can't kick you out." Deverell might be speaking to him. He might be speaking to Deverell. The pale wraith was standing on the *estrade*, the Wedgwood-blue, discarded from Aunt Charlotte's drawing-room, did not quite match her eyes. She stood behind him. But that was another picture. It was the *Blessed Damozel* that she said he hadn't thanked her for. He had never thanked Lizzie.

"Speaking of salutation," said Gabriel, still kneeling on the broad seat of the settle, "don't you like Lizzie?"

William Morris did not answer.

Gabriel Rossetti turned, "I asked you a question," he said.

William Morris said, "I heard you." The blue shirt and the rough beard did not alter his manner; on the other hand, they seemed to emphasize an Oxford insolence that Gabriel had not noticed while Morris was at Oxford. William Morris was more assured, he seemed much older though it was less than a year ago that he and Edward Burne-Jones had moved into Red Lion Square. Said Rossetti, "the first sketch I did of Lizzie was in this studio. It was Deverell's place though I elbowed my way in."

"So Ted told me, but he didn't put it that way."

"Ted tells you everything?"

William Morris did not answer.

"No doubt, Ted told you why Lizzie swep' out and went to live in Hampstead. Did you see Lizzie in Spring Cottage? You might have popped in after a judicious, professional visit to Keats's House—only two minutes walk around the corner. You are interested, I believe, in restoration—or should I say preservation?" Gabriel stepped back as if to view the blocked-in blue and crimson on the wooden panel. William Morris remained stretched in what Gabriel had called (at their first talk in Chatham Place) undergraduate abandon. Morris had an air of independence which he had lacked while he was in Street's office. He had given up the office and spent his nights and days at life-classes and poring over old manuscripts and records. Gabriel did not spoil his gesture, his stage-business, by too prolonged a survey of the panel. "*Fra Pace*," he said, "was done in X—a sort of chess-board idea, I was working on. I built the *Return of Tibullus to Delia* on single arches. It was a later development, experimental really. *Hamlet* and *Ophelia* and *Cassandra* (the first ones) were pure chess-board. Would water-colour technique take better on this board? Do you remember *Galahad at the Shrine, The Blue Closet, The Tune of the Seven Towers, The Marriage of Saint George*—all water-colours. Will a wooden panel go with my first *Dante's Dream*? To whom belongs the panel? It's your Ark. If I paint my sublime masterpiece on its front-door, is the Ark mine?" Rossetti turned round. "But I asked you some time back, another question."

"I remember *The Tune of the Seven Towers*," said William Morris.

"Your poem was my inspiration—perhaps it is only fair, that my inspiration should be your poem."

"You have many inspirations," said William Morris.

"Man does not live by bread alone," said Gabriel, "and contrariwise— well, inspiration, as I had occasion once to tell you, does not wear me out. It wears out other people. Do you remember my speaking of inspiration, the first time I saw you?"

"I remember everything you said, if you mean the first time I saw you alone."

"Which being the case, why should you assiduously avoid the opportunity of seeing me alone, since?"

"Since when?"

"Since the beginning."

"There were too many people about."

"You mean Gus?"

"I can't say that I have anything against him."

"I have. But all that in time. By what miracle, are we alone here?"

"Ted had those commissions. Didn't you ask him to go to Oxford?"

"Where's Red Lion Mary?"

"I told Mary she could have the day off."

"Expecting—anybody?"

William Morris did not answer.

"But to return to the question," said Gabriel. "What came between you and Lizzie?"

Was this fencing? Was this single-stick? William Morris heaved out of the low chair.

"Don't prowl," said Rossetti, "you make me nervous. I was painting and you were prowling that first time I saw you alone. 'Let by-gones be,' says

Mrs. Birrell when she smashes my blue bowl—a collector's item, you can't replace. Canton? Ming? No, that's *aubergine*, a wonderful word—there's no English for it. I have heard it translated mad-apple. You couldn't call *aubergine*, egg-plant. Melon-gourd perhaps, suggests it better? You're not interested in china?"

Rossetti poised his brush like a toreador about to fling the dart. Why wouldn't the fellow answer? It's true, Morris could if he wished, turn at any moment and trample his tormentor. Rossetti studied his palette. He examined his brush, turned to the table and carefully chose another. Then he laid down the palette. "I can ask you," he said, "what I asked Ruskin, after I came back from Paris. Lizzie and I were in Paris. She was happy. No doubt, she told you we had been to Paris."

"Yes," said Morris.

"I advise you to sit down," said Rossetti. "I wish to do the prowling. I hold forth to a vast assembly. My father wrote librettos for Rossini. My father was at one time, curator of marbles and bronzes at the Naples museum. There were the Carbonari. There was proscription. Gabriele Rossetti the poet, was hidden in the slums of Naples. An English gentlewoman, one Lady Moore, inquired diligently for the poet. Why? He might have died there. He was brought to Malta. The London Foreign Office wouldn't have suspects stationed on the still seething island. Why must Gabriele leave Malta? He could live in England. Did Gabriele Rossetti patriot, poet, art-expert and musical collaborator want to live in England? Well, he could live, anyway. Sir Graham Moore brought him to Spithead in 1824. Rossetti (Gabriele) was then almost forty. He had left his heart's dream in Malta. He and one John Hookham Frere had uncovered between them, the clue to Dante's entire system. Don't ask me what the clue was. They never met after. They corresponded for twenty years in a sort of code that neither Bill nor I can make head or tail of."

"This is all very interesting," said William Morris dryly.

"You are not interested. Do you care for Dante? But that is not what I want to ask you. I want to ask you what I asked Ruskin when I returned from Paris. That was last November. Was it? Or November before last? It was the winter you blew in, out of the snow. But that was January. It was, it turned out, the Peace Year. Can you work that out?"

"No," said Morris. He bit off the monosyllable.

"Don't growl at me," said Rossetti. "Where are your beastly matches? Since you won't sit down, I'll lean against the table. Or, thank you—the settle—"

He went on, "Have you ever had small-pox?"

William Morris was looking out of the window. He did not turn round. "I remember every word of that first talk," said Rossetti. "Must it be the last talk?" Still, Morris did not answer. "I asked if anyone had painted your mug and what as. I've done it since, as Lancelot before you grew your beard. There was a chance then, for chatting, only Ted interrupted—or was it Lizzie? She was in and out, then. She wasn't so unhappy. What unhinged her was Ted talking about an old plan you'd once had. It wasn't exactly my idea, but she blamed me. We would all get together, on the lines of some scheme you'd mapped out at Oxford."

"Thelema," Morris condescended to growl. "Abbey of Thelema."

"A sort of monastic order—yes—but with wives. Ted's Lady Greensleeves was already in love with a place she'd found in Kensington—I think it was—somewhere. Cedar Lodge or Cedar Villa—we'd call it Cedar Abbey. I had been over the ground so many times with Lizzie. The last time was in Paris. I concluded that it bored her—the idea of getting married. I was for chucking it all here and taking her to—"

William Morris turned round. Rossetti wanted to tell him something. He couldn't say it. Morris knew the feeling.

"Where did you want to take her?"

"Florence," said Gabriel Rossetti.

"Why didn't you go to Florence?"

"Why? Why? Why? Why did I come back to England? Why did I let Lizzie come back?"

"I am glad you came back," said William Morris. The words caught in his throat but he had to say them. He produced a box of matches. He laid it on the table. Gabriel did not see it. "When I close my eyes, I see things in my head, here," said Gabriel. He beat at his forehead with the inner wrist-bones. His hands were clenched, showing the tendons as Morris stood above him. He wanted to lay his hand on the bowed head. "I never had small-pox," said William Morris.

"The Polidoris were very kind," said Gabriel. He was seated in the unpainted corner of the settle. He leaned his head back, against the bare wood. His eyes were still closed. "Aunt Charlotte got her doctor to say it was chicken-pox. Aunt Charlotte is a saint, really. Gabriel must be moved before the other children caught it. But when the fight came, it was Tibbie who won the battle. She wasn't Tibbie, then. I can't even remember her name. She married Tibbs afterwards. She was a country-girl. She would have the young gentleman in her own bed-room, apart from the rest of the house.

It wasn't right with people in and out like, and Madame with her church-work. But I didn't mean to say this. We were talking about Ruskin."

"We were talking about the Abbey scheme."

"It came back to Hunt and Annie Miller. How could anyone suggest, Lizzie said, that she could live with Annie Miller? God—Annie Miller! She knew it wasn't Annie Miller—but how tell her? How tell her that I raved in the night and a country-girl with braids like ripe corn lay down beside me . . . would anyone believe me?"

"No one," said William Morris. "No one knows what children go through."

"The brat in me cries in the night—and there's—But I couldn't tell Lizzie. She might get small-pox. That's how my mind works."

Rossetti opened his eyes. They were wide, staring, the grey iris blotted out with the black pupil. "That's Lilith, that's Adam's first wife. You know all about it," said Gabriel Rossetti.

William Morris was still standing by the table. The black pupils seemed to grow larger; in a moment, unless he broke the tension, he felt the pupils would be superimposed on one another and he would be staring into a single circle. He would be hypnotized, caught in a luminous black crystal. The curious lids over his own eyes quivered. He shut his eyes upon ordinary darkness. Out of the crystal, the voice was speaking.

"Lizzie. Do you know her name, really? She is Blanchelys out of my *Staff and Script*. Do you remember? The other is Lilith from *Eden Bower*. You've read my poetry?"

Morris turned, as if looking toward the window. He propped himself against the table, his eyes still closed. "I remember," he said, "I have read your poetry. I had occasion one day, to speak of Algernon. I said Algernon's poetry was only to be compared with Shelley. I meant, he had no living rival. I meant it or thought I meant it. But Algernon—how shall I say? There is hope for Algernon."

"There is no hope for Rossetti?"

"None. Not an atom. And there is no hope for those who give in to Rossetti."

"Abandon hope, all ye who enter here."

"There was something about her. I had seen her somewhere. I had written about her in my first poems and romances. She answers the description. You invent her—or imagine her—she appears. It's startling. You didn't want the picture. It was an unfinished sketch in *pervenche* blue—"

"I called it Wedgwood," said Rossetti.

"It was propped on the floor behind the curtain, that first time I came in, out of the snow. It was January, the Peace Year, as you say. I was looking for something and I found it. You asked if I was seeing things. I was seeing the picture. You didn't want it. Later, it came to life again, unexpectedly, and you said, 'I wondered where that frame had got to.' You only wanted the frame, you didn't want the picture.

"But she would not give me the picture. She was saving it. I thought she was saving it for you. But she said she was in love with someone—someone else—not Gabriel—"

"She told me the same in Paris."

"I didn't want to intrude. I thought that I could save her. I called her Lis, she never knew it—she thought Lis was the sister of—of a friend. He's in India. He may be dead, too."

"Dead—*too?*"

"His sister was killed in an accident. He thought he was responsible. He communicated with his sister—for a time, that is. He was concerned—how shall I say it? He was in a way, connected with the Light Brigade. He lost—well, many friends, and a certain friend who was to have married his sister. He lost his—well, you might say, his generation. He said the Light took heavy toll of the—Ayton, it was—hunting-families. He communicated with this Carew who was to have married his sister."

And why was he telling this to Gabriel Rossetti?

He opened his eyes to the room and the room outline. It was a high studio-room. There was the precious north-light that Gabriel had spoken of, in the beginning. There were the other windows. There were the three rooms, a bedroom and another. Framed in squares, like separate painted pictures, or set there in stained-glass, was the light, luminous on the tangle of the garden—thorn-bushes, marigolds and lilies.

"That you should call her Blanchelys and that I should call her Lis, is no accident," said William Morris.

"There is no accident," said Gabriel. "That's what I was working out or trying to work out, with my chess-pieces. But you can only see the pattern after the game is over. I was born in England. You have heard of Little Italy? Soho, I mean. There was the delicious smell of onions; garlic was a passion of my father. Does garlic go with Dante? What would you do, if it went round, whispered from Lavinia (my mother) to Maria (my elder sister), from Maria to Gaby, from Gab to Bill, from Bill to little Christie? What would you do, I mean, if Father Gavazzi and Guiseppe Mazzini both turned up together? You could sit on the floor with your crayons. We had the answer. It was Maria's idea. 'Say, yes we have had our supper and whisper under your breath (when Father Gavazzi asks you), yesterday.' It wasn't a lie, then. Perhaps Rolandi who dealt in old books, or the coal-man Faro, might drop in at the same time. 'We've had our supper,' was a code-word—pass friend. Faro and Rolandi would sit with us by the fire-place. We were always hungry. So were Faro and Rolandi.

"There had been the grand tour before Napoleon but Gabriele Rossetti came in too late for aristocratic coaching. But there was a new flutter and sympathy for Italians in England, due to the attempted revolution and the prison stories. Gabriele had gout. Gabriele took snuff. It was suggested if he called himself *cavaliere*, he might ask ten bob for a lesson. He taught during the day and worked all night at Dante.

"I was going to ask you a question, the same question I asked Ruskin when I first came back from Paris. But that question can wait. I have another question.

"Why did Gabriele Rossetti leave Malta? Why was I born in England? Why did I shriek in the night, 'they don't understand, they don't understand'? I had forgotten my English. In my delirium, I thought I was lost. I was lost. I cried to an English country-girl in Italian, but she understood me. I am speaking a strange language to you who do not know Italian, but you understand me.

"I have found the clue to something that is more important than I or you or—Lizzie. Yet, it is I and you and Lizzie. It is others but I can't collect them—or recollect them. What did you say your friend's name was?"

"I didn't say," said William Morris, "but his name is Lushington, Godfrey Lushington." He added, "there was another chap, Rolando."

"What I mean," said Gabriel, "art is being hungry. When you're starved, you can paint a picture. The two go together. Deverell wasn't starved, not in that sense. But they say I killed him."

"That is impossible."

"It was his studio. Lizzie was his model. Lizzie wouldn't come here. She said the place was haunted. She went off to Matlock, after she left Hampstead. I won't ask her to come back. Lizzie is at heart, conservative. She winds the clock."

William Morris saw them sitting in a row, watching the clock. Their eyes widen and grow anxious as the bell rings. "It's only the newspaper boy," says Maria. "It's maybe, the man with the monkey—" "St-st," says Gabriel, "you mustn't speak of the man with the monkey, Willum. He left a message last time." It was Lavinia, "come children, say good-evening to Father—" What did Gabriel say his name was?

"I see it all so clearly," said William Morris, "ah—er—that is—Father—what did you say his name was?"

"You mean Gavazzi? I was talking about Lizzie."

"I understood she went to Matlock. I don't know the country. I gather, it's cliffs and downs, rather rough and rugged—north Derbyshire?"

Gabriel said, "I read some of her letters to Ted—parts of them—before you left Street's office. In fact, as you know, my spending so much of my time here with—Ted, was actually what sent her off to Hampstead."

"I may have sent her off to Hampstead. We had a sort of—sort of—well, explosion on my part in Hampton Court, last summer. It was my fault. I led her on to tell a story. It upset her. It was a story she started, she said, before she went to France. I first heard of it from the letter that you read to me that first evening I blew in. I was curious about the story. I saw Miss—ah, Lis, as I called her, perhaps a dozen times altogether, counting the times I met her at Chatham Place. I didn't see her again after—I wrote a number of times with suggestions for the story, but she ignored my last letters. I heard from Ted that she seemed better (from your account) and was visiting Sheffield and seeing some of the old places in the neighbourhood. I couldn't go on with the story. It was her story. It was troubadours before Dante. Algernon started it really—at least, as far as I was concerned, with some books he lent me, old French and a play he wanted to write. He doesn't seem to have gone on with it. It seems to evade everybody. But it's the same story."

"Do you mean—"

"He called it *The Albigenses*."

"Do you mean to tell me that your little Algernon has blundered onto the Albigensians?"

"Why blundered?

"It's an *impasse*. No one gets any further."

"Any further than—what?"

"Why the idea, the title, the beginning—the what do you call it—the prologue."

"She called her story, you remember, *Gold Cord*."

"She would, somehow," drawled Gabriel Rossetti.

He went over to the window. The light was fading on the lilies, and the marigolds were turned in on themselves like marsh-buds lost in their thick leaves. Gabriel did not want to talk about the Albigensians, the troubadours, the Kathars. It was all in Dante. How talk about it to a fellow who didn't know Italian? He would have to explain from the beginning. It was madness. And it was—it was—it was his father's Dante.

"You think me impertinent," said William Morris, "to come crashing in on—on—"

Gabriel did not answer. Then (but toward the window and half whispered), "*l'amor che move il sole e l'altre stelle.*"

"*What—*" said William Morris.

It was very still in the room.

Gabriel thought, "Oh God, what would I not give to have the answer." There might be hope yet, though they had gone over the papers, and studied the cramped notes and entrances in their father's earliest edition and the later printings of the *Commedia*. This was his country. Lizzie might have picked up a few crumbs, hearing him and Bill shouting at one another. Gabriel forgot that when he and his brother argued about Dante, they shouted in Italian.

"It was the names," said William Morris. He could let it go now. He had offended Gabriel. He could let this go now, but he couldn't . . . not now. He had committed himself to the story, to Lis and the *Gold Cord* that bound them, that bound them all together. Gabriel was whispering Italian.

"What are you saying, Gabriel?"

"*L'amor che move il sole e l'altre stelle,*" said Gabriel.

II

"I don't have to borrow money," said Rossetti, "commissions are rolling in, but I've lost my model. Can you work that out?"

"No," said William Morris. But he was lost now.

"I think I've heard of—er—Lushington. I must have met him."

"I don't think so."

"I'm sure I've met him somewhere. He was around with Ted. He was working on the paper, the *Oxford and Cambridge.*"

"You might have met his brother. He was back and forth from Cambridge. Godfrey was at Balliol." And now, William didn't want to talk of Godfrey. He did not want to talk of Vivien and the King's Wood. It seemed far away, thin, tenuous, colourless, embroidered as he had first visualised the scene in faded blue, grey and dull brown. The crimson and sea-purple of Gabriel Rossetti's least expression, his intimate, trivial or even base experience, burnt out the fawn and sepia like a fire sweeping through a forest. He had felt Godfrey's

> *My heart aches and a drowsy numbness pains*
> *My sense,*

but in retrospect, Godfrey's experience was a dream, a cold delirium. How could Godfrey turn the simple warning of Carew and Vivien into a battle-cry, another plunge in perfect form, to death?

He said, "do you happen to know if—if Ted has seen or heard from Vernon recently?"

"Vernon?"

"Godfrey's brother, Vernon Lushington."

He had said to Godfrey that they were out of Shakespeare, enchantment,

Belmont from *The Merchant*. Had he himself opened the wrong casket, choosing Godfrey, neglecting Ted and the other chaps of the old Galahad circle? Had he himself plunged ahead, dazzled by Godfrey, as Godfrey had followed Carew? He had moreover, made it part of his story, he had gone over it in his imagination and jotted down impressions, lest he should forget the sequence of their talks together, lest in leaving London, Lis should have broken the thread that bound them. "I may have appeared sullen," said William Morris, "I have kept out of your way, you say you wondered. Yes, I was angry about—about—Ted said it was one of the best pictures you had done. It was your calling it—"

"*Bocca Baciata,*" said Rossetti.

"It was that that sent me raving in the Palace—the royal room at Hampton Court. It was the last time I saw her alone."

Even now, though the sun had sunk behind the plane-trees, to his left (he oriented himself as he stood there), across and behind Kensington and the river at Kew, he felt the flame—or heard it almost—

"*The marigold that goes to bed with the sun,*" said Gabriel Rossetti.

"Couldn't you have called it *The Marigold*?" said William Morris. The voice came from far off, yet it was his voice speaking. It was his voice speaking, "Couldn't you have called it *The Marigold*?" It wasn't Shakespeare, it wasn't Dante speaking.

The voice matched the long wooden trestle-table, the blocked-in outline of the enormous cupboard-settle. It was the same voice that had said to Elizabeth Siddall, now almost a year ago, "These forget-me-nots are funny, aren't they? I am almost certain that we had this very tea-set in our nursery."

"You said there was another chap, as well."

"Rolando."

"English?"

"Roland was—is French. I never met him. He tried to keep Godfrey away from communication."

"What put Lushington unto communication in the first place?"

William Morris did not want to talk about it, not now. Yet the communication had led to Lis, led to his intimate talks with her, those times at the *Tudor Rose*. He had gone over them, assembling, re-assembling the scenes, repeating their talks together and continuing unfinished conversations. In his reverie, he had talked by the hour in the galleries of the Palace, although he had said and affirmed that Hal, as she called him, Halberd or Hallebarde, had another companion in the story. He could never dismiss Gabriel from her background, and as well, she had said, "it was being in love."

But most poignant, most tragic was the voice that stammered, "I like simple things and nice curtains, as much as you do."

"You've put a new idea into my head," said William Morris. "Or the Ark has. I want to do designs in stuffs, flower-patterns, but simple meadow-flowers. I would like to do a strawberry-flower, a periwinkle, daisies flung down as if a child had spilt a basket on the grass—all leaves."

"I have that job for you at Oxford before you get onto your leaves," said Gabriel Rossetti.

"I don't paint well enough to help in your Union venture," said Morris. "Ted is wild about it."

"You paint as well as some of the chaps. Faulkner is putting his mathematical mind to work, on some line-patterns. You can begin painting your flower-patterns on the ceiling or fill up the bays."

"Sun-flowers," said William Morris. He thought of hollyhocks, cream, rose, pale-rose, black-purple. "I could do a mallow-pattern."

"Better stick to sun-flowers. What did you say her name was?"

"Her name? I don't remember—"

"The girl, the sister he thought he had killed. You were saying it was the names."

"I was thinking of the names in the *Gold Cord*. At least—"

"What were the names in the *Gold Cord?*"

"She called herself Fleur, then Flor. Florence came in. I had called myself Florian in the *Hollow Land*."

"Who was Florence?"

"A page, a—a troubadour. It—it was a name out of *King Florus*, an old French story that Algernon had lent me."

"How did Godfrey come in?"

"I didn't say he came in. She had to have a hero. She called him Gregor. He was a sort of St. George, really. She must have been thinking of your picture, *The Marriage of St. George*. I said she could be the Princess Flora."

"Has Flora inspired the flower-patterns?"

"It was you really, saying that I could paint."

"Well, you can come along to Oxford as soon as Ted makes the arrangement for our rooms in the High. I tell you, you can have the whole ceiling for your sun-flowers."

"What are you doing, Gabriel?"

"We have the run of the place. I think Woodward must have been mad when he said we could do the Union in tempera. I know nothing of it. I intend to do a Guenevere, as usual. Brown says he won't come, he's too busy. I'd like the whole ten bays given to *Morte d'Arthur*. Princeps, Stanhope, Pollen and Hughes are all waiting for their orders. Ted took for granted that you were working with us. There's costume, as well, to think of. I'll take a box of old drapes and properties from Chatham. They're paying for the paints—would they pay for some new armour? You fellows have all got to serve as models. What we'll do without Liz, I don't know."

The light was going in the studio.

He supposed he would go to Oxford and help them mix paints. He thought of the suit of armour, real armour, he had had as a child. He said, "I suppose there's a tin-smith or an ironmonger around Oxford, or a black-smith who could beat out some metal for us. I can see about the armour." He wanted to get out now. It was evening on the river.

"There's so much to be seen to. I should like some lapis-lazuli," said Gabriel. "Do you know anything about grinding lapis?"

"No," said William Morris. He was holding out against something. He was holding on to something. Gabriel must not have everything.

"All right," said Gabriel, "but it was you who started the talk about communication."

William Morris said, "It was a conversation that was never finished. I suppose it never will be." He had seen himself stretched in Godfrey's arm-chair. He had seen Godfrey light the candles. He said, "I have some of my old stuff I brought down from Oxford. I keep it for occasions." He saw himself stoop to the wall-shelf for the decanter and the glasses. He saw himself reach in his pocket for the matches, but they were on the table. "Shall I light up?" He could not move, even to the match-box on the table.

He had pulled out the stool from under the table when Gabriel had moved over from the window. He jerked to his feet. "I'll light up." There was a row of candles on the wall-shelf. "Something autocratic about sticking a candle in a saucer. But Mary doesn't approve." He placed the unmatched saucers on the table.

He struck a match. He felt the eyes of Gabriel Rossetti though he knew that Gabriel was not watching him. Gabriel would know. Gabriel did know. He had said to Godfrey, "Rossetti is, to use your own expression, in on this." Gabriel was the whole story, though Lis, out of a sense of self-preservation, had kept him out of the story.

"You were the whole story though you were not in the story. Algernon knows Italian. Algernon ought to finish his play. *Amor*—I know that much, from your quotation. She said she had read it somewhere. You spell it backward and it's *Roma*, or you spell *Roma* backwards and it's *Amor*."

"It's other things as well," said Gabriel. "It's *Ramo*, a branch or bough, the *Golden Bough*, you remember."

"I don't remember."

"Virgil is Dante's guide. You have a guide. I suppose you might say that fellow—did you say Carew?—was your friend's guide. A bough, a branch of wood. It opens doors. You can make *Mora* of it, Moira, the Greek Fate. You can say *Orma*, that's Italian for trace or track or foot-print. *Mora* might be a Moor, an Arab, the—the Astrology and all that came in from the South of France, Spain, or was brought over by the Crusaders, the Templars."

"It's what the table told us."

"The table? Then it was a table. I stay awake, literally all night, sometimes, going over the words. Of course, if it's a secret, you can't give away the secret. That is, if you're one of them. Occasionally, some old bloke gets daring in a foot-note to a foot-note. Generations of commentators . . . I found a French fellow who gave a clue, apropos of Dante in the *Vita*, quoting from the first book of the AEneid. I didn't confirm the Virgil. You just knew the old fellow would bust if he didn't hint to someone, in a foot-note to a foot-note that he had found a fresh clue."

"What was the foot-note—to the foot-note?"

"*Le trépied de Phoebus*. It's in what for convenience, we call section XXV of the *Vita*. I have so far, run my translation along without breaks. There's no use giving these hints in English. There's Romeo in Paradise VI, a Pilgrim from Provence. You remember Romeo? There's the *Sacred Wood*. What is that but the communicating table?"

William Morris had said the story belonged to Gabriel Rossetti.

"There is *Alfa ed O*, as he writes it, the alphabet."

"Alpha and Omega."

"Perhaps."

William Morris poured the red wine carefully. "The first time I saw you, we talked of the colour of the—Elixir of Life, you called it." He had talked to Godfrey of Gabriel, before he had the messages. "It was the fellow from Paris who introduced Godfrey and Vernon to the table. But Vernon left—King's Wood was the name of the place. Then Roland went back to Paris. Godfrey went on alone."

"He must have loved this fellow or there would have been no connection."

"He loved him and he felt that he had killed his sister. She came first."

"You Galahads had the table?"

"Only for experiment in Faulkner's room. Godfrey had asked (across another question) if we should go on with it. Well—it wasn't altogether satisfactory. Ted and Dixon were both bored, in the end. Talking over the matter afterwards, alone with Godfrey—"

It was after all, very friendly.

Gabriel had moved over to the low chair. Where were they? It was a work-shop, the table or the carpenter's bench was like the one in the King's apartment where he had last talked alone with Lis, at Hampton Court. It was a stage-scene, he had said. The candles drew blocked shadows, but they were still twilight shadows. It was back-stage or in the wings, as he had said to Lis, the last time in the Palace. "Funny, I remember everything she said, that last time. She spoke of Othello."

"The Moor of Venice, *Mora*, Amor indeed. There is Guenevere, Ginevra and Lancillotto. He reported them in the Inferno, but in Paradiso, there is mention of Ginevra. They slide in and out, they change character or costume. But it's simple things I'm after, words rather than people. The *arcano*, the Revelation comes through the alphabet. It means so much to me, that I haven't been near Sloane Street since—"

"Sloane Street?"

"Lizzie and I went there to lectures, at one time. They had circles, psychic-investigation. But it is, as you say Ted and Dixon found it, boring in the end. Besides, before I went to Paris, I had the—the revelation. A simple chap there. He was leaving. He gave me a message of a certain sort. I couldn't go beyond it."

So it was confidence for confidence. But Gabriel was always generous.

"There's Homer, too. He mentions him once in the *Vita*. The Italian *Omero* is *Romeo*, Amor again. Someone's got to do a new translation of Virgil and of Homer."

Rossetti went on, "Dante makes much of Mantua in the greeting."

"I don't follow."

"Virgil, the Mantuan. Romeo was banished to Mantua. Don't you suppose it was Virgil started the Roma-Amor? I have never tried to trace it."

Gabriel Rossetti said, "*Mora* is feminine, really, but we needn't be too pedantic."

William Morris thought, "*The School of Night*. But this is going too far, too quickly."

He flung out at random. "I spoke to Godfrey of the Minnesingers. He was working at translations, Marie de France and—someone else. De Fontenelle was studying the originals—"

"De Fontenelle?"

"Roland, Rolando. He was working at the *Bibliothèque* in Paris."

Had he interrupted Gabriel? Had he interfered with his train of association?

Gabriel was gazing at the red wine in the goblet.

He had not tasted the wine.

It was true, the candle-flame might be marking a ruby on the table.

"These are not properly speaking, wine-glasses," said William Morris.

Still, Gabriel did not answer.

"Ruskin was talking of stained-glass. Why shouldn't we experiment with thick-glass—the colour of the wine—for goblets?"

"Did you say Roland de Fontenelle?"

"He was the chap who introduced Godfrey to the table. It was in the country, Ayton. Roland was staying with them. Godfrey was a dark horse. I thought he was diplomatic, he fenced with Carew at St. James's. He must have been on the fringe of the Brigade, or a—what would it be?—reserve. We talked of the Brigade. I offended him. I said it was Byronic nonsense."

"It was damned Byronic nonsense," said Rossetti.

"He may even have been swotting up on Hindu dialects. I knew nothing of him. He was my best friend."

Rossetti said, "I was saying to this fellow I just spoke of, at Sloane Street—that you couldn't stop war. Or he was saying it to me. That was the first black mark I gave Gus. What I mean is, Gus wormed his way into the Society as a sort of private secretary to the then principal or director, an astute, honourable American, named Ely. He was a doctor by profession. He got caught up in some chivalrous notion that a lady he knew—*clairvoyante*—was being imposed on. But messages had come through her and her sister that determined him to go on with the work. The 'movement' as he called it, was getting into bad hands. He wasn't afraid of persecution from without. It was a swamp. There were talking-tables, he said, right across the country, that is, America—and now they had spread to Europe. He blamed himself, in some way. He was trying to check up here, on the 'submergence' as he called it.

"I had run across Gus first at one of their lectures. I had had two private sittings with Dr. Ely. Gus tried to cut across, or he blackmailed me, rather. If I introduced him to people, he would get me a third private sitting. Well, it wasn't as simple as all that. Yet, it was even simpler."

Apparently, this was something that Gabriel felt intensely. "You better sample that wine," said Morris. Gabriel lifted the glass. He set it back on the table. He said, "This is going to be difficult to say. I'd better say it. Bill and I were brought up on codes, secret signs and pass-words. I'm not official. Bill, in a sense, is. The Board of Trade has other irons on the fire. I didn't want to report Gus. I don't officially report people. I gossip to my brother. I did not want to gossip to my brother about Ely. Ely asked me to confirm a letter that Gus had written in French. Ely knew no French. It was exactly as Ely expressed it; there was, Ely said, 'a boudoir-air' about the letter that he didn't like. Later, I went over other letters for Ely. Ely needed no hint, no prompting from me. I didn't even tell him. It was that old worn-out derelict idea, they were after—Louis the Seventeenth."

"Louis the Seventeenth?" said William Morris.

"It goes too far. I don't even know that Louis wanted to be King. Louis Naundorf in the old days, used to turn up sometimes, at the *casa Rossetti* gatherings."

It was *casa Rossetti*, as he said it, that caused William Morris to blurt out abruptly, "If there's anything I can do—"

The words were commonplace, but what could he say? Something had stricken Gabriel. William Morris realized that he himself had been guilty of maligning Gabriel—in his thought, anyway. All the fellows had criticised Gabriel, in one way or another.

"Just run me down, to Ruskin. I must watch Gus," said Gabriel Rossetti.

"Why—why Ruskin?"

"I sent Gus around to Ruskin. Gus knows something about Turner."

Gabriel added, "I said to myself, 'honour among thieves.' His father was a copyist at the Prado. But I didn't like Gus cashing in, on psychic investigation. It was easy enough to see what he was up to. The game was well worth the candle. My game—my candle. I'm thinking of the others."

III

"But names," said Gabriel, "before we go any further—de Fontenelle?"

"I didn't mean to blurt out Roland's full name. I—er—Lis told me you had mentioned a de Fontenelle in Paris, at a restaurant. She didn't think you knew them. The name slipped out. I meant to stick to Roland."

"Why so cautious—or conventional? You remind me of Dev. Always doing the right thing. I didn't know he was de Fontenelle. For the matter of all that, I only guessed that she was. But I don't quite follow. Is this another sister?"

"Sister-in-law, *belle-soeur*, the other fellow was his brother."

"I come into this, if I do come into this, because of a letter. Ely at Sloane Street, asked me to confirm or criticise a letter, written by Gus to a Madame de Fontenelle. Gus was putting Ely's dictated English into French. I thought the letter a little—well, familiar. 'Dear Princess'—Gus began it. Ely was put off at the start by the 'Dear Princess.' He could read that. It had to be explained that the lady's maiden-name was—well, never mind the *née*, after her own signature. She had been a Princess, as I explained to Lizzie, on the occasion that we saw or didn't see her—but the Princess was Napoleonic pinchbeck."

"Lis said, you said she was Velasquez. Lis said (I remember how she said it), 'it is odd how Gabriel sees things.' She was telling me how happy you had been in Paris. She told you about the Palace?"

"Palace?"

"Hampton Court and how we went there."

"She told me nothing of the Palace."

"I had a sort of *crise*—a crisis. The thing the fellows laughed at, when I pretended to smash furniture—and did sometimes—at Oxford. I felt—I *felt* a rose-spray tapping on the window. Afterwards, in the tea-room, when she was talking of your trip to Paris, she mentioned de Fontenelle. It seemed too—too apposite to be accidental. De Fontenelle (Roland) had introduced Godfrey and Vernon to the table. When Vernon left and Roland went back to Paris, Godfrey went on with the table—but I told you. That is what I told you. I don't want to go on repeating. Mary must have left that half-chicken and some cheese and cress sandwiches somewhere. I better light the hurricane-lamp. I bought it in—"

"Don't say Portobello Road or Brixton—I couldn't stand it."

"It was—"

"Don't tell me—"

"I don't mean the hurricane-lamp. I mean Valérie. Her name was—is Valérie, your *belle-dame*."

"What has this got to do with the—tapping?"

"I left all that after Godfrey went. I mean, any idea of going on. I was waiting unconsciously, for Godfrey to turn up. It's a sort of—sort of—well, troth. I mean, with the table. I had plighted my troth to Godfrey's table. I couldn't go to another, it would be the last discourtesy."

(The table? The lady? The *Vita*? The fellow didn't know about it. That's what made it so important. He must not guess how important. It might break the spell. He knows all about it. He doesn't know a word of Dante. He doesn't know Italian.) Said Gabriel, "Your—ah—brew is excellent."

"Forgive me. I was talking too hard. It was the rose-spray tapping in a sort of—a sort of ghost-hush. A sort of icy moment in mid-August. I was afraid to count the taps. It was saying something. 'Are you saying something?' I had to ask that. 'Yes,' ever so tenderly. Then I thought, 'I'm a fool—it can't be true—it's the wind.' There was no wind."

"*Wind, wind thou art sad, art thou kind*—" said Gabriel.

"There was no wind, I tell you. 'It's the wind' I had to *think* it. Well, you know, you ask a question, without speaking out loud—"

"*Wind, wind, unhappy! thou art blind*—"

"That's what I said. I was deluded. '*Is it the wind*?' The rose-spray tapped, but firmly, *no-no*. I suppose everyone has these yes and no-no signals. O, no-no, it seemed to say. 'But the damned place is haunted,' I thought and I turned on Lis. I was trying to make it right afterwards, in the tea-room. It was then that she began talking about your trip to Paris. It was then that she spoke of de Fontenelle."

"*Yet still thou wanderest the lily-seed to find*."

"It was as if her mentioning de Fontenelle at that moment, and for no apparent reason, was a sort of—sort of confirmation of my first—"

"Things do tap," said Gabriel, "rain-water drips."

"It's true, it had been raining, that's why we took shelter in the Palace. It might have been the rain. You think it was the rain?"

"My dear fellow—"

"I said to myself, 'it's Godfrey come to tell me.' Then afterwards, I argued round it. I went over my poems, my stories. There's death and ghosts in so many of them. Something she said, Lis said, made me feel worse—then better. She was telling the story, *Gold Cord*. They were trapped. He was after them. They would delay the army of the Inquisitor by taking a last stand by the altar, so the rest of us could escape. Well, she might have read it. She said, she might have read it. We were burrowing through a tunnel. It was rock-wall, carved rock. It was hard rock. It was the suffocating feeling, made me say burrowing. Perhaps the chambers or tunnels, having been closed for so long, had—had—it happens in mines. I mean, perhaps some kind of gas had accumulated and just that crack of light—of air when I lifted the stone, might have set up some chemical change. What is air, anyway?"

"Who took a last stand by the altar?"

"Gregor, she called the fellow—obviously, she meant George, don't you think so?"

"I don't know the—"

"It was the fellows. I told Godfrey that Carew or one of the other officers, should have ordered them back."

"Did Gregor order them back?"

"That was different—that was just the difference. The Knights Credentes were—how shall I say it? I told Godfrey I admired the fellows. But don't you see the difference? You do, Gabriel."

"Whose story is this?'"

"Well, I don't know. Algernon started it, I told you, as far as I was concerned. Then there was Godfrey and our few sessions with the table. I don't think Godfrey altogether agreed when I said they were the Templars."

"Who were the Templars? These fellows by the altar?"

"Yes, the Knights Credentes, the Knights of Malta, the Crusaders. I felt that Carew (when he came to Godfrey) wanted to start something new. A new approach to the old things, anyway. I didn't feel that Carew wanted the thing to go on any longer—as it was. Of course, I had only been—been introduced to the table, when Godfrey vanished. I wasn't particularly concerned, at the time. Godfrey often disappeared for weeks, during term. Then I got a letter, sent on by his brother. There was no indication where Godfrey had gone, where he had written from—my letter had been enclosed in one to Vernon. It might have been sent from Portsmouth or Marseilles. Only he had gone—to India."

"*In-dia*," said Gabriel Rossetti.

"India, I said," said Morris, "did you say India?"

"I said *In-dia*, it is one of the clue words of Dante. I'm sorry I interrupted."

"How—clue?"

"It's just one of his countless rubrics, anagrams, enigmas. *In-dia* can possibly be translated in-spirits, in and Deus, in-God."

"That's what I was trying to tell Godfrey, that my one message—or two (actually all I had), were—well, he said Roland called it *télégraph to Dieu*. My words were abbreviated. They were Latin. Godfrey said he had had no Latin."

William Morris knew that Gabriel Rossetti would not ask him what the words were. He searched his pocket for a pencil and ripped open an old envelope. The candle drew the ruby on his own page, now.

"TEMP.   LUM. IN.   TEMP. OMN. U   N   ,"
he printed.

"It's nothing," he handed the paper over. "But it's all I had. It's all I have to go on. It's enough. It's everything . . . but after . . ."

He rose abruptly. "Do you want the lantern? The candles are burnt down."

"Haven't you any more candles?" said Gabriel. He was looking at the paper. "Why don't you gulp that wine down?" said Gabriel.

"I was looking at the—the ruby on the table."

"*Qual fin balascio in che la sol percuota*," said Gabriel Rossetti.

"And that's a funny thing," said Gabriel, while Morris found and fitted fresh candles in the saucers, "Dante speaks of the ruby, *rubin* or *balascio*, as he calls it in this instance, in connection with an alleged leader of the so-called crusade against the Albigensians. He says Folquet is like a fine ruby, or a fine-cut or fine-turned *rubis balais*, on which the sun strikes or through which the sun shines. He puts him in the Paradise, in the third heaven, the heaven of Venus."

"Then Dante—"

"No. The whole *Commedia* is a sort of Bible or Book of Hours of the so-called heretical church."

"But this—"

"Folquet de Marseille was a troubadour. Dante followed his pattern in some of the early canzoni and the *Vita*. It was Folquet, the later Bishop, who is said to have inflamed Rome against the Albigensians. But Dante put the somewhat disreputable Cunizza, mistress of Sordello, in the same heaven, and Rahab the harlot. Their utterances are all ambiguous."

But Gabriel Rossetti was marking time. It was easier to explain or try to explain the sibylline obscurity of Folquet de Marseille than to make a simple statement. "Guido Guinizelli and Arnaut both personified Amor. They began it," said Gabriel. But he'd have to say it. "Swallow that wine and sit down," said Gabriel, "till I work this thing out." He spoke as if he might be trying to find the answer to a nursery-riddle or conundrum. "Why don't you just write TEMPLUM?" he said. "Why do you cut TEMPLUM?"

"I don't follow."

"You've got templum, for the first word."

"It's not templum," said William Morris, "it's abbreviated, it's two words, it's TEMP. LUM., as I've written it."

"Why did you write it that way?"

"It was words spelt by the table. It stopped when it finished a word. Godfrey would ask, 'Is that all?' to be certain of the pauses. It would say yes or no-no, as happened, and go on with the word or part of the word. I called it tomb-stone Latin—if you can call it Latin. Godfrey called it mile-stone."

"I told you about the chap at Sloane Street," said Gabriel. "He was in trance or half-trance. But he was talking to me in—that is, he gave me messages from an older brother of my father's, a priest in the Abruzzi. The last messages were in Latin, Church Latin," said Gabriel.

The words as Gabriel spoke them were matter-of-fact, almost commonplace. "But of course, that was a different method," Gabriel went on, "the fellow was in trance or half-trance. He didn't know Italian or French. He might have known a little Latin. In any case, these experiments are interesting."

"I would hardly call—call Godfrey's and my *experience* an experiment."

"Well, except for some pleasant, dull evenings at the Howitts in Hampstead, and one or two trivial essays with a mixed group at Sloane Street, I have had no experience with this table-tapping—"

So Gabriel was dismissing it—*table-tapping*? Morris cut across, "You don't mind my saying so, Gabriel, but this is different." Why had he told Gabriel about Godfrey?

"Different from what?"

"Why it's the thing the—the chaps and I had decided in the beginning, to work for—"

"In the beginning?"

"Our—our circle—"

"But why did you come to me with this?" said Gabriel Rossetti, "I'm no Galahad."

He had said it. He had said the worst thing he could think of. It was possible to drive Tops raving. He had watched others at the game, though theirs were for the most part, the stings and arrows of unconscious stupidity. If Tops raved, what would he say? He might blurt out more about the table. He might give the clue he was waiting for, that would clear up his own—that would give the answer to his own—"What was it who said what to?" said Gabriel. "I mean, the fellow who asked a riddle that had been the death of countless intrepid idiots? You know what I mean. Or was it the thing that asked him the riddle? The Sphinx. When he got the answer, it was ludicrous. Didn't you always feel that the answer to the Sphinx-riddle was an anti-climax? But who gave the answer? Was the Sphinx answered? A play by one of those Greek fellows. This is what I ask you. How is it that Ely, Norton Ely, at the Sloane Street psychic hang-out, gave me something of the same message that's been given you here?"

He had said it, at last. It would only have delayed the issue, to have sent Tops raving. Was he raving?

"The thing—the thing shattered me more than anything that has happened since—since Gabriele—"

William Morris had thought from the beginning, that he had never heard a voice so beautiful. He said, "I was upset about—"

"That fellow Lushington? Well, I missed Ely, when he left London. The worst of it was, I couldn't go back to anyone after Ely—for—for confirmation or for comfort. But worse even than that, I had to take a specious outside interest and turn up at some of their so-called circles, to keep an eye on Gus. Madame de Fontenelle had brought a fortune with her. I was able to check up on the family through old Ida de St. Elme. Ida was a Russian really. She had been a friend of one of Napoleon's marshals. The de Fontenelles had lost everything. Well, so for the matter of all that, had—what did you say her name was? But her loss was irreparable. That sort of woman will go anywhere for consolation. She would have been a gold-mine for old Gus. Ida described her half-Spanish mother to me, Ida knew of course, nothing of the—the story. If it wasn't—did you say Valérie?—then it was someone so like her as to belong to—to the story. Ivory-white, did you say?"

"Ivory-white? I didn't say anything. I never saw—Valérie."

"But Godfrey described her to you?"

"Godfrey had not seen her."

"Well, hang it all, somewhere there was comparison."

"Lis said she was a candle, or Godfrey said it. I don't remember. Lis said, you said she was Velasquez. Someone said, Godfrey maybe said that Roland said—but no, I may have said it, that she was a white camellia. I got that impression, anyway. Ivory."

"As I say, she would have been a gold-mine for old Gus, if he could have got in with her. But I managed properly, to put a spoke in his wheel, through a little judicious postscript work on later letters. I didn't have to warn Ely but I had to warn her."

"This was the Lady that you saw, then?"

"*Qui lo so*? Yes, it was the Lady."

"It's all rather difficult to reassemble. Godfrey was telling me the story as Roland told it to him. But I do remember some reference to her mother. Valérie was one of them, I gathered, through her mother."

"One of them—you mean *ancien régime*? But through *emigrés*, returned from the West Indies. Ida knows everything."

Gabriel said, "there's nothing so white as a white tropic-flower." He was thinking of Gabriele and the orange-groves in Malta. Gabriel had never seen an orange-tree in blossom.

William Morris had called Lis a snow-flower. In some inexplicable manner, the white tropic-flower and the snow-flower merged in a new dimension, as Gabriel finished speaking.

Gabriel went on, "I come back to your poem, *The Wind*. I was thinking of orange-blossoms, really.

I shrieked and leapt from my chair, and the orange rolled out far,
The faint yellow juice oozed out like blood from a wizard's jar;
And then in march'd the ghosts of those that had gone to the war."

"That's what I meant," said William Morris, "when I said that I went over my poems and romances, after I had parted with Lis. I saw ghosts everywhere. It was how my mind had been working, I argued, and she had put a spell on me in the throne-room. I mean, in the upper gallery, the King's apartment. There were those Queens, I argued, and everyone knows that Hampton Court is haunted. She said it was *The Wind*, too. I mean, she talked about that poem, the first time we got caught in the rain. There were two times in the rain, when we sheltered in the Palace. Once, we went on the river to an island. I could imagine their river. I imagined them caught in the rain, there. Godfrey had said (always remember Godfrey is quoting Roland) they had boating-parties on the river. I imagine that Godfrey told me the story pretty well, as he knew it. Roland would not tell everything."

"They had—parties?"

"That's how the thing started. Her cousin had a cottage, a boat-house, a sort of summer-house—I don't know. Imagine it for yourself. They met there, a group. They had formed a circle. It dwindled down and some of them dropped out. It always happens. But I told you all this?"

"When would you have told me?"

"Well, just now. I seem to be repeating myself. I have told myself the story so often, in the past year. It was luminous when Godfrey told it, like pictures seen in crystal. I felt Godfrey was shut up in crystal. But you make it seem real."

"It's real enough," said Gabriel. "They could have been had up for conspiracy."

"Conspiracy?"

"Yes—believe it or not. The girl was so desperate that she wrote Dr. Ely of their meetings, their circle on the river. Ely had saved her letters. He had smelt a rat in that 'Dear Princess.' Would you say the girl was a fool?"

"Why—Gabriel—"

"The circle had dwindled down to three of them. Trust me—Gus had found out who they were."

"What harm was there in that?"

"Harm? An empty cottage—"

"Perhaps not quite a cottage, a cottage in the *Petit Trianon* tradition was Godfrey's phrase, as I remember."

"*Tant pis.* So very much the worse. A girl of the *noblesse* (I don't mean the new nobility) meets her lover—"

"There was Aurélie, her cousin."

"Hardly a duenna, I should imagine."

"But surely Roland—"

"*L'amor che move il sole e l'altre stelle,*" said Gabriel.

"But conspiracy?"

"It already has a name," said Gabriel. "Orsini. But forget it. It's known already as the Orsini Plot. Ida knows everything. They plan to do away with the third Napoleon. Gus had her—or would have had her—both ways. Her father's people were ennobled by the first Napoleon. The *émigrés* were—well, about as near as you can get to the last Louis—Sixteenth. I imagine her mother had left her with no illusions about thrones and princes. It was her mother's father who had escaped the guillotine."

It sounded like a dream or fantasy as Gabriel told it, William Morris remembered an ironical phrase that Gabriel had used that first eventful evening, "*casa Rossetti*," he had said, "no place for Walter—revolutionaries, shady kings and princes." Was Gabriel thinking of *casa Rossetti* or of Valérie de Fontenelle? It was a question of fine-thinking, *ancien régime* (to use his own expression) and honour. Had Gabriel seen Valérie again? Had he warned Roland? It was an impossible juxtaposition of coincidences, his talks with Godfrey, his last talk with Lis.

"You—you—"

"Well, you might as well hear the end of it. Where are those sandwiches you spoke of? I shadowed Roland."

"It was Roland?"

"It couldn't have been anyone but Fontenelle. I'll tell you about it, later. I asked, when we started talking, why I came back to England. Why? Why? Why? I came back to keep an eye on Gus—and on Ted and Tops," said Gabriel Rossetti.

IV

"Yes," said Gabriel, "we can live in our affinities. Or as Lizzie said on that august occasion, we can watch ourselves reflected in mirrors. Eighteenth century? I can't say that I see you there, nor Lizzie—except in a reflection of a reflection, seen through double rows of candles. We made up a story about Versailles. Lizzie played herself into it—or a new waltz (from Vienna, she said) played her into it. She kept talking about the candles in the mirrors, 'and each set of candles lights a separate room, and you can't prove it but you can see it. We are in separate rooms,' she said. It's too damned prismatic."

"That's a little of what I felt of Godfrey. Roland's story seemed to have been seen through crystal."

"Fontenelle wouldn't tell Godfrey the whole story. And even if he had, as you say, Godfrey would have reflected or refracted it—a frigid fellow?"

"I—I hadn't thought of Godfrey as—"

"A little like Blanchelys—what? I mean Liz, Lizzie. We must get someone to match up with Lizzie—not you, brave champion Launcelot, Lancillotto del Lago—what about Sir Godfrey de—de—what sort of place d'you say it was? That octagonal look-out is a good invention. The Lady Lis and the Seigneur of—For myself, I don't for one minute think the fellow's dead yet. He wormed his way into the East India Company, disguised as an honest down-at-heels accountant. What these fellows won't do. You should hear Bill on the subject. Our spies are all right. I don't mean to imply that the Seigneur de la Tour would stoop to add up numbers. I wouldn't. Not that that's anything against Lizzie, knowing the day of the month, the price of a postage-stamp and winding the clock. It's how their minds work. Octagonal."

"What's that—eight? One over the—why eight? Neglecting my duties. You can sleep in Ted's room."

"I'm not going to sleep yet. You've only changed the candles five times. I counted. One over the—you said eight. Yes, thank you. Have you got two by two more candles to go in those wax-sockets, eight less five times? Ha-ha. I caught you."

"Nothing of the sort," said William Morris, "we changed the candles when you spoke of the ruby on the table. *Rubis balais* you called it. Out of Dante. Well that was the second set. But we started talking in the day-light."

"It was you who saw the ruby on the table."

"It wasn't there really, it was like Godfrey telling me of Roland, reflected from the crystal wine-glass. We'll make some red glass. I knew you were lying when you said you shadowed Roland. You could never be a shadow. What—what's light in ruby?"

"Watcher mean? Light in ruby?"

"What you said, when I changed the candles for the first time."

"*Qual fin balascio in che la sol percuota* wasn't Richmond. Did you call him Richmond? She called him Gregor. Ain't they the same person? I don't care for history myself. I called Gus, Calliostro. I had to talk about him, there in Paris, or bust, so I called him Calliostro. Couldn't see myself at Trianon. So I set the scene in Venice. I had to follow her around, in my imagination. An island-story? Sicily? It works out. Count Robert was a Frank. You'll find him and Manfred too, in Dante. D'you see what I mean? A foot-note to a foot-note or bust. I mean *le trépied de Phoebus*. It's very simple. Who were you anyway in the circle?"

"I—I was Pal—Pal—"

"Pal—that you are! You can't say Palomydes. You ain't him, anyway. Wasn't he the chap that was after Iseult? The chap, I mean, that got left? You won't get left. You're too good a trencherman. Have we eaten all the sandwiches? In vino, what I always say, is veritas," said Gabriel Rossetti.

"As I was saying," said Gabriel as Morris refilled his glass, "our spies have no end of fun. He's probably dressed up as a Rajah and riding a dromedary in the desert. Who invented Godfrey, anyway? That tower is an invention, out of your poem—"

"Up—up and away—through the—the—"

"—drifting rain. I know your poetry better than you do. *Let us ride to the Little Tower again,*" said Gabriel. "It doesn't rain in the desert. He'll get sick of the sand-dunes, you mark my words."

"It's not—it's not sand-dunes, it's Holy Mountains and tea-planting. What they call Paisley. I had silk-worms. Must start some spinning—spinning—always wove hammocks at school. We'll start spinning—"

"*Rota*, a wheel, don't go on about Dante—got his ideas from the heathen, *si come rota ch' egualmente è mossa*. Well, Fate, Life, *Rota*, *Amor*, don't spell it backwards. *Mora*, a Moor, she came I tell you, from the West Indies, *India*."

"I don't—don't see con—con—what you called it—told me not to remember—"

"Orsini. *Orsa*—Lady Bear. Ha, ha—*rosa*. I spell everything upside down. I can't help it. Not that the estimable Orsini ever heard of Dante. You mean what advantage for her to be in—in the conspiracy? It wasn't her idea. She never heard of the plot. It was Gus who was the blackamoor, blackmailer. He had (or would have) their comings and their goings—or he would bluff her. Not that she cared for what people thought or might think. She was desperate, I tell you. But if Gus could put a spoke in her wheel, *Rota*, *Amor*, involve her in a pseudo-circle or even in a so-called private-sitting with some other blackamoors, she-bears or blackmailers, he could cut her adrift from any hope of ever seeing Roland. Unless she promised to rope him in too. They would be watched everywhere. What they really wanted was to involve Rolando."

"All too—too com-pli-cated—don't care for politics."

"No heel-taps, you said politics, you're getting sober. *Rota*, a wheel, to wheel, to go around. What Dante says—the she-bear *Orsa* goes round the pole—the heaven, the north-pole that is—*rosa*, a rose."

"What Godfrey said, the rose was the round, the table."

"Shouldn't think Godfrey could spell—"

"But it was his table."

"You said it was Rolando's *télégraphe*."

"Mechanical inventions, I asked if inventions would go further. I remember my very question, 'all these new mad inventions,' I said, 'I suppose something will come of it, in time?'"

"You said you only had that one message, or two—*templum in templo*."

"I had a few answers to some questions, yes and no. Those were the only words I had spelled out. It was your message, not mine, I told you mine was TEMP. LUM. IN. TEMP."

"That's just what I was saying, TEMPLUM IN TEMPLO, the temple in the temple. It's the same message."

"I asked if TEMP, was for Templars, they said yes. But I told you all this.

I told you—or you told me—it's the same thing. It was only about religion, it's being all one, OMN. UN."

"I said it was the dative. Have you got a Latin grammar? I said it was, *templum in templo* to the Omnipotent One—dative Omnip—Omnip—*Uno*, anyhow, is one."

"Well, anyhow, Godfrey didn't agree about the Cross and Crescent."

"Maybe he's right, for him, right. Those were Credentes by the altar, not Illuminati."

"But it was Godfrey's table—"

"You said it was Roland's—"

"We've said all this. But Roland tried to stop him—"

"What I said was a foot-note to a foot-note or bust. What it asked was, what walks on four legs, then on three, then on two? No, I mixed it. What walks on four legs, then on two, then on three? Anyhow it's a damn' silly question. If you asked for the question and didn't have the answer, your forfeit was death. A silly question, I always thought, an anti-climax, and the answer was as silly. 'Why Man,' says Oedipus, 'does that.' Do you see the reason? Now I'll be blasted if I give away the secret—I mean a thunder-bolt will dash me to perdition. Can you stand the answer?"

"Answer—to—"

"I told you, Egypt. It was the Sphinx in Egypt. Oedipus asked the question but it wasn't Egypt. I mean, IT asked it. If you couldn't give the answer, the forfeit was death."

William Morris pulled himself to his feet. He jerked open the window and stood with his forehead, resting on the frame. From the shadowed garden, there was the cool scent of summer. Here, in Red Lion Square, with the distant traffic silenced, they might almost be in the country. He could clown it with the best of them on these occasions. Gabriel was superb, really. But he would cut the rest of the brown loaf now, and get Gabriel some coffee.

. . . .

"Statesmanship and authority," said Gabriel, "doing things across chess-boards—Credentes maybe. They believe in it, anyway some of them believe in it. The Illuminati ain't always better people. They just know.

"But what they fetch in the lottery of knowing, ain't anybody's business. It's got to last their life out. Once they get the answer. But you go on getting answers, like that rose-spray on the window. But didn't you say Lizzie recalled how Mrs. Howitt had those messages—I remember those lingering evenings—from the Gold Coast? Why couldn't the—watcher call it?—double do the dealing? You had the answer—lumen, you call it, LUM anyway. It was the last part of my TEMPLUM but you can have it. *Lume* is light, lamp anyway. Is that Latin or Italian? Have you got a dictionary? Words, words, words. That's the devil of it. You go on getting answers but you can't share them. Only sometimes, perhaps once in a lifetime, you find another fellow going not so slowly crazy. He wears a blue shirt. He makes a clothes-line of his white ties and hangs his brushes in the window.

"But why bother about reincarnation? I don't say you do. We go on re-incarnating backward in time, ordinary time, one's own childhood. I found my own delirium in Dante, in the *Vita*, though he presumably was grown-up when he had his.

"Then remembering . . . you remember the clock ticking . . .

"I didn't need any proof of Norton Ely's good faith. It was genius really. Then why do I get this—*grace* as the Church would call it. It's true, I said in the beginning that I wanted confirmation or comfort but I couldn't ask for confirmation of the—the greater from the lesser oracle. Do you notice how people fall off when you've had your great experience? When your knowing is—what shall I say now?—concentrated, crystallized, concentric—O damn, as I said where's your dictionary? What I mean is, there's something about that in his *Rota*, his circle—he puts it in Latin in the *Vita*, a sort of spiritual geometry, all points of the circumference equi-distant from the centre—then you have your—final—answer."

"Is any answer final, ever?"

"You've got to believe it or you get out of your own circumference. You're kept in it by—affinity."

"Some people have—or seem to have more than one affinity." William Morris wished he hadn't said it. "I mean—"

"Never mind what you mean. There is our Lis. Does it make any difference to the picture that there's Lilith? Lizzie swep' out. She would never understand, though in Paris when we saw Madame de Fontenelle she confessed, she shared her with me. It's the old pattern; there were three ladies in Folquet's *amoros pensamens* and in Dante's *Vita*."

William Morris was back at the beginning. Now he thought wistfully, of that last scene in the Palace. He was sure of himself then, at least sure insofar as—as the *Bocca Baciata*, the Kissed Mouth was concerned. "Does it make any difference to the picture?" Gabriel had just asked. There was Miss Herbert, too, but she was widely admired and an artist. "Ted said there was to be a benefit performance of some sort, with Miss Herbert appearing, in Oxford," he said.

"I'll do some sketches from the stalls," said Gabriel. "She promised to sit for me for the triptych. I'll finish that too, sometime. In the meanwhile, I can only sketch her across the footlights."

Thought Morris, "Was it after all, delirium, fantasy on my part?" He had not seen the picture, he did not want to see it. *Gold at her head and gold at her feet*, but that was his poem *Crecy*, not Gabriel's picture, *Ah, qu'elle est belle la Marguerite*. And he had had it all out with himself, going over and over every minute of their time together. Just twelve meetings. He called it twelve anyway, to go with her twelve castles, her star-signs, most poignantly remembering, *we wouldn't know—at least, I wouldn't know, not knowing my birthday, not even the month. It would help to know one's birthday.*

"Ah, yes—her beautiful face. I believe Ruskin admires her vastly." The candles were sputtering again, double candles reflected in double mirrors, did Gabriel say she said in Paris? Had he seen her across the footlights? *Lyddy used to say I ought to go on the stage, after my doing Aunt Day for her.*

"You'll—you'll remember me to Miss Siddall when you write her."

"Miss Siddall? I thought we were talking of Miss Herbert. And why suddenly so—so stiffish, as Liz once reminded me I called Wykeham Deverell. Liz had an uncanny way sometimes, of remembering. She could repeat whole conversations. Lord knows, what she and Dev talked of. He told her her voice wasn't strong enough for the stage. Whoever thought it would be? She's too tall, anyway. Did Liz talk to you of acting?"

"Only in connection with a story about her sister—entertaining her sister when neither of them could sleep."

"It isn't such a bad crib. I went over there. Lydia's another stunner but she's getting married to some newspaper fellow. Lydia would do for Oxford; I used her for a Queen of Cyprus, but I didn't see the Roman after her engagement—not unlike Lizzie but with brown hair."

"Candles reflecting double candles, did you say she said?"

"She said, 'And each set of candles lights a separate room, and you can't prove it but you can see it.' Is that what you mean?"

"There's something so—so human about her."

"Inhuman, you mean. Bill says she's fey."

"Fey—faery. She used the same word, only she called it *wayy*."

"How way—the Faery Queene? I'll have to do Guenevere from memory."

"It's w-a-y-y, a word out of a Herald Book I gave her. She sent it back, it's around somewhere. It's *wayy* or *undy*, curved like sea-waves. She's like Undine."

"Even Ted said something of the sort."

"*Even* Ted?"

"Not that it matters. Our Liz swep' out. But Ted could have brought Lady Greensleeves in to meet Lizzie, while she was still around at Chatham."

"I never thought of—I mean, wouldn't Lis find—"

"Greensleeves boring? No, she's a pet, the only thing I have against her is that she won't do for my pictures. No doubt, Ted will find Maid Marianne in her or a faery Goosegirl. He wants to do the Beggar-maid and Cophetua—he'll get there in time—and a Mermaid, dragging a man down to the depth. Do you think he thinks Lizzie is a Mermaid?"

"I never talk to Ted of—of Lis."

"Nor I, neither. But Ted will be on the line before we know it. I told Dev it was a rotten picture, his first, *Entracte* or *At the Ball* or something of that sort, he called it, and the one after that was Lizzie. Lizzie and me and Dev himself, as Orsino—my God, what a coincidence. I mean Orsino is the Duke, you remember in *Twelfth Night*. Dev did his own portrait for it. Lizzie was Viola."

"I—I remember."

"Did you see the picture? Hanged if I know where it's got to. I finished *The Marriage* after—after—"

"The Marriage?"

"*Of Rosalind and Orlando.* Fancy Dev, Orsino and Gus in this Orsini business. Could anyone have invented that? Did she ever tell you how she met Dev?"

"Someone, perhaps Ted, said it was his mother going to a bonnet-shop."

"I don't mean that. Everyone knows that story. I mean, did she tell you who put Dev onto his mother buying a bonnet, in the first place?

She was standing on the *estrade*. It was in this very room. He had come in that door. Dev immediately suggested, as he had done that first time in Kew, that they go out together. He unrolled his drawing-paper. "I can work and talk at the same time, if you can't," he had said. Now he said, "Deverell would have kicked me out, the first time I came in."

"In?"

"In that door. I dropped my kit in the corridor—what was left of what I had then. They'd sold up my books but they were Bill's mostly, and some sticks of furniture I had at the last place. I'd been staying at Brown's. When I got back, I had no place to go to—no place to work in, I mean; I could always sleep in Bill's room, at home.

"She was standing on the *estrade*. Dev lifted his hand. His gestures were always perfect. He wanted her to clear out. The same thing had happened the first time, when I saw her in Dev's old studio at Kew. He said he had promised a friend—I remember how he said it, 'the lady is not a model, I promised a friend, when she consented to sit for Viola, that she was not to be approached by any other artist.' What I want to know and never found out is—who was this friend?"

"I confess, I wondered myself. We were talking about that—that Gregor—"

"Call him Godfrey."

"She didn't know Godfrey. She said, could you be in love with someone you'd never seen? She volunteered, it wasn't Allingham."

"I wonder."

"She said it wasn't a fellow called Garth, a stunning name—I don't remember—"

"Garth Wilkinson. Damme, it might be old Wilkinson. He was somewhat struck with Lizzie, I thought, when we went to see him. It would be someone upstanding and conventional, I'll bet."

"She said, someone said he was tall and upright as a spear."

"As to falling in love with someone you've never seen, what of butterflies?"

(He had said, "Is there anything so white as a white tropic-flower?")

"You mean—"

"They sense each other with their whiskers, don't they? Antennae, I suppose you'd call them. Thousands of miles off—"

William Morris thought, "I felt them come together in a new dimension—the white flowers."

O Gabriel—Gabriel!

"I told you, didn't I, that we live in our affinities," said Gabriel Rossetti.

PART VI

I

It was the same sort of room that she had had at the pension with Mrs. Kincaid, above the stone steps by the olive orchard. Perhaps that's why her thoughts went back to that time, the last time she had been alone. It was spring but the rain was sweeping across the olives; it was spring that is, for the South, but the almond-blossom was drowned out. She had drawn back into her room thinking, "I might better be back in England, I'd have a way of getting a fire, Mrs. Tozer had a fender even in the office. There's no way of getting a fire, fancy not even a fire-place, I don't believe in the whole house and the stove only in the downstairs room, where you can't breathe for stuffiness."

Not that she would have put a match to a fire if it was laid there. She would huddle in Weymouth Street in the basket-chair with the bed-quilt wrapped around her, sometimes even, with the window open, to the horror of Ellie passing; Ellie said she could feel through the crack under the door when the fire wasn't going proper. They let her fetch the small kindlings herself, from under the stairs at any time, not even counting what she took, until she recalled it to them, "well, say eighteenpence for the week's sticks," Mrs. Bailey would say, and Elizabeth would protest "but you didn't count the coal in, I told Ellie to keep count, she laid the fire at least three times anyway, without my telling." Not that she would light the fire, when laid. Ellie would creep in when she heard her on the stairs or lingering maybe, in the hall, saying good-bye to Gabriel. They were always very pleasant to her at Weymouth Street and understanding about Gabriel.

She didn't want the fire lit and it was summer anyway, well "the days are drawing in," they remarked now, at the shop where she got her pencils, a corner-shop, shaped somewhat like Aunt Day's, but stationery, chiefly, though it wouldn't seem out of the way to ask for candles or even matches; Aunt Day's was chandler's, really. There was the chemist too, obliging with the laudanum.

The days were drawing in. She had conscientiously explored the neighbourhood and then taken Lyddy over the ground again, when she was with her. She had stayed in Sheffield before she came to Matlock, with the Ibbitts, relations of Dad's auctioneer cousin. She had done Antique twice a week, at the School of Art and gone about, visiting the various sites, the chasm, the shale hill, getting almost to Hope one day, on an excursion with a group of students. Lyddy wrote home that Lizzie had never looked better.

It was getting away from Gabriel and all of them that made her look better. For a time, she played her small part in a small town—or rather her large part. She was important. They listened to her. She had been to Paris.

She was not unusual looking, not for Sheffield, and she adopted herself to the fashions, with just those artful, almost unnoticeable touches that made all the difference. She was one person, Elizabeth Siddall, connection of the Ibbitts; Sara taught drawing and was impressed with her, her brother worked at music when out of the factory. She was a student with other students, none of whom were particularly gifted.

Not that she needed the laudanum, the pain wasn't that bad. It was being reminded—funny! While Lyddy was here, she was too occupied taking Lyddy about, to be reminded. Not that there was much to do compared to London, even compared to Sheffield. She was glad that she would no longer be forced to take an interest in what they called in Sheffield, the development. She could keep out of what was fast growing to a resort, and fashionable, mostly for rich invalids. Perhaps, that's why she felt she could rest now, it wouldn't be thought out of the way, if she made no effort, now Lyddy had gone home. Some of the Sheffield acquaintances had been on holiday and helped make things bright for Lyddy with excursions. There was Mr. Sykes and Mr. Green from the School and Annie Drury, friend of Sara, staying with friends. It was the Wheelers actually, who had suggested the Derbyshire hills in the first place, and Lyddy had settled her in this same lodging-rooms or pension, not so unlike the one above Nice, as she was only just now thinking. This was her second visit, really.

It was cold when Lyddy brought her and it was quiet, but she didn't like what they called "the waters," and then Mrs. Ibbitt heard of it and said she better come to Sheffield and be with company, in the winter. Perhaps it had been better. It left her free now.

Or did it drag her back, now? She couldn't rightly say which, yet. It was their being interested in her for herself, like a person who had never heard of Gabriel Rossetti. She had asked Lyddy not to talk about him, but briefly, "yes, Lizzie is engaged but doesn't want it talked of." It was the little stone-houses with gardens at the back with rows of hollyhocks, old-fashioned, that reminded her of Hastings. It was the sea at Hastings, this was mountains, well, rightly speaking, hills really. What would have happened if she had, as he put it, accepted his gentians? It was how he said it that came back, "I was born to mourn over what I can not save." Well, she had told Mr. Ruskin she was not worth saving, the last time she wrote him, insistent on not taking the money again, having done nothing really properly to show for it. But the cheque came back, she had to get away, she thought she would have died, even in Hampstead where Mary found the rooms for her, in Spring Cottage. She had to see Gabriel sometimes, even if she kept away from Chatham Place, and she couldn't help thinking what was going on there. It was his talking of them all taking a house together—though he said afterwards, it was an idea really of the Oxford fellows, as he called them—that sent her right off. She couldn't speak for stammering.

What if she had gone to Switzerland that winter? It was now, the comet-year as they called it, but the comet hadn't come to much, though it was an excuse for staying out on the river and having midnight picnics, with some of the older ladies along for chaperone. It was what she had called "next year," when she did the cards for Mr. Morris in the tea-shop. She just hadn't thought of Mr. Morris. She answered his first two letters, as she was explaining how she was sending the book back and some of the papers he had sent to her. They were relative to the story *Gold Cord*, that he had had ideas for. Well, he better finish that story. She didn't want to recall it.

In Sheffield, once she started the art-classes and got acquainted with the students, it might never have happened, hardly any of it, that is. Hastings came back, in the beginning, because of these lodgings and the pension at Nice. Nice was of course different, but there was something reminiscent in the up-hill stone-steps at the back. There, she first began on her story and was serious enough to argue a date with Gabriel, that he got wrong. As if it mattered!

Hand and Soul, he called his story and it was beautiful and no one could compete with Gabriel, not even Mr. Morris and Mr. Jones. She didn't count Hunt and Millais and Ruskin, they were already set, you might say. It was Gabriel who was flaming with inspiration.

And what did inspiration do? It got inside you, even thinking of Gabriel and how she saw Halberd snatch at the green-jacket of that twin, her equal, they threw stones at, with red hair—Algernon, they called him.

Not that she liked Mrs. Ruskin from the beginning, though it was reported back that their Annie or their Lucy, the girl in the white apron, said Miss Siddall was lady-like in her deportment. Mrs. Ruskin meant to be kind really and they were so mad at Effie, though they never named her, that they would accept anybody and she was with Gabriel anyway, and there was no question, but old Mr. Ruskin (he wasn't so old really) said he wished he'd had a daughter like her. Mrs. Ruskin sent around some bone-powder afterwards, funny, with directions how to use it. She meant to be kind really but she had harsh manners, though she took her through the house and as good as said, she should be free of it, to walk there if she wanted to come out at any time. They had some old trees and one Lebanon cedar, but Gabriel didn't like Denmark Hill, nor anything about it. Mr. Ruskin showed her rock-crystals and those pictures he did in Switzerland, but she didn't go back.

Maybe, she was putting it all on to Ruskin (Dr. Wilkinson said you invented or put one thing on another), relative to her terror of Mr. Greenacre, that is, relative to the person who would take away her terror. Maybe, she had put it all on Mr. Ruskin or even on Dr. Wilkinson—that person, standing by the altar.

When it came to that, you might put it on anybody. They worshipped heroes, Mr. Morris had told her that last time in the tea-shop. Well, it was the last time, anyway. Whatever she got over, she would never get over his turning on her that way in the Palace. Of course, she'd read the poem and memorized some lines, like she did with his poems, but she thought nothing much about it, one way or another, nothing personal that is, seeing with her mind always that it wasn't her that he was thinking of—till he turned on her, making it obvious, as Gabriel had shown him sketches of her as Guenevere (so he told her, the time before) that he wanted, since she wouldn't give him that first picture that he asked for. She had told him that Mr. Ruskin had the sketches, he might get them from Mr. Ruskin, but he said he couldn't do that. Putting that together with the fact that she saw he had been listening to gossip, had struck her like it was the knife of Mr. Greenacre; though she said she wouldn't talk about it, she came back to its opposite in the tea-room, his friend who he had told her was a fencer and associated, in some way, with the Brigade. Then getting that associated in her mind, with death, because his friend's friend was killed out in the Crimea and thinking of Godfrey as dead.

Thinking he was dead even that first rainy day, when she did the cards for him . . . why did she have to put all that unto a stranger, someone she had never met and even were he living, that she hardly cared to meet now. It might be anybody, she herself said Gregor was a sort of Saint George. So would anyone be, like Dad talking about Wellington, having made a God of him, Dad being only fifteen for Waterloo. But she couldn't think somehow, of the Duke of Wellington nor any corresponding to him, being in the story. It would be more like Nelson, taking away that period-uniform, like that portrait she saw with Gabriel at the National Gallery, a loan collection, she remembered, for she went back, something striking her in the way his eyes looked out, but the portrait was gone with the others of the period. Dad and James had never talked much of Nelson. Perhaps that's why she could claim for herself her personal discovery of him. Dad was only five when Lord Nelson died on the *Victory* at Trafalgar. She remembered the date that way, subtracting ten from Waterloo.

Waterloo meant nothing to her but talk of the new station. She didn't know who did the portrait, his right arm was gone that he lost at Santa Cruz, but both eyes blazed out. Perhaps it was an ideal portrait made up, but it looked real. There were decorations (she wouldn't know what) and what looked like a cut-steel cockade on his admiral's hat that fitted on his grey hair, a wig, she supposed, being that late eighteenth-century, but it was the way his grey hair and the steely decoration on his hat, seemed to bring out the light in his eyes.

It was a steel *aigrette*, comparable to that hawk-feather her out-rider wore in the forest, but this was the sea. It was making someone the opposite of the terror of that knife striking, it would have to be a soldier and she didn't know any soldiers. But she was always watching the ships at Wapping, looking (as she had told Mr. Morris when she tried to get his thoughts away from India) for the Prince out of her story. It was just a story and it might as well be Nelson for it (whose portrait at any rate, she had seen), as Godfrey Lushington.

Why go back so far as something before Dante? She remembered those dates, having caught Gabriel out on quoting Dante, in *Hand and Soul*, before Dante was born. Not that it mattered, really. But there was something about numbers, you could work wonders with them. Well, wasn't it numbers, her doing accounts for Dad, that had really recommended her to Mrs.

Tozer? There were plenty of girls about, for bonnets. But she got preference, as Mum explained how she had helped Dad in the shop with the accounts, and besides, there was Mr. Tozer, as Mum for a joke, reminded Mrs. Tozer (an old friend from Mum's Euston Road days) inviting Lizzie to work in the shop when she was only *that* high.

Maybe it familiarized her with the period, working it out, wondering long after Mr. Tozer was dead, if she got the dates right. Yes, she had worked it back, he could have been a boy who just remembered. Well, perhaps later, she imagined what he might have seen, getting the guillotine mixed up with thoughts of—but she was done thinking of Mr. Greenacre. Gabriel and she had made up a story there in Paris, but it was music that she thought of, making out that Lady was a Princess.

Mr. Tozer was a little old gentleman when she was a child. He had talked of Paris, though she must have made some of it up, out of terror herself, afterwards. Say Mr. Tozer was twenty years older than Dad, he would be nine for 1789, a date anybody could remember.

It was like *The Old Curiosity Shop*, though she would never read a word of Dickens, after what he wrote of Mr. Millais' *Carpenter Shop*, for all Dad used to read the instalments out aloud to them, gathered in the sitting-room under the lamp. The hideous red-haired boy, Dickens had said, and his common-looking mother would have disgraced a gin-shop. It was how they had thought of the Pre-Raphaelites, in the beginning.

And now she was back at her own beginning, and that last talk she had had alone with her father. Wasn't it just like her? It was what Dickens called the "loathsome minuteness" of their paintings. She was, for all her talk, siding with them—who could help it, after what someone called Mr. Dickens writing superior about art? Charles Dickens—it was Dad's name and Charlie's, and maybe it all came back to an older brother who she lost before she saw him, being there to protect her, a red-headed child, "wry-necked" (Dickens even called Him), what they were always talking about in Gabriel's pictures of her, that is, what they had talked about before Mr. Hunt had his big success with *The Light* and Annie Miller in *The Awakened Conscience*.

Maybe, it was her conscience that was awakened, with Mr. Morris drawing attention to a lady maligned by vicious gossip. Yes, now she saw it, "wry-necked," peering around, why, even Mr. Morris spoke of Guenevere being twisted or walking away like one lame, an impression she got anyway, from the poem. She sent back the *Defence of Guenevere* with the others. And now she saw what she didn't dare see before. It was Dad gave her that blow, suggesting someway that honour in their family was something inherited, along with those *Three Birds* on the 'scutcheon, as Mr. Morris called the coat. It was on her like an icy-finger, like Mr. Morris said something touched him in the Palace. It was Death touched her, Dad suggesting her being dishonourable and with Gabriel. It was being alone, standing there by the table with the music-folder on it, and for all her blind infatuation of him, when she was *that* high, and him playing the violin and reading aloud to them, and speaking as anyone could see, like a gentleman, she knew that she must walk out of that room with her head high, because it wasn't only Gabriel but Mr. Ruskin, Professor Ruskin of Oxford, thought well enough of her to offer her like it might be almost seven times what Mrs. Tozer offered her, what Dad was about to offer her to go back to the shop.

And "wry-necked," like Charles Dickens called the Christ Child in John Everett Millais' *The Carpenter Shop*, she had looked back, only with not enough "loathsome minuteness." It wouldn't make any difference anyway, whether she wrote Mr. Morris or not, she wasn't writing anyone but Lyddy and Gabriel just to quiet *his* conscience, and keep him from rushing up, on an impulse, to Matlock. But she could think things out here, and what did it matter if she got into a fever? It was worth it.

II

She stood frozen there, by the table and it was like she said in Paris of those mirrors, you were in different rooms or reflected in different mirrors, and you could see it but you couldn't prove it. But it was almost a relief to see it, to feel it, rather. It was Dad, it wasn't Mr. Morris, though she was there too, in the royal bed-room, herself struck cold, in a brocade chair she couldn't get out of, though (she remembered) a moment since, she had planned drifting to the door-way, through the narrow corridor with the windows looking out on the Dutch garden, and across the grass through the brick-walled rose-garden, to the little door at the far end—or through the wide court-yard under the clock-tower, out of the Lion gates. It was like it was yesterday.

But yesterday too, she was standing by that round-table in their sitting-room at Kent Place, and it was summer, the summer before she went to Paris. It was last year, the Peace Year that Mr. Morris struck her, and now she blessed him like she had blessed Harry, way back in the beginning when she first fancied she might be something other than the ginger-cat, he called her. Mr. Morris was right. She had seen things through a distorting mirror, that flawed two-piece mirror in the little ante-room, off the glassed-in section where the vine was (planted, it was said, by Henry), where they sat the first time they were caught in the rain.

You could see it but you couldn't prove it, she had said to Gabriel of the mirrors reflecting candles while there was music playing. But you could prove the flawed surface of the two-piece grey-green glass, "Don't look in it," Mr. Morris had said. Right across her memories now, if she looked close with that minuteness Dickens carped at in them, there was that dividing line, now she came to see it, where the mirror was divided. What would she be but frozen for-ever, standing by the three-feet round-table in their sitting-room, if it hadn't been for Gabriel?

You might say if it hadn't been for Gabriel, she wouldn't have been struck down by her own father talking about honour, as if it was a word belonging to them, in some set way, because of that shield. But she had been struck down long before that, though it wasn't Gabriel struck her and it wasn't Mr. Morris, but it hadn't (that first time) divided her life in half, she was still at Kent Place for all the terror stalking her round the tan-yards. She still had Lyddy to talk to nights, before Lyddy quieted, sitting propped upright in bed. But when Dad spoke of honour and "my favourite daughter," she knew that she must walk away from that table and get to the door somehow, away from him who had always till now, stood between her and the terror. She walked away in her sleep—her nightmare, she had called it to Mr. Morris in the royal bed-room.

Dad was no longer there between her and the terror, so she worked herself into a story—it was the very night she came back, sitting alone in the basket-chair in Chatham Place, thinking of the cholera.

She had made up stories for herself and sometimes for Lyddy. But for the first time, the story was outside her, she had only to watch it happening. O, it wasn't so clear, it didn't go on like a proper page in a book, more like a dream it was, but she was awake when he came out of the forest with her hawk-feather in his cap. There was that coat too, with *Eagle displayed* as well as *Three Birds* and the word *Honour*.

She thought of Walter Deverell and that picture he hadn't even begun, but talked much of, *The Flight of an Egyptian Ibis*. Why should she think of that now? Was it thinking of Lord Nelson and his *aigrette*, or maybe, the Battle of the Nile? But in what Mr. Dickens had called "loathsome minuteness," little things stood out and she never seemed to get on with the story proper. She could never get over Mr. Dickens calling Him (for the Carpenter's Child was the Christ Child to her) hideous, and Mr. Dickens with Tiny Tim and Little Nell, who seemed so fond of children. If it had been anyone else, she might have thought no more of it than of their speaking of Gabriel and his school, as decadent; Gabriel had first spoken the word to her, there in Paris, though she didn't know rightly what it meant, *décédé*, in her little dictionary, meant dead. It didn't seem they were dead, if anything, they were too much living.

She had her choice now, Dr. Wilkinson had as good as told her of it. He was Swedenborgian really, but even people who weren't of the new faith, spoke highly of him, considering him a very clever doctor. He had new ideas, correspondence of the mind and body and of dreams even. Mrs. Howitt had taken her, in the first place, and Gabriel had escorted her to the house, on several occasions. It was Garth Wilkinson first said, she would burn out.

She hadn't then properly left home, but she could live walking across the river, in some way, so that she could imagine lilac-bushes where the decayed wood-steps were and the old barge, drawn up at low tide. It wasn't always pleasant and she would hurry past the wharves, boys sometimes shouted at her, but there was no use wasting time, anyhow making herself conspicuous, she was on a secret errand. She was walking across the river to Mrs. Tozer's but that wasn't the secret errand.

Dr. Wilkinson seemed to know somehow, that she was somewhere else, when she was about her business. She must give up her work. She had already almost as good as given it up. She did not tell him that the fever burnt her out more—well, she never blamed John Everett Millais for the floating draperies.

"In proportion," Garth Wilkinson had said, "as your mind over-clarifies with acute, cerebral perception, your body weakens." He explained exactly what he meant by cerebral perception. It was a special sort of thinking, he said, but it wasn't the consumption. She knew they thought she had consumption, when they took her to him.

Yes, it might have been Garth Wilkinson in the forest, but it just wasn't. He wasn't in his way so unlike Mr. Ruskin, both of them tall men with those eyes, set like glass-agates.

But Mr. Ruskin wasn't satisfied and sent her to Dr. Ackland. That was some time after, but Dr. Ackland said more or less, the same thing. She couldn't see herself then, staying on at Oxford, but now that she realised that she could have a place in Sheffield, she could even think again of Oxford. Gabriel had written to her, telling her of the wall-painting they were doing for the Oxford Society or the Oxford Union, as he called it. He and Mr. Morris and Mr. Jones had rooms together in the High. He had, he wrote, regretted her at first. He was doing the Guenevere from memory, though they had found a model. Her father kept a livery-stable, at least, Gabriel called him a *palfrenier* and in her little dictionary *palfrenier* meant groom. Gabriel wrote that this girl rode her father's horses, but it would hardly be a girl from one of the big houses who would sit for them, and an ordinary groom wouldn't have use of the horses, she didn't imagine, to lend out to his family, so it must be that he kept stables. The name Gabriel said, was Burden.

They would be on their painting, the whole summer and on into the winter, he thought. Should he come up to see her? This is just what she was trying to avoid. She wrote more cordially to tell him she was quite happy, and as if eager for news, who was there and what else did he plan painting? There was quite a group of them, he wrote back, they were being much talked about, he sent her a page from one of the Oxford papers. Some of the names were unfamiliar to her. He was sending two of her pictures, *Clerk Saunders* and *The London Magdalene* to an exhibition in America. He was still wearing his plum-coloured coat. They had seen Miss Herbert in a benefit. There was a new fellow turned up, called Swinburne. Tops had read them a stunning poem, *Peter Harpdon*.

Of course, she might know if she asked for news, she might expect to get it. She had tried to keep cordial, if she was what he called stiff or shrewish, he might think she was having one of her old attacks, like Mary Howitt wrote him that summer when she was at Hastings, and he might think he ought to come up to see her. It was before Lyddy left that she last wrote him, so she could say Lyddy was with her, and Lyddy wrote at the end of the page, "I have never seen Lizzie looking better." That was while she was still half-living, though physically, she was more "natural looking," as they told her. It was only half a life, she felt now, talking of ordinary things with kindly people, perhaps her body was more living, but her mind was dimmed out. What could you do if your mind ate up what reserve of strength you had? "I mean," thought Elizabeth Siddall, "could I for long, really live like I thought I might live when I first went to Sheffield? Was it really living? But who can decide that for me? But it needn't be decided. In any case, they are all away from London."

For the first time since she left London, now almost nine months ago, Elizabeth Siddall had a sudden pang of longing. Perhaps she had thought of London, but if she had, it was always with a prayer under her breath, "Dear God, you let me get free." Her prayer went further back than nine months ago. She was loyal and she always asked Lyddy for news. Yes, James was taking over the customers, it gave Dad time now for his new department. Funny, Dad at his time of life, taking up new interests. It was lenses, Lyddy explained, until he got his papers they weren't speaking of it, optical. It was for glasses and he was interested in working up the profession. Funny, he never thought that she remembered, spoke of outside interests. But she had been gone a long time. Perhaps that's what he was asking her back to the shop for, that last time she saw him, really alone, so that he could be more free for—whatever it was. "Papers?" "Like a chemist, you might say," Lyddy told her. "Not ordinary glasses, fitting and giving tests in far and near sights, with charts and alphabets." So Dad was optical, almost like a doctor.

Well, she needn't have worried, they had got along without her. But—had she been sitting here all this time, and the light going? Mrs. Cartlidge was calling from the stair-head, "Don't let me disturb you, Miss Siddall, but the kettle's boiling."

III

It came back. She couldn't remember how many times she had had that same dream. It was always of course, different and she forgot the details, or the dream altogether, till it came back. This time, she would try to remember it; perhaps if you remembered it and didn't let it go for very terror, you might rid yourself of it. It might never come back. She didn't want to write it down—could she? A dream vanished when you tried to recollect it, or you let it go, if it was the nightmare.

It would be better to go out, with the sun shining. They brought her breakfast on a tray, she only had the tea and toast and a boiled egg that Mrs. Cartlidge insisted on. She had set the tray on the dresser in the hall and now she sat, half-dressed, with her house-robe wrapped around her. It would be better to go out. She was really stronger and she liked the old town and looking in the windows of the new row of shops, too, on the promenade. The old town wasn't changed much, so Mrs. Cartlidge told her.

She needn't actually write it. Dr. Wilkinson had said that one thing reminded you of another, and he could diagnose even from dreams. It was a new idea, but Garth Wilkinson was Swedenborgian. It appears, some can live real situations in dreams, repeat old memories and go back in time. But that was at the Howitts, someone asking him if he believed in lives repeated. It wasn't a consultation.

"We repeat in this life, what we have lived, or haven't lived out, in another," she remembered him or someone saying. Well, she was repeating what she had lived already. There was Mum coming along behind them, and she and Lyddy would rush on, for the stones that began, like shingle on a beach, seemed to have spread. There were small stones, clean as if sea-washed, but they were far from the sea. Maybe, that was recollection of stumbling along, the last part of the excursion to the Peak. There was no mountain in sight, but endless clean stones, on the up-hill slope.

They went on, she and Lyddy; they would find a way down. She looked over the edge where the shale stopped suddenly, and it was a sheer ledge, but below, was a shelf, a small valley, trees growing and a path to some-where.

She and Lyddy went along, and then she lost Lyddy. It was a throng of people, young ladies, no one elderly. What surprised her, they were all in green but different stuffs and patterns. She wondered at the elegance of the costumes, they were all cut different, different sleeves and neck-lines, not one design repeated, nor one whole length of plain colour, but a jacket maybe of dull contrasting velvet to what might be a skirt of taffeta. One had wings inset of another material, round her hat—not the rim—the—the— she couldn't think of the word for it, the *bowl* of the hat. It was like *appliqué*, not embroidered wings. But every variety of green, no one whole costume of unrelieved plain colour; one had wide sleeves of half-transparent chif-fon, contrasting with the basque jacket. They were none exaggerated, but of a quiet elegance and distinction no one could imagine. She was caught in with them. There was no crowding, though there were so many, all la-dies and young-ladies. They were in a town, as if going to a reception, but it struck her, it was more like expectancy before a theatre, the *matinée*; they were not evening dresses. For the theatre, *matinée* is afternoon, but the word means morning, and it was morning when she woke up, after the dream, with the sun making a ladder from the shutter-slats, on the wall op-posite her bed. And she sat up, wondering if this time, she would really die of terror.

It started with her getting separated from the ladies. Yes, it must have been a theatre, but she had got in the wrong door. There were curtains hanging, as it might be before rooms, three sets of hanging curtains, like stage-curtains but it wasn't a stage. The wind blew out the heaving hang-ing of the middle curtain. It was a long, dim hall, pleasant enough, though she was alone and somehow implicated. In what? She might look behind the middle curtain that was anyhow, lifted at the edge, with the wind. This idea took hold of her, but frightened her. She lifted the curtain, the wind had blown it, anyway. There was nothing in the middle room, furnished if at all, sparsely. As she dropped the curtain, a voice came from somewhere, maybe from a distant stage or maybe from the next division or partition, behind the closed curtains. She did not look behind the other curtains. It was a man's voice, singing.

Lyddy wasn't with her but Lyddy cropped up, outside. There was no division. They were in the country. From the elegant entrance and the crowds, she had gone through the side-wings, and straight from—Paris, it might have been, only it was home; the ladies were more elegant than Paris, but they were her own people. She jotted down the sequence of the dream in her note-book. She would fill in the details, afterwards.

There was Lyddy, and they must get somewhere, find a house where they could all stay. They came across a cottage, straight from Paris or the heart of London. It might do. Well, it was more of a loft, the room they got to; they looked out of the window. There was a large comfortable manor-house or farm-house, outside, low-lying with elm-trees. But cattle were coming home, she was afraid of the long-horned shaggy cattle, so Lyddy would jump out of the window and ask at the house, if they could stay there. All the same, she began to undress and standing in her bare feet, she saw the door sway inward. It was not a very strong door. There was only a small catch-bolt. She rushed to the door and pushed herself against it, her weight seemed to have no value but the bolt held. The catch was two-thirds up the door and the lower door was pushed in, so the crack there widened and showed the shaggy pelt of the bull. The animal seemed far wider than the door, his great hairy shoulders must push through. Now, had she time to bundle her clothes together and jump out? She looked down, but there was a bull-calf lying stretched below. He might have been just born, he might be dead.

It was then, she woke, but the terror didn't leave her.

. . . . . .

Maybe, she got green sleeves from hearing Gabriel speak of the girl that Mr. Jones was going to marry, a Miss Macdonald. They called her, Lady Greensleeves. She wasn't thinking of Miss Macdonald when she turned on Gabriel. She couldn't speak for stammering. No, their choice of ladies all together, wasn't possible. What she meant was, you couldn't call Annie Miller (not that her being a model was against her) a lady. How could anyone imagine they could live in security together? She could imagine Effie of them, but Mr. Millais wasn't now of their company; they had first called it their Brotherhood. That was the comfort of that dream, you could see how they were all ladies, they wouldn't crowd out one another. She was perhaps the tallest of them. She did not even know what she wore, being so interested in detail of the other dresses, how they could be so different, all harmonious. Perhaps she hadn't even worn a green dress, she was separated from them. Lyddy might have been there, only she had lost Lyddy. Gabriel called Lyddy, "the patrician" and "the Roman." Lyddy wasn't as tall as she was, her features were more regular. She was quiet in her manner and retiring. "I wonder what that green would be, those green sleeves," thought Elizabeth Siddall. She wrote down, in her note-book, "green sleeves, Lady Greensleeves." Were the sleeves olive-green? No, it was contrasting grey-green, with a hint of blue in it, like clouded aquamarines, it was love-in-the-mist green, she decided, but that was a mist-blue flower. Maybe, it was Miss Macdonald herself.

You might meet other people in dreams; well, there was Mum and Lyddy. Lyddy was almost herself, having the same date given, 1832, and no day nor month. Funny, it seemed. They might even be twins, though she was taller than Lyddy, and Lyddy had brown hair. Their eyes were the same, only hers, Clara called cat-eyes. Well, cats had pretty eyes and they could see in the dark. She knew what Clara meant, not meaning to be unfriendly.

Seeing dreams and remembering them or trying to remember them, is a way of seeing in the dark. Was it Nile-green, that inset of wings on the crown of the hat? It was a contrasting shade; "all the costumes," she wrote down in her note-book, "were contrasting shades and textures." One might be olive-green, the full skirt to the close-fitting bodice that Lady Green-sleeves wore. She had been too busy noting the effect of the sleeves, to remark on the skirt. Nile-green—that reminded her of the *Ibis*, that hat having those wings. She wrote down, *"Flight of an Egyptian Ibis,"* and followed it with, *"Battle of the Nile,* insert description of the Nelson portrait."

That reminded her that there were contrasting or compensating dreams, as Garth Wilkinson had told her. She had indicated to him the effect of the nightmare, and she had told him of—but she couldn't write it, it startled her so much, and she didn't want that name in her book. It was *Greenacre*—the nightmare.

There was the voice singing. Dad's father or grand-father—was it?—sang in the Cathedral at Sheffield, but this song wasn't Church music. It was as if something held them, held her, while she was with them, a tension, an excitement, like before going to a play. Gabriel had written her of Miss Herbert's benefit at Oxford. Miss Herbert was a lady, you could feel it in every word that she spoke.

"Ladies who have intelligence in love," she wrote down in her note-book. It was a line that Gabriel had translated from one of the Dante poems in the

Vita Nuova. It was life, *New Life,* those ladies and she was, for the moment, one of them, in complete harmony and excited, but she lost them. There could be ladies like that, but it wouldn't be Annie Miller or Miss Cornforth, as Fanny Hughes called herself now.

Old-fashioned people called a churchyard, God's acre, sometimes.

The Devil was an old-fashioned concept, Dr. Wilkinson had said. But children are frightened by what some way, they always hear of—the Devil with horns. There was that voice singing, God—"Godfrey," she wrote down. He was silver and a fencer. That contrasting dream, she had had, some weeks back, was of a silver apparition. It might be even, it was Godfrey; "Gregor," she wrote after Godfrey, in her notebook, and "finish that story," she printed in block-capitals.

There was a saint in that book that Mr. Ruskin gave her, called Florian and one called Valerie. That Lady Valerie could be of them, only perhaps of another—"sleeves," she wrote—that's funny. She was Spanish looking, what Gabriel called Velasquez, maybe she was Catholic. High Church Oxford took over the saints, at least certain ones, suitable. George was difficult, being such a common name, and then being National. She was thinking of a defender and from what Mr. Morris said, Godfrey had made a quixotic gesture. But she knew nothing of it nor of him, only what Mr. Morris had told her. It was William Morris gave Godfrey to her. She had to have a Captain or a Commander for the Credentes.

There was Nelson looking out, and not blinded. She could remember details of pictures, like those Calendar *Hours* she discussed with William Morris. It was consoling to find bee-stocks—but not stocks, they used some such word but another name for the thatched houses, in a row, in that first farm, after they turned back from Eldon. The Vale, now she thought of it, was like the painted-in small scene to the edge of a Castle picture, that ledge and path she saw in her dream.

Not that being help in the college, would or would not make a lady of her and of her sister. Mum had been in service in Sheffield, when Dad met her. She felt that Gabriel was trying to bait her—his word—suggesting that she and Miss Burden were in danger of being rivals. "She is as tall as you, Liz," he had written, "maybe taller. The fellows have arguments about it." There it was, they were talking about her, but it didn't matter. It was said Miss Burden was timid and didn't commit herself to much talk. Well, she lived in Oxford.

That William Morris was interested in Miss Burden, was not to be wondered at. It was fitting that he should let go that shock and association with

Lis, thrown and killed riding. Miss Burden rode magnificently, wrote Gabriel.

Of course, there was Margaret in the Saint Book. But particularly, she noted Gereon. Gregor didn't quite appeal as a name, now. She would follow back the association, like remembering a dream, but "Gereon," as she wrote it, opened a new vista. The old story would be incorporated, but fitted to her *New Life*.

Gereon. The book was on the table at her elbow. Gereon, she read, was one of the commanders of the Theban Legion of the Roman army, "which numbered 6,666 soldiers, all Christians." It was back in Roman times, but it was the same story.

She did not know how many ladies there were of the Greensleeves. Men got together in regiments and even, like Gabriel and his friends, in a sort of Brotherhood. Even if they quarrelled with one another, they somehow stuck together and new ones came in, like the group joining them from Oxford. You could imagine different forms of Brotherhood, like the old Guilds that Mr. Ruskin described in his *Nature of Gothic*. But you couldn't imagine a Sisterhood, except nuns or maybe nursing-sisters. She had wanted some such thing, that is why she was so stricken, seeing how that Abbey of Thelema idea, as they called it, might work out. But it couldn't, not the way they saw it. She did not quite yet know how she saw it, but she saw it. The dream of Greensleeves had been the second part of the sequence—were those three curtained rooms, three circles? Yes, it might be a sort of Greensleeves circle; she was caught in the midst of them, standing, she remembered, not going on with them, against the wall, watching.

The Greensleeves more than tempered the last horror. Was it death, simply?

The Greensleeves came between the horror and high vision.

What did she mean by that?

The apparition was a dream; waking, she recalled nothing before or after, only the silver of him, standing. She had never had a dream experience so refined—by refined, she meant that text from Scripture, like gold refined in the furnace, only this was silver.

It would do, if she were a nun or in a nun-story, for a Saint. Someone appearing, whose apparition would suggest a sanctuary or a chapel, built to record the vision. But it was personal, as if she had known the Saint or Soldier.

But it might be, as she had said to herself, after hearing of Godfrey Lushington from William Morris, the idea of a fencer, a soldier, a defender standing between her and terror. She had walked away from her defender, walking in her sleep, out of the door of Number 8, Kent Place, that summer day, two years ago now, saying she had a commission and paid for by Mr. Ruskin.

What could she do about the soldier? War was a thing that Gabriel abhorred, utterly. Not that she could condone it, but there were ladies, Miss Nightingale, who helped now.

She hadn't the temperament to do proper nursing, but Dr. Wilkinson had given her an idea. If the terror struck her so that her heart weakened, it might be the same with other people, and not heart only, but other afflictions as well. She had only partly confessed to Dr. Wilkinson and hid from Dr. Ackland how her heart took her.

They wouldn't notice, for she took care to go to them for consultation, only when she was well. It would go on for days sometimes, after the terror, and for the most part, it was dream-terror. She was certain you could die of a dream, but she felt exultant. Garth Wilkinson had given her the idea.

The Greensleeves were the ladies that belonged to the Credentes.

I V

She needn't make an effort, not yet. She could sit there, in the morning, in her house-gown and felt slippers, after finishing her breakfast. They didn't disturb her, only Mrs. Cartlidge when she brought in the letters. Gabriel, it seemed, had never written her so often. It was odd, if he was, as he said he was, so busy. And now, it was all Algernon, she must meet him. She did not tell Gabriel that she knew Algernon, at least knew him through the story and those talks with William Morris. But she tried to see Algernon now, as Gabriel and as others would see him, not compensating for the pain she had felt and the grief of William Morris at his friend's affliction. Her *idea* of the golden page was just imagination but it was compensating, to use Garth Wilkinson's word for those real dreams. But you might say the nightmare was more real, for the effect that it had on her heart, though she wasn't going to let it go now. She could even see its likeness to one of those stories of *Greek Heroes* that Mr. Kingsley had sent to the Howitts, at one time. That bull-beast, devouring the chosen and dedicated young men and girls.

She didn't want to make a fancy of it, or a fairy-tale. She wanted to take what was true, that is, what really happened. Though it happened in a dream, still, it was in its effect on her, at any rate, more frightening in the one case, and more of a miracle in the other, than could ever happen in life. It was to her, as she had said, *New Life*; though restricted and limited, it was after all, what Dante had in his Heaven and Hell. Purgatory might be the ordinary life here.

She tried to see Algernon here and now, in this limited existence and with the wrong body. The effort made her feel weak. But no, she wasn't going to let go this reality, not now, no matter how it took her. What she had was a solution, it was an answer, it was that thing—well, call it religion and you got nowhere. It was, as she remembered saying to Gabriel in Paris, "he kissed her and it was God and she walked." She was thinking of Elizabeth Barrett Browning when she said that, but beyond that, she was thinking of—No, she couldn't fancy Robert Browning.

What she meant was, she had something. She had not written very much in her notebook but the jottings served as reminder and she would go on. She sat for the most part, indoors, in the morning; she would feel better in a few days. Now she was going out regularly, every afternoon to take tea. It made a change, though it was extravagant. There was *The Gate* and *The Treasure*, both moderate. *The Treasure* was combined, a new departure, it was tea-shop and curiosity-shop. Old candlesticks and pewter were tastefully set out on old farm-dressers, but for sale. It was pleasant sitting just off the bow-window, at the single table against the wall; she was inconspicuous and the ladies already inquired (if she didn't turn up) if she had been kept in yesterday, and did the climate suit her? One of them even volunteered that she had known relatives, to the north, of Miss Brontë.

There wasn't a Godfrey in her Saint book. Funny, there being Florian. She had worked out that Algernon was Florence, the name of the Italian city where Dante was born. William Morris said he was more gifted than Gabriel, or than any living. Well, Algernon was troubadour in that story, and he was now, a gifted, rare poet. The mind was more real than the body, but she wanted to get them in relation to each other. There was the "double" that Gabriel had talked of. That "double" might do the dreaming or be the person in the dream. Then go on, after.

She had exchanged her *Gold Cord* with the wing-clasp, with Algernon for his dagger. Maybe, she had a dagger, could do her own defending. William Morris had sent her suggestions for the story, which she glanced at before returning to him. They would be of a height, he had written, and she would crop off her hair and it would be as from *Twelfth Night*, only one was later, captured. Confusion would come on, as to which was which, but he said, that same sequence was in other stories of old France. He had confused two of the stories; Florence was out of a *King Florus* story, not the *Amis* one of two friends. Well, it was, as he had said, all written, the stories were the same stories out of old legends. Then, why write this one again? But there was something she didn't think was written, the Real Dream.

Perhaps you might find, if you knew Italian, that Dante wrote it, but Dante was a classic and far off, and she didn't know Italian.

The *New Life* would be the *Real Dream*.

Purgatory, this life here, was not all unpleasant. She had been happy, though it had been an effort, stumbling over the stones, in the first part of her dream, with Mum and Lyddy. Then, she had been without them, and wholly wrapt up in the Ladies. They had *intelligence in love*, and that was Heaven. The last part of the dream was remarkable for the likeness of that long-horned bull to the Devil.

She would do without the laudanum. Did the dream bring on the pain? Or did the pain bring on the dream? Could she find out which? She wrote down, "three—the dream sequence—Purgatory, Heaven, Hell." They could be explained somehow, even if you didn't know Italian. There were influences that brought the dream, but it need not be Astrology. You did not need to know anything about the stars, nor even your own birthday.

You could follow it out.

You might find your dream was suggested by day-happenings or remembering. She had associated the Greensleeves with Gabriel speaking of Miss Macdonald. Miss Burden might not have had the advantages of Miss Macdonald, but no doubt, she had other qualities. Gabriel speaking of her, as considered timid, meant that she was retiring and perhaps not unlike Lyddy.

Yes, she was beautiful. Elizabeth was not one to take Gabriel's word for it, but it was the way he went on about their being the same type, but Miss Burden with dark hair. Gabriel had made a sort of fashion of her—fashion? But unfashionable. Those Greensleeves—how was it they could appear so—so worldly, but worldly wasn't the word for it. That is, though they were spiritual and dedicated, any one single one of them alone, might appear at an assembly and not be remarked on, except perhaps for the very modest elegance. But modern. They were living in our time. Yet, they were out of time, eternal.

It was not ambition that had brought them all together. She had been ambitious. Scribbling in her stitched-together notebook, she had thought herself a poet. It would make her outstanding, different from Annie and the others. She had been different from Annie and the others.

But her difference had led nowhere, that is her ambition. It was due to outside influence that she became *Ophelia* and *Sylvia*. *Viola* was not so good, but Walter Deverell was still very young and he was painting an Academy piece for exhibition.

She had wanted to be different from the others, until the dream of Greensleeves.

They had that Voice, that is why they were all together. In that, she was like them, but the Voice in her case was the Vision. It was the soldier standing there, not in shining armour, but perhaps soldier suggested silver, their constant talk of Knights and Malory.

They were living Malory, Gabriel wrote, and she had talked to William Morris of Sir Galahad. The *Order of Sir Galahad* was the name of their original Oxford Brotherhood.

She wasn't sure of the legend. Was it Galahad found the Grail? There was the poem; William Morris called it *Sir Galahad, A Christmas Mystery*. There was that Christmas message she had had at Sloane Street, when she remembered afterwards, the French name, D'Evrolles.

Walter Deverell was more like Galahad; Galahad was not Godfrey (or the Knight she called Godfrey) in her vision.

It wasn't a vision, in the sense of making up a story, awake, like the scene after leaving home, that evening in the basket-chair, alone in Chatham Place. That was her first waking-dream; she wrote down, "assemble first waking-dream—forest—hawk-feather." The character in the vision or the Real Dream, was from the Round Table; though she couldn't describe what he wore, she did know that he was in no way "in costume," nor was he in the uniform of to-day or of the last war (that is, the war before the last) of the Nelson period.

Deverell was one of the Round Table, as well as of Gabriel's first group, their Brotherhood. Was her dream Deverell, D'Evrolles? One of the Green-sleeves might well companion D'Evrolles.

Who was her knight? She knew him as her knight, whatever happened.

That "questing beast" was always a mystery. They were always out to slay it. She wrote "questing beast—symbolical?" She could not bring herself to write, long-horned cattle and the Devil.

You didn't need the mediums. It was a long time ago that she had last been to Sloane Street. She wrote down, "Mary Howitt and William Alling-ham."

Perhaps outside events might have something to do with the dream sequence; she remembered how she had spoken of the comet to William Morris and how he had started when she said "next year." She didn't mean the comet really, by outside events but the general news and worry about the future. The comet had a name but she couldn't spell it, so she couldn't write it. And now, she couldn't even remember it. But she argued, if a name stops you, or a word like the *crown* of that hat, she had first called *bowl*, there was a reason for it. But why name the comet? Just wondering why she couldn't name it, stopped her. They spoke of it in Sheffield.

Not that she felt superior to the Ibbitts, and they were well-informed at

the Art School. And not that she had ever really felt superior, only different.

The people here too, were pleasant, but they brought her breakfast early,
and Mrs. Cartlidge understood her not wanting to sit about with the house-
guests after dinner. The Cartlidge boy sketched. The guests in the beginning,
had invited her to join in, on their excursions, but she explained that her
sister had tired her out and she was resting after a visit in Sheffield. She had
relatives there, her father's people; she had stayed with Mrs. Ibbitt, Durham
Road. Mrs. Ibbitt was a second cousin, only distantly related, through her
first husband. People like to know things. They were not unfriendly.

Edward Jones or Edward Burne-Jones, as he called himself now, would
come in. There had not been much sympathy between them, but she saw
things differently and from a distance, having been away for so long, and
there was Lady Greensleeves. William Morris had sat to Gabriel for Launcelot, but she did not altogether think of him as Launcelot, and still less as
Palomydes. He had brought Palomydes into his *Christmas Mystery*. Palomydes was the knight unloved, not William Morris.

She was glad she had had occasion to mention him to Gabriel, Gabriel
having written so fully of his attachment to Miss Burden. If he could, she
wrote Gabriel, would he speak to Mr. Morris, conveying as he best could,
her pleasure in his happiness. Gabriel had written that he had done the
first Guenevere from memory, but now they had her father's consent and
Miss Burden could sit to them. "It is fortunate," Gabriel wrote, "that your
property-dresses fit her."

They were property-dresses and Elizabeth Siddall would like to have
gone on the stage. It started with *Twelfth Night*, but now in some unexpected way, she was very happy. William Morris was not wasteful of affec-
tion. He had been long devoted. He would not turn nor be swayed easily. It
was rumoured, Gabriel had written, that Morris (when the group of them
gathered around the new Guenevere) wrote on his canvas, "I cannot paint
you but I love you," and handed the canvas to her.

He was, now she thought of it, a kingly person. Gabriel had written, he
seemed much older and had grown a beard. He might even be, for the sake
of her sequence, the King; it was he who had gathered the group together.
She wrote down, "Arthur—" and hesitated. Not that she resented this constant insinuation of Gabriel's last letters, that Miss Burden was younger and
more beautiful than she was. There were readjustments, but she had her
idea. She would follow the Dream.

But she put aside her notebook. She was later than usual, but she had had a short walk this morning. She could go on with her thought, her reverie, in *The Treasure*. She slipped into her light mantle. She opened her handbag to be sure of the silver. She turned back at the doorway, remembering her letters on the table. There were voices in the sitting-room, the door was half-open; could she slide past? Her hand was on the latch of the front-door when Mrs. Cartlidge called, "Miss Siddall." She had come into the hall from the dining-room. Mrs. Cartlidge closed the door of the sitting-room.

"It's the doctor," Mrs. Cartlidge whispered. "Mrs. Weatherall has been taken—by the news."

"I—I'm sorry—" said Elizabeth. She added automatically, "is there anything I can do?"

"No; only talk, if you could spare a minute, to our boy, about his sketches."

"*His sketches?*" She tried not to seem surprised, but she felt her words showed her bewilderment.

"There's no use giving in to him," said Mrs. Cartlidge, "he's too young to go out. He went off, by the last afternoon coach, to enlist in Sheffield."

She had hung her bonnet, by its strings, over her arm. She unclasped her bag and slipped the letters in it, keeping an eye on the door.

"I mustn't keep you. But I thought I'd just ask if you had heard any details from your sister, Mr. Wheeler being a city-journalist."

"Lyddy said, they were keeping the news back." It was a long time ago that Lyddy had said that. "I'm sorry—it was confidential, whatever Mr. Wheeler told my sister."

"I'm glad for your sake," said Mrs. Cartlidge, "that it's not been the shock to you that we've had. Mrs. Weatherall having her married daughter out there—"

Elizabeth Siddall could only think, "I'm thankful that I didn't let that door swing to." She must get out quickly.

"—as well as our men, the ladies being cut down in the compound," said Mrs. Cartlidge, "the *Indian Mutiny*."

PART VII

I

Insistence on her being Guenevere—but the story was complicated, that *Order of Sir Galahad.*

Galahad was the son of Elaine, another, not the lily-maid. Magic gave her the appearance of Guenevere, or some trick enchanted Launcelot. Galahad was Launcelot's son, anyway.

She saw it all happening again. Gabriel is no Launcelot but he breaks up Arthur's circle, outwardly at least, Jane being Guenevere. But she was Guenevere, in the beginning. It was Jane wore her property-dresses, as Gabriel called them, but those pictures had faded and peeled off the walls of the Union library or Society at Oxford.

It was only five years ago that they had done them. It was symbolic and like Pisa, she thought.

That person standing by the altar that she had had a dream of, at Matlock, not long before the Mutiny and that shock, was Launcelot. He was *King of Arms* in the Round and that, she had decided, the day she did the cards for Mr. Morris at Hampton Court, that first time in the rain, was Godfrey. Well, she had had no time to talk of that with Mr. Morris, but that was the story, *Gold Cord,* how she and Godfrey, like Guenevere and Launcelot came together; it was dishonourable in the old days and broke up the circle, but it might happen the other way (there were so many meanings put on the old legends) and the two might bring back the kingdom. Arthur was king. Why did she call him Mr. Morris? Was it remembering the first days and those talks in the rain?

Galahad was their child, somehow, but it was confusing, making out that Launcelot had Galahad with Elaine, not the lily-maid but another, who magic transformed into an image of the queen. Wasn't it just a way of hiding the fact that Guenevere had that child with Launcelot? There was that Child. That was the name of his circle, the *Order of Sir Galahad*, but whatever happened and Gabriel had that power of enchantment, he couldn't break up that Round.

It was there before her on the table. Funny her stopping in that toy-bazaar, thinking she might find something to take out, that last time, to the Red House, for Janey.

In fine print on the back of the box (she could hardly read it) it told how they were gypsy-cards or from Bohemia.

It was there in the cards, somehow. She couldn't rightly explain it, how Launcelot had that Child with Guenevere. That is, Launcelot as she could make out, being Godfrey as she first thought of him. There would be no insult to Arthur who was his friend. There he was, in that card, the *Emperor*, it couldn't be anyone but William Morris. William the Englishman, he called himself in a story. He was king of Britain.

Herself, she was true to Launcelot because of that Child. Wry-necked, Dickens called him and his mother, and red-headed like Algernon who was, as Gabriel now called him, her *cavaliere servente*. That was after—

He was always with her. No one could take offence at "little Algernon." Gabriel had almost finished that portrait of him and it was just the head—you saw Algernon as he might have been, like the tall page, troubadour he was in the *Gold Cord* that was never finished.

It was him standing by the bed that had brought her back to life. How did he get in? She had often wondered. Opening her eyes on what she thought was death, she saw like a Child, standing with a fiery halo. It was out of *The Carpenter Shop* of John Everett Millais, but more beautiful, more like an Angel. Like it might be, the child they had taken away was not dead. It was Algernon.

Funny how none of it mattered, all coming back to that time. It was war that had shattered her at Matlock, but except that Gabriel got to hear of her condition and rushed up from Oxford, leaving them to get on alone with the painting, as best they could without him, the Mutiny might never have been. No one ever spoke of the Indian Mutiny, still less of the Crimea. There was talk of war now, in America, but war didn't now concern her, except that Godfrey was a soldier and *King of Arms* they called him, when they did the first fortune-telling—if you could call it fortune-telling, that talk in the bedroom in the Palace and afterwards in the *Tudor Rose*.

She couldn't quite remember. Was it the last time she saw him? That is, saw him before—before Gabriel wrote of Top, as he still called him, being so taken with Miss Burden. Jane Morris, she now was.

It was those paintings brought him and Jane together.

It was all there in the cards, she laid down. Or was she making it up?

They were old-fashioned, ladies and knights, cups and sceptres, swords and rings.

It was as if the pictures suggested things to her, crude some of them were, and drawn as if copied—why, they might even be out of the *Triumph of Death*, that procession on the wall at Pisa. Were they older than the wall-paintings? And how did they come to be in a toy-bazaar, it was hardly a shop, skipping ropes, nets and pails. It was more like a booth at the sea. It was at Hastings that she married Gabriel.

That was in the spring and less than two years ago.

Now it is February, she thought, and to-night though she might have been upset at Gabriel being late for meeting Algernon, their quarrel and Gabriel bringing her back early and then flaunting off to the College, she was—she could hardly say what she was. Perhaps it was Gabriel's words that broke her, but it was good. All of it was nothing, she couldn't seem to remember anything since his coming from Oxford and leaving them to finish as best they could without him, and then—and then, Algernon.

He was coming to-morrow for a sitting. She would explain to Algernon and perhaps tell him of these cards. The picture was almost finished. You forgave Gabriel everything when you saw the red-chalk drawing that he had done of Algernon.

It was Algernon started that talk of the *Unknown Church*, though he had written his own story before he met Algernon, so Willie told her. Yes, it was Willie that she called him afterwards, and in a poem that she wrote at Matlock, before she was quite sure that they would come together. She hadn't thought so much about him, only when Gabriel wrote her that he was so taken with Miss Burden, it all came back. She lived back those talks they had had together, the story that he asked her not to tell him; his name was, he said, as she spoke it, Halberd.

He said it was French and she looked it up and wrote it in her notebook, *Hallebarde*. It was important with names. They had talked of that, too. She had thought of him, but briefly in that poem she wrote, but Willie was only part of that poem, *Apple Gatherers* or *An Apple-gathering*, she called it—how Lilian and Lilias were happy, that was Georgie and Burne-Jones (she could not even yet, call him Ted) and how plump Gertrude was helped along with her basket, by another whose voice was *More sweet to me than song.*

Yes, it was his voice that held enchantment, and now Mr. Ruskin had helped publish the book he had been working on, ever since she'd known him and earlier, the *Vita* and the translation of the poets in *Dante and his Circle.* It was enough for any one person, just that, and there was the painting as well.

William Morris had the *Defence of Guenevere* come out, the year before he married—that was the year before she married. The *Defence* wasn't the success it should have been, they said, because of Tennyson and the *Idylls,* appearing about then. She couldn't think of the *Defence,* without remembering that last talk in the Palace.

It was all there in the cards before her—or was she making it up?

It was remembering and at the same time *remembering in the future.* Had she thought that, or had someone thought it for her?

I am so happy. I have found everything. It is what he said, "we have everything," when we spoke of the star-patterns, the signs from the herald manual and the Saint book.

Looking at that card, the *Wheel,* you might be looking at a picture of St. Katherine, set above an altar. Then looking at it, you got into a state of *remembering,* like she was now, *remembering in the future.*

She was glad Gabriel had gone out.

One of these cloths is heaven, and one hell,
Now choose one cloth for ever

he had quoted to her from the *Defence,* that last time at the Palace. She said, she had no choice then, but she had it now, and it made her feel strong and well and able for anything, to think how she had stood up to Gabriel. Perhaps, he never would forgive her, but this was different, not plump Gertrude, Fanny Hughes who called herself Cornforth now, out of the poem she had written, just before Gabriel came to her at Matlock.

She had no choice then, there in the Palace with Dad and Mum so worried and Lyddy getting married. She thought she had choice at Matlock, when she first got away from Sheffield, but that shock of the Mutiny had struck at her. She remembered how she had said "next year" to William Morris in the Palace, and how it happened "next year," the very year too, that he met Jane Burden, and Godfrey out in India and her remembering the dream or picture of a soldier, a Knight but not noticeably in armour, it was just the light, but silver, and having known from the first, there in the Palace, that "next year" would be her—what word did she want for it? Her testing, her trying—she had no choice anyway, Godfrey was dead; though she never saw him, she might have met him one day, and Georgie and Burne-Jones were married, and Janey and William Morris and she married Gabriel.

It was as if she was only half-married, all the time, and he must have known it. That is why after—well, a proper wife would have made scenes about Fanny, but she never saw her and Algernon stayed with her, those long evenings.

He must have found his way up the other stairway, the door was cut through, as Gabriel had first planned. There were two house-doors and two stairways. If you blocked up the hall-door and put the shelves back where they had been . . . where was this taking her? She looked round the room for the first time, and saw it as part of another house; was she thinking of the Red House, he had designed and built for Janey? It was out in the country, not too far to get there by coach. They were going out to-morrow.

Mrs. Birrell had stopped her on the way up, to say Mary—Red-Lion Mary as they still called her—had run round with the mantle, as she knew Mrs. Rossetti would be wanting it, in time to try on. It was lying on the bed there, presently she would try its effect over the house-gown she had slipped into. Gabriel was still talking to her but she stepped out of her street-dress, hung it deliberately, in the built-in wardrobe and went on brushing her hair. She didn't do it to attract him. He had been wild over her hair-brushing, but she was not interrupted now, to pose with her arms bent in some awkward posture. She lifted her arms and the full sleeves fell back to the elbow.

It was green-blue, the lining. She saw the contrasting colours as the loose sleeves fell back. She saw the white arms, reaching out like a Mermaid. Undine was a mermaid, she remembered he said, when she said she was *wayy* or *undy*. She might be overgrown and sensitive, though she was a married woman, not young, now almost thirty. Even, she might be thirty, this being February of the new year and not knowing her own birthday. It fell from her, even as the wide sleeves fell back, the silt and weed and entangling encumbrances of past desolation.

Her arms were free now—empty? She would convey it somehow, she didn't know how that Gabriel must never see Janey again. It wasn't a thing you could fight openly, but she could fight it. Shrewish, he had called her; it was not the first time. It would be their last trip to the Red House to-morrow.

All that Gabriel had said, before he swept out in a temper, was there to draw on. He had said she had lost her reason, reminding her of poor Harry.

She had gone mad. Long ago, he had thought of doing her as Medea. He didn't want to paint her—but thank you, I have an idea for a new picture. She went on brushing her hair.

"I said, in the beginning, she was younger and more beautiful. That is what set you off in Matlock."

She turned in her chair. She laid the brush down on the table. Now she dropped her arms and the sleeves covered her wrists. She was not really cold. Katy had kept the fire in, while they were out at dinner.

It was that triptych he had never finished. Miss Herbert would no longer sit for him, but Jane Morris would do.

She laid the brush down on the dressing-table. Everything seemed the same. "Jane Morris will not do," she said.

She was looking at the cards, her hands clasped under the table. It was the same table, William Morris had said. He asked if she would keep it for him. He might want it, later. No, he had not touched on the matter again, nor spoken of it to Vernon, only to Rossetti.

It was the way he said Rossetti.

"Does Gabriel know this is the very table?"

"I don't think so, it looks quite ordinary. Vernon was keeping it for me, with some books. Do you mind having it here?"

He flung a bit of blue cloth over it that he was measuring for the curtains. "I'll have the square hemmed when Mary does your curtains. Are you sure this is the blue you like best?" There were strips of blue, green-blue, peacock, wedgwood and what he called delphinium, spread out on the low couch he had had built in, with the wardrobe, while she was in Paris on her honeymoon.

"I'm fastening the mirror flat in the wall and you can move this square table yourself, or the other for a dressing-table. It's in one piece," he said.

Why had he said that?

She remembered afterwards, the old flawed glass, with the dividing line across it, in the little room off the Orangery, at Hampton Court, that first day in the rain.

She had chosen the delphinium. It was like that. His garden was full of them.

It was Upton, Kent. They were going there to-morrow.

He had started the shop, the idea anyway, while the Red House was building. It was designing furniture for the new house that put the idea into his head of taking over the Red Lion premises. It was Number 8, Red Lion

Square where the shop was, woven cloths and dyed to his liking, he spoke of pottery and later, the glass and stained-glass that Gabriel was to help with. Gabriel threw "Morris and Company" at her, along with the rest of it. Was she breaking that up, too?

She did not want to leave England.

She looked at the cards on the table. She had put out the lamp after Gabriel left her, and lighted the candles on the mantle. William Morris had had the fireplace set with Dutch tiles, ordered especially for her, little scenes, a blue tulip and a small ship. There was a ship in the *Emperor* card. He was looking out, seated on a throne, over the sea. There was an eagle, that is, banner-decoration, like her *Eagle Displayed*. The cards took you back and forward.

The candles threw that soft light, so the drawings blurred sometimes, giving you new ideas of the shapes and pattern of them. She was glad they were not coloured. She could imagine better what was in them.

She would wait till the candles burned down, before going to bed.

There was comfort in the table. She stood books and her work-basket on it, on the blue woven square that he had had Mary hem and bind for her with a contrasting pattern, key or wall-of-Troy, they called it. *One of these cloths is heaven, and one hell.* Guenevere in the *Defence*, chose the blue, as she remembered, but it was confusing, symbolic; somehow, he had made out she chose the wrong one. Or it was a fear she might not choose right? She felt herself grown tense in her chair. She must not think about it. It was all right. Algernon would help her.

She had swept off the blue cloth, the books and work folded in it, many times, that first year.

She had sat, many times when she was alone, before—

But except for the comfort it gave her to feel this was Godfrey's table and that the two of them had sat together, she had had no messages. She had never heard of anyone, alone with the table. There had always been a group at the Howitts. But William Morris had spoken of Godfrey and their group, the *Order of Sir Galahad*, and of how from the seven or eight of them, he and Godfrey had "crystallized out." It had been the same, he said, with the group in Paris, but Roland de Fontenelle who had first started Godfrey and his brother, seemed to suggest danger somehow—and that Godfrey shouldn't go on. It was the impression as she remembered, from that time when he tried in the *Tudor Rose*, to make it right that there had been talk about her and Gabriel.

He had made it right, coming that day with the blue strips for her to choose from. *One of these cloths is heaven, and one hell, Now choose one cloth for ever.*

He had chosen the blue for her.

She knew she couldn't take over entire responsibility for Gabriel, but she had made it clear that he must break with Janey. Help would come. She needed what they called in the old days, guidance. She couldn't go to Mrs. Howitt with it, it being about Gabriel, and Janey implicated. She knew she could trust Algernon and he would help her. Could she and Algernon sit here with the table? Was that *Wheel* that she thought of, with St. Katherine, the table?

Not that there was anyone that she would wish to talk to, with the table. Dad had gone, the summer before she was married, and Mrs. Browning, last year in Florence. Not that she would *not* want to talk to them. She picked up the cards. It wasn't proper fortune-telling, just going round in a circle. It would be something general, yet specialized.

Algernon would help her. It would be Godfrey, but *King of Arms.*

For all his affliction, Algernon had wanted to be a soldier. They were Navy people, mostly.

But it wasn't war in that sense, it was his *Ships sail through the Heaven,* which (she had reminded him) were *Carrying the planets Seven,* when he had said there in the Palace or over the tea-cups, there were no star-patterns in his poems.

It was that *Star* she had put down, some time back. It was number seventeen, a large star or sun, with seven stars around it. You added the numbers, one plus seven or eight. There were eight points to the large sun or star. It was something she'd read of, the seven bowing to the one. Jacob? Joseph?

There were many meanings.

Mrs. Browning was an ardent believer; she said, that first time in Paris, she must call her by her own name, Elizabeth. But what she'd heard, round about, through Mary Howitt, of their communications and the Hawthornes, there in Florence, wasn't what she wanted. The messages might be spiritual, inspiring, coming to Elizabeth Barrett Browning. But what she wanted—

What was it that she wanted?

She swept up the cards. She would begin over. Can you begin *over?* She found she was watching her thoughts. She had lost her reason, he said. She had gone mad.

Someone could tell her that she was half-in-love with William Morris.

But it must not be Gabriel. "This will give you your chance," he said. She stormed at him, it was all understood, he was in love from the start, with the sister of his best friend, out in India.

"Ah—*Lis*," said Gabriel.

How did he know that Lis was the name of Godfrey's sister?

"So he told you about Lis?"

"Blanchelys," said Gabriel.

"That's one of your poems—"

"So I told him, it was no accident."

"Her being thrown?"

"I am talking of Blanchelys. It was a long time ago, but *ma chère*, I can still help you."

Was he laughing?

"Gabriel—"

"It will even be in accord with the strictest laws of the *Commedia*. And easy with the Red House, my studio and your room here, planned to his taste—"

"*Gabriel*—"

"It is an angel's name. Did you ever stop to wonder?"

There was the *Angel* in those cards. But it wasn't Gabriel.

The *Angel* was fourteen, seven plus seven. Dad said she was good at numbers.

The laws of the *Commedia*? Did he mean the *commedia dell'arte* that he sometimes spoke of?

"Do you mean Columbine, Harlequin and those clowns?"

"I am speaking of the *Commedia* of Dante."

"The Divine Comedy?"

"Dante called it the Commedia. They added *La Divina*, two hundred years later."

"I can't see that that has anything to do with—with—"

"You don't know Dante."

"You can't take away the ideal. I was Beatrice, I was the Damozel. If you'd known me less, you might have kept the ideal. You can't—"

"Jane Morris is coming to the studio. You can keep out of her way and she can keep out of your way—"

"It won't work. Even if I wanted it, it won't work. He loves Janey."

She threw out the suits, hearts were cups; she had read on the back of the box, it was modelled from playing-cards or playing-cards were modelled from these; maybe it was just a legend, their hinting on the back, the cards were so old. She kept the court-cards separate, then decided to include them with the others. They were the usual, with a page added.

The cards that were numbered, they called the *Arcana*. They were Roman numerals, I to XXII.

Like a clock, she thought, as she sorted them, laying them out, from I to XII, then making an inner circle of the XIII to XXII. That meant two cards had no doubles, the XI and the XII.

There was a reason for that. It was part of pictures, peeled off from a wall at Pisa. The *campo santo* it was, and that procession or series or circle was *The Triumph of Death*.

But *Death* didn't triumph. You passed him, the XIII, and went on to XIV, the *Angel*.

It was a clock ticking; Mrs. Howitt called them rapping Spirits.

It was the *Gold Cord*. It was the circle she was to cherish in the story.

She and Algernon were twins there. Goldwings, he called us.

We were Flor and Florence in the story. He was Florian de Liliis in the *Hollow Land*. He was Hallebarde in the story.

She had finished the story.

You do not have to write the story when you have the answer.

It was all there on the table.

Algernon could put it in his play, the Albigensians, the *Albigenses*, he called it.

"Lizzy—Lily," Gabriel had mocked at her.

So he had loved her. She could live that story.

She didn't have to paint any more. She had striven too hard to justify herself, her position, Mr. Ruskin's faith in her.

There was Mr. Ruskin. They hadn't seen so much of him lately. He had been, in the beginning, set against the new faith. Mary said, now he had comfort in communication.

There was Mr. Ruskin. Algernon would help her. It might even be that Gabriel and she might go to Florence. Florence was Algernon, that page in the green jacket. Perhaps Algernon could come with them.

She looked round the room. She didn't want to leave it.

She had talked to William Morris alone, for the first time, in the long room when Gabriel was looking out his sketches. She had slipped in the unfinished picture that he wanted, among the pieces that Gabriel had put together for their wedding-present.

She remembered how she had propped it up, in Weymouth Street, before her mirror and read the poem he sent her.

She still had *Red Roses*, folded where it had first been, in her work-basket.

"Rossetti—roses," he had said, "my rose is a lily."

She had seen him alone, those times at Hampton Court, and only once, after. They had talked together at the Red House, but not properly alone.

It was here in this room, that she had last talked to him.

"I think I should tell you," he said, "I told Gabriel about the circle—"

She wondered why he thought that he must tell her.

"—and de Fontenelle, in Paris."

"That was a long time ago."

"It was part of the table that I'm leaving with you."

She must not look any longer, at the cards. If you went on wondering about them, it only brought confusion. It was as if an hour struck, when you found the right card. It was the *Angel*, XIV.

That second circle or inner circle, passed *Death*, XIII and went on, out of clock-time.

She collected the cards, counting them in their order, I to XXII.

There were those Roman numerals, she remembered, the date of her birth, on the folder of the drawings, and Florence was Firenze; she remembered the basket-chair and her worry about cholera and about Gabriel and Fanny.

There, she started on her story. It was her out-rider in the feather-cap. It wasn't William Morris.

William Morris had given Godfrey to her, and the table.

It was the Knights Credentes. It wasn't just one person. It was Godfrey. She had called him George, Gregor and Gereon, but she had wanted a name, in case she showed the story. But it was Godfrey, the Crusader.

There was some such Godfrey, King of Jerusalem. Maybe the dates were different, but it was that Godfrey.

She had called him Don Gregor but it was just a title, like Childe Roland.

It was Roland started Godfrey. He was part of this very table, and that thin girl, Valerie, she was.

William Morris said he couldn't explain it, it was political. In confidence, William Rossetti had helped.

"Were they entangled in some—some scandal that you hinted of, when

I told you of the summer-house and talk about Gabriel and me, out at the Hermitage?"

"I want you to know," he said, "that Gabriel helped them."

Why just then, did he tell her just that?

It brought her back, to her new mantle flung on the bed, to the blue cloth she was holding. The books and basket were set on the chair by her bed. She must have put them there. She couldn't remember doing it.

Yes, the room was as she liked it. It might almost be part of Red House. She saw now, with Godfrey there or waiting, there would be perfect harmony. She placed the card-box on her dressing-table. She moved the round-table to its usual corner. There would be someone for Gabriel, but it wasn't Janey.

Odd, his reminding her of those two in Paris. She didn't quite place Roland . . . *to the dark tower came.*

There was that *Tower* in the cards, XVI, it was.

Last night, before falling asleep, she had run round them. She knew them off, by heart. But there was some special consolation, laying them on the table. She placed the books and her work-basket, back on the blue cloth.

Now choose one cloth forever.

It was that way with Gabriel; as they said of him, he was the ruby-glass in the window. You couldn't decide against him.

It wasn't only his painting and his poetry, he was following on his father, a Dante authority and a scholar.

"You don't know Dante," he had said. He was jeering at her, but it didn't matter. There in Florence, Algernon would help her with Italian.

Dante Gabriel Rossetti had never been to Italy.

He had talked of Florence, that first time in Paris. Perhaps, she should have gone with him, then.

But then, she would have missed the story.

It was his story, *Hand and Soul*, he called it.

Or it was *The Hollow Land* of William Morris.

She never did make out why Margaret—but Margaret was Lis. She was Margaret.

She was Margaret in *The Hollow Land;* he explained that he met her after they were both dead. But Janey was *Beata mea Domina* in life, now.

She was older than he was and already engaged to Gabriel, when she met him. Not that that would matter, being older. She had not thought if

Godfrey would be older. It was Venice, Gabriel talked of, that first time he met her, out at Kew, sitting for Walter Deverell in *Twelfth Night*.

It was Venetian glass, the little goblet, so he told her, an odd one, lost from a set, or the last unbroken. She lifted the glass.

Should she get undressed first?

The candles could burn on and out, after she was in bed.

She measured the drops from the glass phial, re-set the stopper and swallowed the laudanum.

She wouldn't try on the mantle. She hung it in the wardrobe, stepped out of her house-gown and flung it over a chair. She liked to sit half-dressed, over her breakfast. Mrs. Birrell brought it to her room here, as Gabriel slept late.

She drew off the couch-cover and folded it. It was a blue, just off the curtains. She shook the pillow and her nightdress out of the pillow-holder that he had had Mary work round with that same key-pattern, as the square cloth on the table.

She folded her under-linen.

She slipped her feet into the fur-lined slippers.

Should she sit up, longer? Gabriel anyway, would be late.

She slipped the house-gown on again, over her night-dress.

. . . .

How long had she been sleeping? The fire had almost gone out but one candle was still burning.

Where am I? She remembered. She had quarrelled with Gabriel, then the cards and thinking about Florence. She remembered her disappointment over dinner, being late and Gabriel bringing her away, early.

But Algernon was coming. There would be time to talk of all this, they would go together to the Red House.

Yes, she had had a trying day. No wonder she fell asleep in her chair.

It was just a slight stitch in her side, probably a cramp from the way she had been sitting. But she didn't want to run the risk of pain to-morrow.

She walked over to the dressing-table. She un-stoppered the glass bottle.

She set down the little wine-glass.

She picked up the glass-stopper.

"But it's empty," she thought, "I must remember to stop in, at Mr. Keates, on the way out to-morrow, for fresh laudanum."

L'ENVOI

William Allingham stood somewhat apart from the small group. He had not really been invited. Mary Howitt had told him of it, as she knew he would want to be there. For once, she was conspicuous, in grey. He remembered that the family were originally, Friends.

There was a slight fall of snow. It was Highgate. She was to rest with Professor Rossetti, in his grave.

Mary had told him that her cold hands were folded on the *House of Life*, the fiery sonnet-sequence that Gabriel wished buried with her.

He might have thought of Ophelia, but remembered an awkward, tall girl in the dim circle, cast by the street-lamp.

"It's Miss Sid," they said, laughing by the lamp-post.

He was standing with Walter Deverell. She was lifting a box onto a shelf. She turned, with her arms still lifted.

"I trust Walter does a faithful likeness of Miss Siddall," he said to Mrs. Deverell. He did not look at Elizabeth Siddall.

None of them had been invited. It was a private matter.

He did not see Gabriel.

He must make his way out, before

We lose into the ground
Her face we knew.

Works Cited

Barringer, Tim. *Reading the Pre-Raphaelites.* New Haven, Conn.: Yale University Press, 1999.

Bednarowski, Mary Farrell. "Women in Occult America." In *The Occult in America: New Historical Perspectives,* edited by Howard Kerr and Charles L. Crow, 177–95. Urbana: University of Illinois Press, 1983.

Berg, Maggie. "A Neglected Voice: Elizabeth Siddal." *Dalhousie Review* 60 (1980): 151–56.

Bickley, Francis. *The Pre-Raphaelite Comedy.* London: Constable, 1932.

Braude, Ann. *Radical Spirits: Spiritualism and Women's Rights in Nineteenth-Century America.* Boston: Beacon Press, 1989.

Brown, Ford Madox. *The Diary of Ford Madox Brown.* Edited by Virginia Surtees. New Haven, Conn.: Yale University Press, 1981.

Burne-Jones, Georgiana. *Memorials of Edward Burne-Jones.* London: Macmillan, 1904.

Challem, Jack Joseph, and Barbara Reed-Stitt. "One Pre-Raphaelite Legacy: An Analysis of the Personalities of Dante Gabriel Rossetti and Elizabeth Siddal as Seen Through Their Handwritings." *Journal of Pre-Raphaelite Studies* 7, no. 2 (May 1987): 12–24.

Cherry, Deborah, and Griselda Pollock. "Woman as Sign in Pre-Raphaelite Literature: A Study of the Representation of Elizabeth Siddall." *Art History* 7, no. 1 (1984): 206–27.

Christ, Carol. *Victorian and Modern Poetics.* Chicago: University of Chicago Press, 1984.

Doolittle, Hilda (H.D.). *Asphodel.* Edited by Robert Spoo. Durham: Duke University Press, 1992.

———. *Collected Poems, 1912–1944.* Edited by Louis L. Martz. New York: New Directions, 1986.

———. "Compassionate Friendship." H.D. Papers, Yale Collection of American Literature. Beinecke Library, New Haven, Conn.

———. *End to Torment: A Memoir of Ezra Pound*. New York: New Directions, 1979.

———. *The Gift by H.D.* Edited and annotated by Jane Augustine. Gainesville: University Press of Florida, 1998.

———. "H.D. by *Delia Alton*." Edited by Adalaide Morris. In *Iowa Review* 16, no. 3 (1986): 179–221.

———. *Helen in Egypt*. New York: New Directions, 1961.

———. "Notes." H.D. Papers, Yale Collection of American Literature. Beinecke Library, New Haven, Conn.

———. "Pre-Raphaelites." H.D. Papers, Yale Collection of American Literature. Beinecke Library, New Haven, Conn.

———. *The Sword Went Out to Sea (Synthesis of a Dream), by Delia Alton*. Edited with an introduction by Cynthia Hogue and Julie Vandivere. Gainesville: University Press of Florida, 2007.

———. *Tribute to Freud*. Boston: David R. Godine, 1974.

———. *Trilogy*. New York: New Directions, 1973.

———. *White Rose and the Red*. H.D. Papers, Yale Collection of American Literature. Beinecke Library, New Haven, Conn.

Doughty, Oswald. *A Victorian Romantic: Dante Gabriel Rossetti*. London: Frederick Muller, 1949.

Eliot, T. S. *Four Quartets*. London: Faber and Faber, 1960.

———. *Selected Prose*. Edited by Frank Kermode. London: Faber and Faber, 1975.

Faulkner, Peter. "Pound and the Pre-Raphaelites." *Paideuma* 13, no. 2 (1984): 229–44.

Ford, Ford Madox. *Ford Madox Brown: A Record of His Life and Work*. Longmans, Green, 1896.

———. *The Pre-Raphaelite Brotherhood: A Critical Monograph*. London: Duckworth, 1907.

———. *Rossetti: A Critical Essay on His Art*. London: Duckworth, 1914.

Friedman, Susan Stanford, ed. *Analyzing Freud: Letters of H.D., Bryher, and Their Circle*. New York: New Directions, 2002.

———. *Penelope's Web: Gender, Modernity, H.D.'s Fiction*. Cambridge and New York: Cambridge University Press, 1990.

———. *Psyche Reborn: The Emergence of H.D.* Bloomington: Indiana University Press, 1981.

Gregory, Eileen. *H.D. and Hellenism: Classic Lines*. Cambridge and New York: Cambridge University Press, 1997.

Guest, Barbara. *Herself Defined: The Poet H.D. and Her World*. New York: Doubleday, 1984.

Hanft, Lila. "Woman in an Artist's Studio: Pre-Raphaelitism, Female Authorship, and the Construction of Gender." Ph.D. diss., Cornell University, 1991.

Hares-Stryker, Carolyn, ed. *An Anthology of Pre-Raphaelite Writings*. New York: New York University Press, 1997.

Higgins, Lesley. *The Modernist Cult of Ugliness: Aesthetic and Gender Politics*. New York: Palgrave Macmillan, 2002.

Hollenberg, Donna Krolik, ed. *Between History and Poetry: The Letters of H.D. and Norman Holmes Pearson*. Iowa City: University of Iowa Press, 1997.

Hulme, T. E. *Speculations: Essays on Humanism and the Philosophy of Art*. London: K. Paul, Trench, Trubner, 1936.

Hunt, Margaret. *Magdalen Wynyard, or, The Provocations of a Pre-Raphaelite*. London: 1872.

Hunt, Violet. *Wife of Rossetti*. London: John Lane the Bodley Head, 1932.

Isaacs, Ernest. "The Fox Sisters and American Spiritualism." In *The Occult in America: New Historical Perspectives*. Edited by Howard Kerr and Charles L. Crow, 79–110. Urbana: University of Illinois Press, 1983.

Laity, Cassandra. *H.D. and the Victorian Fin de Siècle: Gender, Modernism, Decadence*. Cambridge and New York: Cambridge University Press, 1996.

Mancoff, Debra N. "Is There Substance Behind the Shadows? New Works on Elizabeth Siddal." *Journal of Pre-Raphaelite Studies* 1 (Spring 1992): 21–9.

Marsh, Jan. *Elizabeth Siddal: Pre-Raphaelite Artist*. Sheffield, U. K.: Sheffield Design and Print, 1991.

———. *The Legend of Elizabeth Siddal*. London: Quartet Books, 1989.

———. *Pre-Raphaelite Sisterhood*. London: Quartet Books, 1985.

———. *Pre-Raphaelite Women: Images of Femininity in Pre-Raphaelite Art*. London: Weidenfeld and Nicolson, 1987.

Materer, Timothy. *Modernist Alchemy: Poetry and the Occult*. Ithaca, N.Y.: Cornell University Press, 1995.

McGann, Jerome J. *Dante Gabriel Rossetti and the Game That Must Be Lost*. New Haven, Conn.: Yale University Press, 2000.

Morrissey, Kim. *Clever as Paint: The Rossettis in Love*. Toronto, Ontario: Playwrights Canada Press, 1998.

Nunn, Pamela Gerrish. *Victorian Women Artists*. London: Women's Press, 1987.

Orr, Clarissa Campbell, ed. *Women in the Victorian Art World*. Manchester, England: Manchester University Press, 1995.

Owen, Alex. *The Darkened Room: Women, Power and Spiritualism in Late Victorian England*. London: Virago Press, 1989.

Paget, Violet. *Miss Brown*. Edinburgh, Scotland: 1884.

Pound, Ezra. *Literary Essays of Ezra Pound*. Edited by T. S. Eliot. London: Faber and Faber, 1960.

———. *The Selected Poems of Ezra Pound*. New York: New Directions, 1957.

Prettejohn, Elizabeth. *The Art of the Pre-Raphaelites*. London: Tate Gallery Publishing, 2000.

———. *Rossetti and His Circle*. New York: Stewart, Tabori and Chang, 1998.

Rainey, Lawrence S. "Canon, Gender, and Text: The Case of H.D." In *Representing Modernist Texts: Editing as Interpretation*, edited by George Bornstein, 99–123. Ann Arbor: University of Michigan Press, 1991.

Rossetti, Dante Gabriel. *Collected Poetry and Prose*. Edited by Jerome McGann. New Haven, Conn.: Yale University Press, 2003.

Scott, Bonnie Kime, ed. *The Gender of Modernism*. Bloomington: Indiana University Press, 1990.

Shakespear, Olivia. *Rupert Armstrong*. London: 1898.

Spoo, Robert. "Editing H.D.'s *Asphodel*: Selected Emendations and Notes." *Sagetrieb* 14, nos. 1–2 (1995): 13–26.

St. Jean, Amy Ujvari. "Unearthing Elizabeth Siddal: The Voice and Vision of a Pre-Raphaelite Artist and Poet." Ph.D. diss, Kent State University, 1999.

Sword, Helen. *Ghostwriting Modernism*. Ithaca, N.Y.: Cornell University Press, 2002.

Taylor, Beverly. "Beatrix/Creatrix: Elizabeth Siddal as Muse and Creator." *Journal of Pre-Raphaelite Studies* 4 (1995): 29–42.

Taylor, Georgina. *H.D. and the Public Sphere of Modernist Women Writers, 1913–1946: Talking Women*. Oxford, England: Clarendon Press, 2001.

Waugh, Evelyn. *P.R.B.: An Essay on the Pre-Raphaelite Brotherhood, 1847-54*. Westerham, Kent: Dalrymple Press, 1982.

———. *Rossetti: His Life and Works*. London: Duckworth, 1928.

Williams, Isabelle. "Elizabeth Siddal: The Health Issue." *Journal of Pre-Raphaelite Studies* 5 (Spring 1996): 53–70.

Yeats, W. B. *Autobiographies*. Edited by William H. O'Donnell and Douglas N. Archibald. New York: Scribner, 1999.

Zilboorg, Caroline, ed. *Richard Aldington and H.D.: The Later Years in Letters*. Manchester, England: Manchester University Press, 1995.

Index

Abélard: birth date of, 97; Siddal on, 73–74, 75, 88, 97, 227

Abolitionist movement, 63, 65, 67

Academy for Spiritual Research (Sloane Street), séances at, 26–27, 258, 303

Ackland, Dr. Henry Wentworth, and treatment of Siddal, 105, 145, 169, 173, 290, 299

Ackland, Miss, 169

Adelphi (journal), H.D.'s contributions to, xliin22

Aestheticism: and morality, xxxiii; of Victorian poetry, xxxi

"Aesthetic Poetry" (Pater), xx

Agincourt, battle of, 151

Albigenses, The (Swinburne), 114, 217, 251, 318

Albigensians, 213, 264

Aldington, Richard: H.D.'s correspondence with, xii, xvii, xxxixn1; and Imagist movement, xxxixn1; knowledge of Pre-Raphaelites, xx; as Rossetti, xxiii; on *The Sword*, xxviii; on *White Rose and the Red*, xix–xx, xxxixn2

Allingham, William, 226; on Caliostro, 83; *The Cold Wedding*, xxxiii, 33, 84, 322; Customs post of, 19, 35; on Deverell, 34–35; discovery of Siddal, 15–16, 20, 202, 322; letter to Mrs. Howitt, 33; in London, 26; and Annie Miller, 40; on Pre-Raphaelites, 49; and Rossetti, 33, 40, 43; and Siddal, 32–36, 91, 200;

at Siddal's burial, 322; Siddal's importance for, xxiii

Alton, Delia (pseudonym). *See* H.D.

Amis and Amile (old French story), 214, 238, 301

Amor, anagrams of, 212, 221, 257, 258

Amor (Swinburne), 257

Andersen, Hans Christian, 227

Anglo-Catholicism, Morris on, 125–26, 220

Aphrodite, xix

Apple Gatherers (Siddal), 311

Architectural restoration, neo-Gothic: Morris's interest in, 89, 117, 119–20, 206–7, 244. *See also* Gothic architecture

Arnaut Daniel, 265

Art, transformative potential of, ix

Artists: decadent, xxi, xliin25; during war, xln5

Artists, female, xi; creativity of, xxxviii; Pre-Raphaelite, xxxv–xxxvi, xxxviiin2, xln8

Arts and Crafts movement, xlvin46

Astrology, 181, 182; in *Gold Cord*, 192; relationship to heraldry, 190; Rossetti's interest in, 179; Siddal's interest in, 184, 191–95, 199. *See also* Zodiac

Aucassan and Nicolette, 230, 238

Aurélie (cousin of Valérie de Fontenelle), 138, 139, 145, 268; circle of friends, 231; and Roland, 186, 230

Alison Halsall is an adjunct professor of English literature at York University, Toronto.

www.ingramcontent.com/pod-product-compliance
Lightning Source LLC
Chambersburg PA
CBHW020930020726
47495CB00002B/435